FOR A SACK OF BONES

FOR A SACK OF BONES

LLUÍS-ANTON BAULENAS

Translated from the Catalan by
CHERYL LEAH MORGAN

HARCOURT, INC.

Orlando   Austin   New York   San Diego   London

www.HarcourtBooks.com

This is a work of fiction. Names, characters, places, organizations,
and events are the products of the author's imagination or are used
fictitiously, and any resemblance to actual persons, living or dead,
events, or locales is entirely coincidental.

This is a translation of *Per un Sac d'Ossos*
First published in Catalan in Spain by Editorial Planeta, S.A., 2005

The translation of this work has received a grant from the Institut Ramon Llull

Library of Congress Cataloging-in-Publication Data
Baulenas, Lluís-Anton.
[Per un sac d'ossos. English]
For a sack of bones/Lluís-Anton Baulenas;
translated by Cheryl Leah Morgan.
p.   cm.
I. Morgan, Cheryl Leah.   II. Title.
PC3942.12.A85F6713   2003
849'.9354—dc22   2007037893
ISBN 978-0-15-101255-8

Text set in Adobe Garamond
Designed by Liz Demeter

Printed in the United States of America
First U.S. edition
A C E G I K J H F D B

A NOTE ON NAMES

Under Franco's regime, Catalan was strictly prohibited from being spoken anywhere outside the home. For this reason, characters' names appear in both their Catalan and Spanish forms, depending on context.

To my uncles Xavier and Ramon,
who were kids of the House of Charity,
in memoriam.

————————

L'ignorance est un sac vide qui peut se remplir. La stupidité est le même sac, mais avec un trou au fond.

—SENEGALESE PROVERB

Clara was the answer. But to get to Clara I had to cross the sea.

—L. TONY WHALES,
News from Brooklyn with a Parrot

PROLOGUE

Franco's Regime makes me sick. I find it despicable. The General's dictatorship is authoritarian, Fascist, docile, ignorant, vengeful, and rancid. It's extremist and priestly, confusing the worship of God with service to the State. And vice versa. This sinister Regime is based on corruption and abuse of authority, not to mention plain and simple bullshit. No matter what anyone may say, it's a dictatorship run by the meek and irresolute. It doesn't matter whether it's government officials, ecclesiastics, military, or civilians. Nobody takes responsibility for their actions, because they consider, with reason, that there will always be someone higher up to cover for them. It's a vast sea of useless people paralyzed by a crushing inability to make decisions. This creates enormous internal conflict. The Fascists hate Communism and its atheism fervently, but oddly enough, the very terror of drawing attention to themselves or taking responsibility makes them act like a bunch of Communist bureaucrats. I laugh out loud at their ludicrous attempts at justification. During the Ribbentrop Pact with Stalin, they kept their mouths shut in a stupor of uncertainty. And the Fascists, like grateful puppies, shed tears of happiness when Hitler invaded Russia. They told themselves it wasn't possible. The Führer, superior being that he is, had fooled us all. He'd planned it that way from the very beginning. . . . It's the same thing with the clergy. The Church is very aware of the fact that it's won the war. Its leaders consider it their sacred duty to carry out the divine punishment God chose to inflict on Spain. They also believe they've helped bring peace to the land, or rather their version of peace. The State is beholden to the Church, which gives the religious authorities free rein to instill a new set of moral values among the masses, rife with downtrodden Reds who are forced to wear a kind of cultural camouflage. Nobody's denying that scores of clergy and believers were persecuted and slaughtered during the first years of the war. But the Republicans never sanctioned or condoned such acts of homicidal terror. And what irregularities they did commit certainly didn't spur them on to further bloodshed. Now, on the other hand, the Church has actually sanctioned and legalized murder, incorporating it into its roster of traditional Christian values. That's hypocritical, but why care? It fits right in with the overall outlook of the rest of Spain's current ruling class. Because the Regime is, above all, hypocritical, and this hypocrisy infects every aspect of life.

I'm obviously a hypocrite, too, an obedient child of the Regime. My own father advised me to shamelessly pretend I had become one of them. It was the only way to get even. He also told me to keep quiet around people who seemed to pay too much attention to me and to watch out for those who talked too little. And so I've been living in Melilla for almost eight years, six of those as a soldier in the Legion. All this time I've been waiting for a chance to carry out the promise made to my father.

Circumstances forced me to leave for Africa in November 1941. I was only sixteen, but that didn't stop the Baron of Remei from sending me to Melilla, placing me in the service of a friend who was a captain in the Legion. The plan was for me to volunteer for the Legion in a couple of years, as soon as I'd turned eighteen. Obviously it's not as if I was dying to do so, but the alternative was even worse. Much, much worse. The baron may have veiled the hard facts with fancy talk, but he made it clear that I was destined for the sea either way. I could either get on a ship bound for Melilla, or end up at the bottom of the port with a block of cement tied to my feet. He was capable of worse. If it hadn't been for his daughter's intervention, he'd have slaughtered me like a pig days before. So I didn't have much of a choice.

I had never left Barcelona before. Standing on deck the day of my departure, I watched the gray docks enveloped in a low and undulating mist and began to plan my return. The shacks and warehouses hugging the docks began to file past. It'd been over two years since the end of the war, but the boats sunk during the fighting were still being dredged up. It wasn't so much to make more room for the loading and unloading of passengers and goods, as the need to actually put the vessels to good use. With such an overall lack of raw materials, even these piles of rusted iron were absolutely indispensable. If the ships couldn't be made seaworthy again, they were used for scrap metal. The ever-widening strip of water between my ship and the dock was rife with a murky sheen of oily filth. And amid the iron, motors, and turbines, they were bound to encounter a few corpses. So much the better for the relatives. It didn't mean anything to me. None of them were going anywhere.

That all began in a half-ruined tower erected on top of an apartment building roof on Caputxes Street, right in front of Barcelona's cathedral, Santa Maria del Mar. That's where I watched the No-Sister-Salvador meet his cruel fate while the baron stood by. Salvador, my friend and companion, was practically a brother to me. The baron's daughter, a nun, was another witness to the murder. The nobleman was so ashamed, he agreed to spare my life on the condition that I'd pack off immediately for Africa and keep my mouth shut.

I swore that someday I would avenge my friend's death.

Eight years have passed since that day. Now I'm a sergeant in the Spanish Legion. As a Legionnaire, I can go anywhere I want in Spain with my head held high. I stick to my father's advice: "Keep them fooled."

Three years ago, in 1946, I found myself back in Barcelona. I was on leave, bringing my son from North Africa to Catalonia to place him in my mother's care. Some of my buddies who'd been in the city not long before told me that Barcelona hadn't changed at all. Supposedly it was as bustling and hectic as always. . . . But it seemed completely different to me. Because of all the electrical cuts, it felt like a city of shadows. The streets were desolate, as if they'd just been bombed. Offices went about their business beneath the dim glow of candles, grocery shops were illuminated by carbide lights, and restaurants made do with kerosene lamps. But then, my impressions might have also been altered by the fact that I saw the city through my father's eyes. My father, Joan Aleu, was a commercial sign painter. When I was little, he'd often let me keep him company on Saturdays as he worked. He would lay a plank across two stepladders, placed side by side, and climb right up onto this makeshift scaffolding. It was set at just the right height so customers could go in and out of the store without having to hunch down very much. Usually I'd scramble up there with him, taking my place on the plank next to the paints and brushes. I'd sit with my back to the wall, facing the street, legs dangling. And as he put the finishing touches on some sign, I'd listen to his views about the world:

"Being up here on the scaffolding is an ideal place to observe people, Niso. Everybody goes about their business pretty much the same way, repeating a series of unconscious gestures. That's not some sort of coincidence. The way we hold ourselves makes us who we are. And we are who we are because of the way we move. But it doesn't matter. You'll understand when you're older . . ."

He was of the opinion that important aspects of city life such as customs, history, and language were continuously evolving, all the time, if only imperceptibly. What never changed, according to him, were the movements and gestures. And these were what defined the character of a society, since these behaviors were spontaneous and unconscious. We are mere passersby, walking in the footsteps of other passersby like us, repeating ourselves a thousand times and copied by others a thousand more, and all of us completely unaware. They were the vestiges of our collective lives: pulling out a handkerchief to blow your nose as you walk, slamming a window shut by accident but actually doing it intentionally; lazily slipping a jacket off in the middle of the street when it gets hot out. . . . My father was quick to defend his theory that the citizens in Barcelona wiped their noses in public differently than those who lived in Madrid. I can offer countless other examples. I remember them all. He was a layman's philosopher, who dreamed up his theories eight feet above the ground while painting storefronts.

On returning to Barcelona that May of 1946, I remembered what my father had said and realized why the city seemed so changed. People blew their noses differently, didn't bang the windows so hard, and men had stopped lazily removing their jackets and throwing them over their shoulder when it got hot. Those behaviors, which according to my father were a kind of citizens' identity card, were radically altered. Maybe I was the only one who noticed. And I know how it must sound when I say that, bit by bit, as if following some unseen code, Barcelona had undergone a transformation simply because its inhabitants didn't wipe their noses the way they used to. But maybe it was true, because the Regime had taken our very snot away from us. We didn't even own the mucus in our own noses. How could anyone be expected to blow them the same way?

During that leave I realized that those who'd lost the war were still struggling to survive amid tremendous repression in Barcelona. No one was above suspicion, anyone under suspicion could be easily sent to prison, and every prisoner had to face a daunting new justice system. And it was no longer necessary to take the law into your own hands; the new justice system set up by Franco's Regime made it possible to seek revenge without breaking the law. Poverty and an utter lack of the most basic necessities were the norm. Endless lines, rationing, and hunger were a part of daily life. The streetcars were old and there weren't very many. They were so packed with passengers that people, for lack of a ticket or standing room inside, would risk riding through the streets hanging off the doors, windows, and running boards.

The winners, on the other hand, were a completely different story. The new ruling class ostentatiously threw their money around in the latest nightclubs and bars. The worst were capable of seeking out the small perks proffered by the Regime: jobs, promotions handed out at the expense of workers from the losing side, permits, and concessions. More than anything, people would benefit from privileged information leaked by a corrupt administration. You could see it every day in Melilla, and Barcelona was no different, filled with people who struck it rich overnight, thanks to the black market.

How could anyone claim that Barcelona hadn't changed? I took a walk over to the tower on Caputxes Street. Nobody recognized me with my thick Legionnaire's beard. I stood on Plegamans Street gazing up at the little hideaway—it's the only spot where you can get a glimpse of it from the street—but I didn't want to go up there. I still have the image burned into my brain of No-Sister-Salvador on that roof, wounded and limping, trying to escape the police. But it didn't end there. Salvador, despite his disability, had spent the whole war scared to death of being taken off to fight. And that day the Baron de Remei ordered the police to terrorize him. And that instant he fell straight into the void. Or, I should say, was made to fly off the roof and onto the ground. I'll return to the tower someday. But it will only happen once I'm back in Barcelona for good. Once the rage has settled deeper into my bones.

Right now, it's impossible.

No-Sister-Salvador was like a big brother to me. I'll never forgive those who were responsible for his death. Or for the death of my father. He died of a heart condition. And he developed that heart condition during the two and a half years he was imprisoned in the Miranda de Ebro concentration camp.

This story, among many other things, is about two men who are gone from the world but are still very much mine. Their deaths occurred after the fighting stopped, but the war still got them in the end.

This story is also about keeping promises.

And it's about revenge.

CHAPTER ONE

"Let me tell you about my friend Bartomeu Camús," my father said, out of nowhere.

He was resting his head against the pillow, his eyes closed. At the time neither of us could know that he had only seven days left to live. It was the second and last mention he ever made of the concentration camp. A staccato of short sentences fell from his lips at a steady pace; he paused occasionally to rest and sip from a glass of water.

"Bartomeu was from Barcelona. He was a young man, younger than me, with a pale, gaunt face and a ready laugh. He'd been taken prisoner in the region around Terol in February of '38. He showed up at the prison camp in the early '40s, after I'd already been there for almost a year. We quickly became friends. I was the only one he trusted. We slept in the same barracks. The two of us shared everything, talked about all the things that we'd do together in Barcelona once it was all over . . . I don't know why, but the soldiers were extremely cruel to him. He was always the first to be punished. They assigned him the most thankless tasks and beat him for no reason . . . Bartomeu hadn't been classified yet, despite the fact that he'd been there longer than most of the other prisoners. Whenever there was a surprise search, they always rummaged through his possessions with particular zeal. I asked him why they had it in for him, but Bartomeu Camús just shrugged his shoulders and smiled. That I'm here today, that I've managed to live just a little bit longer, it's thanks to Camús. He saved my life.

"One day they took us to work in a quarry, outside the camp. As we were about to pack up, a strange feeling came over me. I couldn't catch my breath, my head reeled, and I fell to the ground. The soldiers tried to kick and club me back onto my feet, concentrating their blows on my head, chest, and kidneys. They split my lip, gashed my cheek, and practically shattered a couple of ribs. Just breathing made me feel dizzy with pain. By the time they realized that they'd gone too far, a lot of damage had been done. The soldiers wanted to finish me. Dump me on the mountainside like a piece of dung. It was the most practical and simplest thing to do: They shot you up with a couple of bullets and then claimed that you had attempted to escape. I wasn't so much afraid of dying as I was of being wounded and then abandoned by those scum in the middle of nowhere. That I would perish slowly, and alone. Bartomeu Camús begged them not to do it. The soldiers were so taken aback by his reaction that they came up with another diabolical idea. Bartomeu's kindness spurred them to more wickedness. They told him that they would spare my life if he was able to carry my body on his back all the way to the camp infirmary without once letting my feet touch the ground. Laughing, they said that since he was so brave, he could either accept the task or both of us would be shot on the side of the road. Bartomeu Camús accepted. The other prisoners were scared to death and began to mourn us before he'd begun. It was an impossible feat. Clearly they were going to lose two companions instead of one. They helped me climb onto Bartomeu's back. I held on as best I could, despite the agonizing pain in my ribs. It wasn't only my body he was hefting; it was the exhaustion of a full day's work. But slowly, dragging one foot after the other, as the soldiers taunted and prodded him with rifles, he reached the infirmary without once slackening. Bartomeu Camús saved my life.

"As soon as I recovered, we were separated. Before I was transferred to another barrack, Bartomeu showed me a small blue folder emblazoned with a dragon drawn in crimson ink. He told me in a grave voice: 'Now they're splitting us up. Here are some papers of mine that I want you to keep safe if anything should happen to me.'

"I thought it was strange and replied that the opposite was more likely to be the case. After all, I was the one whose life was most at risk, I was the one who was leaving, abandoning the numbingly familiar routine of camp life. Bartomeu Camús replied with a placid smile:

" 'The way things are going, you never know. If anything should happen to me while you're away, the papers will be in Purgatory. Understand? Do what you see fit with them.'

" 'Purgatory' was a safe hiding place where we used to stow small items temporarily. It was a hole in a tree that was very discreet and practical, as it was out beyond the barracks, well out of the sight of other prisoners. Normally we would stash food there, pieces of bread, a potato, a handful of carob beans . . .

"My battalion was sent off with orders to rebuild a convent near Valladolid, some one hundred and twenty miles away. The daily regime was no different than that of Camp Miranda: shouting, beatings, and constant humiliation. We worked from morning till night, subsisting for days on a crust of bread and a broth of boiled turnips or potato skins. They worked us to the bone. We cut stone and heaved the blocks, built walls, cleared away rubble . . . Our lack of strength led to accidents: crushed hands, broken arms and legs, head injuries. The wounds would often get infected and the already weak prisoners died quickly. They were buried like dogs in unmarked graves right where they fell. Sometimes the military wouldn't even bother to register their deaths. We were back at the camp in two months' time. It was a bitter cold winter day. Everyone was anxious; a prisoner had tried to escape, which was strange. The soldiers had been given orders to shoot to kill. And if they didn't execute the fugitive on the spot, he was beaten and kept tied to the flagpole that stood in the central plaza for all to see. In winter being bound and exposed all night with the thermometer below zero meant pneumonia. In summer being out all day under the hot sun led to heatstroke. Either one could be fatal. We all knew that if you did manage to escape, your family outside would pay for it in the form of threats, reprisals . . . Nobody wanted to take that chance. It didn't take long to capture the fugitive. In the distance we could see how they dragged him, semiconscious, to the river. The man barely twitched when they threw him in headfirst. The Bayas River is narrow and the water scarcely goes up to your waist. He couldn't manage to pull himself up. Once he had gotten good and wet, they stretched him out on a sort of bench by the riverbank. They tied him up like a sausage, with his head hanging out one end and his feet the other. Then they just left him there. The prisoner spent the whole night like that, soaked, frozen, and, I imagine, terrified.

"The next day, as always, they called us to order for the flag raising in front of the barracks with a barrage of shouts and clubbing. Our castigated companion was brought over. He was completely rigid. The man looked like a block of ice. He had frozen to death in the exact same position that he had taken on the bench. It was Bartomeu Camús. They forced us to go through the daily ceremonials as though nothing had happened: formation, roll call, raising the flag, and singing their anthems with all the appropriate cheers thrown in. And all the while Bartomeu seemed to be watching us intently, with

his eyes wide open and his face stretched tight, as though he longed
to sing with us . . .

"The military didn't even wait for the corpse to thaw before they
buried him. I was lucky enough to be chosen to do it, together with
a couple of other inmates. Bartomeu's body was loaded onto a handcart. I pushed him while the other two men carried picks and shovels. We left camp heading toward the river and walked along its banks
for a while, without knowing where we were going. Three soldiers,
guns loaded and at the ready, guarded us closely. Maybe they were
afraid that we would try to get even. The morning was clear and
bright, but very cold. And we were going to give Bartomeu Camús,
my friend, a most indecent burial. As his body defrosted, the wheels
of the cart sank deeper into the ruts in the road. We followed a pair
of train tracks until reaching a fairly large thoroughfare. We walked
along the side of the road for another three quarters of an hour until
they made us stop at a dusty fork, marked by a round rock that was
flattened like a small millstone. We headed down a dirt road that disappeared into the landscape. The cart banged against the rocks and
ruts in our path. Bartomeu Camús's body, no longer frozen, jerked
about like a man with convulsions. It took yet another good half hour
to reach a pine forest. We started to dig a hole before a pine tree whose
two great branches made it look like a giant letter Y. The earth was
as hard as a stone, but we were able to carve out a sufficiently deep
cavity. Perhaps too deep, but the least we could do was to keep the animals from ripping open his grave and desecrating the remains. We
lowered the body with great care and began to cover it with earth. The
soldiers, furious, interrupted our work. All three of us prisoners, lined
up in a row, bowed our heads in silent terror. They were yelling at us
because we had begun to bury Bartomeu without having pronounced
his last rites. We were forced to kneel down in front of the chasm, facing the body, while the soldiers offered a muttered rendition of the

Lord's Prayer. Only then did they let us carry on with our somber task. Once we had finished, I asked a corporal for permission to fashion some sort of cross, no matter how simple, even if it was just a pair of branches bound together. He wouldn't allow for any sort of marker, let alone a cross. Bartomeu Camús, like many others, was laid in the ground as you might bury a common beast . . . But yes, his assassins had the delicacy to recite the Lord's Prayer before sending him off to the great beyond.

"I tattooed the outlines of that place onto my memory. As soon as I returned to the concentration camp, I wrote down as many details as I could remember, especially the Y-shaped tree. A few days later I reached my hand down into Purgatory and felt for the folder with the dragon outlined in red ink. Within was an envelope with various receipts, documents, and a sheaf of papers that I had never seen before.

"I fell ill not long afterward. I had been feeling weak for days. My heart would either beat frenetically, or seem to stop altogether. I lacked strength, couldn't catch my breath, and felt faint. They took me to the infirmary, but I noticed that they didn't bother to give me anything stronger than aspirin, which meant that I wasn't expected to get better. They only tried to cure those who had good prospects for a full recovery. I was being left to die. Prisoners with some hope of making a full recovery were sent to Haro, a concentration camp for the injured and disabled between Miranda and Logroño. The government didn't restore prisoners to health just to save money; they were trying to turn a profit . . . But thanks to one of the nurse aides, Eusebio Fernández, I was able to write a few parting words to you and your mother. I was convinced that I would never see either of you again. Eusebio was a civilian from the city of Miranda. He went in and out of the camp every day and didn't mind doing small favors for the ailing prisoners. I asked him for some paper and a pencil, and he complied. He also agreed to mail you the letter if it came down to that. He was a good man. There are actually a few good people, you know, in among the dung heap of humanity that is the Regime. The problem is that you don't see it in their faces, Niso. Remember that. Eusebio was as tense and straight as a telephone pole. His only conversation was 'yes' and 'no.' But he was a good person. He used to sneak me pieces of cheese and, once in a while, even a book."

After speaking for so long, my father took a sip of water, leaned his head back, and fell asleep. He had made a considerable effort. He had been talking for over twenty minutes straight. I had never heard him say so much, or speak so long, in my entire life. Over the next seven days I couldn't stop thinking about how my father seemed to be truly haunted by Bartomeu's death.

He passed away a week later. It was on a June morning, and I was only fifteen and a half. I was out on the Manning patio, in the middle of Señor Giner's gym class. One of the nuns came outside to fetch me. She told me to hurry up. I was wanted urgently at home. Making no effort to conceal her complete disinterest in the matter, she said: "It appears that your father is dying."

She didn't tell me anything I didn't already know. For over a week my father had been more out of this world than in it. But it had been a long time since there'd been anything left of Joan Aleu, the Letter Painter, as we knew him. War and the concentration camp had reduced my father to a pile of skin and bones, graced with a couple of gray cells but not much else. He had simply ceased to exist. Nonetheless, in that moment, I still felt cheated.

"I know that, Sister . . ."

"I should have said that he's receiving his last rites. And you should consider yourself a lucky young man."

"Really?" I replied, taken aback.

"Oh, indeed! It hasn't been very long since your father got back. In a manner of speaking, you haven't had the chance to get attached to him again . . . If he must die, he might as well do it now. You'd feel it more keenly later on. I doubt that Our Lord minds taking him a bit earlier. On the contrary, with so many Reds to absolve, He mustn't slacken his pace . . ."

The nuns at the Charity Home had just that sort of pragmatic vision of how Our Lord conducted his day-to-day activities. At the same time, it felt strange to hear someone speak of a living man as though he were already dead. Their ready knowledge of the afterlife was equally curious. They were experts on everything about the next world, especially concerning matters of organization. Which saint went on the Lord's right, which went below, and where each angel and archangel could find its rightful position. It wasn't a bit surprising that they should die so peacefully. To a believer, death was little more than moving your household, a mere change of residence. They applied this all-encompassing logic to everything. The religious types had often struck me as odd, capable of unusual behavior or of saying just about anything. After January 26, 1939, they began to seem contradictory and simply incomprehensible. A boy just a bit older than me had gotten quite sick not long before. The adults thought nothing of talking right in front of him, even if we were within earshot, about how the poor soul's days were numbered. I overheard the same nun who had called me a lucky young man inform him: "You may be dying, but that doesn't mean you shouldn't be happy. You have every reason to smile and feel content. Don't you realize that it won't be long before you meet Our Lord?"

The boy began to sob, horrified. The nun found his fearful cries terribly impertinent. The child wasn't yearning to see Jesus Christ! And she not only neglected to comfort him, she actually became angry, dismissing the boy as a coward and an atheist. She told him he should follow the martyred Bishop Irurita's example, executed by a FAI firing squad in Moncada: "The bishop blessed each bullet, because, according to legend, he said that those slugs of lead were his keys to heaven. Why should you be any different, ungrateful wretch?"

The sounds of screaming nun and crying boy wafted out into the hallway for a good while longer.

The Charity Home was no stranger to death. It was a part of our daily lives during the war, but in peacetime typhoid fever kept it ever present.

I said good-bye to comrade Giner, went upstairs to get dressed, and headed home.

My mother's eyes were reddened when she opened the door, but her gaze was curiously firm. She looked at me as though I were a stranger. Then, wiping her face, she said, "Now go on in there and say good-bye to your father."

"Where is he going?"

I was being purposely obtuse. We'd all known for days where my father was going. Not deigning to answer, my mother opened the door to their bedroom and nudged me inside. I was just a fifteen-year-old boy visiting his dying father. And I felt awful about it.

It was shocking to see him in that state. His condition had worsened considerably since my last visit. Both eyes were sunken deep into a crown of bruised purple flesh that contrasted sharply with the pasty whiteness of his face. I remembered how, not a week before, he'd been bursting with vitality despite his illness. While telling me Bartomeu Camús's story, he'd glowed with an inner radiance. Now that light had been snuffed out. My father no longer looked sick; he looked like a corpse. The bedcovers were pulled up to his face, so that all one could see were his eyes shut tight. I could hear his breath rattling in heavy gasps. It was odd how little space the man seemed to occupy in the bed, almost as if he'd shrunk. He looked like a slightly oversize porcelain doll.

"Niso . . . ," he called out.

"What?"

"You should say, 'How may I help you?'" my mother whispered fiercely.

"How may I help you?" I parroted.

No answer came. He opened his mouth wide and told me to move closer, but this time I kept silent. My mother gave me a sharp push from behind. I took a couple of steps forward. My father turned his head toward me and attempted a smile. He managed to free one of his hands from the sheets and motioned me toward his side. This time, instead of a shove, my mother cuffed me so hard that the impact sent me reeling against the bed. I may have been about to lose my father, but my mother and her blows were there to stay. Resolutely, I drew nearer. One never knew, maybe he wanted to pronounce his last words. At the cinema I'd seen how important these parting statements could be plenty of times. I paid close attention so as not to miss something and then regret it for the rest of my life. My ear was practically touching his cheek. I could feel his breath. Then, in a voice that sounded more like a whistle, he said, "I'm fucked, Niso. It's over."

"What?"

"It's over. I'm fucked. Understand?"

"Yes," I said, not understanding a thing.

"What did I say?"

"It's over. I'm fucked . . ."

A laugh jumped out of me before I could stop it. My dying father said "fucked." I turned, all smiles, to my mother, but the look that she shot me wiped the grin right off my face. She hadn't heard. Who knew what she thought he might have said. . . . I moved back to the bed. My father spoke again.

"I'm fucked, Niso. People don't go to heaven or hell when they die, they're just fucked, it's over. Listen to me . . ."

I paid close attention. Maybe now he would stop joking and pronounce the real last words, the serious ones. But instead he sank back into silence. His eyes were closed and his mouth hung open. I glanced back at my mother, but she didn't return my gaze. Her eyes were trained fixedly on the sick man. She motioned me away from the bed. I was just about to move away when my father suddenly revived and grasped my hand.

"Don't move!"

Then he ordered my mother to leave the room, insisting that he wanted to talk to me, and only me. She hesitated for a moment, not knowing what to think, but in the end she gave in. What else could she do? Everyone complies with the last wishes of the dying. When we were alone, he said: "You'll be all grown-up before long. You have to swear to me that you'll take care of your mother and behave. Be just as good to her as she was to me. Do you promise?"

"Yes."

He leaned his head back against the pillow and closed his eyes. The man could hardly breathe. He murmured a few more words after that, but I couldn't make them out. He fell silent, with his top two front teeth gnawing at his bottom lip. He looked just like a rabbit. He stayed like that for about a minute and a half. Then he shifted, opened his eyes, and stared right at me. He tried to sit up a little bit and made as if he wanted to whisper something in my ear.

"Niso . . ."

"What?"

"Do you remember the story I told you last week?"

"Which? The one about Bartomeu Camús?"

"Yes. Now listen. As soon as you can, when you're older, I want you to find Bartomeu Camús's remains. Take them away and give him a decent burial . . ."

"What?"

His request took me completely by surprise. What was he asking me to do? I started to get nervous and, silently, began to cry. He didn't even notice. And as tears began to slide thickly down my cheeks, my father gulped some air and went on:

"If you can't take him away, mark the place well so there can be no mistake. Make sure you'll be able to find it again. Even if you have to wait a lifetime. That's what I want you to do. I would have done it myself, but now I won't be able to. You'll have to do it. So he's not lost to memory. Bartomeu would've done the same for me. He wouldn't have left me to rot in some unmarked pit on the mountainside. Burying a dead man like that, without his loved ones even knowing where to mourn, it's a crime. When you bury someone that way, you deny the humanity of the dead. It turns man into an animal, a thing. It's very important that you understand that. Do you promise to do what I ask?"

I stopped crying and uttered yes, loud and clear.

"How will I find him?" I added.

My father pointed to his armoire, telling me to push a chair over and climb onto it.

"Look around up there."

I could barely reach. My hand felt around blindly. After several attempts, I finally hit upon something. I stood on tiptoes and pulled it toward me. It was a thick paper envelope.

"What is it?" I asked.

My father didn't reply. There wasn't much time left and he was already off in his own world.

"You'll have to be very careful. Don't tell anyone, not even your mother. Remember, Niso, don't ever trust these people. They've no sense of compassion or pity. Don't believe them. No matter what they may say, the truth is that they'll never forgive us. Franco's supposed clemency is a lie. Play along, fool them into thinking you're one of them. They're so arrogant that they'll never know the difference. Do what I say, and there'll be treasure for you at the end."

Treasure? I took a hard look at him. He was overwrought by the circumstances of the moment. I'd just promised to find the bones of his dead friend, but he hadn't even told me where to look. He just lay there, eyes shut tight and mouth hanging open, breathing in that hideous manner. I watched him for a while. He spoke in an ever-weakening, rasping whistle that continually lost strength. I heard someone come in and turned around. It was my mother. We stood there staring at each other. All I could think to ask was:

"Is he dead yet?"

"No . . ."

She pulled me out of the room and left me in the hands of No-Sister-Salvador. She went back in and closed the door without noticing the envelope my father had given me for my inheritance.

I thought how someday I'd tell my father's story, just as he'd told me, about Bartomeu Camús, who in turn would have had another tale to tell. It was like a set of Russian nesting dolls, each one fitting neatly into the other.

Of course I opened the envelope right away. There was a piece of paper folded up inside. I flattened out the creases. On one side was a pencil-drawn map of the Miranda concentration camp, very crudely done, with rows of rectangles that were labeled "barracks," an undulating line that stood for the Bayas River, a dotted line that was meant to represent the train tracks. In one corner, next to the fence, almost touching the railroad track, behind two barracks, was a perfectly visible cross along with the word "Purgatory." The fact that my father had taken pains to draw out and mark the exact spot of his hiding place meant that there must be something important there. It might even have something to do with the location of his friend's burial place.

So there you have it; a map leading to a corpse with a story to tell. And, yes, maybe treasure.

In one corner of the sheet, I could make out the words "Eusebio Fernández, nurse," and the name of the village, Miranda de Ebro. But nothing else. Not even an address or telephone number. Nothing.

What had happened to the blue folder with the dragon in red ink?

My father died at dawn. My mother had been preparing the body for several hours by the time I woke up. When I saw him next, he was stretched out on the bed with an old coin on each eye to keep his eyelids firmly closed. Those ungainly pieces of tarnished copper had the unsettling effect of making my father look like a doll. His cheeks were shaven and his hair was combed. And his skin was whiter than ever. I took a close look, but couldn't see those rabbitlike teeth. His mouth had been carefully shut. My mother asked me if I wanted to kiss my father good-bye. I said yes, but I couldn't face up to it. I simply dropped down into a chair as the apartment began to fill up with strangers. My mind kept turning over the promise I'd made. I meant to keep that pledge, no matter what and no matter when. I would go find Bartomeu Camús's grave so that his memory would never be lost. That act would preserve my father's memory as well. And mine, too. It occurred to me that if he ceased to exist, then the part of me that was connected to his past ceased to exist, too. I decided that nobody was going to call me Niso anymore. That was all over. No longer would I be known as Niso, the Letter Painter's son, or Little Letter Painter. I told my mother and No-Sister-Salvador to call me Genís from then on.

My mother was deeply distressed. I felt so sorry for her that all I could do was scream.

"What do you want?" she replied.

"Yesterday Father predicted that I would find a treasure."

Her gaze was full of mourning, dripping with sadness. She hadn't even bothered to put on the pretty sunglasses that she wore to conceal her wandering eye. I put them on for her myself. My mother ruffled my hair, smiled, and said to me:

"Your father was very sick. Don't get any funny ideas. A treasure is something you're never going to have, ever."

She was completely mistaken.

CHAPTER TWO

Tuesday, October 18, to Thursday, October 20, 1949

The journey to Miranda isn't bad; a long trip, but enjoyable. I look out the window at the countryside going by. It's good just to stare and brood a bit. The ship out of Melilla dropped me off at the Barcelona docks early this morning and I was on the train by midday. I've gone clear across Catalonia in the blink of an eye. After being holed up in a pit like Melilla, you lose a sense of distance and start to yearn for wide-open spaces. Your eyes get sick of always getting caught up in houses, trees, animals, people, or objects. Melilla has about as much horizon as a matchbox. Outside the city, it's different. There are mountains, and beyond the mountains there is the desert. There aren't many open stretches in the Spanish Protectorate, but once in a while the French let us cross over into their zone, and they've got plenty. The desert lets you expand your vision, but you're forced to face the void. That vast expanse can make your head spin; the same thing happens to me out at sea. That's why I enjoy traveling by train. I get a glimpse of a flat-topped mountain, almost devoid of vegetation and crowned by what looks like a shepherd's hut. I also see a whole line of gray metal barracks set up for the railroad workers. I watch them at labor, wearing uniforms. But these guys aren't company men. They're inmates, political prisoners; Reds, condemned to forced labor. It's been ten long years since the end of the war, and you still see that sort of thing. At first, around 1939, 1940, they were everywhere. Endless rows of men set to clearing the rubble out of bombed-out buildings; rebuilding highways, roads, and churches; whatever was needed . . . my father was one of them.

The express is getting close to Lleida. Two peasants doze in front of me, mouths wide open. Their faces are ruddy and splotched. My eyes burn and my ears ring from the constant clamor of the train. We pass by the remains of an old castle on a hill and a herd of goats grazing in a dry riverbed. Villages are scattered here and there along the tracks. Rows of dark green trees stand like cutouts against an immobile, dark blue horizon. It's only October, but a chill has set in. Every so often the car is suddenly engulfed by the telltale stench of pigs. I'm hypnotized by the blanched white smoke that escapes out of a factory chimney. It spreads out slowly as it rises, like thick lava sliding down the side of a volcano. Everything is half hidden by a rainy mist that cloaks the landscape. The train screeches to an abrupt halt in the early hours of the morning. Some passengers exit in different directions. Since I wasn't paying attention, I have to make a mad dash for the train-car door and bang my forehead sharply against the lock. A direct hit followed by excruciating pain. For a few seconds I detest that lock as fiercely as one can hate an inanimate object. I look out the window. We're in the middle of nowhere and it's beginning to get light out. A few seconds later, four Guardias Civiles appear as I rub the rising bump on my head. The men move slowly among the passengers with their firearms poised and ready. They peer into the faces of the crowd. They check a few people's papers. There is a retarded boy sitting a couple of seats behind me. The other passengers, including his mother, try to keep the child amused as if he were a little puppy. But the boy doesn't laugh one bit. He just concentrates on scooping up the bread crumbs from supper with one hand and transferring them to the palm of the other until they begin to sprinkle the suitcase on his lap that his mother set up as a makeshift table. After having collected a good handful of crumbs, he drops them down his gullet listlessly. Now he's lying curled up against his mother, tightly wrapped in a woolen shawl. Three guards stop and stare at him, but the fourth heads in my direction. It seems that my beard and the scar on my head have excited his attention. He asks me where I'm going. Without answering, I pull my wallet out of my jacket and show him the documentation that identifies me as a Legionnaire, rank of sergeant. I hear one of the guards hit the child and laugh. The boy screams like a lamb brought to slaughter. The guard at my side gapes in wide-eyed wonder after having looked over my papers. The poor fool immediately stands to attention. The other three follow suit. I stand up and head toward the guard who struck the still whimpering boy. I give him a hard stare. He's young and probably doing military service in La Benemérita. The kid is quaking because he has no idea who I am. All he knows is that his superior has just saluted me. My arm is itching to smack him across the face. Speaking very slowly and never taking my eyes off his face, I make sure to douse him in a thin film of spittle as I ask:

"Why did you hit this child?"

The young guard is truly terrified. He says that he had no idea that the boy was slow. I have to control myself so as not to attract unwanted attention. I order him to apologize to the boy's mother, a woman swathed in widow's weeds from head to toe, her gaze trained doggedly to the floor. The guard does so, doling out the same pathetic excuse that he used on me. The woman nods her head almost imperceptibly. I keep them standing to attention for the fifteen seconds that it takes me to get back to my place. I sit down and, without even bothering to look back, order them to be as they were. Then I tell them to get out of there and stop causing trouble. They leave the carriage quickly and quietly. Tension lingers in the air for a few moments. The other passengers had watched the confrontation with curiosity. They keep quiet, too. Now the boy dissolves into peals of laughter. His mother lifts her head, gives him a hard glare and then a sharp whack. Such is her right, she's his mother. It seems to calm the boy down. I go back to gazing out the window and can't help but overhear the speculations of the other passengers: Maybe the Guardia Civil is looking for black-market traders, or rebels on the run. Maybe I'm some kind of VIP. All of a sudden they remember how the guards seemed afraid of me and fall silent. They don't have any idea who they're dealing with. Just in case, they switch from their own Catalan language to Spanish. Nobody wants trouble. But it's no use; the Catalan peasants barely speak Spanish and soon give up talking at all.

The carriage falls silent. Farmhouses, villages, factories, telephone and electrical poles, plowed fields, fallow land, patches of forest, goats, and sheep all flash past. The retarded boy's leg starts to twitch. The spasms frighten him. His mother makes him bang the limb against the floor. Finally he calms down. I try to concentrate on my plan, my vision of the future. If all goes well, it won't be long before I'm far from here, starting a new life.

I still have plenty of work to do. And I'll need to be careful. I figure that a few days will be enough, eight or ten at the most. I have two objectives. First I've got to find and then somehow transport the body. Two people in Barcelona are waiting for word that I've uncovered the grave. Then they'll come up and give me a hand. Another contact who works at Barcelona's cemetery on Montjuïc will help me put an end to all this in an honorable and decent way. The next step is to find Camús's papers, which I hope will contain the dead man's last request. But then that blue folder has been hidden in a tree for eight or nine years.

When all that's done, I'll get the hell out of this country.

Tomorrow I'm expected at the Basic Combat Training Facility that the Regime has set up at the old concentration camp, Miranda de Ebro. Two and a half years ago it was officially closed, once the last inmates had been transferred to the Nanclares de Oca Work Camp, right around the corner, near Vitoria. It was up and running for around ten years. Thousands of political prisoners lived and died there. Then, for two years it was left to rot. And just when it looked like it would stay empty and forgotten, they decided to transform it into a boot camp. All the better, since it gives me a chance to do what I have to do without attracting too much notice. For the past six months, the very same barracks where my father was held prisoner have been teeming with a bunch of kids going through basic training. I've supposedly come to Miranda to talk to these youngsters; give them the usual harangue about the virtues of the military life. Above all I'm supposed to convince them that signing up for the Spanish Legion is a highly advantageous and attractive option. It didn't take very much to convince my superiors in Melilla. I requested a transfer to this region of Burgos for personal reasons. And since I would already be in the area, I offered to spend a couple of days at the training camp, in order to enlist some recruits in the corps of the Spanish Foreign Legion. They were thrilled with the idea. So was the major in chief of the boot camp. He was proud to invite a real live Foreign Legion man, complete with beard and unbuttoned shirt, to stir up his future soldiers. As I've said before, I'm the biggest hypocrite in the world.

I arrive at Miranda de Ebro at daybreak. The station opens onto a wide avenue, flanked by new buildings and rows of trees. Everyone probably refers to it as the train station street. Actually, it's been dubbed Francisco Franco Avenue. I check into a pension near Calvo Sotelo Park. It's called Campillo, and I choose it because of the sign. The paint job is excellent and done with style. They probably spent a pretty penny on it, and right now some sign painter in Miranda de Ebro must be very pleased with his letters, just like my father when I was little. But the management wasn't content with just one sign. I see the same sharp outlines painted across the side doors of a cream-colored Chrysler with an eight-horse engine in mint condition, parked outside the entrance. The pension's reception desk is presided over by a wizened old lady with a white bun and a sky blue woolen shawl draped over her shoulders. The lady doesn't lift her head as she crochets behind the counter, holding the work at arm's length to avoid eyestrain. I say hello, but she doesn't reply. There isn't anybody else attending the front desk. The pension doesn't seem to have been in business very long, but the rugs and curtains give it a certain presence. One of those imposing grandfather clocks is set against the wall. Just as I'm about to leave, a tall and reedy man in his fifties, with languid eyes of a nondescript color, appears. He's wearing a green wool vest. A narrow pair of rectangular spectacles rests on the tip of his nose. He looks like he should be a tailor instead of an innkeeper. Instead of asking for a room, I should ask to be fitted for a jacket. While halfheartedly suppressing a yawn, he tells me to disregard his mother.

"She lost my father to cancer a few years back now, and ever since, she's done nothing except crochet and brood. At this point she's so old, we're not sure what's really going on in her head. Either she's taken refuge in her memories or she's gone stone deaf."

My face probably can't hide my disgust. I don't like it when a man is disrespectful of his mother, especially when he's standing right in front of her. If I wasn't so dead tired, I'd get the hell out of here right now. The hotelier looks stunned after glancing through my documents. Now my beard seems to make sense to him. He also stares at

the scar on my head with its thick, pink, raised welt of skin. Everyone is fascinated by it. There are some things in life that you just can't
avoid doing. For example, if you walk by a bicycle with its wheels in
the air, the temptation is to set one of them spinning. Staring at my
scar is another one of those inevitable compulsions. Somebody will
be talking to me, and as they chat, their eyes drift upward. I'm used
to it. It's a sizable and obvious blemish. People often assume that it's
a war wound. Even though I'm too young to have seen combat, I
never contradict them.

The hotelier says, "We've had all sorts of military men, especially
during wartime, but never a Legionnaire."

The place is apparently named after its proprietor, also named
Campillo, who is like one of those chatty old-fashioned shopkeepers
who greet their customers with a bow. I cut him off, letting my irritation show.

"I've just gotten off the train. It's seven o'clock. I'm tired."

"Of course, of course . . ."

He orders a maid to carry my luggage up to the room. The valise
stays with me. Among other items, it is full of guns and ammunition: my officially issued military pistol and a handgun bought on
the black market in Melilla. Upstairs, the room is austere. There's an
antique chest of drawers of heavy, high-quality wood and a walnut armoire with a mirror. A table in the corner has a brazier crackling beneath it. They've given me a double bed. Once alone, the first thing
I do is find a place to hide the handgun. Forget the water tank of the
toilet or above the armoire. I yank the bedside table away from the
wall and pull a carpenter's drill and two pieces of rope out of the suitcase. I make two holes in the table back and thread the cords through
them. I tie a knot and pull the strings tight enough so that both the
butt and the barrel of the gun are cradled between the ropes. It won't

fall, even if the night table were to get rocked somehow. I return the table back to its original position and, only then, stretch out on the bed. I fall asleep almost instantly.

I don't wake up until noon the next day. I go down to the lobby, where the old lady still hasn't let up with her crocheting. Her son is there, too, and immediately asks if I've slept well. I tell him that I'm hungry.

He accompanies me into the dining room. It's crowded, despite being small and not very attractive, since it doubles as a regular restaurant and bar with a separate street entrance. The tables are filled by travelers or workers from the neighborhood. The place reeks of disinfectant.

As a starter, Campillo brings out a pot of traditional Catalan garlic soup with all the fixings. It's heaven on earth, the best I've ever had. I congratulate him, and after offering thanks, he can't resist saying:

"It's not actually Catalan garlic soup; we call it Castilian stew. Our kitchen makes it with ham, sausage, salami, and a poached egg. That is in addition to the usual ingredients of garlic, toast, and essence of cumin."

Good for him, I think. I hadn't meant to offend, but the end result is the same. On such a frigid October day, a warm soup like that warms the body and puts color in your cheeks.

After dinner I ask if I may place a call to the training camp. The man, forgetting my earlier offense, practically knocks over his decrepit mother to grab the telephone. He looks pleased, as if to say of course he has contacts at the camp. . . . I'm put through to the major in person. His name is José Carlos Cedazo, and, judging by his voice, he's probably middle-aged. For all intents and purposes he really should be a colonel by now. I'm sure it won't be long before I'll find out why he's not. As expected, he greets me heartily over the telephone. He's a full-fledged major and I'm a mere sergeant. But the Legion possesses a certain mystique. After all, General Franco began his career of military glory among our ranks. So the major behaves accordingly. I treat him with the utmost respect, quickly gaining his trust. The man speaks quickly and it's hard to catch everything he says. I gather that he's also served in Africa. We agree that they'll send a vehicle around tomorrow to pick me up.

I go for a stroll around Miranda. It's a Spanish provincial city, neat and dignified. The oldest section of the city is divided by the Ebro River. The train tracks cut across the center, separating a relatively new neighborhood from the rest of the town. The atmosphere isn't much different than that of other cities of its size. There's a deep quiet, a kind of stillness, in the air. The war brought a fear that has nestled into everyone's bones and still remains. It's like when you get caught in the middle of one of those violent summer downpours. You duck patiently under some balcony to wait for it to stop raining. All you can do is hope that the clouds will pass soon. And then you continue on as if nothing had happened, as if every last trace of the storm had been blown away by a gust of wind. But the chill in the air remains. We've been huddling under a balcony for over ten years now, and there's no sign of it letting up. And I'm losing my patience.

I enter the Miranda Social Club, a sort of casino that's dimly lit and full of smoke. A bunch of men play dominoes or cards. Six or seven more are in a corner hunched over shots of anise, listening blankly to the radio. The pompous voice of the Spanish National Public Radio announcer is reporting on Franco's upcoming trip to Portugal. All of Spain is in an uproar over Franco's travels. Our great leader never goes anywhere, and even if it's just Portugal, the trip is unprecedented. The Regime officials are running around like chickens with their heads cut off, getting in each other's way and giving each other updates. The casino owner steps out from behind the bar and goes over to turn up the radio so that everyone can hear. Even so, the men sitting around the radio don't budge.

> "And now, an update on Franco's journey through Portugal. A program of ceremonies has been organized to pay homage to Spain and Franco on the occasion of his visit to Lusitanian lands and promises to display untold splendor. As usual the Portuguese people and their government are prepared to pour forth their feelings of fraternal affection. As soon as Franco sets foot in Portugal on Saturday, the military will have a show of arms and a band of trumpets will play the national anthems of Spain and Portugal. Afterward a parade of troops will march past His Excellency, who will then finally travel on to Queluz by way of Lisbon, escorted by a regiment of motorized cavalry. Tomorrow, Thursday, October 21, the distinguished lady Doña Carmen Polo de Franco, wife of the Generalíssimo, and Señora Martín Artajo and Señora Regalado, the respective wives of the Spanish government's minister of foreign affairs and the minister of marine affairs, will arrive in the Portuguese capital. Other ladies and high government officials, in addition to special envoys from various Spanish organizations and newspapers, will also travel on the same train . . . His Excellency will set sail from Vigo for the port of Lisbon Friday night, onboard a Spanish squadron warship called *Miguel de Cervantes*. They are expected to disembark the next day around noon . . ."

One of the casino regulars, an old man of about seventy, with a pasty, misshapen face dominated by a pair of watery blue eyes, downs his anise in one gulp, coughs, and asks out loud, more to himself than to his companions, "Why is Señora Franco traveling by herself, and in a train no less?"

The patron, trying to strike a path through the dense cloud of smoke that engulfs the casino, waves one arm about as if trying to scare away a horde of ghosts. With the other, he carries a tray decked with more shots of anise. He overhears the old man and says, "It's obvious. This way, if anything happens to His Excellency, at least they won't kick the bucket at the same time . . ."

The old man looks at him, grabs his drink, and snaps back callously, "So what if they both get rubbed out? Nothing's going to happen to His Excellency, anyway."

He gets to his feet and ambles toward the men's room. Maybe he's one of the vast majority of citizens who voted for the Popular Front back in February 1936. That's the contradiction that everyone here must live with: Miranda de Ebro was Red. On July 18 of that fateful year, the city government was left-wing. In the face of a military takeover, it was natural that they should remain loyal to the Republic. The town had strategic importance because of its vital network of railroad lines. There was no time to waste or fool about, and the various factions were quick to take a stand. The Guardia Civil was sent in from Burgos and managed to put down any resistance from the opposition in less than twenty-four hours. The reprisals that followed were particularly brutal. They treated honorable and decent people who happened to be Republicans like common delinquents. Once the worst of the dissidents were out of the way, they got to work, setting up a military hospital, a training academy for officers and subordinate officers, not to mention the concentration camp. The town was even designated as a headquarters for Italian Fascist troops. After ripping out the wild weeds, the Fascists set about laying down manure and planting new seeds.

All this in a city that had been left-wing.

A lot of people had to be killed. They eliminated leaders and officials. Entire families were decimated in order to sow fear in future generations. Inevitably that kind of widespread terror always lurks beneath the surface of official propaganda. And these days that fear cleaves Spain in two. There might as well be a dividing line, drawn with pencil and a ruler, separating friends and enemies. Those who have to be afraid and those who don't. Those who live in fear are forced to seek refuge in those they can trust; an inner circle of friends and family. Essentially it boils down to a pact of silence, a quietly simmering resentment. And silence is a symptom of sadness. The Spanish don't need to express their sorrow because, ultimately, it has no voice. We are all equally mute. Mute and disconcerted with our current situation. It is an ever-present and chronic silence that the Regime, complacent and glutted, doesn't even need to control. The fear takes care of that all by itself.

I linger over the newspaper. By the time I leave the casino, it's already dark out. Above the Ebro, the sky has begun to clear, and the tufts of clouds rip apart, allowing a glimpse of black sky and some stars. The air is brisk. It is October 20 and we're not quite halfway into autumn. Cold settles quickly over this land.

CHAPTER THREE

One year before the war broke out, we went to live in the apartment on Caputxes Street, right in front of the Cathedral Santa Maria del Mar. It was small, but I liked it. The front door opened straight into the living room, which doubled as an entrance hall. There were moldings on the ceiling and red clay tiles on the floor. My parents' bedroom was off to the left. It had a set of French doors with apple green shutters that opened onto a small balcony facing the street. On the right, a narrow passageway led into a room that served as both my sleeping area and what my father proudly referred to as his workshop. A tiny kitchen and a water closet were wedged in between. And that was it. My parents squabbled for a while about the placement of my bed. It could go either by the window that opened onto the air shaft or on the other side of the room, next to the door. They were actually arguing about my health. The fumes from my father's paints might not affect me as much if I slept by the window. But then again, the smells might tend to linger longer in the air if all his supplies were shoved in the back of the room. . . . In the end they decided I should sleep next to the door. My father would keep the window open while he worked.

My father was a big man, with a sharp, prominent nose and long, jagged bangs. His massive hands ended in tapering fingers. His dark hair and skin were set off by a pair of vivid blue eyes. Since the color was so intense, they could be unsettling if you didn't know him. He had an eerily transparent stare. My mother had fallen in love with his striking features. According to her, he looked just like a gypsy. Always making sure to add, "But a handsome gypsy though . . ." But I always thought my mother, a petite redhead covered in freckles, was the pretty one. When seen holding hands from a distance, my parents could have been mistaken for father and daughter. My mother was a bundle of nerves. I would watch her little form in amazement as she did all sorts of heavy housework, like batting a mattress on the roof or airing out blankets on the balcony. Whenever she was angry or sad, her right eye would drift slightly toward the center of her face. And, of course, that always made me want to laugh. That roving orb served as a clear indicator of her mood. Before she'd even get a chance to say anything, it would begin to veer toward the center. Where there's lightning, there's thunder.

My father would always jokingly claim to be an expert in Catalan literature. Then he'd quickly specify, "But only the letters! I don't know anything about the words or phrases!" He loved his work, but he limited himself to signs and such, never painting anything figurative. He argued that in the twentieth century, it was ridiculous to go and paint people when photography and cinema could replicate humans down to the last detail. But letters . . . now letters were something entirely different. The work may not be as important as trying to photograph a person or capture a moving train on film. But it could be considered an art form, an art of the people, he would say.

He especially detested those oversize, florid letters that some editors commissioned to highlight the first word of a chapter. Or, for example, those sugarcoated illustrations that the Catalan illustrator Junceda drew for children's books: a little boy swinging from the top horizontal of the letter *Z;* another child running around the base of a capital *A;* a fat man in a vest, carrying a trunk on his back while stepping through the curve of an uppercase *U.* He didn't even want to hear about it. "That type of work isn't one thing or the other," he would say. "That guy is a toy maker, not a typographer!"

Stenciling up a wall border was about as decorative as he would get. He'd work on the small projects at home. For example, one of his regular clients was the neighborhood lottery store. It was an establishment called Confidence that'd been around forever. A blackboard hung in its storefront window announcing the daily winning prizes. The proprietor hired my father as needed to add nice, festive, rounded characters such as "Third Prize, so many thousands of pesetas, Christmas 19 . . ." My father would stop by, unhook the blackboard, and carry it carefully home with him as if his life depended on it. I'd watch his labors from bed until my eyes drooped shut with exhaustion. Whenever there wasn't other work, he'd experiment on devising new letterforms, inventing and fabricating his own templates. Often he'd rip off a part of a poster whose lettering had attracted his attention and bring it home. He'd give my mother a kiss, exclaiming, "I fell in love today."

"Do tell! And with whom, may I ask?"

"With this letter *S.*"

He'd show her a scrap of torn paper and proceed to whisk it off into the workshop. Then he'd tack it up on the wall with wads of chewed bread and set to replicating its forms with paper and pencil. After producing an exact copy, he'd tinker with the design for a while. When he was satisfied, he'd paint a final version on cardboard and cut it out. Then he'd hang the sample up with clothespins on a rope that stretched across the room. Every morning my eyes would be greeted by the same sight: half-finished signs, letters scattered about like socks, and piles of torn posters on the floor. And sometimes I'd find my own father, asleep with his head at my feet, a pencil in hand, a sketchbook chock-full of different characters fallen at his side. The pages were crammed with all sorts of typography. Designs copied from the package of the Ideales cigarettes, as solid as stone blocks; a poster from the Pau Casals Orchestra, with the letters ripped in half so they looked more like decorations on a box of Chinese tea; the elongated characters of Rialto Shoes that teetered forward as if they'd just been stopped dead in their tracks; the gravely gothic forms of the Catalan Chorus poster; the *T* in the word *Netol,* whose horizontal formed a kind of roof for the rest of the word. The *I*'s in the Iberian Ink ad had tails that slithered downward, writhing like snakes. . . . I especially loved the Maja Myrurgia Soap poster. The right stem of the *M* in the word *Maja* curved up and around *aja* as if in embrace; the *J* dipped deep down. The two *a*'s were so rounded that the word *Maja* appeared to stare fixedly at me like an owl.

My father often worked late after supper. He converted two bedside lamps into a set of spotlights to illuminate his evening vigils. My mother pieced together a homemade sleeping mask for that very purpose. It was cut out of an old curtain, with bits of elastic to keep it in place. I'd put it on and fall asleep listening to him curse under his breath if a letter didn't come out just right. "This damned *R* can go to hell and back thirty times." Or he'd try to egg himself on, saying, "Come on, come on, pretty *R,* I've almost got you now . . ." And as soon as he was satisfied with the results, he'd run and show them to my mother.

That was my father all right, a stubborn man in love with any letter that had been carefully designed, drawn, and painted.

He carried his equipment in a three-wheeled bicycle that a rag-man on our street kept in storage for him. Whenever scaffolding was needed, he'd bring along a pair of stepladders and a thick plank. The tricycle had been adapted in such a way that all this paraphernalia was lashed to a set of supports that he himself had soldered onto the sides. His supplies were strapped onto a wooden box affixed to the back: paints, brushes, turpentine, et cetera. My father always worked alone and took his own sweet time to finish each job. He was forever scrambling up and down the scaffolding to see how a sign was pro-gressing. Even variations in natural light were taken into account so as to ensure that the colors stayed consistent. He was a familiar fig-ure in the neighborhood of La Ribera. Everyone knew him as Joan Aleu, the Letter Painter. And they called me Little Letter Painter. The first thing I'd see on waking up on many a Sunday morning would be my father's form blocking the morning sun. He'd be on his way out the door, loaded down with all sorts of apparatuses, and ask me if I wanted to come along. I never once said no. I'd jump into the tri-cycle's storage box and away we'd go. There, in among the paints and brushes, I'd imagine that the bike was a tank, crossing enemy lines. I was just there to keep him company, and spent the day kicking stones, leafing through comic books, and listening to him talk about life. . . . Sometimes he'd call out, "Niso, go across the street. Back up more, farther, farther, now, that's good there. Stop. All right, take a look at this *S*. Pay attention. What do you think? Is this green the same shade as that one?"

Most of the time I didn't have any idea. I would reply that I didn't know, they looked the same to me. That would really get him angry. . . . One time we were down by the train station. I remember it perfectly well, even though I was only a young kid. A couple had taken over a restaurant and wanted to replace the old sign with a new one. The original announced the establishment as THE PAELLA SPOON,

FOOD AND LODGING. My dad was of the opinion that the sign was marvelous just the way it was. The man was incapable of painting over such a fine example of his craft. And the thought of taking it down, throwing it out, and making another one to put in its place was even worse. The owners complained that they'd have to replace it no matter what. Paella wasn't on the menu and they didn't let out rooms. Well, he managed to convince them to leave the sign intact by explaining how much more they had to lose than to win in the matter.

"It doesn't make that much difference anyway," he claimed. "If someone asks for a room, just tell them there're no vacancies and that's the end of it . . . If anybody tries to order paella, tell them it's not one of the daily specials. For every prospective customer you turn away, this beautiful sign will attract ten more."

That was my father. He'd rather lose work than destroy what he considered to be a fine example of local craftsmanship.

The neighbors on our floor were practically part of the family. Señor Pau lived in the apartment across the hall. He was a hearty old widower, with a big white beard that smelled like a snuffed-out pipe. The man looked like a painter or a sculptor straight out of the nineteenth century. He'd been a traveling salesman for decades before going into retirement, and suffered from a mild case of halitosis, a fact that he never tried to conceal. Señor Pau claimed it was from his years of wandering all over creation, with only cheap tavern wine to wash out his pasty mouth. He kept the massive sample case that he used to lug from one village to another as a relic of his golden years. It was empty, but I still loved it. It opened in separate sections, each filled with tiny compartments, and was covered in all sorts of handles and buckles. It still gave off the faint scent of ladies' perfume, which he'd sold across Catalonia for over thirty years. After taking retirement, Señor Pau seldom left the apartment. He always wore a dressing gown, beret, and slippers, even to go shopping. The old man raised pigeons on the roof, but not as some sort of a hobby. They earned their keep. From time to time he feasted on pigeons for lunch, done up in a vinaigrette sauce that was the specialty of his departed wife, Señora Nadala. I only had a vague recollection of her. They never had any children. He had to make do with the pigeons, a small pension, and the monthly rent of a young man who worked in the Born Market, No-Sister-Salvador. Salvador slept on a cot in the back room, next to the water closet. Actually, his room was the mirror image of mine. We could wave to each other across the air shaft. No-Sister-Salvador was quiet and reserved, with a hawklike nose and a deceptively languid look in his eyes. In his thick accent from Lleida, he would tell stories about when he worked as a fruit picker as a small boy.

I was awestruck by tales that he'd tell, mostly about his own adventures. They seemed lifted from the pages of a comic book. Our Saturdays always felt like the beginning of a grand adventure because they were spent in an abandoned tower on top of an apartment building roof on Caputxes Street. I don't remember exactly the first time that he took me there. Of course, it must have been before the war, because I was about nine years old. The tower hideout was our own little secret. I wasn't going to tell a soul. They would've had to skin me alive first. And I was very proud of the fact that someone so much older considered me to be worthy of his friendship and trust. The tower door was all bricked up and, in theory, no one could get in. No-Sister-Salvador showed me how to sneak in through an opening at the base of one of the walls. There was just enough room for one person to crawl through on all fours. Our makeshift entrance was easily hidden by a bunch of big earthenware pots and packing crates that lay scattered about on the roof terrace. Once inside, there was a wooden ladder leading up to a tiny garret room. . . . It was a small, boxy space about seven feet high, with one narrow window set into each wall.

They were always open, flooding the room with light. In summer the full glare of the sun made it impossible to breathe. In winter we froze thanks to the frigid air pouring in on all sides. But there, spring and fall were perfect. When No-Sister-Salvador discovered the tower, he had to do battle with all the nasty critters who'd taken refuge there before him. Pigeons are usually the first to colonize, but rats are always quick to follow. It took a bit of patience, but he managed to clean the space up. He fit the windows with wooden frames covered in wire mesh to keep the birds out. He even cobbled together a table complete with chairs, found some candles, brought in a mattress. . . . Often we'd do nothing more than simply be. On one of those quiet days, Salvador told me the story of his past. He was only fourteen years old when he escaped from his parents' home in Lleida. He had run away from his father and ended up in the big city.

"I followed the train tracks until I got to Barcelona."

"On foot?"

"Yeah. That's where my sister was. She'd run away, too. I figured I could move in with her."

"But she didn't want anything to do with you?"

"It wasn't that. I never found her. Barcelona's too big."

"What do you mean by that?"

"I mean, I didn't know where she lived."

"And you just wandered around looking for her?"

"Not haphazardly, no. I would go to a neighborhood and start asking people for her. I spent the first nights on the beach. I wasn't the only one. It didn't take long to find work at the Born Market. Then Señor Pau offered to take me in. At first I kept asking around the market for my sister. I described her to every single customer, but no one had ever heard of her. Everyone just kept saying no. That's why they started calling me No-Sister-Salvador. And now I'm stuck with it . . ."

He never did explain why he'd run away. Even if his father was as bad as they come, what would make a fourteen-year-old kid walk the train lines all by himself? But then again, I never asked.

Then the war broke out. The teachers at school told us that some generals had rebelled because they wanted to take control of Spain and Catalonia. They went on to explain that if the military won, we'd all be forced to speak in Spanish.

My father was still in business for himself. He was extremely proud of his sovereignty. And he was so autonomous that he decided, out of the blue, to go off to war without consulting anyone. He was too individualistic to attach himself to one political party. But, just like so many others at the time, he couldn't resist the call to the front. He threw some belongings into a rucksack and said to my mother:

"I'm going off to the war."

"You can't join the war as if it were some kind of holiday."

"Oh yes I can."

"But you don't know the first thing about it. You have never picked up a rifle in your entire life."

"They'll teach me. It's like painting; all you have to do is limber up your fingers."

"And what about us?"

"You work. You can support the two of you." At that point my mother had a job as a telephone operator at the customs office, down by the harbor. "Anyway, this'll all be over before you know it. The Fascists won't be able to hold out for long."

My father might've been a great sign painter, but he had absolutely no intuition.

My mother was furious. Her roving eye practically rolled up into her head. She told him that he'd lost his senses; he was a thirty-three-year-old man with a child. She grabbed me by the scruff of my shirt to underline this point, practically sending me flying as she shoved me roughly toward him.

"There's no need for you to go!" she cried.

"You don't know anything about what I need," he said harshly.

Those words hurt my mother deeply. As her eyes welled up, she told him to go wherever he wanted, but not to come back until he knew how to act like a man, instead of a child. Then she slammed the door, locking herself in their bedroom. She was so upset that she refused to accompany him to the train station. My father got only as far as Lleida. He felt so bad about going off to war in the middle of an argument with his wife that he caught the first train back to Barcelona, tail between his legs.

The cease-fire didn't last very long. My father was nerved up all summer. He moped around the house. All his friends were at the front. And his job threw him into constant contact with the euphoria of war. His days were spent surrounded by pots of paint and brushes at the headquarters of all sorts of political parties and unions.

By September the lettering on his signs was cockeyed, the colors dull, and the wall borders lifeless. Everyone in the neighborhood agreed that he might as well go off to war if things were going to continue like that.

One day he left for work early and came back that evening as an enlisted man in the Macià-Companys Column.

This time my mother took it fairly well. Secretly, I felt an inner glow of happiness.

My father attended the ceremony in which the Catalan flag was handed down to the troops before the men were sent off to the front line. The festivities were presided over by President Companys. We cheered him on as the troops paraded through the streets of Barcelona. My hands stung from clapping so hard. My mother was at my side, wearing dark glasses to hide her wandering eye. She sobbed while cheering the soldiers on at the same time. She grumbled through her tears.

"What a mess . . . This is horrible . . ."

From then on, when I woke up, all I would see were my father's tools and a couple of preliminary designs left over from his last project. It had been a sign for a carpentry shop. All I had to watch over me was a group of uppercase letters, made to look as if they were different-size planks of wood tacked together with nails.

We kept track of my father thanks to the letters that he sent home from the front. The first was an indignant note explaining how he'd been pulled from the trenches as soon as they realized that he was a sign painter, exchanging his gun for a set of brushes. He was ordered to paint signs for the command post at the rear guard in Alcañiz. It wasn't long before the Macià-Companys Column had the most striking and skillfully painted signs on the front. My father's reputation grew quickly. It got to the point where the officers were trading my dad's services for arms. My father explained that various militias made up of workers, Anarchists, and Communists didn't really trust the Catalan factions. They thought the Catalans were too bourgeois. That's why the Macià-Companys Column had such a hard time keeping up their armament stock. But the FAI needed someone to paint the signs for their revolution. So they requested my father's services in exchange for a few rifles and a machine gun. The Macià-Companys Column was overjoyed. Although my father wasn't quite as thrilled, he followed orders and ended up traversing the entire Aragon front, from the Pyrenees Mountains to Terol. He painted initials on the sides of trucks and tanks, designed revolutionary pamphlets and posters, slapped up highway indicators and village street signs. . . .

They told him, "You should be proud; it's your personal and

unique contribution to the war. There're plenty of militiamen who would love to be in your shoes."

But with every poster he painted, he just grew more frustrated. Until finally he got fed up. One day, when he was going to pick up more paint, he decided that instead of heading back to base, he would just keep on going straight toward Barcelona. They caught him five hours later. He was brought before the Council of War and formally accused of desertion. He could have been condemned to death for the charge. It was a sign of the times that not only was he not executed, he was pardoned on the grounds that his desertion was brought on by an inordinate desire for combat.

At first my mother thought that she would be able to maintain the family on her job alone. She soon realized that it wasn't going to be easy on the meager salary of a telephone operator at Customs. The job didn't bring in much. Taking Señor Pau up on the loan of his old typewriter, she placed an ad in several newspapers: "Typewritten Copies Done. Speedy and Economical. 1 cent per 4 lines." She brought in a couple of commissions out of it. Once in a while someone would hire her to go type texts in person; otherwise she'd bring the work home. The sound of her typing across the hall would ring in my ears on the evenings I'd spend in Señor Pau's apartment. I kept out of trouble by playing Parcheesi and dominoes with Señor Pau and his lodger, No-Sister-Salvador. All of a sudden the typing would stop. That would be my cue to say good night and go home. She'd have fallen asleep. I would come home to find her head slumped over the metal keys. Customs was busier than ever because of the war, and she couldn't keep up. When her bosses down at the port found out that she was a typist as well as a telephone operator, they increased her workload even more. Once in a while she even had to leave Barcelona for a few days, acting as a secretary for groups of politicians or labor unions. The neighbors took care of me whenever that happened. Señor Pau and No-Sister-Salvador wanted to make sure that I was never alone, so they'd lug my mattress into the only free space left in the house—the hallway off the living room. I stayed with them until my mother returned.

We were as poor as rats, but Señor Pau insisted that we shouldn't complain about it very much. Someone might take us for defeatists. It was a good thing that we had No-Sister-Salvador. He always managed to bring something home from the market, even if it was half rotten. If it wasn't a piece of cauliflower, it was a bundle of shallots. Sometimes the cache was only a handful of roasted potatoes or a couple of onions. Everything ended up in my mother's pot. She cooked for the four of us. Around that time, Salvador had a run-in with an overfull fruit truck and ended up with a gimp leg. He never complained about it though. He said that there's no cloud without a silver lining and it was thanks to his leg that he wouldn't be called to the front.

After dinner, while my mother sewed under the glow of a light-bulb, Señor Pau would sometimes ask me to read articles from the newspaper out loud. Aside from war reports, there was plenty of information about the radical tendencies that were sweeping Barcelona. For Señor Pau, who was born and bred in the city, the revolution in dress was one of the worst side effects of the war. He couldn't quite stomach it. Since he was a little deaf in one ear, he asked questions in a booming voice ripe with distrust.

"What revolution are they talking about?"

"The revolution in clothing, Señor Pau," Salvador replied. "The article is about how everybody, guys and girls, all wear those blue jumpsuits for mechanics."

"My God . . . What bull crap . . . ," the old man muttered. He sighed and continued, "Look, I hope Franco and all his military-crazed rebel cohorts go to hell, let's get that straight. But if it's to change over to Communism, then we're screwed . . . I'll never be a rich man, but I'm even less of a Communist. Who are they kidding? Communism and Anarchism are based on complete faith in the inherent sociability of man and the brotherly ties that supposedly come from communal living. Their doctrines were conceived for a world of good, upstanding, and honorable people. If a world like that exists, I can tell you right now, it's not ours. There are far more bad guys than good ones out there. I'm speaking from experience. Humans are competitive and self-seeking, it's in their blood. The instinct for personal property is grafted onto our very skin. And that leads to jealousy, egotism, and inequality. Take it from me; it doesn't matter if we're talking about a republic or the monarchy, dictatorship or democracy. All everyone wants to do is look out for themselves and make money. The have-nots want; and those who have, want more. Unfortunately, life isn't exactly fair. Not everyone can attain the minimum amount of money that they feel entitled to . . . and even when they do, it's usually at the expense of somebody else . . ."

Señor Pau believed that Communism's idea of egalitarianism was doomed to fail. I was only ten years old and listened eagerly as I tried to make out the smudged newsprint beneath the dim glimmer of a twenty-five-watt bulb.

He'd say things like "People are bad. And that's all there is to it. You, me, and him . . . We're all bad. Nobody likes to admit it, but that's the way it is. We're just made that way."

"Do you really think so?" asked my mother, apprehensively.

Then he lowered his voice and motioned us to come closer, as though concerned that someone might overhear, and whispered, "But is that a real revolution? Does revolution mean men going out without a hat and women neglecting to put on their stockings? Does it mean hanging priests up by their balls and setting churches on fire?

Where is the revolution in that? I don't see it around here anywhere. People are taking advantage of war's misery more than ever . . . Take a walk around the center and you'll see what I mean. Go to Pelai Street, the Angel's Gate. All the shops around there have started buying up gold and jewels. Just skim through the personals section of the newspaper; some people are willing to make a profit off the misfortunes of others any way they can, whether it's buying up paintings, furniture, houses, cars . . . Is that a revolution? There are even some who will buy chits from the pawnshop off you!"

"There's nothing worse than the feeling when you're running in the rain that your feet are getting wet from the water seeping into your shoes . . . ," my mother said a bit doubtfully as she carried on with her mending. We all looked at her as she finished her own thought. "When a storm hits, a pair of boots are priceless. Whoever has dry feet in that moment is rich. They possess a treasure."

Señor Pau listened pensively, shaking his head as if to say, "Ain't that the truth," ripped the newspaper out of my hands, and continued reading it in silence.

CHAPTER FOUR

Friday, October 21, 1949

If a dead man's bones have been left underground to rot for over nine years, they should be able to fit into a potato sack. At least that's what a grave digger in Melilla told me.

"And the stench of death is off them too," he added.

I hope he's right, because if not, I don't know how I'm going to be able to salvage poor old Bartomeu Camús's remains. Maybe the grave digger's advice only holds true for North Africa. Miranda de Ebro's climate is a far cry from those climes. But it makes no difference. Bartomeu Camús is going in the sack no matter what. Well, I wouldn't call it a sack exactly. It's a United States Marines duffel bag I bought off a Yank who was passing through Melilla. I've got it folded up in my suitcase.

I glance at my watch. It's early. I look over the map that my father drew of the concentration camp. I've made some copies of it, even though I've committed every last detail to memory. I could locate the tree that my father and his friend called Purgatory on a moonless night with my eyes closed.

There's a knock on the door. It's Campillo, informing me that some soldiers are here to pick me up. I tell him to keep them busy at the bar. Let them order whatever they want, it's on me.

"Make them wait. I still have to put on my uniform . . . ," I say in a somewhat cajoling tone.

His glance blends complicity with appreciation, as if to say, "Don't worry; leave it to me, you've got all the time in the world."

All the better because it's going to take a while. I'm going to deck myself out in the entire getup. It takes me a good twenty minutes to transform into the ferocious Legionnaire that people have come to expect. I trim my beard a little bit, accentuating my mustache by twisting up the ends. My uniform fits like a glove: the light green shirt, with the sleeves rolled up almost all the way and the requisite stripes. I stuff my legs into a pair of tall, brightly polished boots, adorned with spurs and garters. I tighten the wide patent-leather belt with its imposing, Fascist buckle emblazoned with the Legion's insignia, and inspect myself in the mirror. Perfect. I undo the top buttons of my shirt to put a few inches of chest on display. I step back a few feet, take another look, and pace toward the mirror, opening my shirt again to just above the abdomen. I put on my hat and strap on my gun.

Campillo half suppresses a squeal of admiration as I walk down the stairs. I haven't seen any Señora Campillo so far; maybe he's a fag. The two soldiers stop drinking beers and stand to attention. Being a soldier means having to salute twenty-five to thirty times a day. It also means dressing up and ordering others around. Or being ordered. No questions asked. It's the most ludicrous thing in the world.

The boot camp is on the outskirts of town, but isn't very far away. As we get closer, my stomach tightens like a vise. We drive through the main entrance: *"Todo por la Patria,"* or, "Everything for the Nation." Every corner seems to echo and ring with thousands of voices, now long gone. I can't help but think of my father. He tried to describe a very unsettling feeling to me a few days before dying: "It made no difference, even if you were crushing rock, you got bored. Because you knew there was no point to it. And that wasn't all. Endlessly waiting was painfully tedious. We were either waiting to be classified or waiting to be punished. We had to wait for our transfer orders, which actually meant being taken away to be condemned, thrown in jail, set to hard labor, or executed. But mostly we were waiting for absolutely nothing, teetering on the edge of oblivion. That was the best of all. We didn't know what was going on. Nobody ever told us anything. And if you weren't classified, you might as well not exist. That was the most terrifying thing about it, Niso. We were prisoners of war, but our names weren't written down anywhere. And even if we were registered, our names could be stricken off the list anytime they felt like it. Prisoners could suddenly disappear from one day to the next and nobody would be the wiser. It wasn't as if anybody was going to file a complaint."

He was classified as a letter *B,* in other words, a hostile element. The prisoners lived like slaves while the authorities were deciding what to do with them. If they didn't lose their minds first.

The driver parks the truck in front of the administrative building where the major in charge has his office. The show is about to begin.

A private knocks on a smoked-glass door. A voice calls out, "Come in!" The soldier motions me into the office. I enter, closing the door behind me. I'm greeted by a short and stocky man with thick chestnut-colored hair. He has a positively walruslike mustache that populates his entire upper lip, curling up on itself and making inroads into his mouth. So this is Major José Carlos Cedazo. He is sitting by a table, with his feet soaking in a zinc tub. A milky liquid sloshes about his calves. He's wearing a T-shirt, and the pants of his uniform are rolled up to the knee. I pull off my cap, salute, and put myself under his command.

"At ease, Sergeant, at ease," he says in a strained tone.

He stares openly at the scar on my forehead. He points to it with a pudgy finger that ends in an oddly sharp fingernail.

"A combat wound?"

"Yes, sir," I reply. And I dive into the official version of the gigantic scar's origins. "It's not from the war, I was too young to fight. It happened during a mission in the desert against rebel factions . . ."

"The Legion is always at the forefront."

"Yes, sir. I was betrayed by a Moor . . ."

"Oh . . . the Moors, who can understand them? Look at their excellent service record during the war . . ." He becomes pensive for a moment. Then the obtuse and rotund man adds, "The Moors, when they're faithful, are truly faithful. But when they're traitors, they're as treacherous as they come . . ."

I'm struck dumb by such kernels of wisdom. Thankfully, he keeps chattering away.

"Forgive me for not getting up. What's your name again? I'm afraid I don't recall."

"Aleu. Sergeant Ginés Aleu."

"Sit down, Aleu. Make yourself comfortable. You've caught me at a good time. After twenty years of horrible suffering, I'm finally about to cure my foot problems once and for all. I have delicate feet. It runs in the family and can't be helped. When I'm dressed as a civilian, there's no problem; I simply get my shoes widened. Although it isn't exactly a pretty sight, it brings some relief. But I've never been able to stand military boots. Even the service uniform shoes are a torment. I spent the whole war in agony. What do you think of that? My poor feet gave me a lot more grief than the Reds did. I couldn't find a single remedy to relieve the torment caused by my corns, calluses, bunions, and irritated heels. Well, you're not going to believe it, but a few days ago I discovered a new product that's just arrived straight from Portugal. A colleague on detail to prepare for the Generalíssimo's travels through Lusitanian lands sent it to me. Look, Freire Salts, from the Freire Laboratories in Lisbon. They use secret ingredients; all natural and imported from the jungles of Brazil . . . I've been following the treatment for several days now. I add a handful to a basin of hot water and let the preparation do its magic on my aching feet. It's manna from heaven, Sergeant, manna from heaven . . . But I know such things must seem ridiculous to a Legionnaire like yourself."

There's a woodstove blazing in the middle of the room. Even so, it's probably only a few degrees warmer in here than it is outside. While the imbecile of a major rambles on about his feet, may they rot in peace, I silently examine the office. A well-meaning person might describe the space as austere or spartan, but an objective observer would say it was somewhere between run-down and utterly dilapidated. I take an inventory of my surroundings: one table; four chairs (two plain wood, two wood and leather); one portrait of His Excellency; one crucifix; one typewriter, with its corresponding cart; one wall telephone; one upholstered sofa; one wooden filing cabinet with a roll-front shutter door; one Artillery insignia; two earthenware ashtrays; one gray armoire; one coat stand with a uniform jacket and flat cap hanging off it; one gigantic stain from the infiltrating damp. There's a stuffed chameleon with its tongue sticking out on top of the filing cabinet. . . . Neither the Spanish flag nor that of the Regiment is on display. I notice that the major is winding down his little speech. Suddenly he picks up one of his shoes and throws it against the door. The smoked glass trembles. One of the soldiers appears instantly, and, as if it were the most normal thing in the world, picks the shoe up off the floor, hands it back to the major, salutes, and asks permission to remove the basin.

Once the soldier is gone, the major proceeds to dry his feet with a khaki green towel embroidered with the Artillery's insignia. While rubbing away, he says, "I've spoken on the telephone with your superiors in Melilla. It's not that I don't take you at your word, but I do like to know who I'm dealing with. They tell me that you're a very promising young man, an ideal combination of brains and enthusiasm. I don't understand why you aren't interested in attending the officers' academy. Wouldn't you like to be a lieutenant?"

"I'm very proud to be a member of the Legion."

The major stands up, hangs the towel on the coat stand, donning the shirt and jacket of his uniform. He doesn't take a seat behind the desk until every button is fastened. The man is still barefoot. He looks me in the eyes for the first time. There's a hint of sarcasm in his smile that I don't like one bit. It's the sort of grin that appears out of nowhere, as though turned on by a light switch. It has a fake quality to it, as if it might be easily taken on and off. The grin appears to be pasted on somehow, and is downright unnerving. I feel a shiver course down my spine.

"You still haven't answered my question," he says, in response to my silence.

"What I should say is that I have lived every year of service to the hilt, and plan on continuing to do so for the remainder of my contract. I follow the Legionnaire's Creed to the letter and have proven that I'm not afraid of combat."

"I've been told all that. But what's next?"

"I'm not sure where my future lies. But I do know that if I were to become an officer, it would be much more difficult to give up my career in the military."

"You think too much, Sergeant, and in the Army that isn't exactly a positive trait. You're Catalan, aren't you?"

"Yes, sir."

"Catalans have the potential to be great soldiers, but they don't take to the military life. Just look at the glorious Mother of God of

Montserrat Regiment. Those boys fought the war like the best of them, as courageous as they come. And now they're completely disbanded. Once the war was over, all they wanted to do was go back home and start making money again."

I'm of the opinion that, Catalan or not, nobody minds a bit of cash. There are some people, however, who don't like to admit it.

I ask, if it isn't an imposition, to visit the camp for a few days.

"I'd like to observe your recruitment technique firsthand. I understand that it's unbeatable. The Legion in Melilla has heard excellent things about it."

"The Legion?"

"Oh yes. In a mere six months, you've managed to set up a first-rate training camp."

"Oh, go on. I could get you put away for such shameless flattery. And what exactly is it that you'd like to see, Sergeant?"

"Don't worry, I'm not here in an official capacity; it's strictly personal. I'm preparing a kind of report about current trends in instruction methods. Fortunately, I happened to end up in the basic training camp that's received such high praise, even though it's been up and running for such a short time."

The major is visibly mollified. I'm beginning to get an idea about why he's only a major when he should be a colonel; the man's a complete idiot. Now the question is how he even managed to get where he is. He must have been promoted on war merits. The most incompetent soldier can rise in rank during a war. All you have to do is kill more of the enemy than the next guy. And you don't have to be particularly brilliant to do that.

We continue chatting for a while about the characteristics of the ex–concentration camp now transformed into a Basic Combat Training Facility. I'm impatient for him to finish up so I can get a look around.

"As soon as my wife found out that you were coming, she insisted you stop by our house for a cup of coffee. We'll be expecting you this afternoon after your talk with the recruits. Here's the address. Will you be having lunch with us here?"

I respond in the affirmative. He calls to one of the soldiers working out in the anteroom. He orders the young man to attend to all my needs during the duration of my stay at the boot camp.

I bid the major farewell until lunchtime. I ask the soldier to take me on a tour of the camp. I've been assigned a scrawny little Galician with big ears named Rogelio Fontes. The guy's all hat, head, and ears. The first thing he tells me, after introducing himself, is that he's illiterate. As if it were some sort of vocation, or a chronic illness. You can tell he's pleased about the change in routine brought on by my stay. The man can't seem to take his eyes off my chest. He speaks in a very strong Galician accent.

"What do you do?" I ask.

"I'm under the major's orders. Since I don't know how to read or write, I act as his orderly and . . ."

"No, that's not what I meant. What do you do when you're not here? At home . . ."

"Oh . . . Ever since I can remember, I've milked cows, cut and sold firewood, or worked coal up in the mountains. Of course, now it's a different story . . ."

When I ask him if he misses home, he looks at me like I've got a screw loose. He says no, that he's planning on learning to read and write; study and get his truck driver's license. He adds, "And if I don't get kicked out for being an idiot, I mean to stay in the Army."

You can tell that he's proud to be in uniform. If the guy had anything to say about it, he'd have his shirt open to the waist just like me. Fontes explains that the major has been like a father to him, that he'd do anything for the man. . . . We walk along the streets that separate the various rows of barracks. The Galician intones a steady monologue describing the camp's characteristics, but I barely listen. The tour of the rest of the grounds includes the officers' bar and the canteen. The camp's layout is exactly the same as when my father was here. It's an immense rectangle spliced down the middle by an esplanade lined by two rows of white barracks with peaked roofs. The buildings are arranged obliquely along the road and stand facing each other, a path in between each pair. Some smaller structures off in a corner house the infirmary, warehouse, and showers. The Bayas River provides a natural barrier on one of the four sides of the enclosure. I don't see a trace of the infamous wooden construction that it's said the prisoners were obligated to use as a makeshift privy, exposing their backs to the water. Now a building stands in its place. The sign on it says RESTROOMS. The kitchen is right next door. Fontes looks at me in surprise. He doesn't understand why I'd want to visit the most mundane areas of the unit. The recruits observe us with curiosity. They're a bunch of kids, bursting with energy. Everyone was so weak in my father's time that during the winter the frigid cold kept some of the inmates from leaving the barracks, even to get their daily rations. They preferred to go hungry rather than try to drag themselves out and back. We veer to the right when we get to the end of the esplanade, where the drill grounds are located. The water tank is right alongside. Theoretically, if I were to stand underneath the tank, Purgatory should be the third tree facing the train tracks, in the direction of Bilbao. Those train tracks run along the opposite camp wall. For a second I realize that the trees might have been cut down when the concentration camp was transformed into a boot camp. Almost unconsciously, I head off in the direction of the tank. Fontes follows. Although he hasn't bothered to say anything so far, he suddenly asks, "What are you looking for?"

I've got to be more careful. I stop dead in my tracks, smile at him, and say, "Looking for? What would I be looking for?"

We continue walking side by side until reaching the water tank. It's set in a corner of the camp, one of the vertices of the rectangle. We leave the barracks behind. Now all I can see is a slice of open space, cut off by the exterior enclosure. I can't resist checking to make sure that there're still some trees left standing. Yes, there are. Already breathing easier, I stand beneath the tank and count three of them, but I don't know how I'll manage to get close enough to the cache to dip my hand in. The stretch of ground between the barracks and the outside fence is a no-man's-land. There's no foot traffic, and it's completely open. It'll be almost impossible to get close without being seen. We stride toward the grove of vegetation. I pass by the Purgatory tree, even catching a glimpse of the opening in the bark. It's not so much a hole as a fairly wide fissure, about twenty inches off the ground. Fontes cheers up when I suggest we have a drink, on me, at the officers' bar in order to work up some appetite for lunch.

I have to figure out how to get to Purgatory without raising any suspicions. I'm introduced to a couple of sergeants while at the canteen. They're a bit wary about making too much conversation. By now the entire battalion must know that aside from trying to woo the boys into the Legion, I'm also preparing a report about the camp's internal workings. They ask me what it's like to fuck a Moorish girl and if it's true that they'll do anything for the change in your pocket. I respond as expected, letting my words drip with a knowing complicity so common among military men, but inside I'm falling to pieces. As I delve into the crude obscenities, my soul is breaking apart like some sort of substantial but fragile object, like a cup or a crystal figurine. Something that shatters when it falls to the ground. I explain in detail the desert legend about how camels, aside from being a source of milk, are also used to satisfy the sexual needs of the most libidinous fellows. While they burst into peals of laughter, I can feel my heart melting like gelatin, turning to liquid. I can't stand it anymore. Eight years is a long time.

A brigadier joins the group, and the two sergeants repeat every word I've said amid chortles and shouts. The brigadier makes an explicit comment referring to the Legion's mascot, the goat. I don't particularly feel like meeting his challenge, but I have to live up to expectations. My hand drops to my cartridge belt; I pull out my pistol and place it on the bar. The room falls silent. I put my face up to the brigadier's and tell him that, with all due respect to a superior officer, if he's got the balls, he should repeat what he just said about the goat. The situation is incredibly tedious. The brigadier is about fifty years old and soft around the edges. He immediately backs down, offering his apologies. I remind him that the goat is sacred to the Spanish Legion. I pick up the gun and return it to its holster. It's time for lunch. The sergeants act like they've known me all their lives and make excuses for the brigadier, who, according to them, is a bit of a hick, a coarse sort of fellow. It's as though nothing happened. That's how ridiculously, desperately simple it all is.

We go straight from the canteen to the mess hall. As always, there's an empty table set with food in case the major deigns to eat with the troops. He never does.

I can't stop thinking about the Purgatory tree. I don't know how I'm going to get away with it. But I'll figure something out.

We go back to the canteen after lunch for a coffee and cognac before my recruitment speech. Some of the officers convince me to sing "The Bridegroom of Death." At first they listen quietly enough, but finally, after hearing the refrain "I am the bridegroom of Death, bound for all eternity to the most loyal of companions," they practically stand at attention. When I'm done singing, they shout in frenzied unison: "Long live the Legion!" I'm afraid that I've had better luck here than I will with the troops.

They divide the men into two groups of one hundred each. I'll have to inflict my harangue twice, once today and once tomorrow.

They're ordered to sit directly on the esplanade, next to the flagpole. It's the very same pole where they tied up prisoners as a punishment back when the unit was a concentration camp.

The troops are eager, or at least they pretend to be. The corporals and the sergeants are keeping a close watch on them. In other words, they pay about as much attention as they do when attending one of the lectures on military theory that they hear every day. Some of them take notes. Here it goes:

"The Legion is a relatively new outfit. It's only been in existence for thirty years. But as you are no doubt aware, that doesn't mean it hasn't got a slew of military accomplishments and heroic deeds under its belt, not to mention the important figures who have gone on to form part of the Spanish military's glorious history, and thus, the history of Spain itself. Above all, the Legion has received acclaim for its illustrious members: His Excellency, the Generalíssimo, or the founder himself, Millán Astray . . ."

I pace in front of the troops, who are seated in five rows with twenty men each. With a fierce expression pasted on my face, I explain that the mere mention of the word *Legion* is enough to rouse a soldier into a frenzied passion. . . . One of the soldiers keeps falling asleep. He's making a superhuman effort to keep his eyes open. The kid is wearing glasses, so he takes them off, rubs his eyes, cleans the lenses, and puts them back on. But it's no use. A minute later his head is drooping again. I feel sorry for the guy, but he's going to have to play a supporting role in this production. I proceed to glare at him steadily. The young soldiers sitting near him become alarmed and start poking the kid with their elbows. Finally I throw a livid glance at one of the corporals, who strides through the ranks, forces the sleepyhead to his feet, and shoves him out of formation. Three minutes later the soldier appears, fully armed, and begins to march around the precinct at a lively pace. I continue unfazed. Now I'm working them up with the Legionnaire's Creed, saying how the officers and subordinate officers read it almost every day, repeating it out loud while in formation. How there are copies of it pasted up on the walls, on the back of the dormitory doors. . . . I pepper my speech with striking examples:

"Even if it's during a march through the desert, loaded down and under the blazing heat, there's always some anonymous Legionnaire who cries out, 'Legionnaires never complain of fatigue or hunger!' or, 'We are Legionnaires, made to suffer!'" And I add, practically yelling, "The Legion is a religion and its prayer is the Legionnaire's Creed. It reflects on values such as courage, comradeship, friendship, mutual support and togetherness, brotherhood when in the face of enemy fire, and above all the four cardinal virtues: discipline, combat, death, and an adoration of the flag . . ."

A few of the recruits listen agape, drunk on dreams of glory, heroism, and the mother country. Out of one hundred men, three or four will seriously consider the Legion and two will actually join up. The grand finale comes when I get to the part about songs and anthems. I explain how every night, at the hour of taps, the Legionnaires sing in honor of what they hold most sacred, the memory of their departed comrades. Without pausing, I break into "The Bridegroom of Death" yet again. The troops are stunned. I sing nice and loud, pouring my whole soul and all my strength into the music, because I'm the only one who knows why I'm here, in this moment. I sing and sing and sing. I lift my voice to the Miranda de Ebro sun, "I am the bridegroom of Death, bound for all eternity to the most loyal of companions . . ." I think about my father, of No-Sister-Salvador and the unmarked and unclaimed bones of Bartomeu Camús, and sing even harder. This time, unlike in the officers' canteen, I don't hold back that pathetic tremor in my voice that's supposedly so moving and always reminds me of how the nuns sang at the Charity Home. The corporals on guard stand stock-still. One of the sergeants salutes with honest martial fervor. What an imbecile. It's just a load of bullshit!

I'm so used to wearing a mask that it's while watching the sergeant's epiphany that I suddenly come up with a clear and simple way to get my hands on the Purgatory tree. Perfect.

I catch my breath and plunge back in for the kill. I raise my voice a bit higher, as I have so many times before. Come on assholes; listen up good: "I became the bridegroom of Death, we are bound together for eternity and her love is my flag . . ."

I stop short and look up at the sky as the silence settles. What a performance; all that's missing is the applause.

I hear someone clapping.

Behind me. I turn around, and see Major Cedazo waddling toward me like a duck as he slaps his pudgy hands together. Everyone, both troops and officers, has gone quiet. Nobody knows what to do. I stand to attention and salute.

"At your orders, Major."

"Very good, Sergeant. I wasn't aware that Legionnaires were also given voice lessons."

"Forgive me. I got carried away."

He gazes at me for a moment. It's the same as when we met before; he smiles with his lips, not his eyes, which have a glacial coldness to them. Or at least that's how it seems to me. It's only a second. He realizes and the expression is gone. . . . He takes me by the arm and leads me away. I can hear the troops getting to their feet behind me, but they stay in formation.

"My feet are killing me. Don't forget, we're expecting you at home tonight. My wife was furious when she found out I'd only invited you over for coffee. 'A coffee, you're such a hopeless cheapskate. Dinner! He has to come to dinner!' She didn't seem to recall that the coffee had been her idea in the first place . . . Women, what can you do?

Of course, I'm delighted to have you over. Do you want to be picked up at the pension?"

"That won't be necessary, thank you. I'd rather find my own way; that way I can stretch my legs and get to know the city better."

"As you wish. Nine o'clock sharp then."

"At your orders."

I watch him walk back to the major's headquarters. The man seems to receive a small electric shock every time one of his feet touches the ground. I don't notice that Fontes is once again at my side. He was also impressed by my act. He congratulates me with all due respect. He says that I remind him of his uncle from Ourense. . . .

"Because of the way I sing?"

"No, because of the silences in between the notes."

CHAPTER FIVE

That first winter of the war, I remember tagging along behind No-Sister-Salvador everywhere he went. He was like a big brother to me. Sometimes I'd go along with him to the Born Market. He'd grab me and say:

"Do you see that man in a trench coat with his hands in his pockets, walking this way?"

"Yes."

"We don't know him from Adam. He's not a regular. But it's strange to see a guy like that at the market. That means he's got to be a professional chef. It doesn't matter where he works. It could be a restaurant, a school, a convent, or a military mess hall . . . He's a good potential client. If you take into account that he's going to go by Poll's stall before getting to ours, it would seem like fate were against us, wouldn't it?"

"Yeah . . . ," I answered doubtfully.

Then he scratched the scar on his bad knee and grinned triumphantly.

"Well, it's not! That sort of client will take a good look around. He'll spot Poll's stall and then see ours, just a little farther off, next door. The guy will practically bang into Poll's, so he's bound to pay close attention. And he'll notice how run-down it is, with its peeling paint and the dingy little sign that you can barely read. He'll put his bag down and try to appraise the quality of the vegetables, but he won't be able to make anything out since the stall is so badly lit. That's when he'll turn his attention to us. He'll see our magnificent sign (courtesy of your father, to give credit where credit is due) and our cheerful, bright stall. And he'll walk right over to us without thinking twice."

That's more or less what happened. It turned out that the gentleman ran the kitchen of a boarding school for boys in La Garriga. He placed a substantial order, paid in advance, and walked away satisfied. The stall owner was so pleased that he rewarded Salvador with a big bag of oranges. Salvador threw one at me with a gleeful wink.

Both my mother and Pau praised him when I told the story later on at home.

"It's not only that he bought the produce at your stall," the old man added, "it's the fact that he rejected the competition, which aside from being demoralizing isn't exactly good for their business. Congratulations, kid!"

We spent many a Sunday afternoon up in the tower during the war. We shifted the moldy boxes and broken pots out of the way, always putting them back in their place once inside. It was thrilling. Then we'd climb up to the garret under the roof. We'd bring our breakfast along with us and munch it down while keeping close watch on the sky, our hands cupped around our eyes like binoculars, on the lookout for enemy planes. It was on one of those Sundays that Salvador told me about his origins. I was explaining how our school had taken in a group of little girl refugees from Madrid the day before. They were from Alcalá de Henares and had come to escape the Fascist bombs. They were being housed by the Town Hall in the municipal war shelter under the Plaza Sant Felip Neri. (That shelter was later blown to bits by a Fascist bomb and a great number of children were massacred. In other words, the poor children continued to be plagued by bombs.)

Sometimes we'd talk about the war. The topic obsessed him. He was terrified and didn't try to hide it. In an attempt to calm him down, Señor Pau would tell him not to worry. They wouldn't send away a whippersnapper like him to kill Fascists. Salvador's crippled state made it especially unlikely.

But Salvador would keep bringing it up whenever we were in the safety of our tower perch.

"I wouldn't want to go anyway, even if I weren't a gimp," he'd mutter, getting really anxious. He claimed to be a pacifist and said he'd be incapable of shooting anybody, even if his life depended on it. "As soon as they start calling up even the cripples to fight, I'll get the hell out of here. I'll go to France." There was no rage in his eyes, only fear.

Once he'd gotten that off his chest, he'd smile at me and, peering over the tip of his pointy nose, beg, "Whatever you do, Niso, don't repeat anything I've said at school. It's a secret between you and me. The way things are going, being a pacifist is one step away from being a traitor. Depending on what got around, it could cost me my skin."

"We were told by one of the teachers at school that words alone aren't enough to triumph over Fascism," I said ingenuously, but in earnest.

"And she's right, she's right," he replied rapidly.

The truth was that for a while I was pretty worried about No-Sister-Salvador. I would try to imagine his sixteen-year-old self at the front, dragging a rifle and always being the last to arrive at every battle because of his limp. Sometimes I would go through agony just thinking about it. And I came to the conclusion that only the people who really wanted to fight should be the ones to go off to war in the first place. Salvador should be able to stay home, if that's what he wanted. After all, my very own father enlisted without anyone telling him to go.

Maybe No-Sister-Salvador had hopes that if anyone tried to take him away, he could always escape to our secret hiding place in the tower. A guy could hole up there for years if need be. With the blunt pencil that Salvador used at the market, we drew up a solemn document scrawled in my childish handwriting. We solemnly swore to help each other, to the best of our ability, if one of us should ever have to hide out in the tower. In that event we promised not to reveal the other's whereabouts, even under pain of torture. We also mutually agreed to provide food, water, and comic books, if need be.

Sometimes my mother and I would bring the letters that my father sent from the front over to our neighbors' apartment across the hall. There, under the very same twenty-five-watt bulb, she'd read his correspondence aloud, skipping over the most intimate parts. Occasionally my father would include some very raw descriptions of war. As everyone listened quietly, I would imagine him as a hero, defending his brushes to the bitter end. My mother would unfold the notepaper ceremoniously; put on her reading glasses, taking care to pronounce each word clearly.

> *"We passed through a tiny village, not too long ago. It had been decimated by Fascist artillery. The place was a pile of smoking ruins filled with charred corpses. The few remaining survivors were huddled behind the precarious brick wall of the only house left standing. There were about twenty of them, mostly*

crying women and children. They decided to join up with us since we were making a tactical retreat. We had barely enough time to bury the dead in one makeshift pit and get the hell out of there. The Fascists took up the attack once again and the bombs started to fall. We had only a few minutes before the Fascists figured out that we weren't going to fight back. A reticent man with a shadowy complexion announced that he wasn't going anywhere. We tried to get him to see it was suicide. Nothing we said made any difference and there wasn't time. The man was a manual laborer. He'd been working on the roof of a farmhouse not very far from the village when the attack began the day before. He said that he'd seen from up there on top of the roof how a pair of bombs hit his house directly, with his wife and children inside. "I'm not going," he repeated under his breath. And having said that, he turned around and started clearing away the rubble that had been his home; searching for his family's remains. The way things are going, waiting around for the Fascists is the same thing as signing a death warrant . . ."

There was a shell-shocked hush in the room. Nobody mentioned being worried about my father, so as not to upset Mother. After retracing our steps across the hallway, I'd climb into bed with her. And I never said that it was because I was feeling sorry for her that my father might get killed.

And that's how we got through the war.

I became a ward of the Charity Home, known during the Republic as the Francesc Macià House of Assistance, in February 1937. My father wasn't around and my mother could barely provide for me on her own. I didn't want to go, of course. I had my friends in public school. And domino matches with Señor Pau. And my friendship with No-Sister-Salvador. But my mother stood firm behind her decision.

The Sunday before I was dropped off, we all went to the Rambla together to get our picture taken, in order to commemorate the event. We also wanted to send a copy to my father at the front. The great change that was about to occur in my life seemed to affect them a lot more than it did me. For once, Señor Pau actually got dressed, even though he made it very clear that the beret was remaining firmly on his head. No-Sister-Salvador slicked his hair back and popped into his buttonhole a carnation, which he'd wrangled from a flower stall at the market. And my mother, well, my mother was lovely, with her red hair falling in waves over the shoulders of her Sunday coat. She was so happy for me that her eyes were perfectly focused. The sky was fairly overcast on that Sunday of January 31. That didn't seem to bother the photographer much as he stood on a small platform with his tripod and proceeded to shout at the passersby like a carnival barker.

"Souvenir photographs! Step up, ladies and gentlemen! Here's a chance to have your portrait taken with Columbus's statue in the background. Step up, the light is fading. Who wants to get their picture taken? Who's willing to give our troops something they'll never forget? Those young men start as militia and come back from the front as full-fledged soldiers of the Popular Army! Come now, young ladies, give our poor boys at the front something nice to look at!"

There was quite a bit of bustle and activity on the Rambla that Sunday. The crowds pushed their way toward Plaza Catalonia in order to hear the concert given by Maestro Toldrà, the director of the Anti-Fascist Militia's official marching band. Groups of people were heading toward a festival organized by the Friends of the Soviet Union. We even bumped into some visiting Anglican clergy dressed in their lilac robes and escorted by Catalan officials. Señor Pau recognized one of the local politicians. It was the Catalan government's commissioner of propaganda.

I still have the photograph that was taken of us that day. The woman, my mother, is seated with both an old and a young man standing behind her. The boy, me, sits on the ground at their feet.

That was the last photograph to be taken of all of us together. We never had a chance to pose for another. But we look happy in that picture. Obviously, we had no idea that it was to be our last group portrait. You could say that Señor Pau died of bad luck. The war swallowed Señor Pau whole. The war was practically over when he was killed in a bombing that didn't actually take place. The Town Hall had ordered the factories and places of business to stop using sirens to signal changes in the workers' shifts so as not to confuse the populace. They were only allowed to be used at the same time as the official air-raid sirens in order to heighten the sound of the alarm. One day Señor Pau happened to be taking a stroll when one of those sirens went off. He got terrified, stumbled, and fell, smashing his femur bone when he hit the sidewalk. He didn't even make it to the operating table. Those who had been injured in authentic bombings were given first priority. My mother later explained that someone had sabotaged the electrical system and false alarms had been going off all over the city. It took No-Sister-Salvador and my mother a week and a half to locate Señor Pau's body. Nobody could tell them anything. He was good and buried by the time they found him. Salvador was distraught. He climbed up to the roof and let all of the old man's pigeons go free. Then he walked straight down the stairs, went out onto the street, and disappeared. My mother asked around everywhere, even registering him as a missing person with the authorities. She went as far as contacting the railroad company, in case he'd taken it into his head to go to Lleida on foot, following the rails.

No-Sister-Salvador appeared a few days later. My mother found him sitting in his apartment, wearing blue mechanic's overalls, sandals, and a scruffy beard. He explained that he'd been wandering about turning events over in his mind, and ended up down by the docks. Some fishermen ran into the boy and offered to let him sleep on their barge. They wanted to know what he was doing lolling around in the damp. It seems that he told them how his adoptive father had just died in the most ridiculous way and that now he didn't know what to do. The fishermen took that to mean that this peculiar kid with a limp was debating whether or not he should take a short walk off a long pier. Life is hard enough as it is during wartime, so they decided not to intervene. Let him kill himself if he wanted to, enough people were dying at the front.

It seems they said, "Your father's death won't be half as meaningless as your own."

No-Sister-Salvador wasn't exactly suicidal. He was disoriented. Señor Pau had taken him in, and the boy had come to love the old man as a father. He couldn't understand the logic behind so much bad luck. It wasn't fair. It'd been a real shock to walk into the apartment and see the dressing gown and beret hanging on the coat stand as if nothing had happened. From the darkness of the barge, he could observe the other boats and the lanterns strung up along the docks. Those crafts resembled ghostly stains moving across an oily expanse of water. The fluid was full of changing reflections, forever widening, twisting, and then fading away. . . . The next day he informed the fishermen that he wasn't going to commit suicide after all. They congratulated the young man. He lived and worked with them for three days before returning home.

Salvador related the tale bit by bit while getting over the loss of Señor Pau. He confessed that, in the end, the old man talked continually about his wife, who'd died years ago.

"That's proof that they truly loved each other," he said.

Oddly enough, Señor Pau's undying affection for his wife hadn't escaped the notice of even the likes of a distracted little brat like me. Whenever the old man talked about her, which was often, he always smiled. Perhaps I was more attuned to this sort of tenderness, thanks to my parents' example. They also loved each other very much and didn't try to hide it. When my father finally did go off to the front, my mother smacked him a couple of times and burst into tears, but the blows quickly transformed into kisses and embraces. She proceeded to repeat the same pattern of tears, violence, and then devouring him in kisses the two times he came home on leave. I saw my father only twice during the whole time that he was fighting against the Fascists: four days, some months after he left; and just a few hours during the summer of '38. On that first visit, he was there when I got home from school. I found him chatting with Señor Pau, still dressed in his uniform. His eyes were bluer than ever; his skin a toasted brown. His hands were no longer large and tapering. They had become massive blocks. He gave me a shiny golden rifle bullet to string around my neck. I was thrilled. I asked him if he'd come home to stay. His answer was no, he still had work left to do. It sounded as if the war were another one of his jobs, another sign to be painted with his usual calm perseverance.

We went out onto the balcony to watch for my mother returning from work. As usual, she walked up the street with a determined step. She looked up, saw us from a distance, and lost her head. My father waved his cap in the air and she made a mad dash for the house. Even though we couldn't hear her, we could tell she was screaming and moaning. She flung open the door and threw herself into his arms. They'd been together since the age of sixteen and hadn't been separated a single day until the war broke out. They married when they were nineteen, when I was already on the way. She wrapped her arms around his neck and her legs around his waist. Her thighs dug into his kidneys, her hands were buried in his hair, and their lips were pressed tightly together. He cradled her bottom to keep her from falling. They remained like that, lips locked in silence. Señor Pau, No-Sister-Salvador, and I gaped in placid delight. Until the old man practically pushed us out the door with surprising force.

He said to me, "You come along, too, Geniset. Your parents have lots of things to talk about."

I couldn't understand what they could possibly have to talk about that I couldn't be around to hear, but I did what I was told and went with him. They didn't even notice our departure.

A half hour later my mother appeared at the neighbors' door, hair hanging loose, red cheeked, and her eyes sharply focused and shining bright. She looked like the most beautiful mother in the world. In her hands was a package containing all the provisions that my father had brought back from the front. That evening we feasted as we hadn't in a long time; garbanzos, lentils, sardines, cheese, potatoes, a little bit of chocolate, and actual coffee. It was a real banquet. Señor Pau even gave a speech about the fraternity of man and the horrors of war. . . .

CHAPTER SIX

Friday, October 21, 1949, evening

I stop by the Miranda Social Club before going to the major's house for dinner. I want to relax and have a beer. The radio is shut off today. There's a waitress going back and forth to the bar. She does her work with ease. I don't think that she's the proprietor's daughter. She's not the right age—too old, about thirty. She strides back and forth. I hear the regulars calling her Carmela. I glance at her a couple of times and she notices. It seems I've made a good impression. The proprietor heads my way, having remembered me from yesterday. He works up the nerve to strike up a conversation. If a stranger shows up twice, that makes him a customer.

"I hired her to help out on the weekends," he says, while following the waitress with his eyes.

I don't know why he's telling me this. I never asked. Anyway, it's strange, the place isn't exactly busy. But it's none of my business. He can hire fifteen chorus girls for all I care.

He breaks the silence by asking, "A beer?"

"Don't mind if I do . . . The radio isn't on today?"

"No. I heard everything I needed to know at noon."

"You mean about Doña Carmen Polo's departure for Lisbon?"

"No. This."

He grabs an opened newspaper and throws it in front of me. THE SOUL AND GRACE OF SPAIN: SPANISH CHORUS AND DANCING GIRLS RECEIVE A FERVENT AND ENTHUSIASTIC WELCOME IN LIMA.

It's hard to tell if he's joking. I try to figure it out.

"Are you saying that these two pieces of information are comparable?" I ask in a slightly impertinent tone.

The man holds my stare for a second and then goes back to the bar to see to a customer who orders an espresso. He calls over from the coffee machine.

"One of the girls on the Lima tour happens to be the sister-in-law of my wife's second cousin. They're from the same village."

"Right . . ."

"What did you think I meant?"

He turns his back to me while finishing up the coffee. I detect a flash of sarcasm in his grin. The guy isn't half bad. I finish my beer and go.

A young soldier is earnestly standing guard at Major Cedazo's garden gate. I'm not wearing my uniform and he isn't exactly impressed. I let him know that I'm expected, but he goes even more rigid. No one has informed him of my visit and, anyway, it's too late. . . . I insist, frankly annoyed, that it was the major himself who invited me.

"The major has left word that he's not to be disturbed, so please be on your way."

Just then, a petite, attractive woman with large black eyes appears at the gate. She looks to be over thirty. Her hair is short and stylishly swept back. She's wearing a fall coat that isn't particularly flattering and is loaded down with a shopping bag filled with bottles. The woman shouts at the sentinel in a surprisingly piercing voice.

"Is that how you treat a gentleman Legionnaire?" Now turning to me, she says, "You are the Legionnaire, aren't you?"

She brazenly looks me over from head to foot.

"Yes, ma'am."

"I'm Major Cedazo's wife. My name is Carmen, but everybody calls me Menchu. Carmen, like the Generalíssimo's daughter." She adds presumptuously, "She's not much younger than me. But if you want to know the truth, nobody ever guesses how old I really am."

The truth is, she does look her age, but it doesn't matter. She wears the years well. There are plenty of thirty-five-year-old women in Spain; the problem is that most of them look fifty. She offers me her hand, but instead of shaking it, I lift it up to my mouth and kiss it lightly. Her fingers are thin and recently manicured. I haven't seen a woman with painted fingernails in a long time (pale pink on her).

"Enchanted. My name is Ginés Aleu; everyone calls me Ginés, but you can call me whatever you want."

"Hush, you're shameless. Why aren't you wearing your uniform?"

"The major gave me permission . . ."

"The major, the major . . . I'm the major around here. I give the orders, and if you come again, as I hope you do, you must wear your uniform. A Legionnaire without a uniform is like . . . is like . . ."

I smile. This major's wife is pretty cute, even if she isn't very good at making comparisons.

"Don't worry, madame. The next time, I'll be in uniform. Should I bear arms as well?"

The question is asked innocently enough, but she begins to laugh coquettishly.

"You should come armed to the teeth! Oh my, a girl has to be careful around these Legionnaire types . . . ," and then, motioning toward the soldier on guard, "You'll have to excuse the boy. He's only been here a month and a half and hasn't quite figured out yet that the war's over. My husband should be on his way and I just stepped out to make a few purchases. Come in, come in. You can wait in the salon; at least that way you'll be able to warm up a bit. I'm from the Canary Islands and can't seem to get used to the climate. Do you think it's normal for it to be so cold at the end of October?"

"..."

"Don't say anything, I'll tell you; no." Then she addresses the now shamefaced boy, "Get out of the way, you dolt! To think, not allowing a sergeant inside . . ."

"The major neglected to inform me . . ."

"Keep your mouth shut, if you know what's good for you." She turns to me with a smile from ear to ear. "Come on in . . . What did you say your name was again?"

"Aleu. Sergeant Ginés Aleu."

"Very well then, Sergeant Ginés Aleu, in you go."

The house is a small villa, all on one floor, with a vaguely art deco air. The front door is imposing and robust and made from some expensive timber. A Sacred Heart medallion dangles on it, with a caption reading, "I Reign in this Home." The walls are two feet thick and the windows and balcony doors are all shut and barred to protect the room from the supposed chill. The dank, gray day outside is a sharp contrast with the sudden burst of brightness and heat within. All the lights are blazing. It's uncomfortably warm. There's a hodgepodge of items original to the house jumbled together with later additions.

A full-length mirror stands in the entryway. It's the kind that tilts at the center. A combination coat and umbrella stand is placed alongside it.

"Do you want to take off your jacket?" my hostess asks.

I say no. She seems disappointed. She removes her coat, revealing a cardigan. She takes that off, too. Now she's down to a clingy knit sweater that molds tightly to her breasts. She's wearing a fashionably pleated circle skirt that swirls. The sweater and skirt meet at a slender waist.

"Hello, are you daydreaming?" she asks, fully aware that I've been giving her a thorough once-over.

There's no doubt that she's a very attractive woman. I could fall for her in a heartbeat. She leads me into a fussily decorated salon. The living and dining room areas are separated by a simple arch. What catches the eye right away is a buffet with a display case, which, aside from the usual crystal and coffee cups, houses a collection of glass figurines representing a whole menagerie of animals. Another Sacred Heart, this time a framed bas-relief made of plaster, presides over the dining room table. A large chandelier looms overhead. The two sofas in the lounge are separated by a Telefunken radio, complete with its embroidered cover, which sits on a low table. A highly lacquered black piano rests against one wall. She asks me to wait a moment and slips out a side door. Less than two minutes pass before she starts yelling, "Do you think I have to stand being buried alive here in this one-horse town just because you get to go on a day trip and leave me here stranded? Don't you believe it!"

Hearing the argument loud and clear, I listen closely for lack of anything better to do. The major replies in a haggard tone, "It's an official mission, not some sort of vacation." Then it's her turn: "Official or unofficial, the problem is that you don't want to take me." And she goes on to say it's all the same to her if that's how things are, she'll take the bus, all by herself, to wherever it is they're going. The major tries to reason with his wife, saying that the bus would leave her over five miles away from the village in question. But the stubborn little thing proclaims she doesn't care.

The doorbell rings. Letting out a furious yelp, the major's wife, apron cinched tightly around her waist, strides right past me. She doesn't acknowledge my presence on her way to answer the door, and her eyes are blazing with anger. She calls back over her shoulder.

"I'll walk. Since I don't have a husband willing to take me, I'll walk . . ." The door to the street opens and I hear her say, "What the hell do you want now?"

It's the soldier on guard asking for permission to leave.

"Get out of here!"

The major enters the room, taking painful steps, as if walking on glass. He's in civilian dress: a gray suit with the Artillery's insignia on one lapel, the Spanish flag on the other. Obviously feeling the need to reaffirm his authority in my presence, he shouts in the general direction of the entryway.

"You are free to go!"

There's the sound of a door closing. His wife reappears, still fairly upset.

"What, are you going soft in the head? Didn't I just say the same exact thing?"

The major replies that he is the one who gives the soldiers orders. His wife laughs sarcastically, turns toward me, and says, loud enough so that anyone can hear, "Can you believe he doesn't want to take me to San Pedro de Cardeña?" She drops her voice to a whisper and says, "That monastery is famous because it sheltered El Cid's family while he was in exile, but I don't give a hoot about that. It's really just an excuse to get out of this boring old dump." Then she exclaims stridently to her husband again, "Do you think that just because you're the major you can order me around, too? Well, I wouldn't be so sure of that! And listen to this: If I don't get to go anywhere, Rita will be the one making the paella come Sunday!"

The major doesn't move or make a sound. He's sunk down in an armchair, legs resting on a low, tufted stool. This last attack seems to have thoroughly beaten him down.

"Very well then, come along . . . ," he mutters resignedly. "Anything to get you to shut up. But it's with the understanding that we're on an official mission. In other words, don't make a nuisance of yourself once we're at the monastery."

She still had to get in the last word.

"Me, be a nuisance? When have I ever gotten in the way, silly man? And don't you think you should pay your guest a bit more attention?"

The lady vanishes behind the kitchen door after sending a mischievous little wink in my direction. The major lifts up his hands, mutely begging me to be understanding.

"Women. Normally she's as gentle as a lamb . . ."

"You have a lovely home."

"The place isn't mine. It was confiscated by the government. It belonged to one of those Reds who went into exile during the war. Well, I'm not sure whether he escaped or was executed. The bottom line is that the State took possession of his house. For lack of anything else to do with it, for now it serves as the living quarters of the major in charge of the Basic Combat Training Facility."

I point to his feet.

"I see that the Freire Salts haven't been all that successful."

He stands up with some effort, saying, "Don't be so sure. The problem is that my feet require a certain amount of coddling and patience. How about a beer?"

As we drink, he looks me in the eye and comments, "You really made an impression on me today, Sergeant. What eloquence!"

"When it's a question of expressing profound and heartfelt emotion, everyone is eloquent," I reply with conviction.

"Don't say that, after the work I put into preparing all my own speeches. Imagine how that makes me feel . . ."

"If you'll permit me, I must insist that sincerity is the highest form of expression."

We take our seats at the table. Señora Cedazo has taken the opportunity to change her outfit. Now she's wearing an elegant sleeveless dress with a plunging neckline whose cinched waist furls out into a full skirt. I compliment her good taste. She informs me that it's the spitting image of one that Rita Hayworth wore in I don't remember what film.

"I had to go to a seamstress in Madrid, but it was worth it, don't you think?"

She's prepared a roast lamb with potatoes and herbs. That's enough to send her straight to heaven as far as I'm concerned. I'm distracted by the delicious aroma and fail to realize that the major is already telling me about his adventures while serving in Africa.

"I remember the high commissioner, with his white cape, standing in an open vehicle, escorted by a retinue of indigenous guardsmen mounted on camels who were carrying banners emblazoned with the Spanish flag. He inspected the troops standing in formation . . ."

I'm having a hard time concentrating and catch only snatches of his conversation. Right now, I have no idea what the hell he's talking about.

"It was an impossible position to defend. Our soldiers were brave, but unprepared, and, once again, a Moor betrayed us by stealing some vital machine-gun components . . ."

I hear his words without listening. I'd much rather gaze at his wife, who allows herself to be observed, barely making a pretense of not noticing. Cedazo must be twenty years older than her. The man waves about his pudgy hands with their sharp nails as he rattles on. I wonder if I'd be capable of killing him, if it came to that. The answer is yes. I try to focus in order to regain the thread of his conversation.

"We were prepared to comb the mountaintops in order to hunt down those sons of bitches, but the general called all the officers together, explaining he'd had direct orders from Madrid stating that we were not to deploy any troops. The problem was to be left in the hands of the civil authorities and the French . . . Are you listening to me, Sergeant?"

"Indeed, sir. Your words remind me of many similar situations; politicians are always distrustful of the military."

"You can say that again. Two different beasts really. The presence of the Generalíssimo keeps them in line a bit, but if it weren't for him . . ."

"Yes, sir."

"So what're the politics like down there?"

"I suppose it isn't much different from here, sir. There are the sympathizers of the Regime along with some disaffected."

"I'm not concerned about the petty sins of the civilian population. We can't let our united front be denigrated by a minority who seem to derive pleasure from belittling the Nation's most authentic traditions. The State is strong. We have no fear."

"The Generalíssimo has said it himself from the very beginning: Christian mercy."

The major, who's been concentrating on his lamb, stops chewing, looks straight at me, and interrupts.

"Christian mercy is all well and good up to a point, Sergeant, but we shouldn't overdo it. That's what Franco meant to say. But we'll have to see when, who, and how forgiveness or pardons get meted out. The Nation's enemies should not rest easy."

It seems as if I've touched a raw nerve. I back off a bit.

"Of course, of course. Ever vigilant, right?"

"Always."

Cedazo goes back to his lamb. I shut my mouth and smile at his wife. She returns the gesture and lowers her eyes. Then, out of the blue, the major suddenly mentions, "And speaking of forgiveness, did you know that the training facility used to be a concentration camp?"

My reply arrives a second too late.

"No, no, I wasn't aware of that."

"Well, it was. I was there myself."

"You?"

"Not as a prisoner, of course."

And he begins to laugh.

"When was this?"

"Not long ago, I was stationed there a few years before it was shut down. That's why they assigned me here in the first place, I know the terrain. I don't have to tell you that troops are a significant improvement over prisoners. They were just a bunch of Red scum who had to be kept alive . . . know what I mean? The camp had a horrible water shortage, even with the Bayas River right there. There was only one measly fountain for all that riffraff. Once in a while we had a truck come to deliver water . . . You should have seen them all with their tongues hanging out. They looked like dogs."

I'm appalled. I wasn't expecting this, and the major notices.

"What's wrong, Sergeant? Don't tell me that the idea of a few hundred thirsty Red prisoners upsets you?"

"No, no, of course not . . . I was merely thinking that you must have been very organized to have kept them from dropping off like flies. Because, not only that, the detainees had to be in a fit condition to work . . ."

"Work? Oh they worked all right; I can assure you. And, well, it is true that they were constantly dying on us. But even so, they didn't have anything to complain about. After all, they'd survived the war and that was a lot more than many, and I mean many, Red soldiers could say for themselves. Franco added months, even years, to those prisoners' lives!"

"If you look at it that way."

"How else would you look at it?"

Señora Cedazo drops her eyes coyly and breaks in.

"You must have been nothing more than a boy during the war . . . You're so young."

I nod and glance over at the major out of the corner of my eye. He's absorbed in wiping his plate clean with a piece of bread. We finish our dinner and go sit down in the living room for coffee and a liqueur.

"We spent almost the entire war up here in the north," she continues.

"You didn't see any action?" I ask the major.

"Oh yes, I did, on several occasions," he retorts quickly, "but I was kept mostly in the rear guard, in charge of artillery distribution."

"He even organized executions," his wife says proudly. "Whenever they were open to the public, I would go watch. Since I was his wife, I always got a front-row seat. At first I was horrified. After all, I was nothing more than an eighteen-year-old girl, newly married . . ." Then to her husband, who's contentedly smoking a cigar, "Be careful with those ashes, José Carlos." She turns back to me. "The man's always covered in cinder; he should really wear a bib when he smokes, like a child . . . The major had a knack for it, and was very good-looking. And his feet didn't hurt so much back then. You should've seen him waving his saber around, giving orders. I remember once, in 1937, the spectators got a real surprise when we arrived at the cemetery. The military had built a long wooden fence more than six feet high and about a meter away from the cemetery wall. And they'd filled the space in between with dirt and stones."

The lady is having a good time telling her story. Maybe that lamb isn't enough to get her into heaven after all. The major picks up where she left off. . . .

"There'd been so many executions that the cemetery wall was riddled with bullets. The lead slugs started to go right through the plaster. The problem was that the bullets began to damage the niches and get lodged in the coffins. The relatives of the deceased began to complain, as you can imagine. That's when I got the idea of putting up a wooden fence, separating it from the cemetery wall with packed dirt."

"Very ingenious . . . ," I reply, feeling extremely nauseated.

"At first we blindfolded the prisoners. Later on there were so many, one right after the other, that we didn't bother."

"Tell him the story about the Englishman," says his wife.

"You think so? Are you sure we're not boring you?" he asks me.

"On the contrary."

"Very well, but this is the last story. All right, we were about to assassinate a pair from the International Brigades. One was Polish, and the other English. We had them all ready to go when the Polish man started singing 'La Marseillaise' in a horribly screechy voice. Practically every note was off-key. It was enough to make you want to kill the guy just to get him to shut up. Meanwhile, a soldier came up to them and asked the English gent if he wanted a blindfold. He replied with perfect British aplomb. Dead serious, he said, 'Don't cover my eyes; cover my ears! I've had to put up with this bloke's tuneless singing the entire war. I can't stand it anymore. I don't want to die listening to it, so cover my ears, boy.' It was a sort of last request, so I complied. I put the rag behind his head and pulled it forward, carefully covering his ears, and tied it in a knot under his nose. And that's how they died. One with his ears wrapped up, eyes open; and the other with his eyes masked, howling like a hyena."

The major's wife begins to giggle. She's one of those women who turn ugly when they laugh. The kind of face that crumples up into a mass of wrinkles. I can feel the first twinges of a severe migraine. I don't know if this couple is the cause of it or not. It's hard to tell and that annoys me. While sipping her coffee, Señora Cedazo confides that she's had the honor of meeting Doña Carmen Polo, the Generalíssimo's wife. And that, like all Spanish citizens, she's thrilled about Franco's trip to Portugal.

"She's a great lady, isn't she?"

"Oh yes, she is."

"She'd make such a wonderful queen. The normal royalty would be a laughingstock in comparison. Why doesn't Franco declare himself king?"

I give her a sidelong glance. She's not joking.

"He can't . . . ," her husband begins.

"I don't see why not," she answers.

She's absolutely right. I don't see why not, either. He could easily proclaim himself emperor and be crowned by the current pope, who adores him so much. The major's wife stands up, grabbing a newspaper off a side table.

"Now that's class." Leaning over me a little bit, she shoves the newspaper in my face, making sure that I get a good view of her cleavage. She proceeds, as all too many do, to tell me what the article says as if I were blind or just plain dumb.

"Look, it says that the Generalíssimo's wife bade her daughter, Señorita Carmen Franco y Polo, farewell and climbed into the salon car mere minutes before the train pulled out. Do you see?"

I try to catch the major's eye, but the man is bent over, his body hunched under the table. He's probably massaging his feet. All I can distinguish is his back.

"What is it that I should see?" I ask his wife, while taking deep breaths of her perfume.

"It's obvious, she isn't ashamed to express her feelings publicly. In that way she flies in the face of all those high-society people. And when I say high society, I mean the nobility, too. They refuse to show any emotion and stick up their noses at anything that, according to them, could be considered vulgar. Well, what I say, and pardon my language, is they should go to hell. Doña Carmen is the way she is and now she's in charge. Not only that, she shook hands with everybody who came to send her off. And it was a big crowd. And all the spectators, who were mostly women, started waving their handkerchiefs when the train started up, and didn't stop until the whole convoy had disappeared from view." The major's wife lets her eyes drop, sighs, and continues. "I would've done the same thing. And now listen to this. The customized train that Doña Carmen and her companions are traveling to Lisbon on has a baggage caboose, a parlor car, a restaurant car, three sleeping carriages, and a first-class coach. There are two engineers manning the locomotive and one of them is the Railroad Battalion leader, a certain Major Contreras. I'd love to ride in a customized train like that someday. It's like something out of a fairy tale. Doña Carmen is a very special lady. She's a strong woman with real character. Did you know that she married Franco against her family's wishes? The Polos didn't believe that a mere soldier in the infantry would ever get anywhere. They assumed he'd get killed in Morocco. But she stuck with him through thick and thin. That's exactly what I've done with the major. Now if only, instead of being buried alive here, he could be a bit more ambitious like the Generalíssimo . . ."

Her husband pops back up to the table and observes us closely.

"Being in charge of a training camp is an important task, ma'am," I venture.

My host exclaims, "Sergeant!" with a brittle cry.

It's immediately clear to me what I've done wrong. I leap from my chair and stand at attention, as rigid as a telephone pole. I fix my eye on that spectacular chandelier hanging off the ceiling.

"Sir?"

"There's no need for you to defend me; I am perfectly capable of doing that myself. Especially in my own home. Who do you think you are?"

I apologize, keeping my eyes trained on the ceiling.

"At ease."

"And sit down for crying out loud . . . ," she adds.

"But he's absolutely right," Cedazo admits. "Running a boot camp is a huge responsibility. It means assuring that the population's first contact with the military is a positive one." He turns to his wife. "You'd like me to be more like this Contreras character, wouldn't you? That guy does nothing more than play with toy trains all day . . ."

Doña Menchu stands up and removes the coffee things without saying a word.

We finish off the evening singing around the piano. Cedazo has told his wife all about my performance that afternoon. They happen to have the sheet music to "The Bridegroom of Death" and she knows how to play it. Triple whammy, my hostess says while coquettishly twirling the seat of the piano stool round and round with her finger, making sure that her buttocks are shown to full advantage. She sits down at the instrument and the lid creaks a bit as she reveals the keyboard. The major slumps down in a nearby armchair, returning his lower extremities to their resting place on the footstool. That way, he can observe his wife's playing without having to twist his head around if he wants. I stand opposite my superior, in the expected manner, with my arm leaning against the piano cover. As Señora Cedazo bangs out the first few bars, I begin to retreat into myself, as though I'm somehow not here, off in another world. This can't be happening to me, it isn't possible that I'm here right now, singing and smiling at the major's wife while I ogle her breasts yet again. She notices, yet again, but flirtatiously goes on as if nothing has happened. When I get to the final verse, the one that goes, "I became the bridegroom of Death, we are bound together for eternity and her love is my flag . . . ," I can almost feel her stiffen with pleasure, pain, emotion, or lust. Not for me; for the song. The major has a good chance of getting lucky tonight.

I can't take it anymore. I've sung "The Bridegroom of Death" three times in one day.

I excuse myself and get the hell out of there.

It's midnight and the lamb is roiling in my gut. Back at the pension, I'm greeted by Campillo's complacent smile and his mother's inert figure behind the front desk. Before he can begin chattering away, I cut him off with a wave of the hand.

"I need some bicarbonate."

"Of course, right away."

He heads off toward the restaurant. The evening spent at the Cedazos' has left me unsettled. It seems that the lamb didn't go down so well after all.

CHAPTER SEVEN

Montalegre was a narrow and tidy little street. The Charity Home's hulking mass overshadowed everything. A uniformed porter stood outside its massive wooden door. I was greeted by a professor named Ramon, who was so large that he looked more like a square-shouldered athlete than a teacher. He was a pretty funny-looking fellow, with his round face, a sharp part down the middle of his scalp, and delicate, metal-framed spectacles. His crooked nose was what stood out the most. Maybe he was a boxer and his nose had been broken in a fight. When we introduced ourselves, he shook my hand as if I were an adult. My mother seemed appeased by the gesture.

"Don't worry about Genís; he'll be fine. We follow the Montessori method here, I don't know if you're familiar with it." And then he turned to me and said very gravely, "Here, the Catalan government will provide you with food, housing, and education. And in due time, you will also be taught a trade . . ."

The first thing that I was provided with was a bowl of hot milk thickened with crumbled bread. I hadn't tasted milk in weeks. Actually, it'd been a long time since I'd eaten much of anything. A full stomach cheered me up. I never did lack for learning, a roof, or sustenance the entire time they were in charge. But they weren't given the chance to give me a trade.

It was already pitch-dark out and a sort of nurse led me off to a room filled with beds. Little heads began to poke out from under the covers. The young woman was saying something to me with a smile, but I didn't catch it. She realized that I was about to burst into tears and helped me get into my pajamas. Before leaving, she embraced me and said in a soft voice that there was nothing to be afraid of; I was a big boy now. And I should consider myself lucky that my mother would be coming to visit. That was something most of the wards couldn't even dream about.

I listened to the other children moving around in the dark while lying stiffly in bed. One of them mumbled in his sleep; another coughed. My eyes started to well up again as I thought about my parents, Señor Pau, and No-Sister-Salvador. The world of adults is meant to instill strength and confidence in children, to provide shelter. A desperate child goes to his elders for help even though he knows they can't fix much more than a bump on the head or a scratch on the knee. But the child buries himself in the adult's chest anyway, sobbing over the smallest things. What children are really crying about is the black, unknowable, and bottomless well that lies within them. Consolation is impossible. It is the fear of nothingness and the incomprehensible. The Charity Home, an asylum for orphans, or counterfeit orphans like me, was full of lonely and abandoned children; a herd of frightened goats. Luckily, the adults didn't suspect any of this; otherwise they would have been scared to death. That sense of anguish only fades over time, as the child becomes a sluggish and incompetent adult, committing the same stupid errors that adults do. But the memory of that infantile terror remains, hidden away in some corner of the mind.

I'm pretty sure that I dreamed about my father once I'd finally fallen asleep. The next morning they made me take a cold shower, shot me up with vaccinations, gave me a set of clean clothes and two pairs of shoes, along with some polish and a brush to clean them with. I was assigned a number. As the days passed I grew accustomed to the routine of classes and the rituals of community life in general. I made new friends and explored the rest of the Home, which was divided up into different sections (elderly, cripples, the deaf and dumb, women and children . . .). More than a prison, the place was an all-inclusive sewer of humanity. But at least the people who ran it didn't make us feel like a bunch of rats.

We studied, played, and, above all, ate. Ramon taught us calisthenics.

Every time a siren sounded, we had to run down to the bomb shelter that was located under one of the courtyards. First there would be the sound of motors and then, suddenly, the blast of an explosion. The walls would echo and shake around us as we clambered to safety. The shelter was a gigantic basement, jam-packed with all sorts of people from the Home and off the street: boys, girls, educators, nurses. . . . The adults made us sing songs, but it didn't stop us from hearing the bombs. But the music did make it seem like the war was only going on outside, far beyond the insurmountable fortress of the Charity Home. Those walls gave me a sense of security that the adults couldn't provide. They were too busy trying to make sure we didn't notice how terrified they were.

My mother came to visit me as soon as she could, about three or four days later. She paused to watch the children playing in the courtyard and said, "In here, you'd never know there was a war going on."

And she smiled. She came to pick me up first thing on holidays. We'd stroll around, bringing each other up to date on our lives. I read the letters my father sent, if there were any. She'd bring me to the communal dining hall near the customs office where she ate lunch and dinner. The grand hall was always full of men and women just like her. Everybody knew each other. I loved it because my mother's friends were continually telling me how cute I was and sticking bits of cheese and fruit into my pockets. Later we'd make our way back on foot to the Charity Home. Sometimes we'd have lunch at the apartment with our neighbors. They were always happy to see me. On those days No-Sister-Salvador would always go collect cigarette butts off the street as soon as we'd finished eating. We'd talk while combing opposite sidewalks, walking in tandem while never taking our eyes off the ground. If we saw a cigarette, we picked it up. Eventually our wanderings always led us to the tower. Once we had settled in, we set about pulling the tobacco from the stubs, mixing it all together on a piece of newspaper. It didn't matter what the tobacco was like; we weren't exactly picky in those days. There in the half-light, we sifted through the tobacco as if sorting lentils, never saying a word. No-Sister-Salvador had invested part of his meager savings in a packet of cigarette papers. We rolled new cigarettes from the tobacco we collected and then resold them to workers at the Born. He confessed that he was stockpiling provisions in the tower, in case he had to go into hiding. I assumed that he was still terrified of being forced to go to war, even though he was only a sixteen-year-old cripple. But no, it was something else. He admitted that he and another delivery boy from the market had stolen two chickens from a farmer. Now he was afraid of being caught by the police.

"The man had placed an ad in the papers announcing three chickens and four hens for sale. We went so far as to ask what he wanted for them. We thought maybe we could resell the poultry to our best clients at the market. We found out that the farmer was planning on auctioning the birds! He told us to jot our best offer down in a sealed envelope and he'd let us know. We were furious and almost reported him to the authorities. The only reason we held back was because we realized how much trouble he would've gotten into. Too much trouble, if you know what I mean. A bunch of chickens and hens still aren't worth the hide of a scheming peasant. But we made sure to come back that night. The farmer answered himself when we knocked on the door. My buddy, Cors, didn't say a word. He took one look at him and punched the guy right in the face. He knocked that farmer out cold. We only found two chickens. Cors broke their necks right then and there, shoved them in a sack, and away we went. The two of us kept a part of a breast and thigh each. We sold the rest."

I was shocked. Maybe this was one of the many changes brought on by war. Three months ago Salvador and I had been practically living together, but he'd become radically different. He was, in effect, another person; a thief, which was a very dangerous thing to be. Back then, black-market traders, extortionists, and thieves were severely punished in the civil courts in order to maintain control of the population.

We didn't have class on Saturdays. The teachers let us little kids, along with the older children, take a vote to decide how we'd spend our day. In the winter we always ended up going to a movie theater that used to be near Plaza Catalonia. In the summer we'd go for walks. We kids loved to go down to the port to watch the ships and pleasure boats. Everyone could tell that we were wards from the Charity Home as we walked in single file. Once in a while they'd take us on a Sunday day trip somewhere nearby. The buses would be provided by either the Catalan government or the Military Board of Health. We were always escorted by a couple of militiamen. Thanks to them, we breezed through barricades and highway checkpoints as if they were nothing.

The older children were curious about my father. I told them that he was at the front. When they asked me how long it had been since

I'd last seen him, I had to admit it had been quite a while. That's when they began to slash their index fingers across their throats, shouting that I might as well give him up for dead. He was sure to have been killed by the Fascists and I'd never see him again. It made me so angry that I'd start kicking and punching whoever happened to be nearby. They'd scream, "You don't have a father! You've got no daddy!" As if they did themselves . . .

We were weak-willed, defenseless children, without much character; kids who had worn out before their time. Nonetheless, we did the best we could to live up to our role of being charity cases during wartime.

Food was getting scarcer all the time. According to the teachers, we were lucky to get the lentils that the Russians sent us. We were to consider ourselves fortunate. The people on the street were the ones who were really starving.

My mother picked me up on Sundays as often as she could. We'd walk home together and say hello to Señor Pau and No-Sister-Salvador. They were always happy to see me. We ate lunch at their house, under the protection of a diminutive image of Saint Pancrace, which hung above the radio. The print had mysteriously vanished when the war broke out, only to magically reappear not long afterward. Señor Pau wasn't exactly a churchgoer, and, according to him, Pancrace was on display because as saints went, he was the least saintly of the bunch. The old man always said that Pancrace had only asked the Lord for work and health; in other words, heaven on earth. And Saint Pancrace didn't hand out good luck or easy money. So he must've been both very Catalan and very Socialist.

No-Sister-Salvador didn't talk much at home; but we'd go up into the tower together. He'd let me know how his life was going once we'd settled ourselves into our hiding place. He explained how there were more people going hungry every day. Working at the market made the growing starvation obvious. The crowds would fight over the most putrid scraps. I asked him if he'd stolen anything else. He said no, but not with much conviction.

Every time I had to return to the Charity Home, I felt like Cinderella. The difference was that at the appointed time I turned into a little rat instead of a pumpkin. Once again I'd take my place among the pack of other rats that had been waiting for me. We paced around the courtyard in clusters, hugging fearfully close to the walls. We ran in short, rapid bursts, furtively hoarding food and then gnawing on it in a corner or occasionally storing it in some secret hiding place. I knew that having so many people who loved me outside the Home made me a very privileged rat indeed. Those family and friends enabled me to poke my head outside the sewers once in a while and take a look around. The other wards were well aware of my situation. And a few of them, especially the older ones, didn't like it one bit.

One Sunday my mother slipped a packet of cooked chickpeas into my pocket when she dropped me off at the Charity Home. When it was time to say good-bye, she kneeled down and held me in a tight embrace. It was wonderful to be enveloped by her warmth and smell, but I was worried about those chickpeas. I was so concerned about them getting crushed that I kept my arm rigidly straight as we held each other. When my mother left, I dropped the packet in a fit of nervousness. I noticed one of the older kids watching me as I stooped down to collect them. My plan had been to eat them surreptitiously in bed, while everyone else was asleep.

A pair of hands covered my mouth as soon as the lights went out. My attackers grabbed the chickpeas and pulled me out of bed. I couldn't tell who they were. I was blindfolded, and as they held me aloft, I realized that I was being carried off to the bathroom. The air was frigid. Somebody forced me onto my feet, holding me tightly from behind. Nobody spoke. They pushed me down onto my knees.

I calculated that there were three older boys, which meant they'd get less than ten chickpeas per person. That's when the dampness and hot odor hit, spraying over my head, chest, and down my legs. They were pissing all over me. In complete silence. The last one forced my mouth open, shoving in it a piece of paper that still tasted of chickpeas. Then they left. I was soaked in urine and freezing cold. There was no need for them to say anything; we all knew I wouldn't talk. At least they hadn't hit me too hard. By the time I returned to the dormitory, most of the boys were awake, waiting for me. The fact that I'd only been peed on was taken as a resounding success. That's how things are sometimes: simple and clear-cut.

One day, despite all the bomb scares, the teachers took us to see the aurora borealis. We were piled into a bus and driven to Can Frares, a sanatorium up in the mountains around Horta that was run by the same foundation as the Charity Home. With only a lantern to guide us, our teacher Ramon led the line of little wards, bundled in hats and scarves, up through the quiet darkness of the mountain. It was at least a twenty-minute walk. Upon reaching a clearing on the mountainside, we turned around, and suddenly the sky was awash in a curtain of fire, with flashes of light and flames. All the boys and girls exclaimed in unison as if watching a display of fireworks. And while we contemplated the scene, enrapt in wonder, the teacher explained in reverent tones:

"The aurora borealis is considered a rarity even throughout most of Central Europe, but here at home, it's practically unheard of. This is truly a once-in-a-lifetime experience."

We spent the night in Horta, with the colors of the aurora borealis still glimmering in our memory.

The war trudged on. There were nights when we'd hear the dull hum of airplane motors. Then the electricity would go out. Even the air-raid sirens fell silent. Most of the boys and girls would begin to scamper about, squealing in the dark. Some of them hid under the bed. There were others who crawled in between the sheets, cowering beneath their blankets. A bunch of kids would huddle together in a corner of the courtyard, one on top of the other, somehow comforted by each other's presence. The teachers had a hard time calming us down and corralling us in a quick but orderly fashion down into the bomb shelter.

I was at the Charity Home for a full year and a half before seeing my father again. The meeting lasted for only a few hours. He arrived in person to pick me up. It wasn't visitors' day, but they let me go anyway because he was a man in uniform. I paraded him over to the secretary's office just so the other kids could get a good look at him. That day I was the king and the rest of them were just dried-out little pieces of shit. That's the way things worked back then.

While we were rushing off to go find my mother, he presented me with a belt buckle from a Fascist uniform. I didn't want to ask if he'd had to kill a man to get it. The three of us had lunch in a tavern near the cathedral. It was pretty crowded. There were plenty of soldiers around, but not much on the menu. The tile floor was slick with grease and the display case at the bar was empty. The glass that once protected the daily specials and small plates of tapas was smudged with filth. A girl's brazen laugh cut through the tavern's din like a fragment from a dream. She was giggling at something her boyfriend, a soldier with a bandaged head, had just whispered in her ear. I was only intermittently conscious of my surroundings. The sight of my parents together, right there before my eyes, was so overwhelming that I couldn't take it all in.

They served us baked potatoes with a dash of salt and pepper and a couple of canned sardines. To drink, water. We didn't talk much. My father said he was worn out. He was being transferred to Ebro and it looked like the Republic was going to lose the war. And if that was the case, we were in deep trouble. . . . They both dropped me off when it was time for me to get back to the Charity Home. I watched them walk away, arm in arm, like a pair of young lovers.

In the fall of '38, a boy in my section died. His name was Feliu Pallerols. We were pretty good friends. To get a laugh, we'd do this gag together called the gypsy and the goat. Feliu could imitate a goat to perfection. He'd climb on top of a stool and bob his head from side to side, as if chewing cud, with a positively goatlike expression on his face. I pretended to play the trumpet and ordered him around. The other kids thought it was hysterical. Then all of a sudden he started to lose weight and developed a nasty cough. He had a very high fever. The teachers kept replacing the hot compresses on his chest. One night he stopped coughing. All of the children were settled down for bed when we heard him cry out "Mama." This from a child who'd never known his mother. Then silence. A few of us went up to him in the darkness. We softly called out his name, "Feliu," and then strained to listen, without breathing or making a sound. We tried once more, "Feliu." One boy opened the shutters to let in a little moonlight. Feliu Pallerols's mouth hung open slackly. I don't know how, but we all knew he was dead. I touched his body, and could practically feel it growing cold beneath my fingers. Not ten minutes before, his forehead had been burning up. Hair still clung damply to the skin. The sweat was clammy and cool. We pulled the covers off him slowly and just stood there staring, as if trying to figure out what the difference was between a living boy and a dead one. There didn't seem to be much. Living boys wet their beds, too. A kid named Pau Forner tried to pray, but couldn't get out the words. He used to whisper about how if the Republic lost the war, the Legionnaires would commandeer the Charity Home and cut off the ears of all the children who didn't know the Lord's Prayer by heart. So Pau practiced it every chance he got. The boy started to recite, "Our Father, who art in heaven . . ." But he couldn't remember anything after "in heaven." None of us knew how to pray. Our teachers were agnostic, and we'd never been given any religious instruction. But they were good people. My mother said that was what counted.

We couldn't tear our eyes off Feliu Pallerols's dead face. We lingered by his side for a while, without knowing what to do. One boy grazed his knee, another lifted up one of his toes, and a third tried unsuccessfully to close his mouth. Then we heard the night nurse heading our way. She was doing the rounds, checking on the sick inmates. We covered Feliu up again, put the shutters back in their place, and scurried back to our beds. He was the first child in the home to die of tuberculosis. After the war, sadly enough, that illness became all too common.

The nurses had to turn on the lights in order to dispose of the body. They wrapped him up in a blanket, put him in a wheelchair, and pushed him out the door. So long, Feliu. Before turning out the lights again, they told us not to worry, saying that he had been taken to the hospital for a rest cure and was going to get better. They said this to us, the very same children who'd been keeping vigil over his corpse for the last half hour. Outside, bombs were falling and an entire society was in collapse. From within and without, death permeated the thick walls of the Francesc Macià House of Assistance. We were children in the midst of the most susceptible period of our lives. Without our knowing it, our future memories were being forged in that very time and place. Maybe that's why our caretakers put on the whole charade with the wheelchair. Death outside the Home—the images of children killed in the bombings, lined up next to each other, with their eyes or mouths half open, like little dolls on display in a shopwindow. Death within those walls was another thing altogether—the death of a friend.

A general mood of defeatism pervaded that last winter of the war, thanks to the bad living conditions (hunger, cold, shortages of gas, water, and electricity). But to make matters worse, the Home was struck by a serious infection, taking a good fifteen children into its clutches. People said that the illness was caused by contaminated rations from the Russians and supposedly only affected humans and dogs. Everyone was terrified. We were put into quarantine. We couldn't be seen or receive visits from anyone except the doctors and nurses. The infection manifested itself in an outbreak of what looked like massive pimples called furuncles. They spread all over the neck, face, armpits, bottom, arms, and legs. . . . I had the largest and deepest one of all on my head, on the left side of my temple. It was as big as an egg. They had to call in a foreign doctor, because the Catalan ones didn't know what to do. I was very frightened and didn't have the strength to sit up. The nurses inserted a foot and a half of sterile gauze into the furuncle until the gauze was soaked with pus. When they began to pull it out, the pain became excruciating. I hollered and screamed, convinced I was dying. Every time they drained the pustule, I was left with a hole in my head the size of a fist. I howled like a banshee every time they did their best to disinfect the wound. You could tell they were worried by the looks on their faces. They were afraid the infection might spread to my brain. At one point an air-raid warning sounded, but we weren't allowed to go down to the shelter for fear of contagion. Most of the medics stayed behind with us. We could hear the bombs falling down by the docks. Some sounded quite close. The infirmary walls were trembling violently. And as the doctors went about their duties, their hands were shaking just as hard.

My head was in a bandage for a long time. Every time they'd change the dressings, a thick scab, as big as my hand, would appear.

I made it through, and so did the other children. Not one of us died. And yet the relief of having been spared was shadowed by sadness when we were told that the Fascists had reached the Llobregat River. The only thing I cared about was the huge crusty scab on my forehead. When it fell off, instead of a pustule there was a tight, shiny, and pallid stretch of skin. My hair never grew back over the scar tissue.

The war came to an end in Barcelona less than a week after the epidemic was brought under control. One day the teachers, nurses, and doctors disappeared into thin air all at once. By the time the new authorities arrived, the only staff members left were a nurse and one of the chefs. They were the ones to officially hand over the building and its occupants. The human cargo within was a tightly packed and undifferentiated mass of flesh: old crones and widowers, cripples, boys, girls, and adolescents; every one immobilized by panic and uncertainty.

CHAPTER EIGHT

Saturday, October 22, 1949

I've decided to contact Eusebio Fernández, the nurse who helped my father so much when he was already quite ill and nearing the end of his stay in the concentration camp. I need allies. I've no idea where the man might be. It's possible that he's still living in Miranda. But how should I go about finding him? The Town Hall? Today is Saturday. I'll have to wait until Monday. But maybe that's not the best idea. It could arouse suspicion. What would people think if a Legionnaire started asking around for a nurse who had worked at the concentration camp in 1941? I don't know what to do.

I go down to the front desk. Campillo isn't there.

"Good morning, ma'am."

Silence.

I leave the key on the counter and go outside. I find the old lady's son polishing the chassis of his lovely Chrysler with the eight-horse engine.

"Good morning, Campillo. You've got quite an impressive vehicle there. I particularly like the advertisement you've got painted across the side."

He stops and looks at me with curiosity.

"Good day to you, too. And many thanks."

"May I trouble you with a couple of questions?"

"Of course, I'm entirely at your disposal. What is it?"

"Does the name Eusebio Fernández mean anything to you? He might be working at a hospital, as a nurse, an orderly, or even a doctor."

"Eusebio Fernández? Doctor? Let me think. No, haven't heard of him. I'm sorry."

"It doesn't matter. And the second question: Is there a decent barber anywhere around here?"

This time his whole face lights up with an eagerness to please. He walks to the corner and shows me the way with an elaborate choreography of hand gestures. Although it might not seem this way to him, I actually like the guy. If everything goes as planned, he'll get a tip that'll knock his socks off.

The barber has a harried look about him. He observes my scar with the shifty eyes of a guilty man. But he doesn't ask any questions and gets straight to work with a sure hand. The same thing always happens. It's enough to sit in a barber's chair for me to immediately fall into a stupor. I concentrate on the day ahead. That helps keep me awake. But the barber seems to be cutting away at my consciousness as he begins to snip off my hair. He runs his fingers through it at a lively pace. The scissors peck away behind my ears like a woodpecker. I keep nodding off. The barber has to continually set my head straight so as not to make a hack job of the cut, or slit my throat like a pig's. I shove my hands in my pockets in an attempt to fight slumber, but I'm overcome by drowsiness. The man is making a concerted effort to liven me up, but it's impossible to keep my eyes open. He decides to ask me about the scar. The guy's been staring at it since the moment I walked in the door.

Beginning with a wake-up cough he says, "About that scar . . ."

"Yeah?"

"Would you like me to leave the hair a bit longer there? It would make it a little less noticeable if you did—"

I interrupt. "I have no interest in covering it up, thank you."

"As you wish."

He continues to snip away and I drift back to sleep. I go over last night's dinner at the Cedazo residence. The major's wife is a real looker. She reminds me of a lover I had in Africa: Amalia. I was immediately captivated by her when we met a year ago. I was in Tetuán for a time. I'd been transferred temporarily from Melilla to resolve some administrative problems for the Legion. Amalia was a secondary school teacher from Madrid who was there to oversee the Hispano-Moroccan educational system. As a demonstration of his affection for his Moroccan subjects, Franco inaugurated a series of agricultural and industrial high schools. Amalia was twenty-eight years old. She'd been a widow for five. It was ideal; a free and independent woman who could do what she liked. She told me on the very first day that she didn't plan on tying herself down to another man ever again, adding sarcastically, "I like to devour my soldiers whole, lick them clean, and then spit their bones out on the street. All with the utmost discretion, of course. I never miss mass on Sundays and always take Communion. And I'd never dream of touching a married man."

She was as clever as a little ferret. Women like Amalia don't try to keep up appearances. And that's why they're so dangerous, especially in a constrained atmosphere like the Protectorate, where there aren't many European women like her. Society will accept them only if they keep their behavior to themselves and don't make trouble for decent folk. Some ladies just intuitively understand what a real man needs:

sex with a dash of love, the kind of romance that fades after orgasm. Amalia was one of those women. She drove me crazy. New relationships are usually nothing more than a big headache. Maybe it's from lowering your standards because you haven't done it in a while. Or, normally calm, you find yourself in the middle of an argument, insulting someone (or being insulted) when you've never raised your voice (or been yelled at) before. Or maybe you're ashamed to be walking around with a telltale stain on your pants, whose origin is patently obvious to everyone. It can be safely said that I didn't care about any of that. I was mesmerized by her pale face and couldn't get enough of her body. Her extremely slender form contrasted sharply with a pair of full, voluptuous breasts, which seemed to have been somehow transplanted from another woman's physique. Hispano-Moroccan high schools were being set up in Tetuán, Alcazarquivir, Nador, Xauen, and Villa Sanjurjo. I tagged along behind her from one city to another. I have no idea what she must have thought of me. We only made love once. It was at her hotel in Tetuán. The hotel clerk seemed understanding. He didn't like to turn away a Legionnaire in full uniform, gun holstered to his side. I was terribly excited. It was the second time that I'd get to fuck without paying for it. The experience was incredible. When I woke up the next morning, I realized Amalia wasn't beside me in bed. I got scared. I found her soaking in the bathtub, eyes closed. A sharp pang of love shot through me. I looked out the window. The night had covered everything with a yellow haze, or rather a layer of gold. The scene was like something out of a postcard. The desert outside had deposited a thin veneer of sand over everything inside the room, including the two of us.

I couldn't resist ordering breakfast in bed.

It was already midday by the time I left that room. She adjusted the collar of my shirt as we were saying good-bye, taking the opportunity to grab my shoulders and pull me toward her. I didn't want to go. The whole affair was over in ten days. The word "love" never came up. We ran into each other that very night at a reception given by the high commissioner, General Varela. The place was packed with Spanish and local VIPs, not to mention journalists. The drinks flowed freely. She and I danced cheek to cheek, as if brought together by chance. I was thinking, "We make such a good couple." I tried to kiss her on the lips, but she was too classy to let me get away with it. Then I whispered heavily into her breasts:

"I'm in love with you."

She laughed and pulled away, saying, "And I'm crazy about General Varela! Really, the things you come out with!"

My legs started to quake and I had to sit down. By the end of the party, I realized that Amalia was pretty tipsy and didn't remember a word of what I'd said. I thanked my lucky stars and will always be grateful to divine providence for saving me from the utter ridiculousness of rejection. I've never tried anything like that again.

I traveled back to Melilla the very next day. I wrote her a letter, but she never answered. So much the better.

I open my eyes to find the barber's gaunt face peering down at me. I'm startled and suddenly awake.

"Should I give the back of your neck a trim as well?" he asks.

I nod. He continues about his business and I slip back into a stupor. It just takes a certain measure of self-control, but it's no use. All I have to do is imagine the scent of shaving cream and the massage at the end, and I fall back into complete lethargy.

The barber yanks the chair back to give me a shave, jolting me to life. How long have I been asleep?

"Should I trim your beard?"

"Don't touch it."

He sprays my freshly combed hair with cologne and unfurls the towel engulfing my body from head to foot. I reach for my wallet.

"Do you by any chance know a Eusebio Fernández?" I ask casually.

"Fernández is a pretty common name around here."

"But this one was . . . I mean is, a nurse, a health officer, or maybe a doctor or a pharmacist."

"No, doesn't ring any bells."

"Thanks."

There is a military vehicle waiting for me outside. Campillo must have sent it over to the barber's. That guy doesn't miss a trick.

I enter the camp gates all too quickly. There's a holiday atmosphere to the place. When I go to bid good morning to the major, all I find is the soldier Fontes. He tells me that the major has called to say that he isn't feeling very well and won't be coming in today. I chortle under my breath. The soldier assumes that I somehow find the major's indisposition amusing. He glares at me, suddenly serious. Let the little twerp think what he likes. But after seeing his wife on the warpath last night, I have a pretty good idea what's ailing the major. I introduce myself to the officer in charge during the major's absence, Captain Santos Bonfante, and take a seat at his desk. The man is absorbed in a Madrid newspaper and doesn't bother to look up when I come in. He's reading out loud to himself softly and stumbles over the words with difficulty. "Señora Carmen Polo de Franco arrived triumphantly in Lisbon yesterday morning at 9:47. She was received by the wives of the Marshal Carmona and the Spanish ambassador, as well as her brother-in-law, Don Nicolás Franco. Numerous Portuguese and Spanish personages were also in attendance. Franco's wife, clad in an elegant gray gown, was brought directly to the Queluz Palace, where she gave a very stirring speech." He looks up from the newsprint and gives me a thorough once-over. The captain's appearance definitely makes an impression. He's a thickset and coarse military man, with a face that has the tone and texture of a beefsteak. A shock of dark hair is swept back by a liberal application of Brillo cream. The effect is marred by a circular indentation in his hair, left no doubt by his cap. He must've put it on when the cream was still damp. You can tell that he's proud of his thin mustache. They're quite fashionable in certain circles. He's smoking a cheap cigar, the kind that stinks instead of giving off a pleasant aroma. He clears his throat, takes the chewed-up end of his cigar out of his mouth, spits a fleck of tobacco on the floor, and with a straight face asks me:

"When Señora Franco is with her husband's brother, do you think she treats him like a brother-in-law or an ambassador?"

The absurd always takes me by surprise. I don't know what to say.

"It depends," I reply.

"And what does it depend on, exactly, if I may ask?"

"It depends on whether they're in public or alone."

Situations like this could addle the brain of even the most well-balanced soul. They don't bother me. I've been in the Legion for over eight years now. You get used to it. There is logic even in absurdity. It's a question of taking things with a certain amount of levity. Like the first time you witness the arrest of a wooden beam, because it fell on a lieutenant's head; or watch a swimming pool get sanctioned for drowning a recruit; or see a mule being detained for refusing to carry a machine gun and its corresponding ammunition. While under arrest, the objects or animals are held in custody, with a soldier on guard. When you see that sort of thing, your definition of what is considered normal takes a terrifying shift. So when a major orders you to arrest a stone, you salute, arrest the stone, and get some jerk to watch over it.

Without even giving the guy time to reply, I request permission to give my talk. "Permission granted," he concedes without looking up.

I salute and start out the door.

"Where the hell do you think you're going?" he calls out.

I turn around and see him on his feet, behind me. The dark eyes above his Errol Flynn mustache bore into mine. I notice that he's got a gun strapped to his waist. The weapon stands out; it's much larger than a regulation pistol and is probably a revolver. I know all of these guns like the back of my hand. His right index finger glides along the mustache. After dousing me in a cloud of gray smoke, the guy says:

"I watched your performance yesterday from this window right here. It was a goddamn shame. An embarrassment. You Legionnaires are lucky to be the apple of the Generalíssimo's eye. Someone should explain to him that the only thing his Legionnaires are good for, instead of being soldiers, is to sing like canaries, fags, or eunuchs. Are you aware of what a eunuch is, Sergeant?"

"Yes, sir."

"And do you agree?"

"No, sir. And I doubt that Major Cedazo would, either. He didn't seem to hold that opinion last night, when I was having dinner in his home."

Silence.

"You had dinner with Cedazo?"

"He and his wife were kind enough to invite me."

The captain doesn't comment. He hadn't been expecting this. Jerks like him are all mouth and now he's put his foot in it. That type of guy is so easily cowed; after all, the boss is always the boss. He sits back down at his desk and says, "Get the hell out of here. Run off and put on your little show. But let's get one thing straight, I don't want to hear you sing. Understand?"

"Yes, sir."

"If I hear you singing, I'll personally belt you across the mouth. Understand? Now get out!" he growls, his face redder than ever.

I close the captain's door, leaving little clouds of rancid smoke be-hind. Fontes is practically trembling when I catch sight of him.

"I should've warned you that Captain Bonfante was on duty this weekend. He isn't very fond of Legionnaires."

"I noticed. But why?"

"The rumor is that some Legionnaires were responsible for his brother's death during the war. His brother was taken prisoner. The Reds offered to exchange captives. They were willing to trade three Legionnaires and the captain's brother for one civilian, an important politician. The deal was that they'd be either exchanged or executed. The Legionnaires got all up in arms, boasting how they weren't afraid of death. They refused to be swapped. Maybe they thought nothing would really happen to them. They didn't bother to consult the fourth person. That was the captain's brother, a lowly corporal in the infantry. All four of them were put to death before the firing squad."

The war ended only ten years ago. Spain is still full of people seething with hate, like Captain Bonfante and myself. The horrors of that war have been carried over into the present. Today society is at once thirsty for vengeance and bereft of any compassion for the los-ing side. It will take many years for so much resentment to disappear, to simply fade away. It's going to be a long haul. There're plenty of survivors. We're everywhere. And we plan on living for a long time. And it's likely that our children, or even grandchildren, will be the ones to bury the past. It won't be us. That's impossible. There are some, like Captain Bonfante, who'll have double the amount of work to do. That guy isn't content to hate the Reds; he's got it in for the Le-gionnaires, too. He can go to hell.

Fontes walks with me over to the esplanade. The troops haven't assembled yet. I turn my gaze out beyond the barracks, toward the line of trees and Purgatory. I'll try to sneak over there tomorrow. It'll be Sunday. Half the camp will be on leave and the other half will be asleep. I sense Fontes observing me. He could tell exactly what I was looking at, but it was only a fleeting glance. I can only hope that he doesn't put too much importance on it. Luckily, the troops arrive, dividing into three lines of formation. The corporals and a pair of sergeants stand alongside. The troops are ordered to sit in the same formation as yesterday. A bunch of them seem annoyed. I can see it in their eyes. Thanks to my little talk, they won't be able to go home until midday. They can go to hell, too. These kids already have it too easy. Not only have they been assigned to a basic training camp close to where they live, they get to visit their families on weekends. The recruits who are far from home don't care as much about leaving base. These kids were born in either '28 or '29. They were ten years old when the war ended. The statistics show that out of these one hundred recruits, one or two will desert. If they happen to be assigned somewhere close enough to the French border, they'll get the hell out of Spain. More than one or two soldiers will risk desertion in order to reunite with a father in exile. It's one thing to endure the Regime from a civilian standpoint, and it's another to experience it Army style. It can be unbearable. Most of them are caught before making it to the other side. That's where the military police and the Guardia Civil come in. Then the deserters are really screwed; Council of War and all that. They can get at least three to five years, apart from having to finish whatever military service they have left. But, worst of all, they usually end up getting locked up anyway, even if they do reach France. I've heard it straight from some exiled Catalans, now naturalized Frenchmen, whom I know in French Morocco. It makes them furious to see these young deserters end up in French concentration camps, just like their fathers. The Communists and Socialists declared an end to their guerilla warfare last year. The Anarchists are the only ones currently active. They're constantly shuttling arms back and forth between Spain and France, and it really bothers the French authorities. So whatever kid they nab at the border without his papers in order is detained until they can work out whether or not he's an Anarchist. The French aren't very fond of Anarchists, either.

At any rate, every single one of these recruits I have in front of me will soon be swearing fidelity to the flag. Medieval symbolism in the atomic age. They can kiss the flag or the Generalíssimo's ass for all I care. By that time I'll be far away from here, both in mind and body. I don't give a shit about the treasure my father promised me. If it really exists, so much the better. If not, I'll just have to make my own fortune. I dive in:

"The Legion embodies the spirit of camaraderie. We take a sacred oath never to abandon a fellow Legionnaire, even if it means death for us all . . ."

I met two very interesting individuals in Melilla about six months ago. One was an extremely wealthy Portuguese man by the name of Alcides. The other guy's name was Lazlo Stepanovic. I think he's either Austrian or Slovenian, I'm not sure. At any rate, they own vast, and very productive, estates in the Portuguese colony of Angola. After several evenings on the town, lubricated by the conviviality of alcohol and hash, we managed to become friends. They've asked me to go back to Angola with them. They say that now is the best time; if you're not afraid of work, you can really strike it rich. Just like they did, basically. For someone like me with a Legionnaire's experience, it would be ideal. The colony needs whites capable of instilling a bit of authority, but they also need guys with a head for business. Not many people possess both traits. Some men are full of ambition, but in the end they're weak. And some men are just the opposite. I feel I'm up to the challenge.

"The Legion embodies the spirit of combat. You must always, always be prepared to fight. Without waiting for your turn, or counting the days, months, or even years."

They explained to me that in northwest Angola, two-thirds of coffee production is reserved to whites. Cacao and tobacco are just two of the many crops that are easy to produce with a guaranteed market. But coffee is king. At first many European colonists are intoxicated by the myriad opportunities the country seems to offer, but they ultimately get discouraged by the obstacles along the way. It's impossible to exploit the land to its full potential. The difficulty in obtaining loans gets in the way of mechanization, as well as investing in fertilizers and other materials. But my two acquaintances have met with success, and they haven't been there very long. If I wanted to, I could start out working with them. They've got trucks, local manual labor, and tractors; my initial investment would be minimal.

"A Legionnaire will never admit to fatigue. He runs as fast as he can until finally collapsing from exhaustion . . ."

I'll bury Bartomeu Camús's bones in Barcelona. He'll be put to rest alongside my father. He might end up above or below him, but that doesn't matter. They'll share the same grave. Then I'll continue on to Caldes de Malavella and collect my mother and son. If she isn't up for the journey, I'll take the kid by himself. The two of us will start a new life in Africa. I figure we can last for about four or five years on my savings and maybe a loan. According to these friends of mine, that's more than enough time for the plantation to start turning a profit.

"The thirst for death. Dying in combat is the highest honor that a Legionnaire will ever receive. We get to die only once. Death arrives painlessly, and dying isn't as awful as it seems. What is truly horrible is to live like a coward."

I turn and catch a glance of Captain Bonfante a little farther off, behind the plate glass of his office window. I make it look as if I'm about to break into the Legionnaire's anthem, and glance back again. He's getting visibly annoyed. I smile and keep my mouth shut. There's no need to provoke him unnecessarily. The performance comes to an end. This time, there's no applause. The recruits stand up, staying in formation, and go on their way. Fontes comes up to me with a look of disappointment on his face and complains:

"I decided not to go into Miranda today because I wanted to hear you sing."

"If you're a good boy, I'll hold a private recital of Legionnaire songs just for you."

"Really?"

"But you'll have to do me a favor, Fontes."

"Whatever you say."

"I have a meeting tomorrow morning with two officers, a sergeant and a lieutenant. When that's over, I'd like to take some pictures of the camp. It's nothing really, just a couple of snaps for my report and some others as a souvenir. Do you think you could find me a decently priced camera?"

"You want to buy one?"

"Or rent it. It doesn't matter."

Fontes agrees, grumbling a little bit. We decide to meet tomorrow, Sunday, at ten o'clock.

CHAPTER NINE

Barcelona suddenly became an occupied city. We huddled inside as the hours passed, not daring to stick our noses out onto Montalegre Street. The nuns began to arrive the very next day. Their white-winged headdresses flapped in the breeze. They looked like extraterrestrials. We were struck dumb in utter shock. Only the oldest children, the ones who'd been there since before the Republic, had any idea what a nun was. The rest of us, riveted to the ground, stared at those ladies as though hypnotized. They explained that the National Army had taken over Barcelona. The city would become Christian once again. And that thanks to Franco, there would be no more bombardments or hunger. They said that we'd be able to breathe easier from now on. The scab on my scalp was still tender, and I thought about how hard the infirmary staff had worked to save me. I didn't see any reason to breathe easier on that day then I had twenty-four hours before.

They made us line up in one of the courtyards while all sorts of politicians, Falangists, and a military faction of Carlists known as Requetes appeared, all in uniform. There were officers gleaming with medals, priests, and more Sisters of Mercy, decked out in those winged headdresses. . . . The institution's new director was a tall and imposing chaplain sporting a crew cut. Just looking at the guy was frightening. He smoked long, thick cigars right down to the stump. He kept those cigars clenched tight in his mouth until they were too small to hold, and was always burning his fingers. His nails were singed black at the tips. A couple of medals, won in battle, were displayed on his chest. Standing in rigid formation, we felt terrified. The new mother superior stood defiantly before us, a massive chain weighed down by a crucifix hanging around her neck. She was scrawny and petite, with a narrow face and beady, but very penetrating, eyes. The new monsignor started off by saying:

"The war was a divine punishment sent down from above to purify Spain. Its citizens had become a nation of sinners, who veered off the path of righteousness. With God's help and Franco's sword, we will exterminate, liquidate, weed out, cleanse, purify, sanitize, and purge all in our path!"

He went on like that for quite some time. I heard him, but didn't listen. Why was he explaining all this to us, a bunch of nobodies, miserable little rats who were the lowest of the low? It became clear to me when the mother superior started saying her piece. Those people thought we were guilty of something. I wasn't sure exactly what. She told us to obliterate the past. The atheists and the rebels would be chastised. She would beat the devil from our bodies herself, if necessary.

"You miserable imps will be punished in accordance with the magnitude of your sins," she exclaimed in a screeching voice. A thick Catalan accent distorted her strident Spanish.

She told us that it would do no good to whine or beg for forgiveness, because she knew full well the extent of our hypocrisy. She then added:

"You have been forsaken by everyone and everything. A twist of fate has led you to this miserable existence. From this moment on, you will have to work hard to earn your way toward an honorable, Christian future through acts of penitence."

We felt the consequences of our new situation immediately. The girls and boys were separated. They shaved our hair down to the scalp, regardless of age. Our clothing and shoes were confiscated and replaced with a uniform of striped smocks and espadrille sandals. There were hardly any actual teachers. Most of the classes were taught by nuns in their winged headdresses, no matter how old the students were. And all we did was sing their hymns, memorize their doctrines, pray, confess, and go to mass. But the worst innovation by far were the new guards. Those ferocious individuals had strict instructions to instill the doctrines of the new Regime in our tender souls. They'd been granted the mother superior's permission to punish and beat us at will. We did eat a little better than we had during the last days of the war, but we still suffered from malnutrition. What they gave us wasn't enough to fortify starving children (especially in my case, having just gotten over a grave illness), and we were always hungry.

The Charity Home wards were locked up from the time that the Nationals took over Barcelona in late January to the end of the war in April. The mother superior was of the opinion that only shock therapy could cleanse our bodies and souls. She concocted horrific scenes of hell:

"Bolshevism, the Antichrist, and Separatism are like serpents. They are the devils within, which devour the very fiber of our being. We must wrench them out through penitence and, if necessary, by force."

It was terrifying, because we had no idea what these awful things lurking inside us were. Bolshevism? The Antichrist? Separatism?

They made us kneel on the metal benches in the dining hall every day before dinner and say a Rosary to give thanks for our meal. The guards paced between the tables to make sure that we weren't slumping or mumbling the responses. After a few minutes in that position, your knees would start to grow numb and fall asleep until they couldn't be felt at all. They'd swat at us with rods if we so much as moved a muscle. Finally an evening came when one of the children fainted. Weakened from hunger, he couldn't hold himself upright any longer. He swayed backward and forward and then fell. The nape of his neck struck the ground. They carried him off, unconscious, with blood dripping from one ear.

Hunger took the new Regime's first victim. He was a tall and sturdy thirteen-year-old by the name of Narcís. Another ward had received some carob beans from his parents on one of their visits, and Narcís decided to trade some glass bullets he'd been hoarding for extra sustenance. Narcís was starving and bolted them down too quickly. That evening he started to writhe on the floor in pain. The guards mocked Narcís and told him to stop putting on a show. They swatted the boy with a rod to force him onto his feet. By the time the nuns were notified, it was too late. He was brought to the infirmary and died that same night. We were told that the carob beans hadn't sat very well; a stomach hemorrhage. The priests and nuns used the incident as an example of divine justice's response to the sin of gluttony. We could only pray that God would let Narcís enter Paradise. Any God who let a boy die like that would have to be a real son of a bitch not to let him into heaven. He was only a kid, a kid whose thick lips played the clarinet in the Charity Home band. He used to pass love notes to one of the girls in the young ladies' choir during Sunday mass. The savages who'd practically left him to die were only given a reprimand. An orphan is no better or worse than any other child, with one difference. Orphans are alone and have no one in the whole wide world to defend their interests.

Narcís was the first name on a list that never stopped growing. Normally kids died of tuberculosis. Hunger, beatings from the guards, poor nutrition, and unhealthy living conditions all helped provoke continuous outbreaks of the illness. We all felt at risk. Tuberculosis always followed the same pattern. All of a sudden one of the boys would start to cough, then turn pale. His coughing fits would become more severe and his pallor would increase. Then the coughing attacks would worsen and the child would begin to spit up blood. . . . The doctor would proceed to prescribe tranquilizers and transfer the patient to the section of the infirmary reserved for tuberculosis victims, where the child would slowly die. Winter brought chilblains to our ears and fingers, and there was always dried snot clinging to the tips of our noses. Above all, we were weak. We remembered the Republic with nostalgia, as a time of relative ease. Despite the war and constant hunger, it felt like a dream. How could our brief lives contain such separate and radically different extremes of experience? As always, I kept my hopes up. I had parents who would get me out of there someday. Most wards didn't even have that.

Once in a while they would slap identification bracelets on the older children and send us out to work in the city. Normally we'd help out in the countless parades and processions that were going on at that time. Mostly we were assigned to crowd control. Linking each other's arms, we'd form a human chain to keep the masses at bay. We provided backup for the Fascist paramilitary group known as the Falangists. They were always impeccably polished in their blue shirts and red berets. We'd be in our smocks with shaved heads. There'd usually be a Charity Home guard present to keep us to the task and make sure that we didn't escape.

We held back the crowds at the multitudinous mass and military parade that was held by the Regime on Sunday, April 2, the day after the war ended. Two guards prodded us along with rods as if we were a flock of sheep. On the way up to the ceremony grounds on Montjuïc, we passed by a chain gang of prisoners clearing away the rubble from a bombed-out building. With their bare skulls and uniforms, you could barely tell the difference between us. The atmosphere was already charged around Plaza de España. There was a sea of blue-uniformed Falangists with red berets holding aloft banners and standards emblazoned with the names of their villages and towns. Dozens of buses were parked on Parallel Avenue. Clusters of priests and nuns were hurrying toward their destinations. It also happened to be Palm Sunday, and many families, young and old alike, were holding up small twigs to be blessed. Palm fronds were scarce. The municipal band was rehearsing right there in the middle of Plaza de España. The Barcelona police force, in full dress uniform, was lined up all along Lleida Street on horseback. The ceremony itself was still hours away. Charity Home boys were positioned around the altar, right in front of the fountains at the top of Maria Cristina Boulevard. All the officials took their preassigned seats as we moved chairs, unrolled rugs, and hung banners. There were religious figures, military men, Regime politicians, and representatives from Italy, Portugal, the Vatican, and the Führer.

By the time the ceremony was about to begin, the crush of people had reached alarming proportions. Mass was to start at eleven o'clock. There was barely room to breathe. The sumptuous service was punctuated by the somber cadences of the military band. The ecclesiastic governor (for lack of a bishop) blessed the crowds at the end. Then a choir sang the "Te Deum." The parade began immediately afterward, and the Charity Home boys formed a human barrier against the

thousands of ecstatic spectators pushing against us. They were shouting, applauding, and screaming themselves hoarse as they proclaimed
the military's victory. I found the whole thing very strange. Less than
two months before, Barcelona had been a city occupied by these same
troops.

The Moroccan Army Corps was at the head of the march, followed by other military groups. The Guardia Civil passed by in full
dress uniform and the Red Cross was next, followed by various
squadrons of the Falange, some marching and others on bicycle.
There were rows of trumpet players and drummers. Double columns,
twenty rows deep, contained members of different youth organizations, in addition to the Feminine Section and the Social Auxiliary.
Each group filed past with a martial air, brandishing flags that sported
enormous portraits of Franco and José Antonio. Each faction cried
out "Long live Franco" and "Long live Spain" as they marched past
the official bandstand, where the military governor, General Yeregui,
sat. The multitude bellowed in return, "Long live Franco," "Long live
Spain." It seemed like some sort of warped carnival.

The parade began at eleven forty-five and lasted until two thirty.
Almost three hours of nonstop tension, coupled with the fear of what
would happen if somebody broke the chain. Exhausted and exhila-
rated, we were heading toward a meeting point in the company of our
guards when I saw a Falangist, about eighteen or twenty years old,
punch an old man. The Fascist claimed that the man had neglected
to salute the flag. The elderly gentleman took the abuse without saying a word and kept his eyes trained on the ground. His hat had fallen
with the blow, so he bent over to pick it up. That's when the young
thug gave him such a sharp kick in the ass that the elderly man went
reeling onto the pavement face-first. The Falangist added that the
man should consider himself lucky. In honor of the festivities, he

wasn't going to report the incident. The elderly gentleman, hat in hand, struggled to his feet and silently melted into the crowd.

My mother came to visit not long afterward. We hadn't seen each other for almost two months. She looked haggard, as if she'd aged all at once. I didn't even wait to disentangle myself from our first embrace before asking when she was going to take me out of the Charity Home. My mother told me it was out of the question. Apparently the living conditions in the city weren't any better.

"It's as though someone has come along and swept everybody up. People disappear like the tide going out, as if they'd been tapped with a magic wand and turned to dust. The authorities don't seem to care about one more corpse or missing person. And yet the counting and roster lists never stop, whether it's on the radio, in the newspapers, or the talk on the street: how many living, how many dead, how many prisoners, how many detainees, how many fugitives, how many men have returned home . . ."

My poor mother told me all this because at the time she still didn't know anything about my father's welfare. Maybe he, too, had been swept away in the spring cleaning. I spent my idle hours in the Charity Home brooding. Depending on the day, I imagined my father in the forest, sheltered in some hideout high in the treetops or deep in a cave, waiting for the most opportune moment to sneak over the border. One day a mysterious letter in code would arrive from France, revealing vital clues that would lead us to him, alive and well. Other days I was convinced he was dead. I entertained myself by imagining his final, heroic moments, paintbrush in hand. His last thoughts were always of me and my mother. That's when I'd get sad and downright vicious. The other kids figured out pretty quick that they'd have to watch their step with me. They knew that, in those moments, almost anything could get me spoiling for a fight, even if God himself were before me. They'd start chanting "Crater" just to infuriate me. The scar on my head was large and very obvious. It practically shined. I'd gotten used to the nickname and didn't let it bother me, except when I could tell by the tone of voice that they were trying to be hurtful. In those cases, rage would give me added strength. I'd throw myself into the melee and gave back as good, or better, than I got.

My mother went on, but spoke so softly it was as though she were mumbling to herself under her breath:

"I wish you could see what it's like, Niso. Everyone's using whatever means necessary to try and get information about their loved ones who've disappeared. So many people must be in the same situation; waiting for a letter."

My mother buried her face in her hands and began to cry. She'd done the rounds of the military, government, and the Red Cross, asking about my father. . . . She spent her days wandering from one office to another, begging for information. They shrugged her off everywhere she went. Although sometimes seeming as fragile as a little bird, my mother was extremely determined. She could remain standing for hours in hopes of obtaining some shred of information about the husband who'd been her sweetheart since the age of sixteen.

"Nobody cares what happens to a Red soldier. Everyone is struggling to survive. I wasn't an official government employee or anything, so I wasn't part of the political purge. They just fired me. But now the government is concerned about finding jobs for all their supporters who need work. Businesses are being forced to hire Falangists, ex-combatants, and liberated prisoners of war. It's payback time. We've lost the war, haven't we? Well, we'd better get used to the new reality and make do."

My mother said it was best to leave things as they were. She didn't have any money and had nothing left to sell. If it weren't for No-Sister-Salvador, she wouldn't be able to survive herself. And that wasn't the worst of it. She was worried that if anyone looked too closely at the Charity Home files, it would become apparent that I wasn't an orphan at all, and had been taken into the institution as the child of a Red soldier.

"The last thing I need is for you to get kicked out . . ."

It was entirely possible. Back then more and more children were being admitted, often very young. They'd lost everything during the war. It would seem only fair that I be sent away.

When she removed her dark glasses for a second to wipe away her tears, I noticed her right pupil listing toward her nose.

That was the saddest visit of them all.

Around then I made the acquaintance of the man who called himself Señor Roca. My mother introduced us one Sunday morning in the middle of May. She came to pick me up with her sunglasses firmly in place. My mother had put on her only good dress, even though it was really too heavy for the weather. She described this shadowy person as an old friend from before the war who was going to help us find my father. I'd supposedly met him before, when I'd been too little to remember.

We walked together to a café on the Rambla Catalonia. I could tell she was tense. She was wearing a Social Auxiliary badge on her lapel. She explained, rather grudgingly, that the group had been taking up a collection the day before. And that she'd felt practically obligated to contribute, because it was considered very bad form not to give something.

"These days you can end up being placed under suspicion without even realizing it if you don't watch your step. The authorities encourage the population to report each other's wrongdoings. They say that it's our patriotic duty to denounce fellow citizens."

It was odd; our existence in the Charity Home revolved around brutal punishments, the hypocrisy of our Catholic caretakers, and

the propaganda of the new Regime. We also studied, played soccer
with a ball made of bundled old rags, sang patriotic anthems, and re-
cited endless Rosaries. But we had no conception of what life outside
the Home was like. I had no idea how my mother could have transformed into a fearful creature, enclosed like a tortoise in its shell. My
main concern was avoiding beatings from the guards and trying not
to annoy the nuns. May had been designated as the month of the
Virgin Mary. Anyone from the House of Mercy capable of putting
one foot in front of the other took part in a procession while reciting
the Rosary. The monsignor and the choirboys took the lead, followed
by a group of nuns and the Daughters of Mary, who were adorned
with blue ribbons. Behind them were the inmates from the poorhouse, the elderly and the infirm, along with the deaf and blind children. The ladies' choir intoned the mysteries of the Rosary with
tender sentiment, accompanied by the Charity Home band, which
brought up the rear. We paraded across the courtyards, through the
hallways and workshops, all dressed up in our Sunday best. We sang
with what was supposed to be religious fervor, a banner depicting the
Virgin Mary held aloft before us. It was very otherworldly, like something out of a play. But I quickly got used to it. Good training for
blending into the Legion so effortlessly.

All of a sudden my mother sat up stiffly in her chair. I realized
that Señor Roca must have arrived. He was about the same age as her
and elegantly dressed, with a mustache and hat. He seemed to be
nervous as well. My mother got to her feet. They shook hands. Señor
Roca spoke in low tones so that no one would notice he was conversing in Catalan. And whenever the waiter, or anyone else, drew
near, he smoothly switched into Spanish.

"This is Niso, I don't think he remembers you, he was very little
when we last met," my mother said.

We also shook hands. Señor Roca sat down. It was obvious that my presence made him uncomfortable. He saw that we hadn't ordered yet, went to the bar, talked to the waiter, and took his seat again.

"It's been so many years . . . ," he said in a surprisingly reedy voice.

"It's true, and with a war in between," my mother added in an affectionate voice, as if he were an old friend.

"How did you find me?" he asked bluntly.

"Find you? I wasn't looking for you. It was just a coincidence," she said, surprised by his tone. "I happened to spot you going into your parents' house and simply went up and asked if we could meet. You were so well dressed and seemed so important with that big car waiting for you at the door."

"Have you told anyone that you know me? Do you have my name or address written down anywhere?"

"Floreal, why are you talking to me like this?"

"Don't call me Floreal! I've changed my name. I'm now known as Roca. Benito Roca."

"What are you hiding from?"

"I'm trying to start a new life . . . I live in Madrid . . . I want to know exactly what information you have about me and if you've told it to anyone else."

"But Floreal . . ."

"Don't call me Floreal, damn it, someone might hear you."

"Have it your way! I'll forget that we've ever seen each other, that your name is Floreal, and that we're meeting now. And I won't tell a soul. And Genís won't either."

"I'm taking a terrible risk, getting together like this with you! I'm not even supposed to be from Barcelona, or know anybody from here, damn it! What is it you want from me?"

"I need help."

"Of course, you and thousands of other people. There's nothing to fear if you're innocent."

My mother adjusted her glasses. She was definitely on edge. I didn't like this Señor Roca.

"Don't treat me like a fool. They're executing people as though it were nothing more than knocking down a few ninepins in a bowling match! Wives bring potato omelets for their husbands imprisoned on Montjuïc, only to be handed a death certificate stating internal hemorrhage as the official cause of death. What's worse is that they don't even try to hide it. All you have to do is read the newspapers."

"There's been a war! And in a war, you either win or you lose."

That's when he pulled his wallet out of his jacket and rifled through it, removing a few bills.

"Here, I can't give you any more without it being missed."

"I didn't come here to ask for charity."

"What is it you want then? Do you need me to vouch for someone politically?"

"No. If that were the case, it would mean my husband was safe at home. What I don't understand is why you've gone to such lengths to hide your identity," my mother said, a tinge of exasperation creeping in. "Your father may have been an important figure during the Republic, but that doesn't make you a criminal."

"My father really put himself in a fix."

"But you didn't!"

"When he was killed by the Communists, I used false papers to get out of Barcelona and went to France. And from France I crossed back into the National Zone. My past has to be kept secret, especially from my in-laws."

"You're married?"

"Yes. I met my wife in San Sebastián. They've supported Franco from the very beginning. We're practically newlyweds. My in-laws have already taken me into the family business."

"Congratulations. On everything."

"You're judging me. Who do you think you are? I've done what I had to do. I'm alive, in good health, and have a whole future ahead of me."

A silence fell. Neither of them wanted to be the first to talk.

"If you're found out, it won't be my fault," my mother said in a tired voice. "All the pieces of poor Floreal's puzzle are now finally in place."

"Yes. Well, not too long ago you were feeling mighty content and sure of yourself. But now you've had to come pester me. War changes people's point of view. Whoever says different is a liar. In 1937 I was on the run in order to save my skin. Now it's somebody else's turn. But I still can't risk any associations with that time period. It isn't fair. Even someone above suspicion like me is obligated to prove his support for the Regime thirty times a day. Right now there are four different categories of citizens: prisoners, the disaffected, the indifferent, and the faithful. Those in the first group, if they're not dead already, are either close to it or rotting in prison. The second aren't that much better off than the first. The third are starving because no one will give them work. And everyone wants to be a member of the fourth faction. Everyone! Everyone, do you hear? I've discovered that I quite enjoy being on the side of order and discipline. I enjoy it very much."

"We've got more than enough order now in the cemeteries, out in Bota Field for example . . ."

Señor Roca lowered his voice and muttered irritably, "I haven't come here to listen to some political harangue."

"You're right, that sort of talk has gone out of style."

He looked up at the clock hanging on the café wall. Pulling out a handkerchief to wipe the sweat off his face, he said:

"I have to go. Tell me once and for all exactly what it is you want from me."

"Help me find my husband. I need to know whether he's dead or alive. Nobody will tell me anything, they just keep brushing me off. I feel like I'm losing my mind."

"You have to be patient. There are thousands of cases just like yours. The proof is that the Ministry of Justice has been forced to extend the processing of files on missing or deceased persons until December. Maybe he was taken prisoner. Or escaped to France . . ."

"I don't know. I don't know anything! Help me find him. You don't have to implicate yourself any more than that. Someone else can vouch for him if he turns out to be alive. And if he's dead, I'll go collect his body."

"I have friends in Madrid. I'll see what I can do."

"Even the smallest assistance will be far more than I could ever do on my own." She extracted a piece of folded paper from her pocket and handed it to him. "Here's everything you'll need to know about him, including his military assignments. And the date and location postmarked on his last letter. I'd also like . . ."

"Another favor?"

"It's not for me; it's for this little fellow here," she said, nodding her head toward me. "That's why I brought the boy along. I wanted you to see him."

Señor Roca didn't even look at me. His eyes were trained uncertainly on the ceiling. Then, for a brief moment, he shot me an anxious and shifty glimpse.

"Niso is staying at the Charity Home. That's the only way we can survive. I'm counting on taking him back as soon as our situation improves, but right now it's absolutely essential that he remain there. I'm afraid they'll throw him out. He's not an orphan and his father is a Red soldier missing in action."

"My father-in-law, the Count of Montseny, is a personal friend of the president of the government of Barcelona. I imagine he could look into that without having to compromise himself needlessly."

"Thank you very much."

"'Thank you'? Sometimes I get the feeling that words themselves are just empty shells devoid of meaning. If someone were to devise an eraser capable of wiping out the past, they'd be richer than the inventor of the wheel."

Señor Roca stood and signaled to the waiter. My mother clutched at his sleeve. Her hand seemed to have grown a set of claws. Silent tears began to slide down from beneath her dark glasses.

He stared at her in a peculiar manner and then shifted his gaze over to me a bit shamefacedly. My mother continued to cling tightly to his sleeve. She could scarcely breathe. Señor Roca was obviously uncomfortable with the waiter looking on. He cleared his throat and replied in Spanish, "I cannot promise you anything, madame."

Finally she slowly let go of her hold on the fabric, dropped into her seat, and murmured, also in Spanish:

"I'm asking you to do me a favor. I'll do whatever's necessary to make it up to you."

"I come to Barcelona twice a month on business. Perhaps we could see each other . . . Do you still live at the same address?"

My mother lifted her eyes to his face and nodded her head. She seemed to be struck by a mixture of surprise and resignation. The two of us sat there and watched as he walked out the door.

Señor Roca lived in fear, too much fear.

I was so worked up that night, I couldn't sleep.

That very Monday I watched a fly out on one of the Charity Home courtyards. It rubbed its two front legs together just like a person washing his hands. And it scratched its wings with its hind legs, as any other fly might do. I couldn't get Señor Roca out of my head.

We were depending on him to receive news about my father. We were depending on him to keep my place in the Charity Home. I didn't like it. He hadn't made a good impression on me. I reached out for the fly and plucked it up with my fingers. My muscles are capable of working like a set of tongs in those situations. I never miss. Torturing flies was a favorite pastime at the Charity Home. We'd rip off their wings, burn them with matches, and stick them up our bottoms, only to gas them to death with our farts. I could feel the tiny creature batting about within my closed fist. It tickled. I carefully opened my palm and, with the other hand, grasped the fly between my thumb and first finger. As I contemplated the trapped creature, an imitation of Señor Roca's voice fell from my lips. "I've discovered that I quite enjoy being on the side of order and discipline." Then I began to slowly grind the fly's body between my fingers until it was nothing more than a mass of yellow paste.

CHAPTER TEN

Saturday, October 22, 1949

Saturday may be a working day, but in Christian society it is given special status because the next day is Sunday, the day of rest. You can tell by the sort of clientele that's packed into Miranda de Ebro's casino. It's not that late, somewhere between seven o'clock and seven thirty, but the place is hopping. Married couples drink the local wine and nibble tapas. I notice a crowd of young people who seem to belong to some group, but I can't figure out which. And there's a bunch of blue-shirted Falangists who probably just got out of a meeting. I also notice a middle-aged couple. They're a little dressed up, having a coffee after evening mass. The same old regulars are there as usual, playing cards or dominoes. The proprietor serves me a beer right away, without giving me a chance to order it.

"How are things going in Lima?" I ask.

"What?"

"You were telling me yesterday about the sister-in-law of your wife's second cousin . . ."

"Oh, of course. Thank you. I imagine they're a real hit. Remember, 'The Soul and Grace of Spain' . . ."

I think it's worth a try and let my query drop casually.

"Do you by any chance know a Eusebio Fernández? He's a doctor, an orderly, a nurse, or a pharmacist . . ."

The man just stares at me. Like everybody else, he wants to know who I am. And why I'm asking so many questions. After thinking it over, he decides I'm probably not a cop. No policeman would ever have a gouge on his head like mine. He'd never be able to go undercover.

"Nothing's coming to me right now," he answers.

I sip my beer nonchalantly.

"He was a friend of my father. I'm just passing through the city and wanted to say hello, but I don't know where he lives . . ."

"Sorry."

"Don't worry about it."

"Wait. Carmela!"

The waitress draws near. Today she openly stares at the scar on my head without shame. Her look is at once worn-out and welcoming. The proprietor brusquely asks her right in front of me if she knows a certain Eusebio Fernández, a doctor, orderly, or pharmacist . . . The girl coquettishly holds a finger up to her mouth and pretends to mull it over. She says no and walks away. I could ask her what time she gets off work. Or wait until closing time and offer to escort her home. I'm sure she'd say yes. The girl serves me the second round. There's no ring on her finger and her hands are really banged up. She fills the glass but doesn't move away. What's she waiting for? I imagine those rough hands caressing my face or chest. I'm suddenly assaulted by a childhood memory. They used to make us scrub espadrilles in the Charity Home. It was one of the harshest punishments. I had to suffer through it more than once. By the end of the job, your hands were mere stumps of raw flesh. My fingers, swollen with chilblains, would get infected by the caustic soda. That's why my hands are covered in scars. The rage seething within me was the only thing that came close to matching that pain. Carmela keeps glancing at me out of the corner of her eye. Looking at her hands makes me nauseated. She goes to serve someone an anise, and, seizing the opportunity, I stand up, leave some money at the bar, and get the hell out of there.

I head straight to the pension. Thoughts of No-Sister-Salvador run through my head as I walk back. He may have died eight years ago, but he's still very much on my mind. Without realizing it, I've been acting just like him today, trying to get information about someone at random without knowing anything about them. I've asked around left and right for Eusebio Fernández. I'm No-Eusebio-Genís. I miss Salvador terribly sometimes. We could have made a life together. He certainly would have had a family. And so would I. My children would have called him Uncle Salvador and his kids would have called me Uncle Genís. He definitely would've gone to Africa with me. Now all that's impossible. You don't fully comprehend the loss of someone you love until much later, when you get a sudden impulse to call out his name then have to stop yourself. Or until you realize that he's not going to answer back. As a little boy I grew accustomed to hearing Señor Pau's discourses as they echoed across the light shaft. I remember him saying, "It's a shame I'm not a religious man. I don't even have the comfort of believing I'll be reunited with my wife in the afterlife. But if she were in heaven, then my in-laws would be there, too. And I'd be forced to live out an eternity with them." I smile. Señor Pau was a good man. He loved to read and collected traditional, very scatological Catalan nativity figurines. These little red-capped peasants were known as "defecators." The shepherdlike figures squatted by the holy family each Christmas, contributing their own special offering to the Christ child. Once, a very well-dressed individual appeared at his door to inform him, with a great air of mystery, that a small altarpiece had been discovered in a village up in the Pyrenees. On it was painted what was said to be the first example of a defecator in Catalan history. It was thought to be very ancient, a real treasure, etc., etc. He'd bought it off some priests and was now trying to resell the piece. The man was practically giving it away. Señor Pau forewent his usual prudence and fell for it immediately. He was still working as a salesman at the time and, aside from the usual samples, always carried a selection of jewelry and wristwatches in his case. The man insisted that he and Señor Pau should meet secretly by themselves, so as not to raise suspicions. When Señor Pau arrived at the appointed spot, there were three thugs waiting for him. They stripped him of everything he had and then left him like a rat. Luckily, he wasn't carrying very much merchandise on him at the time. Even still, it was a good two years before he'd paid the company back for the lost samples.

As I'm about to enter the pension, I see someone duck around the next street corner. I make as if to go inside, then whip around at the last moment. No one's there, but I walk to the corner anyway. The Legion prepares you to act quickly in these situations. I come upon a little side street that I haven't even seen before and walk down it without thinking twice. It's dark. I stop and listen. Not a sound. I continue on in the gloom. It's a dead-end street ending in a brick wall. For almost three or four minutes, I remain still, holding my breath there in the shadows. If there is someone hiding, I hope he'll think the coast is clear and come out. No luck; only the rustle of leaves being shaken by the wind. There must be a tree somewhere beyond that wall.

I have to calm down.

But I only manage to relax once I'm lying in my pension bed and thinking about my son.

His name is Joan and he's three years old. In a way, he's my son twice over. He's not only my child biologically, but I also paid good

money for the boy. I got a girl pregnant three years ago in Melilla. It
all happened so fast, I never got a chance to figure whether I was in
love or not. She was a nineteen-year-old Muslim, working at her family's grocery store in the same city. Her parents had already found a
suitable husband for their daughter. One day I waited until it was
closing time. I'd been prowling around the shop for weeks. I knew
that the girl's father sometimes left early to make deliveries. She was
the one who closed up shop on those days. I watched her put away
the last few boxes of goods that had been set out on the street. I offered to help lower the metal shutter with one of those old-fashioned
poles with a hook on the end. The clawlike hook fit into a catch in
the shutter so that the whole thing could be lowered down to within
arm's reach. She looked at me, smiled, and handed me the pole without saying anything. I tried to lower the shutter while she switched
off the lights. I didn't expect the mechanism to be so trigger happy,
and used too much force. It clattered to the ground all at once, making an awful din. I was scared, not so much by the noise, as the fear
of having broken something. I didn't want her to get angry with me.
I lost my bearings for a few seconds. I was out on the street, she was
inside the store, and the shutter was shut tight between us. I could
hear her moving around inside. She told me to step back and pulled
the shutter up just enough for her to crawl out. Once on the street she
said simply, "Don't worry. I should've warned you. The catch is very
loose. It practically falls by itself, even if you barely pull on it."

She pressed down on a metal footrest, throwing all of her weight
into it, and closed the shutter all the way. Then she bent down again
to lock a chain affixed to the ground.

I asked her if she'd like to go for a cup of coffee. She had a specific bar in mind, well out of the way of her parents' shop, and we
agreed to meet there in half an hour's time. She showed up dressed in
European clothing. With such light skin, she could have been easily

mistaken for a Spanish girl from the Peninsula who, after a long day of hard work, was relaxing in a café downtown in the company of a young husband, friend, or relative. A Muslim girl would never dare to do that. Not in that bar or any other. We ordered a couple of mint teas and watched the comings and goings of the other customers. Her name was Albaida. She admitted that she'd noticed how I'd been snooping around the shop for days.

"It's hard to miss a Legionnaire in full uniform."

Our affair began with almost unbearable naturalness. We made love for the first time on our second date. It took place in a spartan, impersonal room with high ceilings, gray walls, and apricot-colored curtains. The space was rented out by another Legionnaire for just such situations. It didn't have electricity, so we undressed by candle-light. We could sense the gusts of heat and the din of the street press-ing in from the outside. There was only a cot, a chair, and a nightstand. The toilet was in the hallway. Hours were spent in that narrow, high gray room devouring each other's lips as we panted and moaned. Albaida was a real spitfire. She told me how she was sick of everyone else always making decisions for her. It made her feel like some kind of little dog. And she was terrified to think what would happen when her family discovered she wasn't a virgin. But she didn't say that for my benefit. I hadn't been the first man she'd slept with; she told me some story about her and a cousin when she was thirteen years old. She'd look at me blankly and say that she wanted a house and an easy life. And only a European like me could provide her with those things. She begged me to kidnap her, take her away. She was willing to convert to Christianity if necessary. Albaida was a little liar, but that just made her more appealing. She lied to me and everybody else. While dawdling about the store, making it look as if I were going to buy something, I'd hear her telling new customers the most out-rageous tall tales. She'd explain that her family had Atlas's last two lions locked up in a cage at their farm in the mountains, or that her grandfather made and sold shoes crafted with thread of pure gold, or that her mother was the princess of a desert tribe. It didn't faze me one bit. In Melilla, but especially in the Protectorate, you were always running into fanatical natives who weren't just mean, they were dumb. Stupidity is what fuels fanaticism, after all. But then you'd come across someone like Albaida, who was just as generous, tender, and loving as any Christian. More, I'd say. Aside from despising the Regime, I don't have any kind of political beliefs or doctrines. At most, I've learned to put faith in certain people I've met along the way. And, aside from the fundamental promise that has been central to these last eight years of my life, I make decisions about things as they come along. What I'm trying to say is that in that moment, I made a conscious choice not to hold back my love for Albaida. And if that meant having to kidnap her, I'd kidnap her. Simple as that. I came to that conclusion only forty-three days after the first time we made love. Then, suddenly, she disappeared. I happened to be out on maneuvers and didn't see her for a month and a half. I found the store locked and barred shut when I finally went looking for her. The neighbors couldn't tell me anything. It was obvious that her parents had found out about us and spirited her away. I asked around but couldn't get a straight story. I tried to check out the various pieces of information that she'd given me along the way, but it was all a web of invention and lies, woven by her imagination.

I'd occasionally walk by the store as the months passed. Albaida had been missing for almost a year when, one day, on one of my strolls, I noticed that the place was once again open for business. My hopes weren't exactly high as I drew near the establishment. It had probably been taken over by new owners. But imagine my surprise when I walked in to find Albaida's father himself weighing rice on a scale. I pulled out my gun and aimed it right between his eyes. The bastard thought that all he had to do was wait a year and I'd forget all about it. The few customers in the shop went running. The guy began to sweat so hard that rivulets dripped down his forehead and off the tip of his nose like a leaky faucet, splashing onto the counter. I asked him what happened to Albaida. The man played dumb, saying that he didn't know what the hell I was talking about. His daughter had gone inland to get married. I kept at him, but the guy didn't budge. He begged me, in the name of Allah, to leave him in peace, sputtering that he was nothing more than a humble merchant. I came back the next evening, accompanied by eight Legionnaires armed with pistols and rifles. The grocery store was barred shut. We drove the truck full speed right into the front of the building and smashed that damn shutter to bits. We parked inside the store, surrounded by burst sacks of chickpeas and broken jars of oil, with the viscous liquid dripping onto the floor. Half of the Legionnaires stayed out on the street to disperse the onlookers. Out of the other four, three went into the back room of the shop, returning with a woman and child, both bound up like two sausages. The last guy kept a tight hold on the shopkeeper. I stood in front of the man and watched the sweat pour down his face once again. This time the drops collected on the tip of his nose, only falling once they'd pooled to the point of spilling over. I pointed to the woman and kid and said that he'd better tell me where Albaida was, or I'd set fire to his house and establishment with him, his wife, and child in it.

That got him talking. Everyone ends up talking in the end.

It turned out that Albaida had gotten pregnant (the assumption was by me), and the entire family had packed up and moved inland.

"Is she married?"

"No, she's dead."

I felt riveted to the floor. He explained that she'd died in childbirth, but the infant son had survived. My companions seemed to be paying almost more attention to his words than I was. It was too much information for me to take in at once. But it became clear to me all of a sudden. I snatched up a rag, soaking it in some of the spilled oil, and wiped the sweat off his head and face. I asked my friend to let him go. And while he adjusted his shirt collar, I offered in a steely voice, "I'll buy your grandson from you."

I added that were he to accept, I'd also pay for the damage done to his shop and make sure that the Legion placed some decent orders for provisions. It took the bastard less than ten seconds to accept.

"Oh . . . and if you're lying to me," I said in a threatening tone, "I'll exterminate everyone you love. No one will be spared. I'll chop all their heads off. That includes you and the rest of your family. It doesn't matter if they're in Melilla or the interior. I'll flay every brother, uncle, aunt, cousin, second cousin, grandfather, and grandmother alive . . ."

I listed every possible living blood relative. The oil from the rag lent a brilliant sheen to his face. The sweat cascaded swiftly down his cheeks and onto a pile of sugar, which had spilled out of a broken sack. The salty drops left a small indentation in the mound, making it look like a miniature volcano. His breathing less labored, he asked in a calmer voice, "But why do you want the boy?"

"Because he's my son, you idiot."

I grabbed him by the collar and threw him in the truck along with the eight other Legionnaires. We headed out for the desert. The man was riding in back, with the butt of a rifle literally shoved up against his asshole. I wanted to see Albaida's tomb and I wanted the kid. I was fully aware that I was using the Legion's property, men, and arms in order to solve a personal problem. But I couldn't care less at that point. After a three-hour drive, with the sky darkening fast around us, we arrived at a tiny village in the middle of nowhere. That bastard led me to a graveyard and pointed to a tomb. One of the

other Legionnaires trained a lantern on the marker. I copied down the
Arabic letters written on that stone stuck in the ground. I wanted to
confirm what the lettering said in Melilla. Maybe it really was Albaida in there. But whether she had actually died in childbirth or not
was something else entirely. Those people were capable of having
killed her themselves as a question of family honor. In any case, I decided to let it go. I hadn't seen the girl in over a year. With the other
Legionnaires watching my back, we approached one of the white
houses lining the main street, alert and with our guns at the ready.
The shopkeeper knocked and a six- or seven-year-old child opened
the door. The interior was also entirely white, with a cavelike feel to
it. A fire burning in the corner was the room's only source of illumi-
nation. A woman, her back to the door, stirred the contents of a pot
suspended over the open flames. The space was empty except for a
low table in one corner and the carpets covering the floor. A man
about thirty years old and two children were standing in the middle
of the room, staring out at us from the relative gloom cast by the
woman's shadow. Albaida's father began to speak to the fellow. The
others followed the conversation in silence. The woman, without taking her eyes off me or missing a word of the two men's exchange, kept
steadily stirring her pot.

Finally the head of the family addressed her harshly. She got up
and went over to the group. The couple proceeded to scream at each
other until he punched her so hard that she fell to the ground. Show's
over. The woman exited stage left through a curtain, which served as
a door. She reappeared with the infant. I'd been told by the shopkeeper
that Albaida had given birth to a boy. And in all probability I was the
father, so there was no way I was going to leave that piece-of-shit village empty-handed. When the man showed me the baby, the first
thing I thought was that I didn't give a shit whether the kid was mine
or if he was really the child of that woman in front of me. It was just

as likely that I was stealing, or buying, the boy. I wanted the child, so I took him. We brought both the woman and the baby back to Melilla with us. She breast-fed the infant along the way. Albaida's father explained unconcernedly that the woman happened to still be breast-feeding her youngest child when his daughter gave birth. It was the most natural thing in the world for her to adopt the little one and provide it sustenance. The guy could tell me whatever he liked. The kid could have been Allah's grandson for all I cared. I kept our deal, gave him a good bonus, and put the whole thing out of my mind.

I left the infant in the care of some nuns when he was less than six months old. On his first birthday I brought him to the Peninsula and gave him to my mother. She was doing much better overall and had become a full-fledged peasant. After her mother's death, she'd taken over the land the old woman rented as a tenant farmer. She was still fairly young and was delighted to have the boy. I haven't seen him since. But if all goes as planned, it won't be long before we're together again. I named him Joan, after my father. He has white skin and very dark eyes, which I imagine he gets from his mother. Right now it's hard for me to remember Albaida's face. And I don't know why, but I'm absolutely certain that he's mine. My son is nothing more than a little handful of skin, fat, and bones. He's only three years old, but he's got more history behind him than most old men carry around at the age of eighty. He's often in my thoughts. Every three months my mother takes the boy, at my request, to have his picture taken by the local photographer. Then she sends me the portrait in the mail, which I in turn show to his godfathers, those same eight Legionnaires. On the boy's birthday, which we celebrate on the date that we went to the desert to find him, I invite those eight men to either a good meal or a good screw.

And that's the only military escapade in the history of the Legion that means anything to me.

CHAPTER ELEVEN

There was still no news of my father. We had no idea whether he was dead or alive. My mother's lustrous wavy red hair became flecked with gray. The two of us made quite a sight on the street together. She walked around like a movie star, wearing those dark glasses to cover up her wandering eye even if it was nighttime. And me with my shaved head and livid scar loosely covered by the beret I'd inherited from poor Señor Pau. It was too big for me and slid all over my skull.

My mother couldn't stop talking about Señor Roca. I don't know if it was his doing or not, but I wasn't kicked out of the Charity Home after all. The possibility was never mentioned. And in addition to providing my mother with packages of food, he also managed to find her work as a seamstress working at home.

"I had to find myself a sewing machine," she said excitedly. "I went to the Underwood headquarters on Balmes Street and traded in Señor Pau's old typewriter for a used Wertheim in good condition. No-Sister-Salvador lent me the difference. We agreed that I'll pay him back bit by bit. After that it'll be nothing but profits, Niso. Aside from the orders coming in from Señor Roca, there'll be plenty of work this winter altering clothes for people."

And that's exactly what happened. Customers brought coats that she turned inside out, making them look like new again. She converted men's blazers into women's jackets. Men's shirts were transformed into ladies' blouses. She split into two a pair of pants that had been made for a corpulent gentleman before the war. One half became a new pair of trousers for the now much diminished customer; the other half, a pair of shorts for his youngest son. Once in a while she'd also receive a big order from Señor Roca. Boxes of blue shirts were delivered and she'd embroider them with Falangist symbols, yokes, or red arrows. If there was any time left over after all the machine work, she'd set to unpicking worn-out knitted pieces by hand. She'd turn them into a diverse and multicolored collection of balls of yarn that would quickly be worked up into new sweaters, gloves, scarves, or socks.

The old tools of my father's trade disappeared. All of the brushes, paints, posters, and letter samples were packed, tied up, and hidden away on top of some armoire. Instead, the space was taken over by the sewing machine, bobbins of thread, scraps of fabric, and cardboard boxes bursting with blue shirts.

It came time to celebrate the first big festival since the end of the war. As every other year, it was held in honor of Barcelona's patron saint, La Mercè. The monsignor gave a solemn speech in honor of the occasion. He said something like: "We still recall those tragic days when, scourged by that brand of Marxism, we prayed to the excelsior patron of this city to protect the National Army who was on its way to liberate us." Our celebration consisted of an elaborate mass with sacred music performed by the choir and the Charity Home band. This was followed by a special feast. We started salivating at the mere mention of the main dish, chicken thighs and rice, since we were so used to going around with our stomachs half empty. I was practically dreaming about it. That's why I felt a sharp twinge of irritation when I was told to put my street clothes on because someone was coming to pick me up. All my frustration disappeared as soon as I saw No-Sister-Salvador's unmistakable silhouette waiting for me in the visitors' lounge. My friend was only nineteen at the time. But he looked quite a bit older dressed in one of my father's suits, which my mother had altered for him. Lately, all Salvador wanted to talk about was girls. As we walked home, he asked, "So do you Charity Home kids have much luck with the ladies?"

"Some of the boys get crushes on other orphan girls. We spy on them from a distance, during Sunday mass. But all the nuns talk about is sin, punishment, and penance."

Even with his bum leg, No-Sister-Salvador was a good-looking fellow. He said he was having a hard time getting used to living under all the rules and prohibitions imposed by the Regime.

"It was all so different during the war! Back then girls could come and go as they pleased. Now they're all trying to be saints or nuns." He stopped short in the middle of the street, pointing out a few. "Look at them. They go about in packs, arm in arm. And if you dare say anything to them, they either threaten you with fire and brimstone, or run off screaming."

I liked listening to Salvador even though I didn't understand half of what he said. Especially when he talked about love.

Before heading home that Sunday, we spent some time in the tower. I hadn't been up there in months. Just a whiff of that damp air mingled with my friend's familiar odor gave me such a contented feeling that I wanted to cry. Once we were settled in, I said, "I don't understand why you go around talking to girls in the street. And another thing, why do they run away?"

"What do you think?"

"How should I know?"

"Boy, Niso, I can't tell if you're really an idiot or just acting like one. Well, it's because I whisper sweet little nothings to them. You do know how babies are made, don't you?"

"With lots of love," I said confidently.

"Well, it takes a little bit more than love."

I was absolutely convinced that when a couple really loved each other, their kisses and caresses spontaneously popped a baby into the world—what one of the nuns had coined "the miracle of life." Salvador thought that I was trying to pull his leg. I was shocked when he finally filled me in on the real story.

"That's how babies are made?"

"Yeah. But you don't always do it to make a baby. Sometimes it's just for fun."

"And you have to move back and forth like that the whole time?"

"Yeah."

"That sounds tiring! And it sounds pretty boring and messy, too."

"Tell me if you feel the same way once you've tried it."

"But no girl's going to want me with this huge hole in my head."

"On the contrary. The girls will be dying to be with you, just so they can get a chance to touch that scar. They'll all be itching to run their fingers over it."

We were walking up the stairs to my apartment, and I noticed at the landing that the door was half open. Salvador grabbed my arm and wouldn't let me take another step forward. Just then Señor Roca's voice fell on my ears, clear as a bell. What was he doing in my house? He sounded nervous. I heard my mother talking to him in a trusting voice that was utterly new to me.

"I know how to show my appreciation for everything you've done," she was saying, her voice choked with emotion.

"I wanted to tell you the news in person."

"I will be forever grateful to you."

"I don't want you to be with me only out of gratitude."

"Well, that's the only way I can be."

"Sometimes I wake up in the middle of the night because I've been dreaming about you. My wife asks me what's wrong. I tell her it's nothing, just a bad dream. And then I can't get back to sleep. It's strange how easy it is to hide our deepest feelings. All my frustrations disappear with a touch of your fingertips."

"That's enough. Now go. Niso will be here any minute."

No-Sister-Salvador and I silently made our way back to the staircase and went up to the roof. We watched Señor Roca leave while leaning over the brick balustrade that faced the street. His big car was waiting for him at the door. He climbed in the back. The vehicle started up and drove away.

"What does it mean when people call my mother a kept woman? Why is Roca afraid that someone might find out about him visiting her?" I asked my friend.

He refused to explain anything. It was obvious he was very uncomfortable. Finally he admitted that Señor Roca visited my mother twice a month.

"I already know that. He brings her things to eat and sewing jobs."

No-Sister-Salvador looked doubtful. He said, "He always gets here really early in the morning. And they have lunch together, too . . . And not only that . . ."

"What?"

"Goddamn it, Niso!" He added in a constricted voice, "You've heard for yourself how they talk."

I didn't ask any more out of him. We stayed up on the roof, quietly staring down at the street for five or ten more minutes. It was pretty hot up there under the midday sun.

My mother smiled as I walked in the door. Her eyes were both in the right place, parallel to each other and perfectly aligned. That could mean only one thing.

"Have they found Father?" I yelped.

"Yes, he's alive!"

We hugged each other and started dancing around the room like a couple of idiots. We kept jumping around, shouting: "Alive, alive, alive!"

He was alive, but not free. Roca had located him. From then on, another name popped up in our conversations: Miranda de Ebro. That was the concentration camp where my father was being held prisoner. We sat as closely as we possibly could to one another, and began to write our first letter to my father.

It was a month before we received a reply. My mother and I, despite being overjoyed at having received news, were taken aback. We kept passing it back and forth, rereading it again and again, but we couldn't scratch beneath the surface. It had been so long since we'd seen him that it seemed to have been written by some second uncle in America, rather than my father. But it was definitely his handwriting. He was definitely the one who'd penned those curt sentences in Spanish:

> *I'm fine. I hope the two of you are also doing well. They don't treat me too badly here at the camp. There's enough to eat. I should be classified soon.*

It was as though the note had been dictated to him, word for word.

Señor Roca cleared up the mystery. He told my mother that the prisoners were allowed to correspond with their relatives only if they had been on their best behavior. That permission was taken away at the slightest infraction. The letters would be posted only if they were brief and didn't contain comments that could be construed as critical of the Regime or camp life. If there was the slightest doubt, the letter wasn't sent. The correspondence coming into the camp was also gone over with a fine-tooth comb for the very same reason. That's why all the letters were nothing more than a string of banal sentences. Keeping in touch turned out to be a very difficult and slow process, thanks to heavy censorship. During the whole time that my father was detained in the concentration camp, we barely managed to send and receive letters every two months. And often not even that. The whole procedure felt very odd. We waited anxiously for every letter, fully aware that it wouldn't contain anything of interest. But, of course, receiving it was enough. At the very least it meant that he was still well enough to hold a pencil.

For a while those letters took precedence over everything else in our lives. On several occasions the four standard and obligatory sentences would be mixed in with a few phrases that attempted to actually say something. These would be crudely censored, either crossed out with a thick red pencil or even extricated with scissors. Those ridiculous sheets covered in red blots or filled with holes were far more eloquent than all the writing in the world.

We quickly found out what it meant to be classified. Señor Roca threw light on that matter, too, and my mother relayed everything to me.

"A political prisoner may be classified in five different ways: AA, which stands for an adherent to the Regime, or, in other words, a sympathizer; DA is a dubious adherent, or someone who appears to be a sympathizer but they aren't sure of him; B refers to someone who isn't a sympathizer but hasn't committed any crimes; C and D are Republican military, political, and union leaders. The prisoners classified as AA are released. They go on to live blame-free, normal lives in the bosom of the Regime. The DAs are reeducated and then released. Sometimes they're required to repeat military service. Before being reeducated, prisoners in the B group are usually put to hard labor in order to prove themselves in the New Spain. Those classified as either C or D don't stay in the camp very long. Most of them are sent directly to prison and then sentenced. Almost all of them are condemned to death and executed. The most unlucky ones aren't even put on trial."

That gave me the shivers.

"What about Father?"

"Roca says that he will probably be classified as a B. And if that's the case, it may take a little longer for him to get released. Meanwhile, we have to find someone from the Regime to vouch for him. They'd have to claim that he's a good man who happened to join the Republican Army by accident. The part about being a good person will be easy, but the rest may be a bit more difficult." She tousled my hair and gave me a sad smile, adding, "Actually, Genís, I think that the first part will be a pretty tricky thing to prove, too."

Meanwhile, we killed time at the Charity Home going hungry and praying for the Generalíssimo. We also had to pray for the victory of his buddy, the Führer, who'd started a war against democracy while at the same time allying himself with the Communist demon, in order for them to divide the Catholic country of Poland between themselves. If anybody knew how to make sense out of that plan, I wish they would have explained it to me.

The priests and nuns at the Charity Home decided that they couldn't celebrate the first Christmas of peacetime with children who had been brought up under the scourge of the Red Terror. So they decided to Christianize us en masse. We were told that, come Christmas, our bodies, minds, and souls were to be purified and guided back to Jesus's flock. They were especially concerned about the older wards. The little ones were different; those nine or ten months of immersion in Catholic doctrine had turned them inside out like socks. The younger kids wandered around in an ecstasy of terror thanks to the caretakers' exaggerated descriptions of condemned souls roasting in infernal flames for time everlasting. The children lived in constant doubt, forever asking themselves, "If I were to die right now, would I go to heaven or hell?" We older boys would sneak into their dormitory before daybreak and beat up those little snitches and wimps to get them to descend a bit from their celestial heights. One night we caught a boy praying in the lavatory while taking a shit. His voice sounded strained, since, while conversing with God, he was exerting a certain amount of effort. We could hear him saying, "Dear Jesus, I know that Judas sold you for only thirty pesetas. And I'm sure it must have hurt real bad when they pounded those nails into your hands. I don't want to remind you so I won't go on about it. Let's talk about something else. The nuns keep on complaining that we're nothing but trouble and give them a lot of grief. They think we're really bad children. I'm telling you this because I know that you are all powerful. Make them understand that no family will ever take us in if they go around saying that all the time."

He was right, but that didn't stop us from grabbing the kid and pissing all over him.

The Charity Home authorities held three ceremonies on the same day, back to back: Baptism, Communion, and Confirmation, with sessions in the morning, midday, and afternoon. Some boys were forced to suffer through all three sacraments and ended up completely exhausted. Having already been baptized, I only had to take part in Communion and get confirmed. The Charity Home girls had been sewing white tunics nonstop for a month, under the watchful eyes of the nuns. They decided to make the robes all the same size in order to save money. The tunics barely grazed the older children's knees, whereas the hems of the smaller kids dragged on the ground. No one had been able to receive visitors or leave in over a month and a half, in order to intensify the process of indoctrination. According to the mother superior, we needed to be completely immersed in Christianity, without any worldly influences.

On a Sunday in late November, 120 boys and girls were Christianized in one fell swoop. Those few wards who were in the Home because their parents were destitute were allowed to have them present. The children were of all different shapes and sizes, but each one wore the exact same tunic. It was embarrassing to have my mother there as a witness to the charade. When the afternoon ceremonies were over, everyone gathered out on the courtyard. It was freezing out. A representative of the government of Barcelona gave a religious and patriotic speech. We applauded, sang anthems, and were made to salute with our arms outstretched, just like Franco. That's how we appear in the photo: a forest of raised arms attached to over a hundred muddled heads thrust into badly cut tunics. After my mother hypocritically congratulated the nuns for organizing the event, we managed to talk for a few moments. She wasn't wearing her dark glasses, which was a good sign. She told me that she wanted to go to Miranda de Ebro to visit my father. She glanced about and then said under her breath:

"You need a special permit to go. I suppose I could get my hands on one of those. But money is a problem."

I almost asked what she could possibly be worried about, considering that she could always ask the lord and master of our destiny, Señor Roca, for help.

Contented and satisfied with their new flock of Christians, the Charity Home directors considered that the institution could now safely face the Christmas season. We were still starving, so as on every other special occasion, what really got us into a celebratory mood was

the holiday feast. The priests and nuns at the Charity Home were all
Spanish, so they celebrated on Christmas Eve. They'd organized a
sumptuous meal for us. It was incredible, a complete luxury. First
there would be the traditional Christmas stew of gigantic pasta shells
mixed with all sorts of meat, and then the second dish—roasted
chicken! We started drooling over the menu a week in advance. When
the great day arrived, we were made to say grace out loud, giving
thanks first to Our Lord, and then to His Excellency, the Generalíssimo. We would've done or said anything at that point. One boy was
so overcome with hunger that when the food was set before him, he
didn't know whether to laugh or cry. He finally let out a deep moan
that could have been construed as suffering but actually expressed
happiness. The nuns were amused. They went up to him, asking,
"What's the matter, don't you want it?"

The boy began to cry freely and said, "Yes!"

The nuns laughed gleefully and pretended to take his plate away.
"No, you don't like it . . . all the more for us!"

The boy, a quivering mass of sobs, squealed, "No, I do like it,
I do!"

"Just a little bit or a lot?"

"A lot! A lot!"

Those nuns acted like being in Barcelona wasn't that much different from missionary work in Africa. The little boy couldn't stop
crying. One of the nuns grew very serious all of a sudden, saying she'd
had enough of his nonsense. But he couldn't calm down. One of the
guards went up and slapped the child so hard on the back of the head
that his nose smashed right into the chicken. The kid wasn't crying
anymore, he was screaming. One of the older nuns proceeded to drag
him out of the dining room by the ear.

"Off you go, straight to the chapel and without supper! You're
going to get down on your knees before the Almighty, you miserable

wretch! You demon-spawn brats are incapable of showing the least bit of respect even on Christmas. I want you on your knees until midnight, until the very last minute before Christmas Day. You children don't know how to appreciate anything."

The chicken on his plate disappeared before he was out of the room. After that, we were served long, tubular Christmas biscuits called neules and two types of almond nougat, one hard, one soft. The priests opened a bottle of hard cider to go along with dessert and the adults made a toast. I didn't even know what cider was. The director confided to one of the priests that he far preferred cider over champagne. The priest agreed, adding that it was much more digestible. We, with our shaved heads, observed them out of the corners of our eyes. After all, we were just poorhouse rats, obsessed with taking as much in as we could and storing it for future use.

The next day I had lunch at home, with my mother and No-Sister-Salvador. It was a somber and meager meal, shadowed by absent loved ones. The three of us felt awkward but were very determined to celebrate the holiday together. We also had Christmas stew, but there wasn't much meat in it. Then we munched on roasted chestnuts, which had been prepared on a pan riddled with nicks and gouges. There were some raisins, walnuts, and hazelnuts. And marzipan studded with candied fruit. It was like celebrating the traditional All Souls' Day banquet of nuts and dried fruits, but at the wrong time of the year. We toasted with a bottle of sweet wine, courtesy of Señor Roca. I didn't care for the stuff. It made my head spin. We wished each other a merry Christmas and embraced. We turned the radio on, but it kept blasting German military marches. The evening ended in a game of Parcheesi. Before I went back to the Charity Home, my mother whispered in my ear:

"Next year your father will be with us, wait and see."

"Liar!" I cried.

I could feel rage rise up in my chest. I'd get very anxious whenever she'd talk about things she couldn't control.

There never was another Christmas with my father. The next year he was still locked up in the concentration camp, and the year after that, 1941, he was already dead.

CHAPTER TWELVE

Sunday, October 23, 1949

Sunday morning. The church bells in Miranda ring out loud and clear. Saint Nicholas's, Saint Mary's; the Cathedral of the Holy Ghost would join in the fray as well if it hadn't been bombed. Those godless Reds reduced it to rubble in 1936. The bells, old and new, antique and modern, chime out in order to call together the faithful. Now Sunday services may be attended confidently and without fear. Spain returned to the fold of Jesus's flock ten long years ago. It's Sunday, the Day of the Lord, and all the bells in Miranda de Ebro cry, "Glory to God in heaven and peace on earth to all of mankind." If they could, they'd chime for one man in particular, the general of all generals, artificer of the miraculous victory of the Cross and the Sword. Every single bell in Miranda on this radiant October morning is delighted at the opportunity to ring out in rich and assured tones, calling the population to worship God Our Father, insistently praising "God and Franco, Franco and God, Franco is God, God is great, as great as Franco, Franco . . ."

Miranda's church bells have a point. All you have to do is look at Lisbon's tremendous response to Franco's visit. The spectators fluttered thousands of miniature Portuguese and Spanish flags as he passed by. It was even stranger to hear the multitudes in Lisbon shouting, "Franco! Franco! Franco!" as fanatically as they do in Spain. Marshal Carmona, Oliveira Salazar, Cardinal Cerejeira, every official and practically the entire population of Lisbon prostrated themselves fervently at the Spanish leader's feet in one of the most effusive welcoming receptions in Portuguese history. Thousands of fliers praising the Spanish national spirit and the victory of the Civil War were distributed anonymously. The broadsheets proclaimed Spain to be the last impregnable bastion against the insidious spread of Communism, which is so debasing to humanity.

I'm leaning out my window, looking down on the street. A dense and compact silence descends as soon as the bells stop chiming, which is only broken by a passing train. The tracks run straight through the city. Then there's the warning bell of the railroad crossing and the revving motors of the cars, trucks, and motorbikes waiting for their turn. All grows still once again. I watch a woman stick her head out a door. She calls for her child to hurry up. A little boy appears at one of the entrances to the park, dragging behind him a zinc bucket with a slab of ice in it. Three young ladies bustle up the street, heading toward the old quarter, arm in arm. Equipped with heavy, black-lace scarves, prayer books, and rosaries, they must be late for mass. A kitten, oblivious to the historical moment he is living through, flashes past, hiding himself beneath a tricycle. I can make out the just barely intelligible announcer of some unidentified radio program through an open window facing the street. A set of white curtains blowing in and out of the stark frame protects the occupants from my prying eyes. And then I hear music. It's sacred music, perfect for a day like today. Even a dignified town like Miranda de Ebro feels just as solitary, desolate, and orphaned as the rest of Spain. The Nation's lord and master is away, surveying his neighbor's lands.

There's a knock on the door, and I'm told that some people are waiting for me downstairs. Probably a couple of recruits from boot camp. All of a sudden I have no interest in going. Something tells me that it's not a good idea. Anyway, I haven't heard anything from Fontes about the camera. I send the soldiers away with some excuse about my health. I'll go for a walk around Miranda instead.

While handing Campillo the keys to my room, I ask him again about Eusebio Fernández:

"Are you absolutely sure you haven't heard of him?"

"I'm sorry, Sergeant, but I already told you no. Wait right here, I'll go ask the girl who works in the kitchen."

I observe his mother closely while waiting for him to return. The woman is knitting as usual. When does she eat? I've never seen her partake in either lunch or dinner. She might not need to. Maybe the woman is on to something. No world can beat the one you make up in your own head. Anyway, it's not as if she's missing much. The whole thing is so depressing. Time passes much slower under the Generalíssimo's rule. The hands of the clock drag. That's the way it has to be. These dark years require it, just as happiness calls for momentum and activity. Because there's no hope, somber periods are impenetrable and dull. By not saying anything at all, that old woman proves that she's much smarter than the rest of us. Campillo's going to find her dead one of these days; head slumped over the front desk, knitting needles on the floor. And he'll never know whether, in the last moment, she thought she was just going to take a little nap.

The kitchen girl hasn't heard of Eusebio Fernández, either.

I wander aimlessly around Miranda. Melancholy has settled into the marrow of my bones. I try to dispel it by leaning against the railing of the Charles the Third Bridge to get a little sun and air. The turgid waters of the Ebro River flow beneath me. A row of houses hang over the river's edge. One of their roofs is so completely covered with birds that you can't even see the tiles. A young married couple strolls by at a brisk pace. A little boy in a matching jacket and pants with a pair of carefully shined shoes totters between them, holding their hands. They're all dressed up for the twelve o'clock mass, I suppose.

I like to see everybody on the street dressed in their Sunday best. It gives a sense of continuity and ease. I have a little boy, too. It's hard for me to comprehend why I love him so much. How can a man like me be capable of such emotions? Some days it's almost as if I've taken a vacation from myself. My feelings, along with their corresponding physiological responses such as words or actions, even my very will, begin to freeze up inside. There are times when I don't feel anything, good or bad, for days. As if I was sleepwalking through life. But being suspended in such a vegetative state doesn't impede me from carrying out any of the tasks expected of me. I'm even capable of being the worst son-of-a-bitch Legionnaire that the Spanish Legion has ever known. Sometimes I have no idea who I am.

I head over to the casino after dinner. The place is full of life, the clientele a real mixed bag. You can tell it's Sunday. The old men playing cards are nowhere to be found. There's a group of young men, all sporting the same blazer, sitting around tables and making quite a racket. I go up to them; it's a chess club. I notice several married couples, all gussied up and having aperitifs. The first gabardine and trench coats of the season have come out of the men's closets, whereas the women are clad in coats with those wide lapels that are so fashionable this year. Carmela, the weekend waitress, and the proprietor are behind the bar. He gives me a welcoming nod. I order a beer and carry it over to a table. There is some sort of get-together taking place a few tables over. A group of about ten or twelve men is celebrating something. The fellow who seems to be in charge stands up and waits for the other men to quiet down. But he raises his voice a bit anyway.

He's elderly, about eighty years old, with a shock of white hair brushed back from his face, liver spots mottling his skin. His elegant and erect stance is no doubt aided by the girdle that's probably tightly cinching his form from neck to waist. He's wearing an impeccable English wool suit. To underscore the informality of the event, the man has exchanged the usual tie for a foulard scarf. Raising his wineglass, he pronounces in a hoarse voice:

"Gentlemen, before I go on, I'd like to propose a toast to His Excellency the Generalíssimo, who, as we speak, is spreading the light of Spain's new era throughout Portugal in an unprecedented manner. More than ever, I'm positive that the principles set forth on July 18 constitute a clear and definitive path toward moral and material posterity in Spain."

Everyone lifts their glasses. A voice cries out, "To Franco!"

And the others join in.

"To Franco!"

The old man takes the floor again.

"Friends, before concluding such a pleasurable meeting, allow me to reflect briefly on the stupefaction of the supposedly 'democratic' Europe when faced with the remarkable public acclaim with which Franco has been received in Portugal. The European nations claim we are not democratic. What do they know about the idiosyncrasies of the Spanish? Nothing. There is democracy in Spain, and it can be found in the Movement. This is Spain's version of democracy, our answer to the grave crisis facing the liberal and plutocratic democracies of today. The French and the British can complain all they want. They wouldn't be anything without the Americans. Spain defeated Communism all by itself. And now, thanks to the Movement, it's reinventing the true democracy of the twentieth century. Make no mistake, the Movement isn't some old-fashioned political party with a pack of talking heads, military men, technicians, and bureaucrats running the show while the people remain silent or are made to keep silent. The Movement is much more than that. It's the key to transcending the class struggle. Whoever realizes this will triumph. And as for ourselves and the new path before us, I want you to keep one watchword in mind: discretion. Aside from the immense profits that Franco's leadership has garnered, the last ten years of peace have also brought the ostentatious behavior of certain families favorable to the Regime into the limelight. They're continuously flaunting their new status. This is a grave error. Discretion will be our victory. In the Generalíssimo's exact words, 'A frivolous bourgeoisie, a greedy merchant, or an aristocrat under foreign influence are just as detrimental to the Cause as a materialist Communist.' Do you see? Take note. I'll repeat the watchword then: discretion. Remember, a truly elegant person will always attempt to pass unnoticed. I myself try to avoid any private gathering of more than twelve persons. Believe me, my friends, I find social obligations very tedious, especially those organized by merchants who've won their fortune through speculation, industrialists who've used privileged information to become powerful, or newly rich smugglers. I prefer dealing with those sorts of people through a third party, an intermediary. And if that's impossible, in writing. I repeat, the key word is discretion. That's what will help us break into the European market, which is what we all want. Discretion."

They get to their feet once more and lift their glasses. One of the youngest of the group says, "I propose a toast to the marquis."

The white-haired gentleman is an aristocrat. This marquis is flattered, but still makes a stab at humility.

"And for the company, gentlemen, the company comes first . . ."

In other words, he's a bona fide marquis who's been forced by circumstances to go into business. They clink glasses, applaud, and proceed to attack their potato omelet and Rioja wine.

I drink a few more beers.

"You left yesterday without saying good-bye."

I look up. It's Carmela, with her rough hands and warm voice. She asks me if I need anything. I say yes.

"I want you to sit down next to me."

The answer is no. She says it would make a bad impression and the proprietor won't let her. A few more beers and I'd marry the girl if she asked. She doesn't.

On my way back to the pension, that same old feeling of being followed washes over me. This time, despite all that beer, I don't intend to let him get away. My head is clear enough to realize that, as on the other occasions, there's only one person at my back. I stroll along calmly, like someone who needs a little air after having too much to drink. I slip into the park across from the pension. I head toward a gazebo set up in the middle. It's a bandstand with a public toilet underneath, and I circle it. I go down into the lavatory and wait. I press my back up against the wall behind the door. I hear someone coming and try to avoid the stench of piss that's assaulting my nostrils. He stops just a few feet away from me; I can practically hear him breathing. The guy's making some tough decisions; should he go in or not? I hear footsteps moving away with a decisive cadence. He's leaving. It won't do him any good. I'm out the door in one leap and grab the man from behind, wrenching him toward me. I seize his lapels in both hands. If it's a mistake, I'll apologize and end of story. But I know it's not a mistake. The guy looks miserable. He's got my sarcastic grin shoved up in his face and my fist right between his eyes, where it hurts the most. It's a hard, direct, and crushing punch, the kind of blow that could stun a horse. It's no surprise when the fellow, a tall and scrawny man, falls to the ground, knocked out. I look around and don't see anybody, but just in case, I drag him into the lavatory by his feet. He's not dangerous. The guy struggles a bit, so I slug him hard enough to twist his face around like the head of a doll in its socket. His nose is bleeding. I pick him up by the shirt collar and lean him against the wall. Seeing his bloodstains on my clothes is unsettling. I'm seized by the urge to beat him up even more. He closes his eyes and keeps his head down.

"Who are you and why are you following me?" I ask, beginning the countdown before I start pummeling him again.

He's knocked out cold and I don't know what to do. The guy's as still as a rock. I'm afraid that I might have killed him. Pulling the front of his jacket aside, I put my ear up to his chest. I don't hear a thing. Then I rummage through his pockets. There's a worn-out leather wallet in his jacket. In it is a doctor's prescription, an ID card, and a bill, all belonging to the same person. I take a look at the name. All of a sudden, still not moving and with his mouth practically closed, he moans.

"Don't hit me anymore . . . I'm . . ."

"I already know, Eusebio Fernández. Come on, get up."

I take him back to the pension. I manage to get him into my room without anybody noticing. Well, no one except for Campillo's mother, of course.

For a good while all Eusebio does is cough. He's exhausted. I've got him splayed out on the bed in front of me with a wet cloth on his forehead. He's lucky. I could have really done him some serious damage. Eusebio is about fifty years old with a long neck and a thin, pointy face like a duck's. He wears his hair very clipped. It's almost a buzz cut. The guy looks pretty shabby. His cheap suit has seen better days. It's not what one would expect from a nurse, not to mention a doctor or pharmacist. Things don't seem to have been going very well for him lately. He's taken a couple of aspirins and appears to be perking up a little.

"You're a brute. I was almost killed."

"If I'd wanted to kill you, I would have," I reply. "Why were you following me?"

He barks back, "I wasn't following you." The words seem to give him confidence.

"Don't lie to me."

"It's not a lie, goddamn it. I saw you heading toward the pension and waited. I didn't know how to attract your attention."

I let it go.

"Who are you?" he asks, taking the rag off his forehead.

"Don't worry, I'm a friend."

"A friend who almost smashed my head open?"

"That's one of the risks you take when you follow people around."

He's about to repeat his story about not being on my trail, then thinks better of it. He asks dully, "Why are you asking around about me?"

"My father said that if I ever had the chance to visit you I could count on some bread, cheese, and wine."

"And who was your father?"

"Juan Aleu. He was a patient in the concentration camp's infirmary from January 1941 until they released him, when he was already on his last legs, in April."

"I don't remember him. There were so many prisoners."

"Well, he remembered you very well. On the day my father died, he asked me to do something for him and told me to find you. He said you were a good person."

"Juan Aleu, you say?"

"Yes."

"No. Never heard of him. And you're a Legionnaire, a military man. Why don't you leave me alone?"

"You're right, I'm a Legionnaire—but that's not all I am. Don't be afraid, I won't hurt you."

He tries to get up to leave, but I don't let him. One sharp shove and he's back down on the bed. The guy doesn't weigh a thing. There's no need to hit him again. Eusebio keeps still, a dejected figure lost in the bedding.

I calmly suggest, "Let me tell you my story. Once I'm finished, if you still want to, you'll be free to go."

Eusebio settles himself more comfortably and deposits the damp rag back on his forehead. I tell him who I am and what I'm doing in Miranda. He pulls the cloth away and looks at me as though I'm crazy. I'm not surprised; it's a pretty far-fetched tale. I keep talking. But even then, it still takes quite a while to convince him. He's a worn-out and decrepit fifty-year-old man. Eusebio seems to be suffering from some serious disease. That cough sounds familiar and his breath gives off a sickly sweet stench. He genuinely seems not to have any recollection of my father.

"Maybe you remember someone by the name of Bartomeu Camús. Or maybe he was registered under the Spanish spelling, Bartolomé Camús. He was killed after trying to escape."

"No, I don't know him, either. I helped out a lot of prisoners during that time. They were all the same to me. None of them stood out. I lent them a hand if I could, but if not, tough luck. Once in a while you'd find yourself getting too personal and end up doing something risky. Everyone was starving, so I smuggled in packages of food and clothing that families from Miranda would donate anonymously. The prisoners knew they could count on me. I was forever sending off letters of farewell to future widows. Occasionally the relatives' whereabouts were unknown and I wouldn't be able to get the correspondence through in time. At least the prisoners died in peace, thinking they'd said good-bye to their loved ones. There's a big stack of letters like that in my house; I've kept them all. My way of helping the inmates was to treat them with a little respect. They were always shocked whenever I'd clean up their vomit, wipe their bottoms if necessary. I never thought of them as the enemy; they were my patients. I was younger then. I thought whatever good I did then, someone else would do for me later. Anyway, the nurses had a different perspective on the situation than the soldiers did. We couldn't help but be affected by such a massive scale of death; it didn't matter if it was friend or foe."

He kept his eyes closed, saying he hadn't been the only one. The ties between Miranda and the prisoners were much more intense than one might think.

"First of all, the prisoners' friends and relatives would come to town, often staying for a while. They'd even look for work nearby in order to be close to their loved ones. There were boardinghouses and pensions that practically made their living off handling the transactions between the prisoners' relatives and the concentration camp."

Someone decided that they didn't like Eusebio Fernández's humanitarian activities. Or they'd had enough of him flying in the face of the authorities. Most of Eusebio's good deeds, even his attitude, didn't merely break the camp's rules. Under certain circumstances, that sort of assistance could be considered criminal. So some citizen of Miranda denounced him in favor of order and discipline. He was put on trial and sentenced to three years in prison, which he served to the last day.

"Nobody wanted to give me work when I got back to Miranda. I ended up moving back to Pancorbo, a village not very far from here, to live with my parents and help out with the family bakery. It's what we've always done. I'm sick, but have no idea what it is and don't want to know. A pharmacist friend of mine, we went to school together before the war, supplies me with medication. They released me from prison in 1944. I've spent the last five years driving all over the region, delivering fresh-baked bread in my truck."

Eusebio Fernández is a broken man. And I've just given him a good whack on the head to top it all off. I replace the cloth on his forehead with a fresh one, letting him rest for about ten more minutes. We're both covered in blood. I give him one of my clean shirts and change into a fresh one myself. That was my last clean shirt. I watch him go to the sink and take one of his pills. He drinks a glass of water and sits down by my side on the bed.

"Now what?" he asks.

"I need your help. Tomorrow, Monday, I'm going to try and slip Camús's papers out of the tree. That's the only way I'll be able to determine the exact location of his grave. On Tuesday or Wednesday I'm going to the station in Logroño to meet a couple of men I hired to help transport the body."

"Why Logroño?"

"What do you expect, that we'd hold the get-together here in Miranda, complete with a brass band and speeches?"

"You've got a point . . ."

"From the station, we'll head straight for Camús's grave. It'll all take place in broad daylight, when least expected. His body will be brought back to Barcelona in three parts. We'll divide up the remains between three bags and take three different routes. The challenge will be disinterring the body. I haven't found much information on how to do that . . . We'll just have to put the pieces together like a jigsaw puzzle once we're in Barcelona. I've already come to an understanding with a guy who works at Montjuïc cemetery. The body will be laid to rest in the same grave as my father. We'll break open the niche, slip in the new occupant, replace the slab, and the job is done. Once a few years have gone by, the sooner the better, we'll make it official. Then we'll have both their names carved on the stone. What more can he ask for? There must be thousands of bones out there, like Bartomeu Camús's, that'll never be claimed."

"And what do you expect me to do?"

"I already told you; help me."

"How?"

"Everybody knows your delivery truck. It won't raise suspicions. Be my taxi driver on Tuesday. Take me to Logroño. We'll pick up my assistants and dig up Camús's bones. Then it's a question of you driving one of us to the station in Vitoria, another to Logroño, and of bringing me back to Miranda. You helped my father, now help me. Anyway, as far as I can tell, you don't have much to lose."

That's a lie. The guy's got plenty to lose. There's his elderly mother, his little sister and her husband, not to mention his nieces and nephews. They're the ones who bake the bread. If Eusebio helps me and things go bad, they'll suffer the consequences, too. Of course, I don't mention that to him.

"Let me think about it," he replies.

He gets up gingerly, barely able to open the door. He staggers on the way out. For a few seconds I almost expect to hear him fall down the stairs and break his neck. What I do hear several minutes later is the screech of tires as his truck veers up the street.

CHAPTER THIRTEEN

The winter of 1940 was one of the worst for us little poorhouse rats. There was no respite from illness or the guards' brutality. For punishment, Tomàs Reniu, a very undernourished kid with a big head and little ears, had to pace around the patio in the middle of winter. He fainted. One of the guards hit him so hard on the temple that he became a half-wit. You'd try to talk to him, and he'd just stare quietly at you with an empty smile on his face. Joan Anton Delera couldn't sing anymore in the choir and stopped playing the violin. The guards boxed his ears to the point of bursting his eardrums. He never could hear very well after that. We all had the same rage seething within. But the difference was that when they punished me, I could always console myself with thoughts about my family outside the Charity Home walls. Sooner or later I would get the hell out of there. I could always run away and wander around the world with No-Sister-Salvador. That knowledge gave me strength. The other frightened little poorhouse rats lived a very different reality. They knew full well that they were the lowest of the low and that their misfortunes were of no interest to anybody. And so, it wasn't such a bad thing to have a smashed eardrum, because both of them could have been boxed in instead. If both eardrums did get shattered and you went deaf, all the better; at least you didn't end up an idiot like Tommy Reniu. And even if you did lose your marbles, it was still an improvement over dying from tuberculosis. That's how we kept ourselves going.

Since I wasn't very good in school, they set me to work as a funeral assistant. The Charity Home had no rival in Barcelona when it came to organizing such affairs. There was one known as the "extra deluxe," which involved suspending a gigantic piece of mauve sailcloth across the entire Manning patio in order to block out the light of day, creating an artificial gloom. It was miraculous. Whenever the door onto Montalegre Street opened, a sharply delineated rectangle of blinding sunshine fell onto the darkened patio like a white carpet. From beneath the shrouds of violet half-light, we could see the carriages led by beribboned horses out there in the brightness. The funeral procession filed solemnly in. The aristocrats wore formal attire, the military had on their dress uniforms, and everybody was wearing all the medals and badges they possessed. The ladies wore severe black-lace head scarves draped over extravagant hair combs perched high on their heads. The priests were dressed in the purple vestments with silver and gold embroidery that were brought out only on special occasions. They clustered on the church steps to greet the funeral party and coffin. Inside the church, the musicians and choir (occasionally made up of singers from the Liceo Opera House) created a fittingly somber atmosphere for the ceremony. A heady mix of odors predominated, ranging from the musk of incense to the pungent notes of the ladies' perfume to lingering traces of burnt wax. The truly pompous funerals went on for more than two hours. Apart from all my duties as a funeral assistant, I was also assigned to organ duty. My job was to keep the massive instrument's two bellows up and running. I spent most of the ceremony pedaling my heart out so that the

organ wouldn't lose steam. My legs would get worn out. Undernourished adolescents aren't exactly physically fit. To be honest, all
of us poorhouse kids were just a grubby collection of skin and bones.
It's ironic then that we were actually required to attend gymnastics
class. Our professor, Señor Giner, was a short, sinewy, and jumpy
man. He was missing one arm and wore his Falange uniform reli-
giously, with its blue shirt, black pants, and red insignia. We didn't get
very much actual gymnastics done with him. He would spend the
whole class telling us war stories, mostly related to how he lost his
arm. Oddly enough, at least in comparison to other people, he
showed a certain amount of understanding toward his enemy, the
Reds, if only because they were Spanish.

"A Frenchman would've been shitting his pants after all the abuse
they took, but the guys in that trench were Spanish, lads. They might
have been Reds, it's true, but they were Spanish men, each one en-
dowed with a fine pair of balls. And, of course, I don't have to tell you
how hard it was for us to blast them out of there . . ."

The battle that cost him his arm had also left its mark on his face,
as if a handful of tiny scars had been splashed across it. The fact that
his beard was pocked by a constellation of shiny stains was an endless source of amusement to us. There was almost nothing left of his
right arm. Señor Giner didn't fold up his shirtsleeve with a clothes-
pin like other amputees. Instead, he rolled it up, exposing his stump
with pride. Come summer, the mangled appendage was put on permanent display, moving in quirky and unexpected ways as if it had a
life of its own. It was covered with a black wool sock during the winter. Barcelona was full of the mutilated and maimed; the lame and the
one-handed. People with missing fingers, feet, eyes, ears . . . You
could tell by the crutches and the artificial limbs if the victims had
been on the winning side or not. Those on the side of the Regime
always had access to the high-quality wheelchairs and varnished

wooden crutches with padding under the arms. The false hands of the winners were attractively gloved in black leather. The mutilated on the losing side did the best they could with the sticks and canes they cobbled together from all sorts of refuse. Often they were forced to drag themselves about as best they could. Or beg on the streets with the aid of a guide dog, their eyes gouged out.

Señor Giner didn't seem like a bad person, in the same way that not all the nuns were evil or stupid. For example, there was Sister Paula in the infirmary. I thought she was beautiful. The nun possessed the telltale odor of a good home. I'd noticed her before, with her white nurse's apron, going up and down the halls. She was the one who'd taken care of us when there was a literal plague of bedbugs. The little creatures would jump from one person to another, eating us alive while we slept. They'd creep out of the nests they'd made in our very own beds, sucking our blood like vampires. Nothing worked. You could burn the sheets, enforce the strictest measures of hygiene, use Zotal . . . and none of it would make any difference. Covered in bites, we felt miserable and defenseless. All of us, the young and the old alike, would scratch ourselves as if the very devil himself lay beneath the skin. Sister Paula dabbed Mercurochrome on our wounds. Her prettiness was more obvious since she usually wore a nurse's uniform and cap instead of a nun's habit. In her kindness, she'd try to keep the patients distracted, especially the youngest ones. When telling stories, she managed to make the lives of the saints sound like fairy tales. Unlike the other priests and nuns, she'd attempt to play down the bloodiest episodes of the martyrs' sufferings. She didn't treat those children who obviously weren't very religious any different than the rest. It was difficult for us to have faith in her Lord; he was too good. The God we knew was mostly cruel and unjust.

My mother kept up with her sewing. More than once she was called in by a neighbor to refashion the entire wardrobe of a deceased relative. Not even dishrags were thrown out; everything was put to good use. Those deaths were the last dregs of lost battles, the final victims of the war. But there were still thousands of people infested with illnesses, be they physical, mental, or of the heart. The cleanup wasn't quite over yet.

Señor Roca continued to pay his little visits. I knew for sure, because she never tried to hide it from me. Instead, my mother took great pleasure in showing me the gifts of food and other provisions that he'd bring. This was mostly because she'd quickly pack up the booty and send it off to my father at the concentration camp.

The best Christmas gift we received in 1940 was an uncensored letter from my father. It was brought to us by a boy who'd come straight from the concentration camp. He'd been released after having proven himself sufficiently right-wing. The young man promised my father that if he managed to smuggle the letter out of the camp, he'd go to our house and put it directly into my mother's hands. As usual, my mother read it aloud. In it, my father gave us some idea of his daily life:

> *We're made to file into formation first thing each morning*
> *for the raising of the flag. It's the same routine in the evening*
> *for the lowering. They do a head count after each ceremony.*
> *Sometimes, just to annoy us, they'll make us go into formation*
> *several times throughout the day. They'll have us stand like that*
> *for hours under the hot sun, or in the freezing cold. We've been*
> *trained to salute with one arm outstretched and forced to*
> *memorize their anthems. And we shout "long live this" or*
> *"long live that" at their command. All political discussion*
> *stops as soon as you get to the camp. Nobody's up for it, they're*
> *disoriented and beaten down. Here you talk under your breath*
> *and nobody trusts each other. Don't get the wrong idea; I'm as*

*scared shitless as the next guy. I knew we were in trouble when
I heard the speech that the camp director gave us as soon as we
got here. He told us that the war in Spain had been different.
The National Army hadn't been fighting against another
military. No, they'd fought a bunch of undesirables, assassins,
and criminals; a pack of scoundrels seduced by propaganda.
And that the camp's goal was to reeducate us. We work like
beasts and they squash us like flies. But waiting is the worst
thing by far; the endless days, weeks, and months of waiting
and waiting.*

We didn't receive another letter, censored or not, for three
months. The next one arrived around the end of March. It was from
a priest, writing to us about my father. He let it be understood that
the inmate in question was in a very bad way. We were told that the
sooner my father could be removed from his current situation, the
better. We would need to find someone to vouch for him. If we didn't
make haste, it might be too late.

*Find a member of the police force, Guardia Civil, the
Falange, or your parish priest. This person must be willing to
declare that your husband was not affiliated with any political
party or union before July 18. They must attest to him being
a devout Catholic of right-wing political tendencies and a
sympathizer of the Glorious National Movement.*

We never did have to find someone to vouch for him. We got another letter a few days later, this time from the central administration
of correctional facilities. It stated that in honor of the second anniversary of Franco's victory and for "humanitarian reasons," my father was going to be released at the beginning of April 1941. They

must have figured that seeing as he was in such bad shape, they'd rather get him off their hands, with or without a voucher. The military confirmed that he was in fact very weak and wouldn't be able to make it back to Barcelona on his own. However, they refused to take responsibility for the prisoner's transport. They might as well have been talking about a package.

That meant we had to be fast. Those people were perfectly capable of throwing him out in the street like a dog. My mother wrote to the camp saying that she'd be coming to pick up my father in person. There were the train tickets, one round-trip, and a few nights at a boardinghouse. It would all cost money. She'd been saving up for months in the hopes of being able to visit him. Even still, it wasn't enough. I could tell she was consumed by suffering and anxiety and didn't know what to do. It all made me so angry, especially the fact that I was just a shitty little locked-up adolescent, powerless to help her in any way.

My mother was only able to get the money after working double time at her sewing, pawning all of Señor Pau's clothes, and taking out another loan from No-Sister-Salvador. The day she came to explain those adventures to me, I asked her, "And what about Señor Roca?"

"Your father's coming back. We're all going to be together again."

"But what about Señor Roca?" I insisted, with a touch of malice.

I couldn't stand the idea of Señor Roca continuing to buzz around my mother like a bumblebee.

She fell quiet, doubtful. Her voice shook as she said, "Look, Niso, it's thanks to Señor Roca that I've got work. Señor Roca's negotiations have gotten your father an early release. He would've vouched for your dad, too, if it'd come to that. And Señor Roca's the one who kept you from getting kicked out of the Charity Home. Is that clear?"

"Yes."

"Well, that's that!" she cried. She paused a few seconds and in a more contained, but in no way calmer, voice said, "I want you to know something. Roca isn't coming around from now on, and he won't be here in the future. There's no need for your father to know anything about Señor Roca when he gets home. It'll be our little secret. Do you understand, Niso?"

"I understand."

There was no news from my family for almost a month. It turned out that my father was back at home within the week, even though the journey to Miranda de Ebro took a day and a half each way. He was sent straight to bed for two weeks to recuperate. I can't imagine what my father must have looked like when she picked him up, because the first time I saw him, he was unrecognizable. The man had been in top condition when he'd gone off to war. The Fascists hadn't managed to do him any serious damage in over two years of combat. He was taken prisoner at the end of 1938 and was released two years and four months later. The man who walked out of those gates was the mere mortal remains of my father. He was suffering from an incurable heart condition that was most certainly fatal. It had been caused by the lethal combination of physical hardship, poor diet, and the grueling exhaustion of forced labor coupled with frequent beatings.

One Sunday morning my mother showed up at the Charity Home with a rabbit-faced man with sunken cheeks, ashy skin, and a listless expression in his eyes. He was so painfully thin that he seemed transparent, like a piece of smoking paper. His large hands, with long fingers ending in nails that were cracked and broken, stood out against his narrow frame. This was my father. Standing next to my mother, he grinned at me foolishly, his mouth half open. That smile revealed that there were only four teeth left at the front of his mouth; two on the top and two on the bottom. The person who stood before me couldn't possibly have been Joan Aleu, the Letter Painter. He didn't look anything like the clever, good-hearted fellow that I remembered. He bore no resemblance to that robust and swarthy youth whose intensely blue eyes had frightened the ladies. My father had left home with a full set of teeth.

But my mother was smiling anyway. You could tell she was happy. Her lazy eye looked straight ahead. She gave me a hug and a kiss and chided, "Aren't you going to say anything to your father?"

He seemed more like an uncle to me than a father. I addressed him quite formally, without even realizing it. That made her furious and earned me a good slap on the back of the neck.

That first day we walked all the way to Plaza Catalonia to see the pigeons. My mother kept a firm grip on my father's arm for fear that the first strong gust of wind would blow him away. He walked with difficulty and tired easily. I remembered how we used to go visit the pigeons when I was little. There was a man with a cart selling packets of seed and grain to feed to the birds. But after the war broke out, the poor creatures started to disappear as if wiped out by some epidemic. The cats also suffered a similar fate, and for the same reason. No-Sister-Salvador claimed to have witnessed people hunting the birds down with nets. But now it was a different story. Although hunger was still rampant in Barcelona, there were still a few brave pigeons promenading around the plaza. The other group strolling around on that spring day was a pack of big, strong German soldiers who were in very high spirits. It wasn't surprising. They ruled the world, after all. Apparently an ambassador to the Third Reich was on an official visit to Barcelona and his entourage was indulging in a little tourism around the city. Those soldiers seemed to be hewn out of rock. We slowly made our way between their dazzling uniforms and handheld cameras. I couldn't help but feel that they were laughing at us.

We had visitors that afternoon, but not many. They knocked on the door softly, so as not to disturb. The guests would come in and take a seat, but were practically struck dumb by the sight of my father. To fill the awkward silences, my mother talked about her trip to Miranda de Ebro.

"Half the ladies in the boardinghouse where I stayed were the wives of prisoners. There were pregnant women who had come to town to be close to their husbands and ended up giving birth in a rented room. Most of those ladies were looking for work. Some couples took the opportunity to have a church wedding, since it counts toward lowering your sentence. Overall, the townspeople didn't seem to think badly of these women. A few of the boardinghouses let them rent the rooms on credit until they find work."

After having accepted the offer of a glass of water, most visitors would set to encouraging my father. Some of them started talking about his paints and brushes in an attempt to cheer him up. They'd tell some anecdote about a sign he painted for them. He'd smile, grimace, and add, "I'll have plenty of work to do thanks to the peace that Franco has brought us!"

Seeing his audience's mystification, my mother would interrupt. But pleased that he'd shown an interest in something, she'd exclaim, "Of course, now everyone will have to replace their old Catalan signs with new ones written in Spanish!"

That's when the visitors would smile uncomfortably and mutter something about it being time to go. Everyone, guests and family alike, breathed easier once they were out the door.

I kept asking my father to tell me about his experiences in detail, but it was no good, he kept his mouth shut. He only spoke about the camp briefly, when we were first reunited, and then two months later, on the day he died. That first day, he described his arrival at the camp to an audience of the three people dearest to him: my mother, me, and No-Sister-Salvador.

"They packed us into cattle cars under the blows of their billy clubs. There were so many people crammed in that nobody could move. We slept standing up, leaning against one another. We shat and pissed on ourselves like old men, or small children. Once, the train stopped moving and we were left in the car the whole day with the doors closed. It was days before we got there. We weren't given anything to eat on the entire journey. When they opened the doors and forced us into the open air, a couple of corpses had to be dragged out, too. The rest of us, those who were still alive, were so rank that we were brought straight to the river. It was the middle of winter and the water along the banks was frozen. The soldiers on guard had to use their bayonets to chop up the ice. One of the prisoners was weak from an open wound that had gotten infected. The contact with the frigid water knocked the breath out of him. He fainted, falling flat on his face. The guards didn't bother to pull the man out of the river. They refused to let his companions come to his aid, either. He died without making a fuss, unable to save himself from drowning."

After saying his piece, my father got up and slowly dragged his feet toward my parents' bedroom. He crawled into bed, saying he felt cold. The truth is that my father trembled all day in those last weeks before he died. It was spring, but he was constantly freezing. We couldn't walk around very much when they'd pick me up from the Charity Home on Sundays, because his nose would quickly turn red, his eyes start to water, and his body shake. Once safe inside the apartment, he couldn't tear himself away from the warmth of the kitchen stove. My mother kept their bed warm with a hot brick. That February there wasn't enough gas in Barcelona to keep the streetlights working, so we resuscitated the old cast-iron stove and went back to burning coal or wood. She'd set the brick, which retained heat remarkably well, deep into the fire. Once it was burning hot, she'd pull it out with a paddle, just as if she were taking bread out of the oven. Then she'd run into the bedroom, rub the brick across the sheets and leave it inside the bed. My mother loved her husband down to the very marrow of her bones, the furthest corner of her soul. She resorted to Old Testament tactics when there wasn't enough fuel to heat up the brick. King David's bed had been warmed with young maidens, so she would do the same. Except that in place of maidens, she used me instead. My mother would convince me to strip down and nestle in their bed for a good half hour, even if it was only five o'clock in the afternoon. The truth is I didn't mind my post as a bed warmer at all. I didn't have to see anybody or explain myself to anyone. I would spend those solitary minutes mulling things over and thinking about how strange everything was. Later on No-Sister-Salvador would add to the fun by coming over to tease me, asking if I'd like to go warm up his bed for him, too. Then I'd proceed to chase him around the building. I'd always catch him right away since he was lame. I'd throw my arms tightly around him and threaten to jump into his bed and piss in it.

I've already explained how my father died. No-Sister-Salvador came to pick me up at the Charity Home one day. With a doleful expression on his face, he said, "Your father is in a very bad way. The doctor says that he might not survive the night."

And without saying another word, he started to walk home. It wasn't long before we were on the Rambla, heads down and hands in our pockets. I had to slacken my pace to meet his limping stride. Otherwise he'd have to rush hobbling along behind me. I felt guilty because although I knew my father should be paramount in my mind, I kept getting distracted. The most minor incidents in the street caught my attention. There were quite a few women waiting in line outside the Boqueria Market. I asked Salvador what was going

on, and he looked at me like I was some kind of idiot. Then he remembered that I was a Charity Home urchin who didn't know any
better. He shrugged his shoulders and replied, "It's the rationing. Potatoes are being distributed today. Four pounds in exchange for a
number fifty-two coupon."

That warm spring day in June didn't cost us a thing as we strode
along. Salvador seemed to have his mind on other things. He mentioned that he was thinking of signing up as a volunteer to work in
Germany.

"The Nazis offer excellent living conditions. But of course there's
always the chance that they might not accept me."

"Why?"

"Because I'm a gimp. It seems they're very picky about that sort
of thing."

We continued on our way without talking. After the war Salvador
had continued to work in the Born. However, his confession of theft
still hung in the air between us like a dark shadow. I couldn't hold
back any longer and asked, "Do you still steal?"

He stared at me shamefacedly.

"No, not anymore," he said, "but I have to admit that it wasn't
too long ago that I quit . . . A kid caught me robbing a rabbit out of
a hutch on a roof. I gave him a few coins to keep him quiet and he
agreed. I stunned the rabbit and shoved it in a sack. Then we went
downstairs. The kid followed behind without opening his mouth. It
was only when I was practically on the street that the little shit started
to squeal, pointing at me and shouting, 'Rabbit thief!' There was a
mule-driven cart right at the door. I grabbed the kid and bit him
on the arm. He started to howl. I hit the mule on the head and the
startled animal began to bray. The beast's owner came running, followed by a whole crowd of people. I accused the mule of having bit-

ten the boy and ran off in the midst of the confusion. That was three months ago and I haven't stolen since and don't plan on ever doing it again."

After walking along, we finally arrived at my house, where my father was on his deathbed.

He passed away in the early hours of morning. My mother altered a dress suit on the sewing machine so that he could meet his maker with a little bit of dignity. The less said about the funeral and burial the better. Hardly anybody was there, and the few attendants were a dejected, sad bunch. I was surprised by the high opinion that everybody had of him. People that I'd never seen before, mostly former clients, spoke of my father with real respect. And not just because he was dead. You could tell they'd admired him from way back. That sort of regard seemed like a rare and precious thing in comparison with how gray and dreary everything else was. We were all so used to being treated with disdain and cruelty that it took me by surprise. It made me realize how important it was to gain people's respect.

Sister Paula told me, by way of consolation, that it wouldn't take very long for me to get over my father, considering that we'd hardly seen each other over the last few years. That was an example of the nuns' brutal pragmatism, coming out of the mouth of the only person in the Charity Home who seemed to genuinely have our best interests at heart. She said those words while putting her arm around my shoulders and pulling me to her as a way to express her condolences. The intense aroma of soap, so close and so penetrating, combined with the direct contact of the soft curves of her flesh, filled me with a momentary surge of lust.

And the truth is Sister Paula wasn't that wrong. My father hadn't been around in a long time. He'd returned only to leave for good two months later. So when he died, it felt like just another absence, except this one would be for a bit longer. It's true that it did weigh on my conscience. I decided that it didn't matter if I was only a kid; I wanted to win people's respect. And it seemed to me that a good way to go about doing that would be to fulfill the promise I'd made to my father. And that resolution gave me a sense of importance and maturity.

CHAPTER FOURTEEN

Monday, October 24, 1949

I'm going to the boot camp today to have a talk with a lieutenant and a sergeant, just to keep up the farce that I'm supposedly writing a report. I'm wearing civilian dress to lend a more bureaucratic feel to the conversation. When Campillo brings me my breakfast, I tell him that I'd like to telephone Barcelona before leaving.

"Can you place a long-distance call for me, please?"

"I doubt we'll have a line before midday."

"If I'm not here, have them transfer the call to the camp."

"Very well."

I arrive at the training facility fairly early. Daily announcements are being read off to the soldiers as they stand in formation. There's no mention this morning of the Spanish Army's dead. No heroes or glorious exploits that could somehow be related to today's date are mentioned. Instead, the morning's harangue revolves around a very special and unique event: His Excellency and Head of State, the Generalíssimo of the Armed Forces on land, sea, and sky, is traveling in Portugal and the journey continues to be a triumph. The corporal reading the announcement intones that the noble Portuguese people have recognized the Generalíssimo as being solely responsible for vanquishing the materialist misery of Communism in Spain. It sounds like a broken record.

I stop by to say hello to the major, who receives me barefoot, pants rolled up, and with his dubious brand of cordiality. He asks me how my work is going while pouring a nice handful of Freire Salts into a basin.

"I still haven't gotten a chance to see any documentation about the camp. It would be very helpful for my report," I reply in a perhaps overly neutral tone.

"That sort of thing is of no importance," he responds. "Just a few statistics. After all, it's impossible to capture the spirit of the work itself with raw data. I'll have someone put all the information in an envelope; you can pick it up whenever you want. Have you already spoken to the officers?"

"That's what I was planning on doing today."

A soldier knocks and enters directly. He's carrying a bucket of hot water and pours it into the basin. The salts begin to bubble and spit like bicarbonate soda. The major sits down, placing his feet in the water with a look of complete contentment.

"Well done, Sergeant. It's always best to get your information firsthand, believe me. Forget about documents and research. What's next?"

"I'd like to take pictures of the camp for my dossier."

"Pictures of what exactly?"

"Different shots of the grounds, here and there. That is, if the soldier Fontes has managed to find a camera for me, of course. I left my own by mistake in Melilla."

I wait in silence for the major's response. It reminds me of the first day, when he dried his feet, toe by toe. He's doing the same thing now. He gets up with difficulty and heads barefoot toward the armoire. He opens it and pulls out a magnificent Leica with its very own leather case. The soldier Fontes seems to be in pretty tight with the major. He brings it over and hands it to me.

"Take it with the compliments of my wife. It belonged to her father. When I mentioned that you were looking for a camera, she didn't hesitate for a second."

"I can't accept such generosity," I say.

"You'll accept what I tell you to accept."

"Yes, sir."

"Don't get me wrong, I'm only thinking of myself. If you don't take the camera, my wife will assume that it's my fault. And you've seen how she can get. Make no mistake, she's only lending it to you, it's not a gift. Take all the photos that you want, get the film developed, and return it to me before your departure."

"Well, if you say so . . ."

"Of course, what did you think? The camera even has a full roll of film in it. Courtesy of the Miranda de Ebro Basic Combat Training Facility. What more could you ask for? We won't take no for an answer."

"Thank you."

"I'm curious to see what sorts of photos you'll take."

I observe him for a few moments, but as before, it's impossible to tell if he's being sarcastic or not. I leave the room with the camera in my hands and run into soldier Fontes. He's got the look of a guilty dog on his face. I can practically see his ears shrivel up and fall back against his head. He gives me the envelope containing the camp statistics. Even I'm starting to believe in the existence of this report.

"Good morning, Sergeant. How are you feeling today?"

"Very well, Fontes. Why do you ask?"

"You didn't stop by yesterday."

"Oh yes . . . I hadn't slept well, something didn't agree with me at dinner. But I'm in perfect condition now."

Fontes cheers up when he realizes that I'm not going to chew him out. He points to the Leica that the major has just given to me.

"That's a pretty good camera, huh? Much better than anything I could have gotten my hands on. The major noticed I was asking around the unit for one and wanted to know why. Anyway, I couldn't do anything about it."

"Don't worry. I've arranged to interview Lieutenant Huertas and Sergeant Borrajo. I don't think it'll take me more than an hour and a half. When I'm done, will you come with me while I photograph the camp?"

"Of course!"

"I'll see you later then."

Fontes seems disappointed that I'll be leaving soon. I wait in an office for a while, flipping through the documentation on the boot camp. There's nothing out of the ordinary. It's not even a particularly good training facility. All they've gained by taking advantage of the installations of the old concentration camp is an uncomfortable and not very practical space.

Lieutenant Huertas is the only one who shows up, and he's fifteen minutes late. The asshole gives me an arrogant once-over. He's a good foot taller than I am. He doesn't accept my cigarettes, only smoking the ones he rolls himself. The guy's slender, intelligent, cultured, with very formal manners. He apologizes for the sergeant and asks if we can make it quick.

"There's a lot of work to be done. It's almost time for the flag ceremony, and everything has to be in order."

This brownnoser must be fresh from the academy. He's the kind of guy who doesn't look anybody in the eye when he's talking to them.

Instead, the lieutenant lets his gaze wander around the room, as if searching for a more interesting topic of conversation or something to distract him while burdened with my presence. To him, I'm merely a lowly underling of the Legion, which is little more than a band of savages. He doesn't have any qualms about making his feelings known, either.

"Nothing personal, Sergeant Aleu, but do you really believe that the Legion is still valid in 1949, a day and age when it's possible to wipe out an entire battalion like a bunch of ants by simply pressing a button?"

"What do you mean exactly?"

"Don't play the fool. I know the Legionnaire's Credo by heart: 'The warrior is unique, always attacking with blind ferocity and attempting to get as close to the enemy as possible in order to engage in man-to-man combat, wielding his bayonet.'"

"What do you expect me to say?"

"What you think."

"I'm a Legionnaire. There'll always be a need for Special Forces like the Legion. The English have their Gurkhas. And, anyway, we don't know how to fight any other way. We're suicidal types with guns. Sometimes that's what's needed. Look at the kamikazes."

"Are you pulling my leg?"

"Of course not, Lieutenant. Think about it and you'll realize what I'm saying isn't so crazy."

Actually, I agree completely with the lieutenant. The Legion is little more than dead meat when thrown into modern conventional combat. But I'd never admit that to him. He talks about the war.

"I tried to enlist when I was only sixteen and they didn't let me. The war ended not long after. Despite my youth, I still felt a strong attraction for the Christian mysticism of the Crusade. That's why I enlisted in the Blue Division and went off to Russia, along with so

many of my other companions in the Falange. The struggle continues even now, during peacetime. In order to win the battle once and
for all, we have to stay true to the beliefs that our fathers, and later
we ourselves, fought for. We must follow their footsteps and live by
the same credo."

The lieutenant can't shut up. He truly venerates the war fought
by the generation before him. He's probably one of those people who
fervently believe that the enemy committed every act of barbarity
under the sun, but won't accept that his side did anything untoward.
Military Falangists like him still have faith in the Regime, even
though, once in power, the new government didn't waste any time
watering down the Falange's core philosophy, leaving only a skeleton
of rhetoric. The lieutenant is one of those lost souls who think that
with the war over, now is the time for young idealists like him to take
charge and build a more just and prosperous nation. The lieutenant
is an asshole. He continues.

"Don't think that I'm not aware of the scores of disloyal citizens
who've taken advantage of the situation, with their flamboyant political careers or business success. They equate winning the war with
plundering and pillaging, as though they have a right to the booty. A
lot of people are like that. The Generalíssimo's challenge is to create a
socially progressive country somehow, despite all the opportunists. We
have to be patient and trust that the government will soon implement
one of the Falange's guiding principles, the eradication of the class
struggle. Some power must be taken away from the privileged in order
to create more opportunities for the disadvantaged. The only way to
save the Nation is through a social revolution, which will transcend all
the traditional conceptions of property, commerce, and labor."

I've stopped listening. He's beginning to seem like a pathetic jerk.
Those Falangist slogans sound so antiquated and decrepit coming out
of his mouth. Having to hear those words in an ex–concentration

camp makes me sick to my stomach. The world has been turned up-side down. We end up talking about the Second World War. He shows off the tactical and strategic knowledge he gleaned from studying the major battles. What he doesn't explain is why, if he's so smart, he's been assigned to this shit hole. I finally get him to give me a half-hour lecture on training techniques for future soldiers. He's vain enough to believe that he's actually doing a halfway decent job. Of course, it's a post that, worst-case scenario, could be organized and carried out by the most inept salesclerk of any midsize shop in Barcelona.

Good-bye. You're staying right where you are, you miserable, dried-up old piece of shit. You, with your Falangist pipe dreams, your studies in military tactics. You're trapped within these four walls; stuck in this hole, which echoes with the screams of the tortured, humili-ated, and mortified people who passed through this place.

I stand at attention and salute Lieutenant Huertas, say my good-byes, and go outside. Fontes is waiting right there.

"Are you coming along or not?" I ask.

"Of course I am, Sergeant! Where do you want to start?"

I start taking snapshots pretty much at whim, with Fontes nip-ping at my heels. I keep heading toward the group of trees that con-tains Purgatory. Walking right past it, I note the crevice in the trunk again but don't stop until reaching the outer boundaries of the camp. I snap a photo of the train tracks. The tree is about ten feet behind me. Now is the time. I pull the camera off my neck and hand it to Fontes. Then I ever so nonchalantly walk up to the tree and lean against it, ordering him to step back a ways.

"I want the picture to be taken from far away, so you can see the train tracks in the distance. Let's go."

Fontes shrugs his shoulders and turns around. He takes a few strides away from me. I strike a casual pose of someone about to be photographed and stay still, keeping my gaze trained ahead. Without shifting my body as it rests against the tree, I take the opportunity to reach into Purgatory, which is right within arm's reach. It's only a matter of seconds before Fontes turns and catches me red-handed. I go rigid. My stance looks a little forced, but he doesn't seem to have noticed. He stands still, looking at me. I can't stand it anymore and practically scream, "What the hell is wrong with you now?"

"Is this far enough away?" he cries.

"No!" I roar back. "Get back! Much, much farther back! Perspective, goddamn it! Perspective!"

Fontes continues to gaze at me for a moment. I watch him murmur the word "perspective" to himself and scratch his head. He turns around once more and moves a few paces forward. I'm sweating. My heart pounds wildly. I quickly shove my hands inside, groping haphazardly within the hollow space. And I find it! Trying to stay as still as possible, I pull the bundle out and slip it down the back of my underpants. Just then, Fontes turns around. Now my hands are free. I tell him to stop, he's gone far enough. I flash him a wide grin and he calms down. It takes him a while to find the right angle. After the way I chewed him out before, he must think he's got the photo of the century hanging over his head.

Finally, he calls out, "All set. Are you ready?"

"Yes, damn it; I am."

He pushes down the little button and the job is done.

I can feel Bartomeu Camús's folder pressing against my ass. The worst that could happen is that I'll end up with a red dragon tattooed to my right buttock.

I'm so nervous my hands are shaking when Fontes gives me back the camera. I'm dying to get the hell out of here as soon as possible. We take a few more photos and call it a day. I take the opportunity to adjust my shirttails as he walks me back to headquarters. It's almost midday.

"Do you want me to get the film developed?"

"No thanks. There's still a few left. Maybe I'll play tourist and finish off the roll this afternoon in Miranda."

"As you wish."

I try to bid the major farewell, but they tell me he isn't there. So much the better. I can't wait to be alone.

The ride from the boot camp to the pension seems to take forever. The only thing that keeps me from jumping out of the military vehicle is the fear that someone might notice the folder I've got wedged against my ass. I pay my regards to Campillo's mother as I enter his establishment. She doesn't even look at me. Then I grab my key and bound directly up the stairs, bolting the door behind me. Hesitating for a second, I wonder, should I pull my pants down? I undo my fly, pull out the folder, and zip myself back up again. The paper feels damp and soggy. I place it in the middle of the bed. The folder is made out of blue cardboard and seems to have been fastened with rubber bands at one time. They're long gone now. Maybe they rotted. The poor dragon is a little smudged but still identifiable. It's very cleverly drawn in the Chinese style. Between the ferocious expression on its face and a wide mouth full of menacing teeth, the creature looks as if it were trying to guard the contents within. I sit down on the bed, take up the package, and slowly open it. I'm afraid it will crumble to bits in my hands. It contains an envelope and a sheaf of papers folded in half. Everything's in pretty good condition, considering the changes in temperature over the last eight or nine years. I extricate the sheets with caution. Far from being damp, they're almost brittle. I move the folder aside and place them on top of the coverlet. After unfolding the sheets and smoothing them down a bit with my hand, I realize that there're two separate sets of documents. The first consists of some sheets ripped out of a school notebook. The text is written in pencil and the pages are numbered from one to four. It's headed by a very bizarre title written in Spanish, "Declaration of Bartolomé Camús Concerning the Theory of Absolute Segregation." The document itself fills the two sides of a sheet of paper with cramped script. The other page is taken up by two lists of names. I begin to read:

> These are the words of Bartomeu Camús, which I leave as a testimony of everything that I witnessed as an unclassified prisoner, from the end of 1938 to the beginning of 1940. In the capacity of master carpenter, I was hired to work in the house of Dr. Antonio Vallejo-Nágera, major of the Military Psychiatric Service of Franco's Army. After I had completed various repairs and constructed several pieces of furniture for his house in Madrid, the major, pleased with my service, requested and was granted that I continue to work for him as an all-around assistant, in charge of maintenance and acting as majordomo, in addition to any other tasks that he should require. Over the next five to six months, I heard him discuss with the various visitors who came to the house the basic principles of what he called his "Theory of Absolute Segregation." I served coffee, cleared away cognac snifters, offered cigars . . . and listened. According to him, under the direct orders of General Franco, they had started using political prisoners and prisoners from the International Brigades as subjects in a series of psychiatric experiments. After a few months they began to focus their studies on females and came to some startling conclusions. It was found that all women who take part in political activity undergo a degenerative process, resulting in a depravity of character that quickly leads to irreversible mental retardation. Given the impossibility of rehabilitating these individuals, and in order to save a considerable

sector of the Spanish race from its very foreseeable degradation, it was considered indispensable that the children of these women be radically segregated from them. The major believed that it was possible to correct the children's erroneous biological inheritance through moral values and a traditional Catholic education. He considered that the State should be responsible for taking charge of these young souls. They should be sent to live in centers expressly designed to extricate all past experience from their tender little brains, replacing it instead with character traits that are appropriate and honorable to the race.

From that moment on, Dr. Vallejo-Nágera began to compile lists of prisoners, including pregnant ones, who should have their children taken away from them. I myself was sometimes responsible for typing those rosters out. One of the special centers that the doctor had envisioned was already being set up in Madrid. It was known as a prison for lactating mothers. By sheer chance, I discovered that the lists compiled by the doctor, who was in charge of the Military Psychiatric Service, were being put to a very different use. His office was run by a lieutenant and a subaltern. One day the death certificate of a three-year-old girl fell into my hands. As luck would have it, I happened to have that same child right before my eyes at that moment, and she was very much alive. When I pointed this out to the subaltern, he became visibly upset. He insisted that it was a mere clerical error, but, nevertheless, I should keep my nose out of it if I didn't want to end up pounding rock on a chain gang. Above all, I wasn't to breathe a word of it to Major Vallejo-Nágera. The next day a pair of Germans showed up at the office. They undertook a thorough inspection of that same three-year-old girl, with her blond hair and blue eyes. Approving of what they saw, the men returned to pick her up a few days later. However, according to the official records, the child was still deceased. Similar incidents occurred on several other occasions. The pregnant women were especially targeted. The infants were taken away immediately after birth. The mother was informed that the creature had been stillborn. The whole operation was organized and run by a military doctor, a forensic surgeon, the lieutenant, and the subaltern. The boys and girls were sold off like animals, I imagine to couples who couldn't have children. On more than one occasion, I got the feeling that the purchaser was some kind of pervert. In the office I was considered little more than a mute and half-stupefied slave. They trusted me so much they'd occasionally start talking about their scheme right in front of me, as if I wasn't there.

The mistake that I made, which will cost me my life, was to try to somehow intervene in the whole process. I registered the arrival of a two-year-old boy from a prison in Saturrarán. According to his file, after his father was executed the child was sent to prison, along with his mother, when he was barely three months old. They'd just taken him away from his mother by force. His maternal aunt's address and telephone were listed in the file. I couldn't hold back any longer and called her. I anonymously informed the aunt where the child was and suggested that she'd better not waste any time; otherwise it would be too late. In her shock and confusion, it took the woman ten days before she was able to fully grasp the situation at hand. By then, the best she could get out of them was a death certificate. The lieutenant in question began to suspect me after that. I assume that's why, in a matter of days, I was suddenly removed from Major Vallejo-Nágera's service. The torture sessions went on for three or four days. They wanted me to confess what I knew and find out if I had said anything to the major or talked to anybody else. I kept repeating no to all their questions, saying that I didn't know what they were talking about. They couldn't get anything out of me. The life was fading out of me. It was probably thanks to a few choice words from Vallejo-Nágera himself that I wasn't assassinated right there and then.

Afterward I was sent to the Miranda Concentration Camp. I knew I was still under suspicion and being watched. I discovered soon after I arrived at the camp that they weren't planning on ever classifying me as a prisoner. They made sure that my name wasn't written down anywhere. Officially I didn't exist. In addition, I noticed that the guards inspected my belongings a little too often, beat me at the least provocation, and assigned me the most godforsaken tasks. I was often punished for no reason. It was all meant to be a reminder that they were keeping an eye on me. When they finally come to the conclusion that I really haven't left behind any kind of concrete proof regarding their activities, or that I haven't revealed their secret to anybody, my life won't be worth shit. I know that time is coming, and that's the reason I'm writing these lines and leaving them in the care of my friend Joan Aleu, for him to do with them what he sees fit.

My hands are shaking. I can't get over it. This must be the cruelest irony of all time. Infants, children of executed prisoners, had been adopted by the very same people who'd murdered their parents.

The next sheet contains the names of the military men implicated in the supposed sale of prisoners' babies: Major Doctor Julián Barros, Forensic Doctor Facundo del Pueyo, Lieutenant Valentín

Fresneda, and some subaltern called Aznar. On the other side of the page is a list, with first and last names, of the minors who were sold (about twenty children) and their mothers. It also specifies the prisons where the women were originally incarcerated and the date that they were separated from their children. If this document were ever to be made public, it would explode like a bomb. I fold up the papers and return them to their folder. I'm overwhelmed. This is the treasure that my father was talking about. A subtle mention here and there to the most important people on that list and money would start to rain down. A couple of those names sound very familiar. Some of these guys have become pretty important officials in the Regime. Major Barros is a general now, with the prestigious bureaucratic post of running the Military Board of Health. As for Dr. Pueyo, after receiving a special distinction from Franco's very own hands, he returned to civilian life and currently runs one of the most modern and expensive clinics in Madrid. I don't think either of them would be interested in having their names mixed up in such a sordid affair as the trafficking of minors.

After eight years of living a double life, I've acquired an unbridled thirst for revenge. And if I can honey the pot with a bit of blackmail, so much the better. I'll make them pay dearly for all the suffering they've put me through. I'll destroy them. Rip their guts out. Make them fear they'll be paying up for the rest of their lives. And just when they start to hope that they have gotten rid of me, I'll let the whole country know what they've done. I'll use their very own money to hire the best lawyers to denounce them, if necessary. I'll drive them to complete ruin. . . .

It's no good. I sound like such an idiot. I am an idiot.

These are extremely important people. It'd be better just to extort a big wad of cash in one fell swoop and get the fuck out of here. Get my ass back to Africa. Those baby-selling bastards can stay right where they are, sit, and suffer. Just when they think the danger's past, I'll go public from afar.

I open the blue envelope. There's a sheet covered in what is unmistakably my father's handwriting. It's a map showing where Camús's grave is located. On it are very simple indications marked in pencil: "camp," "river," "train track," "highway," "dirt road," and a cross with the initials B.C. beside it. The distances between landmarks are measured in time. It's hard to tell exactly what locations he's referring to. For example, it doesn't specify which highway he's talking about. Several of the directions are the same ones that he gave me on the day he died: a fork in the road marked by a large, flat stone; a pine tree in the shape of the letter Y. . . .

I sit at the small desk in my room. There's work to do. I grab a notepad and a fountain pen. I copy down the testimony concerning the segregation of children, including Vallejo-Nágera's activities and the team of wiseguys who put his repugnant theory in practice. I'll send it to my own address in Melilla.

I continue writing for a good while. I'm not sure why, but something tells me I don't have all the time in the world to do it.

I stop at a tobacco shop to purchase some stamps and an envelope. I slip the copy inside and send the document off right then and there.

CHAPTER FIFTEEN

Are some people simply incapable of getting over the loss of a loved one? After a reasonable period of mourning, most are able to move on, but a few never do. I discovered that my mother belonged to this minority. She didn't eat. She couldn't work. She wouldn't leave the house. Clients began to complain about jobs not getting finished on time. It wasn't as if she didn't want to work. She simply didn't have the strength to run the sewing machine. We watched her fade away. I couldn't stand to see my mother like that. By the end of summer she'd lost all her customers. Salvador made it clear that things couldn't go on that way. It was just a question of time before someone informed the authorities. They might even end up putting her away.

One September day a guard came to tell me that I was wanted in the head secretary's office.

"Apparently your mother's with him," he said.

It wasn't like her to show up in the middle of the week and during class time.

I found my mother next to Sister Paula, looking terrified in her dark glasses. The Home's head secretary, a government employee, was also with them. He was a fifty-year-old man with gray hair, plump cheeks, big eyes, and a deceptively amiable face. He greeted her with exaggerated cordiality. His manner tried to smooth over any differences but in the end only accentuated them.

"Señora Aleu, I understand that the Home's external appearances are deplorable. My only defense is we ensure that the internal workings of the institution run fairly smoothly, keeping in mind that we subsist solely on the charity and generosity of the nuns and the citizens of Barcelona . . . Ah, look, here we have your son." He began to speak to me instead. "We found your dear mother loitering outside in the middle of Montalegre Street, contemplating our Home as if she were a government inspector." Then the head secretary drew closer to me and said under his breath, "The guard at the door didn't pay any attention to her at first, but when it had been over three quarters of an hour that she'd been standing there, he went up to her and asked if anything was wrong. She was quite disoriented." And then, continuing on in a normal voice, as if addressing the nun, "The guard recognized her as that mother with the dark glasses who comes to visit sometimes. He brought her inside, assuming she wasn't feeling very well, and we took her to the infirmary."

Then he looked at Sister Paula, and she smiled at me, saying in her calm voice, "There's nothing wrong with her, she's just a bit nervous." And then, facing my mother, "Why don't you stay with us for a little while, Señora Aleu? Ginés and I can keep you company."

"Sister Paula, is there anything we can offer her that might calm her down?" the secretary asked, irked at the nun's sudden command of the situation.

"How about some hot chocolate?" she suggested.

"Magnificent!" Then, speaking to my mother, "Stay here as long as you like. Your son is here for you to talk to. I imagine it's him you've come to see . . ."

"No."

"No? Oh, really?"

"Well, maybe, yes."

"Of course. These aren't visiting hours, but I think today we can make an exception. You're a friend of Señor Benito Roca, aren't you, madame?"

My mother flushed as bright red as a tomato. I would've given anything to shove that question down the secretary's throat with a nice big punch in the mouth. The man pulled his wallet out of his blazer, removed a card, and handed it to her.

"Don't hesitate to call if you ever need anything."

That said, he bade us a bright farewell. I felt a stab of envy as I watched the tails of his suit jacket disappear down the hallway. He was the sort of man who always had a business card handy, as if perfectly at ease and confident in the world. A lot of people don't have any idea what they're doing here. But in that moment it seemed to me that I wasn't in the world at all. Sister Paula took us to the kitchen and told the nun on duty that the secretary had ordered a hot chocolate for my mother. Then she smiled, said good-bye, and left. As usual, I could hardly take my eyes off her. It didn't seem possible that I was the only who noticed how special the nun was, if only because of her clean aroma of fresh cloth. Most of the other nuns certainly didn't smell like that.

The kitchen was a cavernous room with high and majestically vaulted ceilings. Aside from an assortment of the enormous pots and pans required to feed so many people, there were also piles of sacks scattered about. They were full of beans, sugar, and rice. Who could they be meant for? The wards certainly didn't get to taste such luxuries very often. We sat at a massive table with carved wooden benches. The nun prepared the hot chocolate. My mother sat in silence. Her face bore a look of suffering.

"What happened to you?" I asked in a murmur.

"When?"

"Now!"

"What do you mean, now?"

I didn't force the issue, because the nun was bringing over her chocolate. The woman placed the steaming cup and a small plate with three ladyfingers in front of her. Since the secretary hadn't extended his hospitality to me, I wasn't served anything. Then the cook sat down in front of my mother, with a very nunlike grin, to ensure that she ate it. My mother dipped a ladyfinger in the cup, brought it to her lips, and grinned at the nun. The nun smiled back. My mother popped the pastry into her mouth. As she was about to dip the second half of the third and last ladyfinger, the nun stood up and said that she'd be right back. She had a small errand to run.

My mother looked so lovely to me sitting there by my side, her lips gleaming with chocolate. She was as petite as a little girl. Running her tongue across her upper lip, she said very seriously, "Ginés, I've been doing a lot of thinking. I'm not at all well. You see what happened today. Knowing you were inside, I found myself standing outside the Charity Home. I wanted to tell you something, but I couldn't work up the courage. Instead, I kept staring at the stones in the wall, the bars on the windows, and the roof. I can't go on like this . . . A little time away would be the best solution. It'll help calm me down. I'm surrounded by memories here and it's unbearable."

She gazed at me from behind those dark glasses and then very slowly, as if carefully weighing every word, continued by saying, "I've written to my mother. She's still a tenant farmer in Caldes de Malavella. I've explained to her that I'm newly widowed, in poor health, and in need of assistance. I'm going to go stay with her for a spell."

She talked about Grandmother Victorina for a while, as if all the anger and disagreements they'd had over the years could simply vanish from one day to the next. I suppose she wanted to put my mind at ease. They hadn't spoken to each other in years. I hadn't even been born yet when they stopped. I'd always assumed that the falling-out had something to do with my father. I'd never even met the woman.

"I'm going to miss you very much. Do you understand? We're going to be separated again. This time I'm the one who'll be going away. What kind of mother leaves her child behind? I'm such a complete failure."

"Don't say that."

"It's true. But don't worry. We'll see each other as soon as possible. Meanwhile, get as much as you can out of these people."

My father had given me the exact same advice.

My grandmother, whom I barely knew, suddenly appeared in our lives. She lived out in a country village called Caldes de Malavella. There had been some talk of me going to stay with her during the war, but that plan fell through. This time she had agreed, grudgingly, to take my mother in. But only on the condition that she would come down to Barcelona to pick up my mother herself. That way Victorina could finish making up her mind right there and then, once she'd gotten a look at her daughter.

I was given special permission to accompany my mother to the train station. No-Sister-Salvador came along with us. The train arrived punctually at noon. It wasn't very crowded. Soldiers on leave, peasants hauling huge loads while chomping on sprigs of rosemary, travelers. A little boy ran to greet a young man who swooped him up onto his shoulders, and my grandmother appeared striding behind them.

She looked different than I expected. I imagined somebody older, a decrepit old woman. Instead, the person walking toward us, although definitely of a certain age, was lean rather than skinny, with steely hair and firm flesh. She walked determinedly, with a strong and masculine gait, a bundle in her hand. I felt my mother tense up.

Fifteen years had passed since the two women had seen each other, and they didn't even give each other a peck on the cheek. Grandma Victorina looked right through me. That's when I realized that she had the same lines on her face as my mother, two deep grooves curving down from the edge of each nostril to the corners of her mouth. She didn't mince words.

"Who's this?"

"Your grandson."

"And the other one?"

"A neighbor and friend."

"And your husband was killed during the war?"

"No. He was sick when they sent him back from the concentration camp."

"It's been fifteen years since you cut me out of your life. You didn't even know whether I was dead or alive."

"You told me that you didn't want anything to do with me."

"Any girl worth her salt doesn't let herself get pregnant by the first fellow who comes along."

"Don't tell me you've come all this way to start arguing about that again."

"You wrote me a letter claiming to be unwell."

"I've lost my appetite. I don't have any strength or my wits about me. I can't work. The best thing for me to do is get as far away from here as I can."

"Thanks to the war, there are thousands of widows in this country. And most of them are perfectly capable of keeping their family going."

"Well, I'm not. I can't even keep myself going. Luckily, Genís is a ward at the Charity Home."

I'd never seen my mother beg for anything like that. Her head hung low as she wiped her nose with a pocket handkerchief. My grandmother took another look at me. I was scared of the lady.

"He doesn't look anything like you," she said in a completely neutral voice, devoid of inflections.

"No. He takes after his father."

There was a silence. Both women refrained from speaking.

"I can barely maintain myself," Grandmother said irritably. "The landowners went abroad right at the beginning of the war. And they haven't come back. No one's heard hide nor hair of them. And of course I don't earn a cent. I get by with the garden and a bit of poultry. But sometimes it's not enough. I trade cords of firewood for salt, oil, and flour. I bake bread in exchange for sewing thread, needles, and buttons. It'll be a real strain to have one more mouth to feed."

"I'll make it up to you once I'm back on my feet," my mother assured her.

"Money isn't worth much these days. You'll have to work hard if you want to stay with me. What exactly do you do for a living, if I may ask?"

"I was a telephone operator at Customs. During the war I worked as a typist."

"None of that will be of any use on the farm."

"Lately I've been taking in sewing."

"Do you have a sewing machine?"

"Yes."

We were startled by a continuous dry and metallic clatter. A railroad worker was walking along the tracks next to a stalled train, banging the bottom of the cars with a steel bar as he went.

"What's he doing?" my grandmother asked.

"He's checking to make sure that there's no one hidden underneath," No-Sister-Salvador chimed in.

It was painful to leave my mother in the hands of a woman who had no interest in getting saddled with a daughter she would barely recognize on the street.

"We'll have your sewing machine shipped to Caldes. You can help out around the house and do some sewing on the side."

"You're just looking for an unpaid servant."

"Ungrateful girl. You haven't changed a bit."

"Neither have you. I should never have come to you for help."

"Really? Well, now you have."

My mother cried out in a burst of anger, "I'm your daughter!"

"I have no idea who you are anymore . . . It's been a long time since you left home."

That's when my mother exclaimed that she'd had enough and squeezed my hand tightly. She told her mother that she'd had second thoughts and didn't want to go stay with her after all. My grandmother smiled strangely.

"Have it your way."

They stared each other down for a few moments. Then my mother, as quickly as she lost her temper, abruptly calmed down.

"You're right, forgive me. Don't worry, I can sew and take care of whatever else needs doing."

"That's more like it. Is there a pension anywhere nearby?"

"You can sleep with us," my mother replied.

"I suppose I could, but it won't be necessary. The train leaves in five hours, around five fifteen. You go home and come back with your things. What about those black glasses?"

"They're for my lazy eye."

"They won't be needed at the farm. No one will be looking at you there. As long as you can see well enough to sew, I don't care."

My mother hung her head and nodded. Most of her pride had been swept away with my father's death. The most my grandmother would allow us to do was accompany her to a pension near the station so she could freshen up and wait for the night train that would take them back to Caldes. No-Sister-Salvador, who'd barely said a word during the entire exchange, carried the bundle for her.

It was growing dark out when they departed. I never saw my grandmother again. And good riddance. No-Sister-Salvador and I watched how the old woman, stiff as a telephone pole, and my mother, her slight form doubled over from the weight of her suitcase, boarded the train together. These two women were joining forces to get through hard times. They were both without men and both equally stubborn. I was a shitty little adolescent, useless, incapable of doing anything. And that made me furious.

My mother signed a document stating that Salvador would be legally responsible for me until I reached the age of twenty-one.

I went back to my manic routine, but my head wasn't on straight. My father was dead and my mother gone, out of the line of fire. She might as well have ceased to exist. In less than three months my plans to leave the Charity Home had been dashed to bits. If I didn't get my act together, those people would eat me alive. I was about to turn sixteen and my whole being was like some kind of time bomb. The problem was that I didn't know exactly when the explosion was going to take place.

There was a guard named Folquet who was on duty in the afternoons. He'd had it in for me for a while. He'd once been a ward himself and had the face of a toad, complete with a wart under his chin. He wasn't very bright. At the least provocation, he'd start poking and tapping me with his club. Whenever the nuns weren't around, he'd make fun of me. I ignored him as much as possible. His favorite tactic was to keep repeating my nickname. He'd say, "Good morning, Crater." "Good afternoon, Crater." "How's it going, Crater?" "So, Crater, is that redhead going to be stopping by for some hot chocolate today, too?" One day when the two of us were by ourselves out in one of the courtyards, something snapped, and I fought back. He hadn't been expecting it. Being much taller, I grabbed him by the collar and dragged the guy over against the wall. Then I forced him to turn around, immobilizing his right arm behind his back. He tried to twist out of my grip, but the struggle only wrenched his arm further, increasing the pain. With my face inches away from his cheek, I screamed insolently in his ear, spitting all the while.

"This is the Manning courtyard of the Charity Home. Here's the same fountain as always. You and I run into each other thirty times a day. But right now, it's just you and me. Why do you keep calling me Crater all the time?"

I had a good hold on him, and he was frightened. He replied in a shaky voice, "Doesn't everybody call you Crater?"

Giving his arm another yank, I answered as he moaned in pain.

"Yes, but you don't have to use it every single time you see me."

"Why not?"

"Because you'll wear my nickname out!"

"But you can't wear out a name," Folquet replied stupidly.

Everything happened really quickly after that. I pushed him onto the ground and sat straddling his back. My hands circled his neck roughly. He tried to scratch, hit, or push me away, but it was no use, I was much stronger. Slowly I began to apply more pressure around his neck and watched his eyes fill with fear, or rather terror. As soon as I was convinced that the bastard had, for an instant anyway, tasted death, I let him go.

As he coughed, I began to stride up the stairs at a dignified pace toward the dormitories. Just as I'd thought, once Folquet had gotten over the shock, he came after me with the club in his hands. The guard didn't expect me to be lying in wait for him. I didn't count on the fact that he wasn't a complete imbecile. He'd gotten reinforcements. There were two of them and they made the most of it. The other guard grabbed me from behind, holding me down and covering my mouth. Humiliated, Folquet socked me right in the stomach. He was blind with rage and might very well have punched me to death. The two of them gave me a good beating. They showed no mercy. One of them kicked me, while the other wielded the club. They went for my face, chest, stomach, and kidneys. Those two got me good. I was bleeding like a stuck pig. A few of the wards heard the racket and realized that something more than a run-of-the-mill punishment was taking place. They went running to go tell the nuns. I was splayed on the ground by the time they came to my rescue, passed out from the last boot to my head. Even the nuns had a hard time getting that pair of animals off me. They were like two rabid dogs. Once the men were finally torn away, they realized that I was soaked in blood from head to foot, a gash on my head and a badly disfigured face. My right eye was filled with blood; the left one was puffy and swollen shut like an old boxer's; my lips were split and swollen. Two of my teeth had been knocked loose. I couldn't sit or lie down, everything hurt too much. After that clubbing, my back, arms, buttocks, and legs might as well have been ripped from my body. The two guards looked on from a distance in shocked silence at what they'd been able to accomplish in ten minutes' handiwork. I regained consciousness a few seconds later. They helped me sit up, leaned me against the wall, and I immediately began to spit up blood. The pain in my chest, ribs, and kidneys was agonizing, and I fell straight to the ground in a dead faint once again. Just then Sister Paula appeared and saw me. She had no idea what was going on. The nun cried, "Oh my Lord, oh my Lord!" and went running for medical assistance.

I was laid up in the infirmary for three weeks after that beating. The first thing I saw on cracking my eyes open for the first time was Sister Paula. She leaned over me, a crucifix and rosary hanging off her waist, running her hands through my hair and speaking in soft, soothing tones; but I couldn't make out the words. I wasn't able to eat or speak because my lips were too swollen to open. My eyes hadn't gone unscathed, either. I could barely see and pissed blood for an entire week. Apart from tending to my wounds, Sister Paula spoke to me as no other nun in that place ever had. She treated me like a normal person. Sister Paula was trying to convince me not to hold a grudge against the guards. She didn't succeed on that score, but we became friends. Sitting up in bed, I would help her fold clean dressings and bandages. Then she'd start telling me quite personal things about her life. That's how I discovered she came from a wealthy and aristocratic family. Her parents were the Baron and Baroness of Remei, and came to visit her from time to time. One day she brought them into the infirmary. They were escorted by the mother superior, the head secretary, the doctor, and a couple of nuns. Much to everyone's surprise, Sister Paula brought them all over to my bedside. Suddenly I was surrounded by important people. I was introduced to the baron and baroness, who seemed very elegant and polite to me at the time. They greeted me without paying much attention to the mother superior's bitter tone as she explained that I'd been a bad boy.

"How did you manage to wound yourself so badly?" the baron asked abruptly.

Despite the fact that I'd made a lot of progress, what with the stitches closing the gash on my forehead, the old scar, and all the other still very evident bruises and marks on my face, my appearance was hideous. The mother superior, the doctor, and the nuns looked on in a nervous and threatening manner, waiting to see what I'd say. I remembered my father's words and my ultimate goal: Leave, get the hell out of there, and let all those bastards eat my dust.

"I misbehaved and had to be punished." Everyone relaxed. The baron wasn't entirely satisfied. The boy in front of him was in critical condition. It was obvious that I'd been given a nearly fatal beating. Regardless of whatever crime I may have committed, it still didn't make sense.

"But what did you do to receive such a terrible punishment?"

"I got into a fight with the guards."

Luckily, the secretary and the mother superior managed to distract the baron with something else and led him away.

It was strange to spend so many days alone in the infirmary, whiling the hours away with such a peculiar nun.

My reward for not having exposed the Charity Home's brutality to the baron became apparent the very next day. They decided that while they deliberated exactly what my definitive punishment was to be, I wouldn't be allowed to leave the building or have any contact with the outside world, for an initial period of six months. Six months locked up! In the end the isolation gave me time to make some decisions. I'd get the hell out of there the first chance I got. Running away was considered a serious crime, at least in theory. The police and Guardia Civil were brought into the matter. And once the fugitive was found and captured, the usual punishment, aside from the inevitable beating, was to send the individual to the Duran Asylum in Barcelona. The name of that sinister institution fell from all the wards' lips with fear and trembling. It was hell on earth. My case was worsened by the fact that the guard had denounced me to the police for attempted murder. It was all the same to me. If they tried to lock me up in the Duran Asylum, I'd just escape from there, too.

One day I told Sister Paula about my friendship with No-Sister-Salvador and how we told each other all our secrets. I also described the death of my father and Bartomeu Camús's cruel fate years before. She responded that war was always unjust. War? The war in Spain ended in 1939. Camús and my father both died after the fighting had stopped, like trash that didn't get picked up on time. Even as we spoke, the Regime was shooting people down with firing squads as if they were targets at a carnival booth. Why couldn't Sister Paula realize that? Nevertheless, I ended up confiding in her about the promise I made to my father. The more I thought about it, the more I longed to break free of the Home.

"Ginés, this is absurd. You're only a fifteen-year-old boy."

"I'm about to turn sixteen."

"Fine, but it doesn't matter. An almost-sixteen-year-old boy can't go around digging up dead bodies. Do you hear me?"

"I've got it all planned out. I'll go up to Miranda de Ebro and find work, settle down, and wait for—"

"Enough, Ginés. Enough of this nonsense. At least wait until the six months are up and then you can decide what to do."

"I can't wait that long."

"Indeed you will, young man!" she cried, furious.

I was able to feel, smell, and look at Sister Paula. And at night, although my body was swathed in bandages, I would think about her and touch myself. And while cringing from the pain in my ribs and kidneys, I knew I was committing a double sin, since the impure act was directed toward purity itself. But the strangest thing is that I never felt any remorse about it at all.

I began, with restrictions, to return to my normal routine. The guards wouldn't leave me alone. Once again I was being constantly needled by Folquet. Sister Paula managed to get permission for me to eat my meals in the infirmary. She claimed that I required a reinforced diet in order to recuperate completely. That kept me in direct contact with her for a while longer. Sometimes I'd stay afterward and help her do the rounds, visiting the patients at their bedsides, as if I were her personal assistant. We never stopped chatting as I wheeled the medicine cart along. She'd get lost in her memories. How she abandoned the boy she was engaged to in order to embrace religion.

How she'd managed to cross over, safe and sound, to the National Zone during the war. I listened, and kept agreeing with everything she said.

My friends couldn't understand what had gotten into me. Nobody had told them a thing about my condition. I was acting slightly touched, and they assumed it was from the beating. It wouldn't have been the first time that a kid ended up losing a few marbles after an incident like that. It certainly didn't create any logistical problems for the Home. Instead of trying to treat the child, the nuns would simply transfer him to another section of the institution. They'd switch the kid over to the section for the mentally retarded and that was that, job done. I wasn't aware of how concerned the other wards were about me. All I wanted to do was go to the infirmary and feel Sister Paula's fingers running through my hair as she said good morning. And sense the growing stiffness around my fly.

That nun did everything she could to get the idea of running away out of my head. She never took her eyes off me. She went so far as to ask me if I'd like to help her and the doctor out in the infirmary.

"We can't manage on our own. The institution's administrators are considering training one of the wards as a nurse."

And that was how I ended up spending a few hours each day with Sister Paula, learning the basic techniques of medicine: emergency first aid, how to disinfect wounds, how to stop a hemorrhage, etc., etc.

I was tangled up in a web and on the verge of being trapped. I'd been hypnotized, half falling into the chloroform-like haze of Sister Paula's aroma: clean soap and a good family.

CHAPTER SIXTEEN

Monday, October 24, and Tuesday, October 25, 1949

I'm informed that the long-distance call to Barcelona has gone through and the voice at the other end of the line confirms that my two men are on the way. They'll be waiting for me tomorrow, Tuesday, morning in Logroño, with a set of collapsible picks and shovels disguised within bulky suitcases. So as not to arouse suspicions, they'll check into a decent hotel and wait for me. If everything goes as planned, in forty-eight hours, tops, we'll have thrown Bartomeu Camús's bones in a sack and be long gone. But now that I've gotten to know Eusebio, I'm worried about him. He'll be fine if the job goes smoothly. But if things go sour and we have to make a run for it, they'll be sure to question Eusebio first. After all, I've been asking everyone about him and the authorities know where he lives. In any case, I'm going to ask him if he wants to leave with us. Maybe he can make a new life for himself in Africa, by my side.

I go down to the reception area, and there's Campillo, glasses poised at the tip of his nose, settling up with a purveyor of siphons, soda water, and other refreshments. He takes me in, wide-eyed, and smiles. I leave the key at the front desk. There aren't many guests around, but even so, the pension doesn't seem to be doing too badly. The staff isn't very nosy around here, either. I've left little booby traps every day before going out to see if anyone's been tempted to snoop around while cleaning up the room. The answer is no.

I stand stock-still at the front desk. My thoughts turn back to Bartomeu Camús's declaration. Obviously my father was aware of its contents. And yet he didn't say anything about it to me. Why? I guess he wanted to make sure that I'd collect his friend's bones out of respect, and not as some sort of blackmail.

The fact that I'm still hanging around makes Campillo nervous. He sends the siphon guy packing.

"You'll have to excuse me," he says. "I'm not accustomed to dealing with purveyors in the middle of the reception area, but this fellow was in a rush . . ."

"No problem."

"Did you want something?"

"Yes, I'd like to hire a taxi. Are there any in Miranda?"

The man takes a second to bring himself under control. He's deeply offended.

"Yes, sir, certainly. We happen to have a taxi stand right next door, in Plaza Prim."

"Do you think you could arrange for one to pick me up after lunch?"

"I'm not sure. Why don't you go into the dining room and let me make a few calls. Exactly what time do you need it for?"

"Somewhere between four o'clock and four thirty."

He's not making this easy for me, and I'm anxious to be driving down the highway, following my father's directions. I need to give the terrain a preliminary once-over. Finding it won't be any problem; I've brought an Army map with me. There's the road that goes from Miranda to the boot camp, the same one that used to lead to the concentration camp. My father said they'd followed the banks of the river, crossing the train tracks a couple of times. The only major highway they could have encountered is the one that goes from Madrid to Irún.

In my excitement, I barely taste a pig trotter stew delicious enough to keep me riveted to the chair. Maybe Señora Campillo does exist after all. He's probably got her locked up in the kitchen, slaving away over a hot stove. But she's got a real flair for home-style cooking.

The taxi arrives before I get a chance to have a cup of coffee. I run up to my room, double check my father's map once more, and go back downstairs. I know those directions by heart, but I still bring the paper with me, along with the original copy of Bartomeu Camús's statement concerning Dr. Vallejo-Nágera.

Campillo is chatting away with the taxi driver. Everyone knows each other around here. The driver's a middle-aged man wearing a brimmed cap, which he promptly removes. You can tell he doesn't wear it very often; it's still shiny and new. Everything about him seems round. He's short and plump and his head, which doesn't have a single hair on it, is round, too. He steps toward me, timid and quiet. Campillo introduces us. The taxi is a Citroën in excellent condition. I congratulate him on his vehicle but am unable to extract more than a few monosyllables out of him.

"What year is that car from?" I ask.

He turns his back on me and answers, "Nineteen forty-two."

We go outside. As I climb into the taxi, I catch a glance of what seems to be someone across the street, but the shadow quickly vanishes among the plantings in the park.

"Where do you want to go?"

"Head toward the main highway."

"But where are we going?"

"Just get on that highway and I'll let you know later."

The man shrugs his shoulders, places the cap on his head, puts the car into first gear, and we take off.

I notice the driver peering at me in his rearview mirror. He asks, slightly annoyed, "Direction Madrid or direction Vitoria?"

My father told me that they carted Bartomeu Camús's body for about three quarters of an hour. They must have been heading away from Miranda; otherwise they would have hit the city itself. They would have been able to walk clean across town. And my father never mentioned anything about that. So they must have gone in the other direction. I point straight ahead to let him know we should keep going north and ask him to slow down. You can't get very far pushing a dead body in a cart for three quarters of an hour—one mile, maybe two and a half, tops. I press my face against the right-hand window and watch the scenery. So as not to give anything away, I pay particular attention to the milestones on the side of the road. I watch one, two, three, four, five, six, seven go by. There's nothing on the right side of the road that matches my father's description of the landscape. I ask the taxi driver to turn around once we've obviously gone too far. This is going to be more difficult than I thought. The countryside might have changed considerably over the last eight years. I may have to comb every foot of this highway. And with the taxi meter running, that's not an option.

We're cruising back toward Miranda. I shift over to the left-hand side of the vehicle to scan the same stretch of highway, but coming from the other direction. A mile or so farther, I happen to spot the rock from my father's description; round like a millstone. It's half hidden by brambles. The dirt road next to it, which I'd missed before, disappears into the fields. The taxi driver asks abruptly, "I might be able to help if you tell me what it is you're looking for."

I flash him a wide smile in the rearview mirror and tell him not to worry. It's nothing. I'm not looking for anything.

"I just wanted to go on a little drive, take in the scenery. We can head back to Miranda now."

The taxi drops me off at the casino. I take a stool at the bar. The proprietor steps up and immediately serves me a beer. I thank him, but he doesn't budge. He uses my scar as an excuse for making conversation. I get that a lot. But he certainly has an original way of going about it.

"That's some scar you've got there."

"Yes."

"It's huge."

"Yes, it is."

"Well, you should take care, especially in winter."

"Why?"

"Scar tissue is very delicate. Cold air whips right through it. Don't ask me for some scientific explanation, because I wouldn't be able to give it to you. All I know is that's the way it is. I have one, too; a war wound on my back. It's even more of an issue for you, since the scar is on your scalp. And you don't want to take any chances with your head."

If he starts insinuating my brain might work slower in the winter, go into deep freeze or something, I'll have to put him back in line. And I really don't feel like threatening the guy. I wait a few seconds. He doesn't continue.

"Thanks for the advice," I say.

"It's nothing."

Leaving, I run into the weekend waitress at the door, about to go inside. She's got her street clothes on and a little too much makeup. It doesn't seem like a bad idea to go right back into the casino. I offer to buy her a drink, forgetting that she's not allowed to accept. She replies, "If you want, we can go to a cafeteria not far from here, on the road to Bilbao. You can order as many drinks for me as you like there."

I give her the once-over, even though I know perfectly well that I won't be able to stand the touch of those mangled hands on my skin. I accept. It's not that late and I have to pass the time one way or another. We walk along, side by side, on this brisk, almost cold, fall afternoon. She doesn't say anything and simply shows me the way once in a while, pointing with a worn finger topped by a chipped nail. We walk a couple hundred feet along the edge of the highway and our shoes get covered in dust. The cafeteria turns out to be a restaurant bar called Venta del Cruce. The name mentions a cross-road, but I see only one wide stretch of road around here. The white one-story building is a typical roadside establishment, built like a shoe box with a peaked roof and bars on the windows. It's agonizingly dismal. There's one car and a Guardia Civil vehicle parked out front. Carmela opens the door confidently and goes in first. As we enter, we're hit by a gust of heat emanating from a woodstove in the corner. A couple of Guardias Civiles, wearing their regulation sleeved capes, have dropped in for a moment while doing their rounds. There's just one more customer and then the bartender. All four of them turn around, only for an instant. Carmela is clearly a familiar face. The bartender greets her with a friendly nod. The customer motions to the girl with an almost imperceptible tilt of his head and she responds in kind. There's a galley window connecting the kitchen and bar, so the smell of cooking mingles with the odor of firewood and tobacco smoke. One of the guards ventures, "Good afternoon, Carmelilla . . . and friend."

As usual, there's nothing I can do to keep them from staring. My Legionnaire-style beard attracts quite a bit of attention when I'm in civilian dress, not to mention the visual impact of my scar every time I remove my hat. But it isn't long before they leave me alone and go back to their conversation. They're discussing what for their profession is the big news of the day: The president of Portugal has appointed Franco as a general of the Portuguese armed forces. The youngest of the bunch can't quite comprehend the situation.

"How's he going to lead the nation that way?" he asks, adding in a perplexed tone, "If Franco is a Portuguese general, he's going to have to swear allegiance to the Portuguese flag."

"Are you an idiot or are you just pretending to be one? Do really think that the Generalíssimo would agree to swear before a foreign flag?"

"Well, I don't understand how you can be a general of a country and not swear allegiance to the flag. And even if it was possible, you'd have to pledge allegiance to two flags. What if one country declares war on the other? You'd be forced to choose and that would make you a traitor to both nations."

"Keep your voice down, you imbecile! You're calling Franco a traitor? Are you out of your mind?"

"You're right, Sergeant; let him promise to defend the Portuguese flag if he wants to. We won't stop him. He can simply break the vow whenever he sees fit. Anyway, it wouldn't be the first time; he already did it once before—in 1936."

"And aren't we lucky he did! Honor before discipline. And enough of your nonsense; you're giving me a headache. It's all symbolic. It's the same as when they declare His Excellency the honorary son of some city or another. What do you think, that the mayor asks him to present a birth certificate so it can be inscribed in the municipal registry? And Franco can do what he likes, that's that. That's the way he won the war and that's why he's the boss."

"But he won the war in Spain, not Portugal, and—"

"Enough is enough, damn it! You just don't get it. This kind of international politics is way over our heads."

The bartender is the only one listening, out of obligation, from behind the counter. The other customer takes his sweet time rolling a cigarette, never taking his eyes off the girl at my side. Carmela obviously feels at home in the gloomy, dust-covered establishment. We are seated at a corner table. A girl of about twenty-five and a sixty-year-old man appear at the bottom of some stairs at the back. The older guy is adjusting his tie. He keeps his eyes trained on the ground. The girl stops short at the bar, plopping down on one of the stools. The man heads straight for the door, without saying good-bye to his companion. Just as he's about to leave, the sergeant from the Guardia Civil calls out his name in a joking tone; Don Cirilo, Don Venancio, Don Fulgencio, something like that. The gentleman, dying from embarrassment, tips his hat without turning, as a sort of salutation, and keeps going. The second girl, a bit chunky, has her eye on the customer sitting at the bar, beyond the two guards. But the guy just keeps staring at Carmela. It's obvious that nice girls don't show their faces around the Venta del Cruce. A lady who must be the bartender's wife fills the kitchen door frame. The mustached and sallow-faced woman comes up to us and takes our order as if we were a couple of deadbeats as opposed to paying customers. Carmela orders the drinks without bothering to consult me. Then she relates a sordid and all too common tale chock-full of private miseries, dashed hopes, and a dismal future.

"At my age, and with a past like mine, I doubt I'll ever marry."

"What past?"

Carmela explains how, before the war, she worked in the office of a lumber company. She was the lover of the owner, an old Republican, who went so far as to set up a little love nest for her in Vitoria. But then the war broke out and the man was detained, sentenced, and shot, all in a matter of days. Carmela ran the company for a couple of months, until the wife discovered, thanks to a set of letters, exactly what sort of relationship her husband had maintained with the young woman. The wife wasn't content to simply fire Carmela;

she also denounced the girl anonymously to the Regime. Carmela was incarcerated in three different prisons around Castella la Vella before it was established that her relationship with the owner had been strictly sexual, not political. By the time she got back to Miranda, she was two years older and her hands were destroyed. She tried to make a life for herself in Madrid, but without much success. So the girl started to waitress at the casino. The proprietor of the establishment had been close friends with the owner of the lumber company. The two men used to tell each other everything. As a result, the proprietor started to chase after her, too.

"The problem is he's a cheapskate," she said, "not like his friend. He was a real gentleman."

She abruptly grows quiet, gives me a stare, and then casually mentions, "That's why I've only accepted to be his mistress sort of halfway. I've got to earn extra money somehow. Do you want to come upstairs with me?"

I stare at her. The thought of what she must do with those rough hands of hers sends chills down my spine. She gives me her price. It's incredibly cheap. I tell her I don't feel like it. She looks really disappointed. I pull a bill out anyway and drop it into the palm of her hand. Our fingers brush. The brief touch disgusts me. Of course, she cheers up immediately. She'll go home today with double pay for half the work. It's pretty obvious that the john in the fedora is hanging around for her. And, no matter how long it takes, he'll wait his turn. The Guardias Civiles keep glancing at me out of the corners of their eyes, but they're still obsessing over the Generalíssimo's spanking new double generalship. Carmela, like a good professional, doesn't give up.

"Are you sure there's nothing I can do for you?"

"You've done more than enough just by keeping me company."

Then a very specific request occurs to me out of the blue.

"Actually, may I ask a favor of you?"

With a coquettish gleam in her eye, Carmela gives me a mock salute, saying, "Legionnaire, I'll follow your every command."

"Perfect."

I rummage through my pockets and find a leftover envelope. I pull out my fountain pen and jot down the address. I give her the paper and she puts it away. The girl bids me good-bye and she stands up. Before I know it, she's heading up the stairs with the guy at the bar. She turns around for a second and waves.

The bartender's wife shoves her face, full of distrust, right up into mine, saying, "Don't get the wrong idea. This isn't some kind of a whorehouse. There aren't any rooms, private accommodations, or anything like that."

I observe the plump young lady at the bar for an instant. She gives me a smile, assuming that Carmela wasn't to my taste. The proprietress doesn't seem to notice and continues on with her harangue.

"Men and women come here for a glass of cognac, or some other refreshment. If they happen to go home together, that's their business. Carmela's an exception. She's like a member of the family. Once in a while she'll come here, do her thing, and then leave."

I look over again at the pudgy little whore and smirk. The proprietress notices, and continues, "Well, Reme also does her thing here, but that's another exception. She's a niece from the countryside. We took her in. She was starving."

I have absolutely no interest in hearing the sad tale of how this fat slut Reme fell into her aunt's clutches. I get up to go and pay for the drinks. The lady doesn't let up.

"This is a decent place of business. Understood?"

"Yes, ma'am, understood."

On my way back, I take one of the streets that runs parallel to the river. I get to a bridge, and even though it leads in the opposite direction of the pension, I walk across for the sheer pleasure of it. Gusts of wind sweep across the fields beyond in a perpendicular fashion, following the Ebro's course. The bridge is a solid-looking structure, about fifty years old, with a pair of majestic stone lions poised on each side, right in the middle. I glare at the one closest to me and he glares right back. The animal sits on his hind legs and observes the bridge's interior with his back to the river. He provides a temporary shelter from the wind. The lions flaunt gaudy diadems on their heads, crowns so oversize they seem to have been lent to the pair just so they could pose for sculptures. I found myself in quite the opposite situation shortly after joining the Legion. The tasseled beanie everyone had to wear seemed too small for my head, so the hat looked foolish on me. It didn't take much for me to feel ridiculous back then. I couldn't care less about the giant scar on my scalp, but I felt awfully silly in that useless beanie. Then I got to know a Legionnaire named Amedeo Rossi. He was an Italian who'd fought the Spanish war alongside the Fascist Expeditionary. He signed up for the Legion in order to avoid the Second World War. We became good friends and spent a lot of time together. I was eighteen and he was twenty-six. We'd often go for walks and end up down by the wharf, watching the ships filled with fresh troops as they embarked for the Peninsula. We'd sit outside at a café downtown that served decent coffee and stare at the young ladies of Melilla strolling by—the Spanish ones, that is. They normally went around in packs, trying to get some soldier to fall in love with them and spirit them far away. And we used to spend hours poking around the Moors' market stalls. You could find anything, from photography equipment to stranger things, like stuffed animals, desert roses, or even live falcons. . . .

One afternoon Amedeo announced that he felt like a fuck. He knew a brothel where the Moorish girls were really clean, and I was welcome to come along if I wanted. I agreed, but said I wouldn't go with a woman, that I didn't feel like catching any of their diseases. But really I was afraid he'd find out that I was a virgin. The Italian was a good-natured guy who assured me that there wasn't any chance of that, it was a very hygienic place. But if I didn't want to do anything, I could just have a soda or some coffee in the brothel's café, relax, and wait for him. He did his business, and then emerged from one of the establishment's little rooms. The madam, a Moor herself, asked him if it had gone well. He replied, *"Benissimo."* As was to be expected, the lady tried to encourage me to join in the fun. But I refused, telling her to leave me alone. To that she replied, "I know exactly what you'd like. Come with me!" She grabbed my arm and led me into a very well appointed room. Inside, there was a little girl. She couldn't have been older than eleven or twelve. Without letting go of my arm, the madam ordered the girl to play with the nice soldier. She pushed me into the room and slammed the door. The little girl removed the long top she was wearing and was left completely naked. Her breasts hadn't developed yet and there was nothing more than a wisp of hair curl-ing over her mound. In my shock, I barely noticed when she began to undress me. In no time, the only thing I was wearing was that ridiculous beanie. Without letting go of each other, we fell onto the bed. It was obvious the little Moor was less experienced than I was. She kept her legs pressed firmly together and simply lay there, her body as tense and rigid as a telephone pole. I was aroused and tried to force the girl's legs open, without success. Touching her like that, I ended up ejaculating all over the child without meaning to. I felt deeply ashamed and pushed her so hard that she fell off the bed and onto the floor. The little girl began to bawl as I ran out of the room, banging the door behind me. I was mad as a hyena and stark naked, clutching my clothes in one hand. The beanie was still firmly planted on my head. As the Italian and I left the brothel, I could hear the madam screaming at the child, whacking her several times for good measure. I was left feeling ridiculous and confused. Had I lost my virginity or not? Once I was back in the barracks and in a calmer frame of mind, I felt guilty about how I'd treated the girl. I went back to that brothel more than once to try to make amends, but I never found her.

Back at the hotel, I drift off to sleep and dream about Carmela and Bartomeu Camús. They're in the Venta del Cruce, hiding a group of ashen-skinned children whose eyes are as innocent as a baby goat's. The proprietress is in the dream, too. She's telling me about how Bartomeu is like a member of the family: "Once in a while he'll show up, do his thing, and then leave." Then she continues to insist that hers is a "decent establishment."

The next morning, when I come down for breakfast, I'm confronted by Major Cedazo. He's waiting for me at the bottom of the stairs. He's dressed in civilian garb, a snazzy hat, an overly snug gray wool blazer with matching pants, and patent-leather shoes worthy of a movie star.

"Good morning, Major."

"Good morning, Aleu. Is Campillo treating you well?"

"Do you two know each other?"

He gives me one of those smiles that somehow isn't a smile and says, "Everyone knows each other around here."

"Well, yes. I'd say I'm getting treated fairly well here."

"Good to hear; I'm glad. I'd like you to come away with the best possible memories of this place when you leave. Have you had breakfast already?"

"No."

"Perfect. May I join you then?"

"Of course."

"Campillo, bring us two hot chocolates and some fritters."

I have no idea what Cedazo wants. The first thing he does once seated is untie his shoes, take them off, and carefully place them between the four chair legs.

"Everyone in town knows that I have delicate feet. Everyone, that is, except my wife. She seems determined to inflict torture by forcing me to wear these shoes every time I go on a trip."

"Where are you going, if I may ask? Is it a long journey?"

"Madrid. Personal matters. Business. Are you a businessman?"

"I don't understand business and I don't ever want to."

He doesn't say anything for a few seconds, observing me with that icy smirk frozen on his face.

"That's very wise of you, Sergeant," he replies with agonizing slowness. "Once you start, it's hard to know where to stop."

Every time this guy opens his mouth, he makes me nervous.

Campillo serves up the chocolate and pastry. I don't care for chocolate and Campillo's known that since day one. Even still, the man sets the cup down in front of me without comment. Cedazo places the napkin against his chest, tying it securely behind his neck. He doesn't want to get stained. He begins to dip a fritter into the chocolate with a curious blend of frugality and greed. You can tell he's relishing every bite. He slows down his pace to make it last longer. Mouth full and midchew, he says:

"I understand. You're not interested in business matters because you've probably made a nice little nest egg for yourself down in Melilla. Am I right, Sergeant?"

"If you're asking me if I'm rich, the answer is no, on the contrary."

"I'm surprised. I understand that you hired a taxi to play tourist. That's a real luxury in this day and age. Why didn't you ask us over at the base for a vehicle, for Christ's sake? We would have let you cruise around all by your lonesome if that's what you wanted."

I restrain myself.

"I didn't want to be a nuisance."

The major's cold eyes, encrusted within an affable face, bore into mine.

"And where is it you wanted to go, if I may ask?"

"Nowhere. I was bored and went for a spin on impulse."

"That's what I imagined. That taxi driver is a good man and a good patriot named Evaristo. We military men give him quite a bit of business; he seemed to think that you were looking for something."

"I just wanted to let off some steam. The truth is I got bored pretty quickly. We only drove a few miles and then turned right back."

"Of course, of course. There aren't many places to go around here. But Miranda is a small town, and news gets around fast. By the way, my wife asked me to mention that she hopes you were able to make good use of the camera."

"It was perfect, thank you. I'll go up to the room right now and give it back to you."

"No need, my good man, no need. There's no rush. You can return it right before your departure. Then you'll have an excuse to come say good-bye to us. My wife was very pleased with your visit, you know. She keeps nagging me to invite you back. And I'm all for it, of course."

"Thank you."

"It's a shame you have to go, isn't it?"

"Yes. I suppose I'll stay until the day after tomorrow, or maybe the day after that."

"From now on, whenever you need something, come directly to me first. Don't waste time and money driving around in circles and paying taxis. That's an order."

"Understood."

"Are you sure you don't want any more chocolate?"

"No, thank you."

The major's really making me nervous. He's clearly suspicious about my little jaunt in the taxi. He doesn't seem to know about anything else. I'll have to be very cautious from now on. The major calmly downs the last bites of his breakfast. After taking an inordinate amount of time to put his shoes on, he gets to his feet. I try to follow suit, but he intervenes.

"Finish, my good man, finish. Don't rush away from your chocolate. After all, you've barely touched it . . ."

There are all kinds of military men. It's a question of figuring out which kind you're dealing with and handling them accordingly. The unpredictable fools and the ruthlessly ambitious types are often the most dangerous. Major Cedazo seems to be a combination of the two. He reminds me of a captain in the Legion named Julián Bajolmonte. When the Baron of Remei sent me to Africa, he arranged for me to be placed in this captain's service, as his assistant, from the age of sixteen to eighteen. The captain was a cold and calculating man, alcoholic and ambitious. He had an image of Christ's agonized face tattooed on his arm. His sorrowful expression was topped off with a crown of thorns, complete with drops of blood coursing down his cheeks. A legend inscribed beneath the image read, "He forgives, I don't." The captain spent his free time smuggling various materials that had become scarce on the Peninsula. One of these was rubber. Fishermen in the Canary Islands harvested it out of the ocean from Allied ships that had been sunk by Nazi submarines. The contraband was dumped on a Moroccan beach and eventually ended up in a warehouse in Melilla, which also happened to be the center of Captain Bajolmonte's operations. The rubber was sold on the black market to companies that desperately needed the material to fabricate car tires and were willing to pay a good price for it. Most of those businesses had been granted lucrative contracts from both the State and various transportation companies. The captain also dealt with gasoline, which, at the time, was more precious than gold. Thanks to his position in the military, he managed to steal gas—in small quantities—from the Army. If there was a delivery of three hundred gallons, two hundred and ninety would go to the Legion. He'd keep ten for himself.

I found myself up to my neck in the whole operation; I never had a choice in the matter. The captain trusted me more than he did his own wife. She was completely oblivious to her husband's dirty dealings and assumed that the salary of a Legionnaire was what kept them in the lap of luxury. Every time a deal went off well, he'd throw an exorbitant tip my way. I became an official member of the Legion after turning eighteen in October of '43. It goes without saying that they placed me under his command. He kept up those fraudulent activities, and I with him, until the end of the Second World War. That's when he decided that it was no longer necessary to nestle beneath the Legion's protective wing. He left the military in order to dedicate himself fully to business. He started a couple of import-export companies to cover up what was actually his new, main source of income—war supplies abandoned by the Allies.

The captain hired a small army of deadbeats to comb the Sahara Desert and the beaches of Morocco, Algeria, and Tunisia in search of equipment that had been cast off by Rommel's Afrika Korps and the Allied troops. There was quite a bit of profit to be made, even though occasionally his men had to literally fight with other interested parties for the booty. He'd asked me if I wanted to be included in this new phase of his career as general director, offering a salary that made me dizzy. He was completely taken aback when I refused. I had another objective in mind, and in order to achieve it, I would need to stay in the Legion for a few more years. Strangely enough, he trusted me when I solemnly vowed to never utter a word concerning his business practices.

About two years ago the captain and his wife were found murdered in their home. Beneath the tattoo of Christ and the inked words "He forgives, I don't," a note had been nailed to Bajolmonte's inert, headless body. It said, "Neither do we." His severed cranium had been attached to his wife's body in what one could only interpret as the last word regarding his manhood. His wife's head was never found.

I thank the major once again for the use of his camera. As I watch him leave, I get the sensation that his icy smile has somehow penetrated my skin. I try to calm down a little. The taxi driver couldn't possibly have figured out what I was up to. I observe the major's labored retreat. Before disappearing through the door, he turns around for a moment, and waves good-bye.

CHAPTER SEVENTEEN

One day in October I received a package. The smallish cardboard box was wrapped in brown paper and tied up in thin string. It was from my mother. This gave me quite a jolt. By that time I'd lost contact with the outside world. I'd practically forgotten all about her, it had been such a long time since I'd had any news from her or No-Sister-Salvador. The package contained an envelope and a small leather bag. In the letter, my mother wished me a happy birthday. She told me not to worry on her account, that she was feeling better, adding, "Your grandmother is a real taskmaster, but it keeps my mind off things. I'm so sorry I haven't been able to visit, but it's impossible. I'm broke." She also said she was sending me some snapshots to keep her face fresh in my memory, that even though we were far apart and couldn't see one another, she was still my mother, and that I was in her thoughts every single day. Most of the pictures had been taken before the war. In one, she and I were both perched on my father's painting scaffold, our legs dangling as we pointed at one of my father's half-finished signs. Another showed the three of us dressed in our Sunday best. I stood between my mother and father with both of them holding my hands so hard that my scrawny body scarcely seemed to touch the ground. And there was that photo taken on the Rambla during wartime, without my father: Señor Pau and No-Sister-Salvador standing behind my seated mother with me at her feet.

I began to weep inconsolably, hardly noticing the tears as they flowed down my cheeks. I opened the little leather bag. It was a wrist-watch. My mother said that, at the age of sixteen, I was man enough to wear my father's watch.

I wiped the snot from my face with my sleeve and took a couple of deep breaths. That's when the scales fell from my eyes. Spurred on by shame and a sense of finality, I saw things as they really were. But it wasn't really the end of anything; nothing had started yet. But it was like being woken from an enchantment or like when the curtain goes down on a play. And it had all come to a head in one exact moment. I was going to get the hell out of the Charity Home as soon as pos-sible. Nobody would be able to stop me, not even Sister Paula. I even had a pretty good idea of how I was going to do it.

The opportunity presented itself three Sundays later. As usual, I spent the entire morning in church. The first two masses were held for the Charity Home inmates and were segregated by sex. Afterward there was a service open to the entire community. It was attended by people from all over Barcelona. They came because it was such a lovely church and the mass had a gaudy solemnity to it, what with the choir and the organ. The worshippers tried to measure up to the pomp, you could see—and smell, too, they were so clean and gussied up. I had to attend all three services. As soon as I'd recovered from my beating at the hands of the guards, they had put me straight back to the onerous task of pedaling that organ. My escape plan was intri-cately simple. I'd take advantage of the public mass and try to blend in with the normal citizens as they filed out of the church. Once on the street, I'd make a run for it.

That Sunday, from my perch up in the choir stalls, I watched the worshippers trickle in and take their seats. The women sat on the right, and the men on the left. I followed the entire ceremony with anxious attention. To help ensure my success, I'd decided not to take anything with me. Well, nothing that anyone would notice, I should say, because my father's watch was in one pocket and the photos sent by my mother were in the other. The idea was to dress like a regular young boy attending mass with his family. I was wearing, hidden beneath the Home's regulation smock, my Sunday best: striped short pants, a collarless shirt, gray sweater, dress socks, and recently shined shoes. I'd tucked a beret into yet another pocket.

The mass ended and the faithful began to make their way outside, first bending at the knee and then crossing themselves before they left. I exited the choir stalls with my companions, making sure to lag behind. In a swift dodge, I pulled away from the group, as if somebody had suddenly caught my attention. Luckily, the mass had been well attended. Leaving in an orderly fashion, the faithful paused at the door, squinting up their eyes against the blinding light that cascaded into the cloister from the Manning courtyard. Hiding behind one of the confessionals at the front of the church, I whipped off my smock. I threw it into a corner and, all decked out in my finery, resolutely lost myself in the crowd. There was a cop from the Barcelona police posted at the main entrance on Montalegre Street. He was even dumber than the others, flaunting his gun and uniform with pride. The guy was having a nice little chat with Folquet, the guard who had beaten me up. I picked out a group of women and a young girl who were heading toward the street with their prayer books and black-lace head scarves. I decided that they would be my family.

Actually, there were only three of them, two older women, most likely sisters, and a girl of about thirteen who must have been the daughter of one of them. I didn't make my move until they'd almost crossed the courtyard and were about to reach the entrance to the street. I stuck the beret on my head. It wasn't so much to cover my scar as to hide my closely shorn scalp, which would've attracted unwanted attention. I waited and then saw that the cop and the guard were busy talking to another man who had stopped to say hello. I had to get past them without being seen. Even if they somehow spotted me, I would have to fool them only for a moment. That would be enough time to get a sufficient head start and make my getaway. And the time had come. Instead of rushing directly for the door, I headed toward the two women and the girl, who were still making their way to the exit at a leisurely pace. I slipped among them as though I were a wayward nephew running to catch up. I even raised my arm a bit, as if trying to call their attention. I walked along next to them as they were about to pass through the street entrance, making it look like we were all together. The two women didn't even notice, but the girl seemed to think it was strange. I gave her a grin and then kept my gaze nailed to the ground. We crossed through those wide doors, painted a bright, chili pepper red. I stayed by their side once we were on the street. That's when the girl, who hadn't taken her eyes off me all the while, said to her mother, "Mama, I don't know what this boy wants."

The two women stopped short in the middle of the street to see what she was talking about. I lifted my head and returned their stare. It was in that exact moment that I heard the guard at the door bellow, "Aleu! Where do you think you're going? Get back here!"

It all happened in a few split seconds. Folquet grabbed me by the arm. I twisted around and slammed my knee into his balls. I tore myself from his grasp as he fell, smashing that very same knee into his face. I left him there on the ground with blood pouring from his

nose, and broke into a run down the street. I felt exalted by a mixture of excitement and fear. I didn't run, I flew. And it was mostly the
vision of Folquet clutching his balls that gave my feet wings. The cop
screamed bloody murder and tried to chase after me. I glanced back
when I got to Carme Street and saw that he was still on my tail. But
I wasn't afraid, he was nothing. Even if the guy had had three legs
and I'd happened to be missing one, he still couldn't have caught me.
The cop was a hulking man, flabby and slow. He kept up the chase
for a little while, but it was no use. The guy lost me in the neighborhood's twisting little streets. As soon as I'd convinced myself that the
danger had passed, I stopped to catch my breath and calm myself
down. I had to get back to the apartment building fast and hope that
I'd get lucky and catch No-Sister-Salvador at home. If not, I'd go
straight to the tower and hide out. I tried to blend in and continued
on my way. It was important to keep my nervousness in check and
not get frightened. Everything looked different, even old, familiar
places. I was a little overwhelmed. It felt strange to be out on a Sunday among so many people who, rich or poor, were all dressed up
and on their way home after having gone for a stroll, buying a pastry, or what have you. It was surprising to see so many adults wandering around aimlessly or, on the contrary, walking with firm
decision, confident as to where they'd come from and where they
were going. I also noticed pedestrians like me who, worn-out, dazed,
and disoriented, simply gazed vacantly ahead. I was afraid of catching somebody's attention, but nothing happened. Nobody paid any
mind to me. The people on the Rambla went along chatting about
their days and drinking their aperitifs.

I turned onto Ferran Street. Now I was getting close to home. I
passed by a used bookstore that happened to be open even though it
was Sunday. They were doing inventory. The very presence of all
those books displayed in the shop window—with their long-dead

writers and pompous titles—annoyed me, but I couldn't say why. There were also etchings of antique maps depicting far-off cities and countries. One had a conquistador in the corner, sinking his sword into the sands of some exotic beach as a lion looked on. The beast appeared to be wondering if such a pallid, discolored human might not be tastier than his normal fare of indigenous folk. Thousands of stories came to my head as I contemplated that shopwindow. Perhaps one of them would be my destiny. Peering through the open door, I noticed an old man at the back of the shop, sitting in a low chair more appropriate for a small child. He was brushing the dust off the most antique, fragile tomes, his eyes focusing intently upward. I followed his gaze and realized that it was trained on the legs of an extremely young woman balancing on the top of a wooden ladder. She was diligently going through the rows of books lining the higher shelves. Each time she reached for another volume, her skirt rose slightly, allowing for a tantalizing glimpse of her lower thighs. She'd grab a handful of books, climb down, pass them to the old man, and climb back up again. Once in a while the clouds of dust would make her turn away, grimacing and screwing her eyes shut. Whenever she sneezed, her whole body shuddered. I stood there staring at her legs like a fool, mouth hanging wide open. They were shapely and white. Finally the old man caught me. I got scared and broke into a run again. I was free. As foolish as ever. Those five minutes of distraction could have cost me my liberty. But I was still free.

In the blink of an eye I was on Caputxes Street. I had to dodge a car, the back end of an autobus, and the front of a double-decker tramcar, the likes of which I'd never seen before. A metal bar connected it to an electric cable; it didn't even need to ride on tracks.

I bounded up the stairs in a flash. I began to knock on the door, crying out in a soft voice, "Salvador . . . Salvador . . ."

I could hear him lurch forward with that uneven gait from his lame leg. No-Sister-Salvador's apartment hadn't changed a bit. It was exactly as I remembered it, from the furniture down to the very odor of the family who'd lived in that house for over fifty years. The smell of Señor Pau and his wife, Señora Nadala. Salvador was living there somewhat illegally. He'd neglected to inform the landlord that the guy whose name was on the lease had been dead for over two years. He just kept paying the rent each month, and nobody seemed to notice.

"They told me at the Charity Home that you almost murdered one of the guards. Is that true?"

"No, I only scared him a little."

"But weren't you punished with not going out for six months or having any contact with the outside world?"

"That's right."

"So what are you doing here?"

"I escaped."

Shock was clearly written on Salvador's face. He'd start a sentence and not be able to finish. Salvador attempted to gently explain something I already knew. This time, if I got caught, nothing would save me from going to a correctional facility, the Duran Asylum. I firmly let him know that I didn't plan on getting caught. I laid out my plan. I'd hide out in the tower for a while until they forgot the whole thing or gave me up for lost. After all, to them I was nothing more than some little rat who'd escaped from the poorhouse. Afterward I'd make my way to Miranda de Ebro in order to fulfill my promise.

"I'll fill in the details while we walk, Salvador. Right now we've got to get over to the tower. The guards could be here any minute. This is the first place they'll come looking for me."

We went up to the roof, jumped onto the adjoining terrace, and pulled aside the ceramic pot that hid the entrance to the tower.

No-Sister-Salvador hadn't been there in a while, so it was pretty dirty and run-down, but I didn't care. All the memories came rushing back as soon as I stuck my head out of the window facing the cathedral, Santa Maria del Mar. The tower may have been a wonderful hiding place, but once inside, you could spy on the world below. The entire neighborhood of La Ribera, a sea of roofs, lay at your feet. All the streets and little alleyways, the carts and tricycles. There were trucks going to and from the Born Market, piled high with vegetables— heads of lettuce, glistening with drops of water; tightly packed cabbages; broccoli; and the red flash of tomatoes. My family had called that neighborhood home for generations. My father had shown me all the landmarks from his childhood. He'd play on the street while the adults enjoyed the fresh air out on the sidewalk. And my mother, also born and bred on those streets, had showed me where she'd gone to take sewing classes or where her mother, my grandmother, had sold oil and soap until she got fed up and went off to Caldes de Malavella to be a tenant farmer. And the tower afforded an impressive view of the lodestar of our existence, the queen of those twisting alleyways: the compact mass of Santa Maria del Mar, the cathedral of the people.

No-Sister-Salvador brought me a little bread and cheese along with a jug of water. He explained that the vehicle I'd been so impressed with before was called a trolley.

"A lot of buses were left idle after the war since there wasn't any gasoline or replacement parts. This is a good way to put them back on the street."

That said, he left. In order to relieve myself, I simply scrambled down to the tower's entrance. Salvador had placed a chamber pot there and would make sure it got emptied on a regular basis. We agreed that he'd bring me newspapers and food. And that he'd exercise extreme caution. I was bursting with pride. For a second it felt like when I was little and he'd bring me up to the tower in the afternoon after picking me up from public school. It was his secret hiding place. He was willing to be friends with me, despite being five years older. If anyone has any idea what it means to a nine-year-old child to be close friends and share secrets with an older, fourteen-year-old boy, then they'll know what I mean. It was pure happiness. Now, for the very first time, I was the one who was setting the pace of our relationship. And, as always, I could trust him. As soon as he'd let me in the door, Salvador realized that it was no longer a question of treating me "as if" we were equals. He'd sensed that we had actually become equals. And, as always, he was determined to stay by my side.

Government officials arrived at our apartment building within the hour. I could hear them banging on the door that led from the stairwell onto the roof. Peeking through the cracks of the closest window shutter, I watched as a pair of Charity Home guards turned everything upside down. They scrutinized the small washing area on the roof carefully, even doing some gymnastics to get on top of the water tower. They went over to the iron balustrade separating one roof from another, and scanned the horizon for me. They didn't seem very dedicated. Since they were lazy and their supervisors weren't nearby, they figured it wasn't worth the effort to jump over the fence for a quick check of the terrace next door. Barcelona could be traversed from Llobregat to Besos without touching the ground; all you had to do was leap from one adjoining roof to the next. And, of course, if they searched one roof, they'd have to search them all. The guards turned on their tails.

Once the guards were gone, No-Sister-Salvador told me that they had been accompanied by the head secretary of the Charity Home.

"I was officially informed, as your legal guardian, that you'd escaped. They said there'd be serious consequences if you didn't return within twenty-four hours. And that I could be sent to prison if I with-held information as to your whereabouts."

"Don't believe a word of it. They're only trying to scare you."

"I suppose you're right."

We had dinner together up in the tower, just like old times. The sounds of the city began to wane. Salvador told me what he'd been doing those last few months. Thanks to one of my father's nice suit jackets, which my mother had altered for him before leaving, Salvador had been able to find work as a salesman for Mandri Laboratories. He made the rounds of all the pharmacies in Barcelona, toting Señor Pau's old sample suitcase filled with bottles of Cerebrino Mandri elixir.

"Not only that, but since glass is so scarce, Mandri Laboratories has asked its customers to return the empty Cerebrino bottles. They pay twenty-five centims a bottle if you bring them directly to the warehouse, clean and label-free. When I stop by the pharmacies to fill their orders of Cerebrino, I always pick up the empties of the lazy clients who don't want to bother bringing them all the way to the laboratory headquarters. I give them ten centims on the bottle, spotless or filthy, label or no label. Once I get them home, I wash them, soak the labels off, and bring them to the laboratory. The result is a clean profit, you might say, of fifteen centims per empty container."

He was still working at the Born Market, too, unloading and loading goods. He delivered produce by cart, even dropping off goods at various grocery stores. Restaurants would sometimes hire him to help out in the kitchen or work as a waiter when they needed backup for weddings, birthdays, and so on. The pay was miserable. But he worked, so to speak, for the tips and food that he managed to squirrel away on the sly. His whole face lit up before I could even finish asking him about what those celebrations were like; he underwent a complete transformation. Striding around the tower as he talked, Salvador even seemed to have a firmer, more even step.

"I got a job as a waiter at the Marquis de Fonter's house, in San Gervasi. It was an incredibly elegant coming-out party for the nobleman's daughter, held outdoors."

"What's a 'coming-out party'?"

"I'm not exactly sure. From what I could tell by the event itself, it seemed like her parents were announcing, 'Our little girl has grown up and is currently available.'"

"Available for what?"

"What do you think? Don't be an ass. Available for whoever wants to court her . . . as long as they're of their kind. Rich people are like that, they keep to themselves. This way, the girl's parents can rest assured that she'll end up with a boy from a good family. Anyway, the marquis and his wife, accompanied by their daughter, greeted the guests as they arrived. You should have seen it, generals, priests, a bishop, grand ladies, people of all sorts, consuls. There was even a pair of German soldiers. Everyone presented the girl with a gift when they walked in. She accepted each package, but didn't open a single one. They were left piled up on a table. The headwaiter told us that some of the most well-known members of Barcelona's high society numbered among the guests, not to mention military men, diplomats, and politicians. They dressed me up in an all-white uniform that was too big for me, with black patent-leather shoes. It had a short jacket with a bow at the neck. I might as well have been hired to sing boleros. What an estate! What a garden! It was grand. They'd hung strings of colored lights in the trees, can you imagine? The house's veranda was illuminated from below by violet lamps, as if it were some sort of monument. They'd set up a wooden platform on top of the tennis court for dancing. I bet you're wondering why they didn't just dance directly on the court itself, right?"

"Well, why didn't they?"

"Because the court's red sand would have stained the shoes of all the ladies!"

"Oh!"

"The orchestra was set up right alongside, the same one that plays at the Monterrey. They went out of their way to get Antonio Machín to sing at the festivities. It seems that he had a performance at an exclusive country club the next week and the marquis convinced him to come a few days early to be able to sing for the guests at the party. The music could be heard throughout the grounds, since there were speakers set up all over the garden. The marquis had a man playing zarzuelas in an intimate little clearing surrounded by trees. A stall serving orxata was set up on the other side of the house, off in a corner. They'd gotten an orxata maker to come expressly from Valencia, along with his wife and son. All three of them were dressed in traditional Valencian costume. The marquis made a speech. When it was over, everybody shouted, "Long live Spain! Long live Franco!" and then the guests attacked the food and drink. The dancing didn't let up all night. Machín's songs, so slow and sweet, helped set the mood. Even though the air was pretty stifling, the young ladies and gentlemen didn't sweat while they danced."

"What do you mean, the rich don't sweat?"

"Look, I don't how they manage it, but that's how it looked to me."

"I don't buy it. Everybody sweats, except for dogs. That's why they've always got their tongues hanging out. Did your rich folks have their tongues sticking out, by any chance?"

"No."

"Then they were sweating for sure."

"Enough already! Who gives a shit if they were sweating or not? The thing is, me being lame and all, they said it wouldn't look good

if I were seen wandering among the guests, canapé tray in hand, with
my gimp leg. So I got stuck behind the drinks table. So much the
better; that way I could relax and take everything in. It was like being
at the cinema. I only had to pour and serve. The guests came up to
the table to ask for drinks in little groups. Everyone looked so assured
and calm; I couldn't help but wonder what they were talking about.
They were probably exchanging the latest news from the world of
business, or maybe politics; intelligent people conversing on intelligent topics. I also noticed how the wealthy seem to be constantly
flirting. The party host came up to ask for a drink, accompanied by
a woman in her forties, as scrawny as a piece of dried cod, but with
one of those enormous filigreed combs planted on the top of her
head. The lady was wearing a very fancy dress of bone-colored silk in
the latest fashion. She was the wife of one of the other guests. The
man was saying to her, 'But what are you complaining about? Your
waist is the envy of all the other ladies here, and I shouldn't be saying that, since I include my wife in that number . . . Shall we make
a toast?' The lady clucked like a chicken, replying in a coquettish
voice, 'Hush, hush, you crazy man. Don't you ever stop?' And he answered, 'To our health—including your husband's, of course.' The
marquis' daughter, whose name was Judith, was wearing a long white
summer dress, even though it was already October. Young men kept
asking her to dance, but she refused them all at first. She also came
up to me at one point with an empty glass. I'd never been so close to
a rich girl before. She was one of those girls with narrow shoulders
and a big bottom, but a really sweet smile. She held out her glass and
I filled it with champagne. Instead of moving away afterward, she remained standing right in front of me. I saw she was looking off in another direction. I thought she must have been embarrassed to be in
front of so many people. But no, she was following the movements
of one of the guests, a young man in his twenties, very swarthy, who

was walking quickly past her. It was obvious that they knew each other and she smiled at him. The kid avoided her eyes, wrinkling up his nose as if he'd caught a whiff of shit. I felt sorry for her—so rich and yet the guy didn't want her. I was about to say something, but luckily she headed off to the dancing platform and didn't stop waltzing all night. Personally, I think rich girls must be more beautiful from the day they're born."

No-Sister-Salvador had told me the whole thing seemed like a movie. And it was for precisely that reason that I didn't think he should be very jealous of the marquis. Everyone knows that movies are make-believe. And maybe everything he'd seen that night had been a lie, too.

He sighed and let his tale trail off, then exclaimed, "I'll be right back!" And he ran off toward his house.

Salvador appeared five minutes later with a package. He undid the brown paper, revealing six sandwiches from that same party, made of ham and butter. He handed me three. The bread was a little dried out, but we relished them as if they'd been the tastiest delicacy in the world. That was the only payment he received for his labors.

"The organizer told me I should consider myself satisfied. That in the long run, it was far more worthwhile to be able to say that I'd served all those important people, instead of having earned a couple of miserable pesetas."

It grew dark around us as we talked and talked. I explained to him how the two guards had nearly beaten me to death. And yet I couldn't be too bitter. If I hadn't been pummeled so hard, I never would've gotten to know Sister Paula so well.

"Sister would lean right over me as she'd spoon soup into my mouth and I'd try to separate out her specific scent from the odor of cooked vegetables. And sometimes it worked. I'd close my eyes, but she'd make me open them again, telling me to stop clowning around. But whenever I did, her eyes would suddenly be so close to mine that my whole body, from head to foot, would be thrown into a confusion of sensations. Despite being so weak from the beating, I'm ashamed to admit the things that happened under those sheets."

"What kinds of things?"

That's when he fell down on the floor in a fit of hysterical laughter. And he told me not to worry. Finally I was beginning to have normal reactions.

"Too bad she's a nun."

"But why does that happen?"

"Damn it, Ginés, because you're a sixteen-year-old boy!"

I convinced Salvador that he shouldn't sleep over, it was too dangerous. I sent him home with the precaution to keep his eyes and ears open. He'd bring news and come check in on me the next day, sometime in the morning.

Our old solemn pact of mutual assistance had automatically been put into effect.

I scanned the sky, curling my fingers into pretend binoculars, just like the old times. It had been two years since the bombardments had ceased. The silence at night in Barcelona, or of any city, is very different from other silences. Silence in the city isn't quiet at all. When a city sleeps, it's like a giant taking a nap, allowing himself a short rest, which lasts only as long as the darkness does and is punctuated by his snores. It's an ambiguous, oppressive silence. And for me, in those moments, it was merely a lull in the battle. It was a silence pregnant with sounds.

I had planned on hiding out in the tower for a month or two, if necessary. As it turned out, I was there for only three days. But I didn't know that it would be so short then. And I wouldn't be alone when

I left the hideout. Two companions, who hadn't been looking for or expecting any sort of trouble, were dragged down with me. The tower had a magnetic quality to it. The space drew people in and swallowed them up. It devoured me, consumed my friend and companion No-Sister-Salvador, and gobbled up the Baron of Remei's only child, Sister Paula. Then the tower proceeded to spit us out in all directions, as if, after having trouble digesting what it had just eaten so ravenously, it vomited us up without thinking twice.

CHAPTER EIGHTEEN

Tuesday, October 25, 1949

I call Eusebio from the reception desk. Because he is from a family of bakers, his house is one of the few in the village to have a telephone. I ask him if he's made up his mind as to whether he'll help me or not, but he dodges the question.

"Why don't we meet?" I suggest. "I want to make you a proposition."

"What kind?"

"It's concerning your future."

"I don't have one of those," he replies, more out of cynicism than resignation.

Desperately in need of his assistance, I refuse to give up.

"I have something very important to tell you. Help me out, even if it's just for old times' sake."

"The old times are so old, they're already dead."

The man bursts into a fit of hacking coughs. It gives credence to his dire outlook on the future. He deliberates for a few more moments but ends up saying yes.

"I've finished the morning's bread deliveries. We can meet an hour from now, if you like."

"Do you know the Venta del Cruce?"

"Who doesn't?" he says teasingly. "I see that Legionnaires have a good nose for sniffing out that sort of thing."

"It's not what you think. Is it discreet enough?"

"Yes. Wait for me outside, by the highway. I'll be on time."

"Understood."

I go back to the dining room and push the cups of chocolate out of my way. The major's cup has been licked completely clean. I tell Campillo to bring me some real breakfast. He hands me today's newspaper. I read that His Excellency, the Generalíssimo, has been appointed by the distinguished University of Coimbra as doctor *Honoris causa.* This crap is going to end up driving me insane. The newspaper says that the students gave Franco, the martial gentleman of letters, a resounding welcome. Before, he was sporting the sash of a general of the Portuguese Army; now he's wearing the cap and gown of a doctor of the University of Coimbra. It's madness. Franco appears in the newspaper photos with a fucking tassel swinging in his face. I can't tear my eyes off the image. The Regime has no shame. And the guy who wrote the article doesn't either. He presents the event as some sort of divine justice. Francisco Franco embodies the fusion of the university and the military—wisdom conjoined with arms. The reporter is probably in love with the Generalíssimo.

Who would deny the Generalíssimo's prowess with the sword? Without it, Spanish culture would have sunk into misery and abject mesocracy. Franco holds Christian civilization and culture, which he saved from catastrophe, in the palm of his hand. Franco is a military genius, but he's a political mastermind as well.

I give up. It's unbearable. The newspapers are drooling all over the place, and so are the politicians. Everyone's slobbering everywhere. Even more than in other totalitarian regimes, the General's subjects seem to be enthralled by an almost insane desire for their lord and master. Countless people, like the writer of this article, are torn between admiration and an almost sexual passion for their leader. This newspaper reporter would gladly drop his pants and be sodomized with pride if that were His Excellency's wish.

> The Generalíssimo of the Army, savior of Spain, has seen fit
> to ram his entire manliness as deep up my ass as it will go. It is
> an undeserved honor. I will refrain from defecating until my
> bowels burst in order to hold that august, forthright, and his-
> torical anal penetration dear to my memory for as long as
> possible.

Campillo has just placed a plate of sliced fried sausage from Burgos and a glass of wine in front of me. He's drooling, too. I show him the photo of Franco tricked up as a doctor *Honoris causa* and ask him what he thinks. Sighing like a lovelorn damsel, he says, "Look, it's not just because he's Franco, but what can I say, he's got distinction, a savoir faire . . . God forbid that I seem disrespectful, but what with him and Doña Carmen constantly being photographed with the Portuguese lately . . . Well, there's no comparison, they look like peasants dressed up in their Sunday clothes."

"Who, Franco and his wife?"

Campillo panics as if I'd called up the devil himself.

"Sergeant Aleu. Please, what do you take me for? I was referring to the Portuguese! We're so lucky . . ."

Campillo thinks that Spain is lucky to have Franco in power. I, on the other hand, haven't had much luck at all. His Regime killed my father, my father's best friend, and my dearest friend. They drove my mother to neurasthenia and made a monster out of me. No, I'm nothing like that reporter from the local newspaper. I'm not madly in love with Franco.

Two truckers, leaning against the bar, have been making a racket for quite some time now. They're massive, tall men, taking up the space of four people and babbling loudly. A couple of giant bags of salted sunflower seeds are set in front of them, ready to be brought on their travels. They're explaining to the waiter how sunflower seeds are the best antidote to falling asleep at the wheel. The two argue, and each time one of them bangs his fist down on the bar, a little bit of the neighboring customer's coffee slurps over the side of the cup. He's a guy with sunken cheeks and a melancholy look in his eye, wearing the dark blue jumpsuit of a laborer. A small case lies at his feet. He doesn't seem to be a mechanic, more like an electrician or a plumber. Whoever he is, he's got a worn face. It's clear he's broken down and depressed. He doesn't give a shit if the truckers spill his coffee. I ask Campillo who the guy in the jumpsuit is, and he instantly jumps to an explanation.

"That fellow's a telephone technician, a specialist sent over from Burgos."

Now I understand everything. Here's a jerk who doesn't get the least bit of pleasure out of traveling far from home to repair some telephone lines, freezing his ass out in the middle of fucking Highway Number One, Madrid–Irún. And worse yet, he has to do it all in that awful blue jumpsuit. I like the guy. I don't have the same opinion of those two truckers at the bar, who continue to force the whole restaurant to listen to their idiotic opinions on a wide range of issues. One of them, a guy with a savage face and fingers like Cantimpalo sausages from years of grappling with a steering wheel, says that life is all about natural selection:

"It's been heard and said many times, but it's true all right, the big fish eats the little fish."

The other one agrees, wiping the beer froth dripping off his mustache while spitting a sunflower seed onto the ground. The fat-fingered fellow continues.

"As long as there are goods to sell, they'll always need truck drivers to haul it around. And that's that."

The imbecile offers a couple of other examples as incontrovertible proof that even if the world were to fall apart, truck drivers would survive. They're getting on my nerves. Anyway, I can't stand people who feel the need to emphasize their opinions by saying "and that's that." I wouldn't mind pulling out my pistol right here, shoving it against their balls, and watching them get scared shitless. The cheap philosophy of a trucker: The big fish eats the little fish. That may be true, but the big fish had better hurry up, because before he knows it, he'll find out that the little fish is all grown-up. And nobody's going to be eating him when that happens. The truckers keep chomping down on sunflower seeds, spitting the shells onto the ground, and drinking beer. They're in no rush. They switch from cheap philosophy to jokes, in bad taste but harmless. They're all about women, of course, as vulgar as they are naïve and passed down from one generation to the next. Those jokes were around before the war, got trotted out for a laugh during the fighting, and still make their appearances today. Not every aspect of life has been drowned in the Regime's sea of mediocrity.

The truck drivers turn around and notice that I'm scowling at them. They don't know quite what to think of me, and I can understand why. A twenty-four-year-old with a beard full of tangles and a buzz cut bisected by a giant swathe of scar tissue on his head, extending from the left temple down to the ear. If these were earlier times, they'd try to catch my attention, either to pick a fight or to offer me something to drink. I'd have become a member of their club, Sages of the Spanish Highways. But now they're not so sure. I'm in civilian dress. They don't know who I am or who I might be. The war has been over for ten years now, but you can still see plenty of fairly young people throwing their weight around—stuck-up rich kids, Falangists, military men. . . . And you never know. Just as I expect, they decide not to take their chances, those little shits. Afterward, out of the corner of my eye, I notice them asking the proprietor about me. When he replies, they pay and get up to leave immediately. I'm seized by an urge to chase them, but I don't. That's what this country is like, filled with blabbermouth Fascists shitting their pants.

Those two truck drivers remind me of old Señor Pau, who was practically my grandfather. During the war he always used to say that people from the country tend to have a very conservative mind-set. And, barring a few extraordinary exceptions, the majority are willing, if need be, to defend the rights and privileges of their masters. Señor Pau based his beliefs on years of experience as a traveling salesman, wandering from one Catalan village to the next. The people he encountered, when faced with a stranger carrying a huge case full of the most motley mix of samples, ranging from cologne and garters to aspirins and gloves, tended to be distrustful. I can only base my opinions on what *I* see. But I have found it to be true that people from rural areas tend to betray their own class when given the chance to change over to the winning side, to join ranks with their superiors. Everyone still remembers what it was like right after the war. The new Regime encouraged and rewarded denunciations. Did the population show any unwillingness to comply? No. On the contrary, a veritable landslide of informers appeared. Just about anyone could accuse his neighbor for absolutely no reason. It was a quick way to take care of long-held grudges and old rivalries. Sometimes it was simply a chance to plunder. It was that feeling of arbitrariness, the sensation that life was hanging on a thread, that drove my mother crazy. A lot of people took it as an opportunity to try to garner favor with the winning side. These were regular Joes who weren't content to stick around with the losers. It's not surprising that this sort of mentality should continue to prevail in a Regime as corrupt as this. Every privilege, down to the most insignificant minutiae of daily life, is still in the hands of the victors. The vanquished are reminded every day of their lives that they're nothing more than the lowest of the low, pure scum.

It doesn't matter. I keep to myself. For the last eight years, I've been living in a bubble. I may have had to wait almost a decade, but now I'm here to finish the job. I will vindicate my father's memory by giving the remains of his friend Bartomeu Camús a decent burial.

When it comes time, I leisurely make my way over to the Venta del Cruce. Walking helps me mull things over. With Major Cedazo monitoring my movements so closely, I don't have any other choice but to snatch Bartomeu Camús's bones and get the fuck out of here as quickly as possible. I'll take care of those son-of-a-bitch baby sellers later.

An old pickup truck appears at exactly the appointed time. It's a run-down model from before the war, its tires worn smooth and with a wooden platform at the back. The driver doesn't shut off the motor or even stop. The vehicle keeps heading toward me and its headlights flash. It's Eusebio. My face is hit with the comforting aroma of bread and flour as soon as I open the door.

"Let's go for a ride," I say, after getting in alongside him.

"Now?"

"Now. Turn around. We've got to get on the national highway, heading north."

He shrugs his shoulders, shifts into first gear, and releases the brake. We leap forward. The truck's transmission lurches badly, as if there might be a scrap heap rattling around inside, but it rides fairly well.

I bring him up to date on the latest developments, including that unsettling breakfast with the major. He's scared to death.

"That declaration is pretty explosive. What are you planning on doing with it?"

"Fuck them. Fuck them hard and slow. I'll make all the names public bit by bit. I won't make any accusations until I'm abroad, of course. That's how I'll get my revenge."

"All well and good, but haven't you thought of trying to squeeze a little bit of cash out of this?" Eusebio sees my face turn beet red. "You've already given the matter some consideration, haven't you? Don't worry, it's only human. I won't tell a soul. As far as I'm concerned, you can bleed those assholes for as much as you can get."

It takes me a couple of seconds to swallow my pride. I clear my throat and reply, "We'll see about that, but in the meantime, we're going to pay a courtesy call on dear Señor Camús. We have to tell him to be patient, if he's waited eight years, another twenty-four hours won't hurt."

On the way I ask him to explain what life in the concentration camp was like.

"My father refused to talk about it. I hardly know anything."

"It's not surprising that he kept quiet. Nobody likes to talk about the shit they've had to swallow. You know, I remember something Franco said, right after the war. He claimed God punishes countries that lead a twisted and depraved existence. In other words, Spain's sufferings weren't just some caprice, but divine expiation. The concentration camps were designed to inflict this pious suffering, but only in one direction—toward the prisoners. Are you sure that you want to hear this?"

"Yes."

"Franco's adherents blamed the war on the Republic. So it seemed only fair that the Republican prisoners should be the ones to rebuild what the war had destroyed. They made them repair train tracks; excavate tunnels; rebuild canals, mines, or bridges; crush rock; build reservoirs; restore churches; fix roads; and remove rubble from bombed-out buildings. Actually, most of the forced labor had little or nothing to do with the destruction meted out by the war. Instead, new stadiums, prisons, and monuments to Victory were constructed. The vanquished soldiers were turned into slaves. Living conditions in the camp were inhumane; filthy men piled on top of each other, cold, hunger, illness, and humiliations of all sorts, beatings, physical abuse, and, depending on the time period, arbitrary executions. The starving inmates were lucky to receive the packages sent by their families or people from Miranda. More often than not, I was the one who'd sneak them in, but it was never very much, since the townspeople had so little themselves. Chronic hunger lowers the body's immune system, and the prisoners were constantly getting sick. They died like flies, out of sheer weakness, normally from tuberculosis, pneumonia, or even diarrhea. But most inmates suffered from constipation, straining so hard that they ended up shitting blood. It was their primary goal not to get sick. The ones who fell ill normally died, especially during the winter. Aspirin was often the only medicine we were allowed to administer."

Eusebio pauses for a moment and begins to cough uncontrollably. He pulls a handkerchief out of his pocket and holds it to his mouth, while keeping the other hand on the wheel. The clean square of cotton is marred by old bloodstains, now faded to brown. When he returns it to his pocket, the stains are once again bright red. His words bring to mind hordes of dejected souls. Those prisoners who had once held such stalwart political convictions must have seemed like a pack of beaten and terrified animals.

"A couple of them confided in me," he continues, "that they were reserving their last ounce of strength to be able to hit the guard at the quarry over the head with a shovel. But as far as I can remember, no one actually did it. They didn't have the strength. The inmates tried to avoid punishment as much as possible. And everybody wanted to get on the good side of the priests and whoever else was in charge. Maintaining an open line of communication with the outside world, with their families, was vital to them. Interrogations were usually conducted by the military, but sometimes they called civilians in to help out, local members of the Falange, distinguished gentlemen. Those were the worst. They'd ask the prisoners if they had served in the Republican Army as volunteers, or if they'd been forced to join; if they'd been taken captive, or if they'd given themselves up; why they hadn't deserted. They were brutally thrashed no matter what they said.

"The guards punched and kicked the inmates out of pure thirst for revenge until their fists and feet were sore. The prisoners were shattered by the time they got to the infirmary. They'd piss blood for days. Some of them didn't make it. Afterward the authorities would tell their relatives that they'd died in some accident, had uremia or an internal hemorrhage."

"Enough!"

"I thought you wanted to know what it was like?"

"Yes, but for now I've had enough."

We drive on in silence for a few minutes. I spot the rock, round as a millstone, half hidden off to my right. On my direction, Eusebio heads down the dirt road. I tell him to pay attention; we're searching for a pine tree in the shape of the letter Y. His ducklike face and long neck are about to burst through the windshield. We have to turn around a couple of times, after several failed attempts.

"Maybe this pine tree got cut down. Is there another landmark?"

"No."

"Then we're out of luck."

We get back on the main highway. My father said they'd walked for a half hour before reaching the pine tree. But it had to be taken into account that they'd been hauling the dead body in a wooden cart down this stony path. They were probably struggling along fairly slowly. I must have miscalculated. The spot has to be much closer than we thought. We have to go back. I notice Eusebio getting nervous. He's probably frightened that someone will see us. The major's distrust didn't please him one bit.

"Why don't you just leave well enough alone?"

"I can't."

We take one of the first forks in the road, which we'd dismissed the first time as being right off the highway. And we hit the nail on the head. Five minutes later, the silhouette of a letter Y appears cut out against the sky. Eusebio rests his chest against the wheel. I stare at the tree.

"Here we are," I whisper.

"How do you know these tires aren't treading over Camús as we speak?"

I'm startled. Eusebio starts to laugh and cough all at once; laugh, cough, laugh, cough, laugh. . . . The son of a bitch is in a pretty good mood now. He puts the truck into reverse and puts his foot on the gas, lurching back about ten feet. The engine sputters to a halt again and I get out of the vehicle, slamming the door with a bang. The whole truck shakes. Eusebio continues to laugh and cough simultaneously. I walk up to the pine and then turn my back to it. A large patch of bramble lies straight ahead. It looks old. Apart from that, nothing. I investigate the plants more closely. It turns out to be rosemary, not brambles. If Camús is under there somewhere, which is very likely, then we're going to disinter the sweetest smelling bones in the world. We can't be seen from the highway and there's no one around. It's a desolate place; all flat expanses of abandoned fields with mountains off in the distance. I sit down next to the rosemary bush. It gives me a deep feeling of satisfaction to know that Bartomeu Camús lies there, six feet under. The promise I made is about to be fulfilled.

Eusebio lowers himself down next to me and, reading my thoughts, says, "The hardest part is yet to come. Aren't you worried about the major?"

"No. Anyway, what is he going to do to a guy who's just looking for a pile of bones?"

He shrugs his shoulders and sets to rolling a cigarette. The guy starts to cough before he can even put the tobacco to his lips, let alone light it.

"What about that proposition you wanted to make me?" he asks.

I give him the full rundown of my plans concerning Africa. How I plan on investing all my savings, taking my mother and son with me. That some associates of mine in Africa have already told me about an enormous estate in Angola that will start turning a profit in no time.

"You could do whatever you want there if you decided to come along: Bake bread, be a nurse, or just watch the world go by."

"Me, be a nurse?" His eyes gleam for a second, but only for a second. "It's impossible. Thanks for the offer, but it can't be."

"Why?"

"Because I'm already a broken man. My body won't hold up. And I don't want to desert my mother."

"Look at it from another point of view. If you come with me, she won't have to watch you fall apart. Since you've got to die anyway, you might as well do it far from here. You'll be doing her a favor."

"You're a cynical son of a bitch."

"I get that from the nuns. Anyway, you must admit I've got a point. They can get along fine without you at home."

"But what the fuck am I going to do in the middle of Africa?"

"Live, work, sleep with the local girls, enjoy yourself as much as you can, smoke until your lungs explode, and, above all, get as far away from this shit hole as possible."

"Not so fast. Angola belongs to Portugal. And you've seen what good buddies the Generalíssimo has become with the Portuguese."

"It doesn't matter. The country is immense; three times the size of Spain. You won't even notice the Portuguese."

Eusebio continues to smoke and cough. He doesn't seem convinced. Suddenly he says, without looking me in the eye, "You're right. I'll go to Africa with you. Spain and the Generalíssimo can go to hell."

"It's not Spain's fault," I reply in a testy voice.

Spain, as an entity in itself, is nothing. But Franco exists. He is a very real, loathsome assassin. Franco is scary. Franco scares me. I scare myself. After eight years in Africa serving in the Legion, I still manage to surprise myself sometimes. My hatred for the Regime stems from purely personal reasons. It's done me so much harm. But it's frightening, because if it weren't for that, it might not be long before maybe I'd be one of those guys who go around saying how the war was a necessary evil and maybe the Regime isn't all that bad, how it's worthwhile to lose a little freedom in exchange for peace and tranquillity. Taking deep breaths, I push those thoughts from my mind. The smell of rosemary is almost intoxicating. Eusebio starts expounding on his own personal theory concerning the nature of the soul.

"I watched a lot of people die during the war. Some of them were aware of what was happening to them, and others weren't. In any case, nobody wanted to accept it. After they had survived shrapnel wounds, mutilation, the entire war, it seemed absurd for them to meet their end in a concentration camp bed, dying from an infection or the sheer physical exhaustion of forced labor. I cared for the patients and attended to their anxious relatives. I remember there was one woman who used to correspond with her husband by means of little notes rolled up and hidden in the handles of the food basket she'd bring back and forth. One time she got caught. I watched the female civil servant grab the note and read it. Then she crumpled the paper and tore it to shreds. The woman was terrified, but the civil servant kept the incident to herself, not doing or saying anything about it. I'll never forget the look of gratitude on that woman's face. One of the guards witnessed the incident as well, and reported it. The civil servant was disciplined. As part of her punishment, the government employee's head was shaved and she was administered a laxative. Then they paraded the poor woman around the streets of Miranda as she defecated uncontrollably. For whatever reason— maybe the laxative was tainted, maybe the woman's health wasn't very strong—she came down with an intestinal infection and never recovered. I was with her when she died. And do you know what happened?"

"What?"

"I felt it. I could sense the exact moment when she passed on. That's when I came up with my spiritual theory about scattered souls. When somebody dies, all of their energy draws into itself for a few moments. Then suddenly their soul is released and scattered about, drawn back into life itself. Whoever happens to be nearby receives part of this energy. I was there and that's what I felt . . ."

I refrain from comment. I wait to see if he's going to elaborate on this extravagant idea. He doesn't. I say, "You're going to feel right at home in Africa. Theories like that seem to be the order of the day over there."

"You think I'm nuts, don't you? What about you? This is the guy who's sitting in this exact spot because the bones of his father's buddy are six feet underneath. And, meanwhile, you know full well that the longer we're here, the more likely it is that some peasant is going to spot us. Aren't you a little crazy, too?"

"Maybe, but keeping the promise I made to my father makes me feel I belong to the world, somehow. It gives me a sense of worth. You don't earn people's respect by just sitting around. Nobody will pay any attention to you if you simply exist."

"That's a pretty lopsided way of looking at things."

"Not exactly. I'd consider myself as more of a realist."

"A realist? I'd describe it as a deadly combination of naïveté and optimism. For all your brains, you're an idiot."

Eusebio is starting to get on my nerves.

"Isn't that a bit contradictory?"

"No."

"Well, I swear, idiot or not, that we're coming back here tomorrow with my associates to dig up those bones and bring them back to Barcelona. Understood?"

"Understood, kid. Understood."

"We'll meet at the Venta del Cruce at nine o'clock and then go pick up the others in Logroño."

"All right then, nine o'clock."

Eusebio hasn't stopped smoking the entire time. Even now, coughing so hard it sounds like he's going to lose his lungs, he keeps puffing away.

On the way back to Miranda, I ask him why nobody knew him in town, since he passes through every day, delivering bread to most of the local establishments.

"You asked around for a nurse named Eusebio Fernández, right?"

"Yes."

"In my village, Pancorbo, I'm known as Piojillo—Little Louse—from Tahona, because my father was called Piojo, the Louse, and he was a baker. My mother's called La Pioja; my sister's La Piojilla; her husband goes by Brother-in-Law Piojo; and their children, my nieces and nephews, are nicknamed the Little Piojillos. In Miranda they call me Piojo from Pancorbo."

"I'm taking you out to lunch."

"Done."

He brings me to a grill near his house, off the highway to Burgos. We eat our fill and drink even more. I end up explaining my strategy of using hypocrisy as a way to survive the Regime. He doesn't quite understand, saying, "I wouldn't have been able to stand wearing such a thick mask for eight years, twenty-four hours a day. To be honest, I wouldn't have lasted eight minutes. I'm a wimp, Sergeant."

Like so many others, he may be cowardly now, but he wasn't during those hard times at the concentration camp, risking his skin so often for the sake of the prisoners. Back then it seemed possible to change his own destiny (his own and that of many others). That must have made him feel responsible for his actions. By helping out so many inmates, he rejected the complacent tendency to deny personal accountability, which is in itself a kind of defeat.

We've drunk quite a bit of wine. Eusebio burps. A coughing fit ensues and he vomits. The guy is a wreck, but at least he's honest about himself. I'm not so sure I can say the same.

He wipes his face, sips from a glass of water, and, calmer now, solemnly states, "Your commitment to the promise made to your father and everything that he represents is a clear indication of your profound loyalty toward others. I wouldn't mind striking that kind of balance between what I say and what I do."

The poor guy couldn't be more mistaken. There are days when I'm consumed by doubt. It's not that I've lost faith in my objective, but that I'm afraid of not being able to withstand wearing this mask for so long. Or, worse, of the mask taking the place of my very own skin without my realizing it. There is a high price to be paid for having worn it so long.

We were doing a roundup one time in a village right outside of Melilla, looking for two Muslims who'd been accused of raping an eight-year-old Christian girl. The inhabitants were all as poor as rats. By the time we arrived, there wasn't a single young man left. They must have been warned. I was already a sergeant. I gathered all the old men, women, and children into the central plaza. The patriarch of the village was among them. I got one of the Legionnaires who spoke Berber to translate for me. "If you don't hand over your men, we're going to shoot everybody here." The man decided to send a woman up into the mountains, in order to explain the situation to those in hiding. The old man offered himself as a hostage, but I refused, saying we'd start by shooting the children. And we'd do it right in front of everybody, to bring shame on him and his village. While waiting for the woman to return, I couldn't stop thinking about what would happen if the men didn't give themselves up. I wasn't planning on killing anybody, but for a second I actually felt that I could have been capable of such an act. After having worn at least two or three different masks for so many years, I had gotten to the point where, for an instant, the lives of those poor souls were worth nothing more to me than some piece of livestock. It was only for an instant, but that's the way it was. The woman came back and the two brothers turned themselves in within the allotted time frame. We took them away to be imprisoned. Fifteen days later it was discovered that they were innocent. When we went back to the village, we were told that the old patriarch, a community leader, shattered by the treatment he'd suffered, had hung himself from a tree. I still haven't forgiven myself. What was I doing in Africa, taunting old men to the point of hanging themselves off the nearest branch? Did my duplicity come at such a price?

It's getting dark out. Eusebio drives me back into town. Before dropping me off, he smiles and asks, "So we're going to Africa, huh?"

"Yes."

"The jungle, lions, blacks . . ."

"Yes, and coffee."

"Of course, coffee!"

He starts laughing hysterically, tears streaming down his face. The deep chortles lead to veritable spasms of coughing. He shifts into first gear, still crying, laughing, and coughing all at once, saying over and over, "To Africa, I'm off to Africa!"

I don't see what the big deal is.

CHAPTER NINETEEN

"The shrewd detective Julio Norma and his faithful sidekick, Pablo Moreno, must use all their cunning to recover the stolen Dragon's Paw from the dastardly bandit Fu-Txong."

"Shirley's papa sends her off to boarding school when he is forced to move abroad. The young girl is sent packing when her father is unable to meet the tuition payments. Her teacher, Miss Lorraine, takes the child under her wing and adopts her. A series of adventures ensues. Mrs. Celedònia, the evil school director, lurks behind every dastardly deed. Miss Lorraine and her servant, the selfless gardener Pasqual, go to live on a farm. She's determined to marry her colleague Jordi Dur, but a black cloud settles over their plans for matrimony. Nevertheless, little Shirley is always at hand, ever ready to find the solution."

The next morning I passed the time half asleep, splayed out reading over and over the old comic books Salvador had left in the tower: the amazing adventures of Tim Tyler in Africa, Detective Julio

Norman's exploits, the ups and downs of sweet little Shirley, and back issues of *Flash Gordon* and *Fantômas.* They were from before the war, and even though the comics were only four or five years old, they seemed ancient. Although such a short time had passed, the whole prewar era already seemed remote and dated.

It must have been nearly midday; the sun shone high in the sky. I was woken by the sounds of people wandering around on the roof. I heard someone moving the pots and boxes that hid the entrance and begin to climb up the ladder. I assumed it was No-Sister-Salvador stopping by after work. The thought cheered me, since, aside from food, he had promised to bring a fresh supply of reading material, including comics.

I recognized her distinctive odor first.

Sister Paula popped her head out of the trapdoor in the floor and gave me one of her best smiles. It knocked the breath out of me; my jaw dropped open. Then I proceeded to turn as red as a chili pepper. Even the scar on my scalp seemed to blush. I was speechless.

"I'd close my mouth if I were you, young man. You don't want to have to go running to the doctor's with a dislocated jaw, am I right?"

She bounded up the last few rungs of the ladder with surprising agility, wearing her white nurse's cape. It goes without saying that Salvador the traitor was right behind. I glowered at him menacingly. She stopped me before I could say anything.

"Wait one moment, Ginés, I know what you're thinking and I don't like it one bit. Salvador hasn't betrayed you. He's your best friend."

"He hasn't, huh? Well, then, what are you doing here?"

Sister Paula, in complete command of the situation, pointed her finger at me and didn't mince words.

"You've betrayed yourself. Or perhaps you don't remember how, not too long ago, you confided in me that Salvador wasn't only a best friend, but a brother? And that if anything was to happen to you, he'd be the first to know about it? Well, that's what you get for talking too much. Since I was so sure that he knew where you were, it wasn't difficult to coax the information out of him. You see, it's not his fault. And don't worry, I didn't tell anybody where I was going."

"I couldn't help it, Ginés, she seemed to know everything about you," Salvador said sheepishly.

"Ginés, I've come to bring you back," Sister Paula stated firmly.

My reply sounded a lot more determined than how I actually felt.

"Well, I refuse to go."

The nun simply stared at me. Even in that hovel, she still looked beautiful while mulling the situation over. Sister Paula was dressed in full uniform, from the traditional winged nurse's cap to the lovely white cape, meant to protect her from some nonexistent chill. She pointed at me once more, saying, "Very well, if you don't plan on going anywhere, then I'm not, either. I'll stay here with you."

No-Sister-Salvador and I stole glances at each other out of the corner of our eyes. This would be my downfall, our downfall.

"But, Sister Paula, you can't be here."

"Why not? Do you own this tower?"

"No, but . . ."

"Then you can't stop me."

She opened her cape, and a leather change purse appeared out of some hidden fold in her habit, just like the story of Saint Tarcisius and his communion wafers. She emptied the contents out onto the sheet on the floor and counted the money. Things were looking worse for us all the time. The nun seemed to have gone a bit soft in the head. She gathered up a few coins and handed them to Salvador.

"We might as well not go hungry, considering that I'll be visiting for a while. Here, go buy us something wholesome, along with a bit of fruit. You decide."

"But the money . . ."

"This is my money. Or it belongs to my family, I should say. My parents give it to me to do as I see fit. Normally I donate it to the infirmary, to supplement the Charity Home's supplies. Now get along, Salvador, my boy, I imagine you have to get back to work."

No-Sister-Salvador grabbed the money and flew down the ladder without saying a word. Once again we were alone. Sister Paula's distinctive scent filled the garret.

"You know perfectly well that they'll start searching for you like crazy once they notice you're missing," I said, deathly anxious. "They'll be sure to blame me if they find you here. If you really want to help out, leave."

"You're mistaken. A boy like you won't get anywhere alone. I'm the only guarantee you've got. I'll defend you if we're found together."

I understood what she was saying, but I didn't agree. I wasn't going to let anybody catch me.

"Nobody will be able to protect me, not even you."

"You're very stubborn."

"I don't have a choice. I'll never get out of the Charity Home alive if I end up going back there."

She laid out a few sheets of old newspaper on the floor, muttering that I shouldn't exaggerate. Then she sat down on top of the newsprint, legs tucked up beneath her uniform. Lazily scratching her left arm with her right index finger, she said out of the blue, "You have all the makings of an intellectual or a writer, did you know that?"

"Me, a writer? With this scar on my head? What are you talking about?"

"You're right; don't pay any attention to me. What I just said is meaningless. A writer is a kind of an acrobat. To be a writer is to be nothing at all."

That's the way Sister Paula was. Her personality revealed itself through the simple, impulsive actions of a young girl. I'd seen it many times. The midday sun filtered through the chamber's narrow windows, lighting her forehead. A thick, pulsing artery coursed down her neck and disappeared into her blouse. I sniffed the air like a dog. Sitting on the newspapers, she left one arm hanging by her side, as if grasping for a leg.

"Well, in sickness and in health, tower or no tower, Our Lord sees all. So I don't see any reason not to say the Rosary the same way I do every day. Would you care to join me?"

I said yes. I felt a little self-conscious at first, but that soon passed. Actually, I was used to it. At the Charity Home, it'd gotten to the point where I could recite the Rosary while keeping up my own parallel train of thought. But with Sister Paula, it was different. I knew that afterward she'd be relaxed and happy. She'd talk to me as an equal, as if I were an adult.

Salvador showed up in the middle of our prayers. His eyes popped out of his head when he saw what was going on. He told us to lower our voices and quietly slunk off.

Once we were done, Sister Paula made herself comfortable and started asking questions about my family and future plans. She could get me to do or say anything. I reminded her that I still planned on going to Miranda de Ebro to fulfill the promise I made to my father.

"I'll get there, no matter what. Whether it's by train, bus, or bicycle. And when I do, I'll find a job and settle down. It doesn't matter how long it takes, I can wait."

"You loved your father very much, didn't you?"

As she had so often in the past, Sister Paula began to tell me stories about her life. She confessed that at first her family hadn't been at all pleased about her decision to become a nun.

"And it wasn't for lack of religion. On the contrary, they're true believers and love Our Lord very much. But of course they'd made other plans for me, since I'm an only child. Especially my grandfather, the patriarch. Do you know what they were hoping I'd become?"

"No."

"An entrepreneur, like them. A modern businesswoman. Can you imagine? I would've squandered the family fortune in less than two days!"

If Sister Paula had continued showering me with her warm gaze and sweet smiles, it would've been pretty difficult to maintain my resolve. I'd eventually had given in and gone back to the Home. She went on, but I'd lost track of what she was saying. It seemed to be a childhood memory.

"I opened the door to my grandfather's office, slammed it behind me, and there I was, inside. That's what children do. They laugh and scamper about as soon as someone chases them. Sometimes the little demons scurry here and there for no reason, without thinking twice about it. I remember the way a wall lamp shook when the door banged shut. I was five years old and can still see the two-part reaction of the people in the room. At first they swerved their heads quickly in my direction with annoyance. But they quickly relented when they saw it was only the little girl of the house. I stopped short and was so afraid, I almost wet my pants. My grandfather began to laugh, and the stranger in the room followed suit. He kept glancing at my grandfather to see when to put an end to his chortles. If my grandfather chuckled harder, so did the stranger; if my grandfather fell silent, the man became immediately mute. I was used to that sort of thing. His word was law at home. Actually, people tended to obey him in general. My grandfather Manel, may he rest in peace, could be very frightening. That's why he never had to raise his voice. The patriarch had a very round face and, now that I think about it, wore a neatly trimmed, but very unfashionable, beard peppered with a combination of white, gray, and black hair. He tended to move in a ponderous fashion, as if his corpulent figure were burdensome to him. What impressed me most were his small, dark, almond-shaped eyes. Alone in my bedroom, I'd imagine them bobbling around like two fat little black olives. The stranger was a young man with the shifty, feline gaze of a house cat. He was tall and good-looking, with the air of someone who's used to being in charge. I remember a pair of green kid gloves peeked out of his blazer pocket. My grandfather said, 'Come here, Neleta.'"

"Neleta?" I asked in surprise.

"I was known as Manela in my secular life. Nuns have to change their names when they join the order. Well, anyway, my grandfather said, 'Come over here, Neleta, I want to introduce you to a friend of mine. His name is Deogràcies Miquel Gambús and he's a business associate of mine. You'll have to watch your step around him though. He's a crook!' Once again he started laughing, with those deep guffaws of his. The youth looked on somewhat distractedly with a pleased smile on his face. Then my grandfather scooped up my little body and carried me over to the table, standing me on top of it. It almost made me dizzy to be placed so high above them. I could see the tops of their heads. Being so small, I'd never actually seen what was on the table. And what I found was marvelous. It was a model of a village or a city. Do you know what a model is?"

"No."

"It's a copy of a sculpture, house, or city, but in miniature . . ."

"Like a nativity crèche?"

"Exactly, very good. But instead of the houses of Bethlehem, there was, according to my grandfather, a whole section of Barcelona. Getting me to hold myself as straight as possible on the tabletop, he asked, 'What do you see, Neleta?' And I answered, 'Houses.' He said,

'What else?' And I ventured, 'Streets.' He went on, 'What else, come on, quick, quick.' I was about to burst into sobs with those two men staring at me. My response was 'Carts and mules. And people.' The model was very intricate, with all sorts of tiny figures and animals replicated down to the last detail. Then my grandfather called for silence, and with his eyes boring into mine and his thunderous voice booming, he ordered, 'Walk, Neleta!' Already half in tears, I pleaded, 'But I can't, there's no room.' 'What do you mean, you can't? Look carefully.' That's when he gave a hard tug on a kind of handle, or lever. And suddenly a trapdoor opened, like one of those ones on a stage. You know, the hole that the devil pops through in that Christmas play about the shepherds?"

"Yes."

"Well, it was the same. The two halves of the wooden platform tilted downward and all the houses, streets, carriages, and carts in that entire section of the model disappeared as if they'd been swallowed by the earth. It reminded me of those antique etchings showing the waters of the Red Sea parting to let Moses and the good people of Israel cross over. Once the table had been taken over by open space, my grandfather raised the trapdoor again until the two halves clicked into place. What was once a labyrinth of contorted streets had been replaced by a single wide boulevard, clean and straight. He exclaimed, 'Do you realize what this means, Neleta? This is the future! A quick and convenient route between the port (*Bang!* a sharp rap on the blue section) and the new city (*Bang!* a sharp rap on a darker area of the model). The port will expand and businesses will grow. There'll be more money all around, everybody will be happy, and we'll end up the richest of all. And do you know why? Because we're heading toward the future. Remember this well and always, Neleta: Only Our Lord, your grandpa Manel, and this young man, my associate, Deogràcies Miquel, know what the future will bring. Normal people don't possess such foresight. That's why they need professionals like us to steer them onto the right road. And if all goes well and nothing gets in the way, our plan will fill our pockets while at the same time making our dear Barcelona a richer and more beautiful place. Isn't that so, Deogràcies Miquel?' My grandfather's associate forced a sarcastic grin and quickly nodded in agreement. My grandfather had me take a few steps toward the open space, which spliced the model in two. He shouted in excitement, 'We'll make piles of money and Barcelona will benefit as well. It'll be the new Paris of the Mediterranean. And if I die, your father will carry on in my footsteps!' I cried, 'No, no, you're not going to die!' 'Of course I'm going to die, it's a law of nature.' Incidentally, my grandfather, who was as strong as a bull, passed away not long afterward. I was too young to fully understand. It seems that my parents weren't interested in his fabulous plan after all. My grandfather's enigmatic business partner ended up taking charge of the whole business himself. And you know how my little interruption into my grandfather's office ended?"

"No."

"With a good, sharp pinch! He picked me up and deposited me carefully back on the floor as if I were a little flower. Opening the door, he ordered me to bid his associate farewell. And while pushing me out into the hallway, he gave my arm a nice, hard pinch. I squealed and burst into tears. My grandfather responded, 'That's for barging in without knocking, or did you think I'd forgotten? Now keep quiet. What you've seen here today is a secret, and you can't tell anyone, not even your mother. Do you hear me?' His words had quite an effect on me, and I went running straight back to my room. My grandfather and I had a secret together!

"My parents don't have much business sense. That's why they were hoping that their only daughter would follow in her grandfather's ambitious footsteps. And, instead, I became, of all things, a nun. What do you think of that?"

I was amazed. My reply came out of nowhere.

"Rich people can be whatever they want. No matter what they do, they'll never stop being rich."

"What do you mean by that?"

I meant exactly what I'd said and quite a bit more, but I didn't tell her that. "Rich people will always be rich. Even if they become nuns, they'll still have a delicious, clean, soft, and tender smell like you do." Once when I was little, while my father was up on his scaffolding, struggling to copy a particularly difficult letter *B,* I called up to him from below.

"Daddy, are we rich?"

"Well. Rich, what one would call rich, no, we're not."

"Then are we poor?"

"No, we're not poor, either."

"So we aren't rich or poor?"

"Exactly. Maybe you'd rather have a rich man for a father, is that it?"

The truth is I considered the matter for a little while and answered him with complete sincerity.

"Yes, I think I'd rather have a rich daddy, now that you mention it."

He broke into peals of laughter and ended up botching that troublesome *B.* But he didn't get very upset about it.

Salvador returned bearing the provisions he'd bought with Sister Paula's money. It was quite a haul: bread, two tins of sardines, apples, biscuits, cooked chickpeas, a bottle of milk and another of wine, which he hid shamefacedly off in a corner. Sister Paula blessed the food and we fell on our lunch with real appetite, as if we'd hiked up Montjuïc, as if that bizarre situation were the most normal thing in the world. After all, the tower was our own special place. And we felt at home there. Salvador's voice rang out.

"They're sure to have noticed you're missing by now."

"Yes," she agreed.

"Why are you getting involved?"

"Because I don't want my little friend to do anything stupid. I plan on convincing him to come back to the Charity Home with me, no matter how much resistance he puts up. And if he wishes, I'll help him denounce those guards who nearly beat him to death. We'll see to it that the guilty are punished and Aleu gets pardoned."

It was exasperating how hopelessly innocent nuns could be. I didn't have the heart to contradict her. Even an ex–poorhouse rat like me was aware that despite being the Baron of Remei's daughter, she wouldn't be able to do anything. Not even God could save me. I'd seen it thousands of times at the Charity Home. Some of the nuns were just plain dumb, blissfully ignorant of everything going on around them. They minded their own business and didn't ask questions. On the whole, they weren't bad people, but they tended to blame everything on God's will. Meanwhile, they kept to their prayers and got as much work done as they could, which was a lot. Then there were the intelligent nuns like Sister Paula. Those women, although perfectly aware of the injustice of our situation, were incapable of breaking their vow of obedience. So they became accomplices of the official Church, Franco's very own brand of Catholicism, which was founded on hypocrisy and revenge.

I wasn't going to let her sweet voice hypnotize me into submission. She could denounce what they'd done to me if she felt like it; I wouldn't stand in her way. But I wouldn't stick around to see what happened. She'd have to fight that battle on her own. She'd chosen to remain in the tower with me, with us. And it didn't matter what the final outcome was, nothing would ever be the same again. Especially for her. Without fully realizing it, Sister Paula was fighting her own personal revolution.

Salvador went off to work, leaving us to our own devices. We spent the afternoon giving the place a thorough tidying up.

"What if someone goes up on the roof and sees us?" she asked all at once.

"It's practically impossible," I answered. "Salvador told me that this building might as well be empty. Two apartments are occupied by a pair of elderly couples and they never come up here."

"When it gets dark, we'll go out and stretch our legs," she said confidently.

I didn't know how to say no. The situation was so out of the ordinary, I was having difficulty thinking clearly.

No-Sister-Salvador came back in the middle of the afternoon, sporting that blazer he wore when doing his rounds for the Mandri Laboratories. He was loaded down with sheets, pillows, and blankets. I recognized the bedding. It was from my old apartment. He was very worried, explaining that Montalegre Street had been in an uproar when he'd walked by the Charity Home. There were all sorts of cars parked outside the entrance and policemen standing guard.

"Was there a shiny silver Buick, with five seats, from before the war?"

"I don't know if it was a Buick, but there was a big silver car, that's for sure."

"It belongs to my father."

"Do you think they'll connect your disappearance with my escape?" I asked.

"Most certainly. Everybody knows how much time we've spent together lately."

Although Sister Paula looked much younger, she was at least as old as my mother. That was the only thing that might keep the authorities from coming to some horrible conclusions. The enormity of the situation got me trembling. No-Sister-Salvador always used to say that the well-to-do never got nervous. "They know they'll land on their feet no matter what, just like cats do." While gazing at her, hair covered and crucifix around her neck, I didn't know what to think. She'd just pulled out a notebook from her bag and calmly began to jot something down. She noticed me watching, lifted her head, and continued. Nuns were supposed to be married to God, at least in theory. Maybe she was explaining to him, in some intimate couple's chat, why she'd decided to risk so much for my sake; put herself out on a limb for a rat. Maybe she was asking him to pardon her temerity. I hope he forgave her. Once the adventure was over, she'd have to return to the fold. And it wouldn't be easy.

It started to get dark out, and we decided not to go for a walk after all. It was too pleasant just to stay right where we were, chatting about this and that. Even No-Sister-Salvador felt like talking.

Suddenly we heard the sound of feet on the apartment building roof next door.

The conversation immediately died on our lips. There were voices. Someone was giving orders, but we couldn't quite make out what they were saying. I peeked out the window and saw three or four policemen. These weren't just some guards from the poorhouse. They were real cops, with guns. And the person in charge looked vaguely familiar to me. Sister Paula took a glance outside and whispered, "My father!"

I observed her out of the corner of my eye. In that moment all she'd have to do was stand up and call out to her dear papa. She stayed still. The baron, on the other hand, was divvying up the policemen to start the search. He ordered two of them to jump onto the other roof, the one with the tower. And that's just what they did. The tower was really the only place someone could hide. The pair went right up to the structure, investigating the bricked-up door. They banged on it with their hands, to make sure it was solid and not some sort of a trick. Then they walked around the tower, pausing right in front of our secret entrance. The men noticed the ceramic pots and packing crates, which covered up the hole in the wall. One of the policemen jerked his leg as if about to kick a crate out of sheer boredom. Luckily, he didn't. They went back to the roof of our building next door and continued to poke around for a few minutes more. That's when the baron decided to call off the search. The light was quickly fading and it didn't make much sense to keep looking. They left. The last thing we heard was the slam of a door.

We breathed easier, relieved. No-Sister-Salvador was extremely anxious. Anything having to do with the police or the military made him sick. He was reaching a state of true panic. Pulling the cork from the bottle of wine, he furtively took a generous swig. Sister Paula noticed, but made no comment. He slowly began to calm down. I covered the windows with cardboard once more and lit a candle that'd been shoved into an empty beer bottle. We watched him take a few more gulps of wine in silence. The candle flame, surrounded by curious little moths, gave off a tremulous glow. Salvador's face, ashamed both for being afraid and for having drunk wine in front of a nun, was distorted by the flickering jolts of candlelight. There in the gloom, Sister Paula looked as blithe as if she were about to go out for a stroll with her little nun friends. We ate some dinner but didn't feel much like talking. By then it was pitch-black outside. The three of us leaned against the wall, with Sister Paula wedged in the middle. We bundled up beneath her cape and one of the blankets. The candle went out and we didn't light another.

It was impossible to convince No-Sister-Salvador to sleep in his own bed that night. We improvised a makeshift pallet on the floor and quietly lay huddled next to each other beneath the covers. The only thing we took off was our shoes. Sister Paula removed her nurse's cap as well. I'd never seen her without it, but despite being so close, I couldn't make anything out. It was too dark. I couldn't tell whether she wore her hair short or long, pulled up in a bun or . . .

We let time pass slowly as we lay there. Once again I could sense the tumult of the city below begin to wane. It couldn't have been that late, but the three of us were already falling asleep. After half suppressing a yawn, I heard Sister Paula ask Salvador, as if it were any old question, "So what is it you want out of life, Salvador?"

"Right now, a bicycle," he replied, after thinking it over for a few seconds.

"Are you joking?"

"No, ma'am," he said, very seriously.

Knowing him as well as I did, I knew he wasn't trying to pull her leg at all. Of course, it would've been impossible for Sister Paula to understand. She merely saw a timid, scrawny boy with a crippled leg. That his sole desire in life was to get a bicycle must have seemed absurd to her. No-Sister-Salvador tried to explain.

"The bicycle keeps me from getting bitter. Even though I don't have two coins to rub together, I like to wander through the Encants flea market once in a while, just to poke around. It occurred to me to look for a secondhand bicycle, only to find out how much one might cost. But there weren't any for sale. I went back a couple of times. Nothing. Then, not too long ago, when everybody was about to close up for the day, I saw a guy packing up his wares. He was loading all the old junk he'd brought to sell into a handcart. I noticed he was holding a bicycle frame in his hands. That instantly caught my attention, and I went up to ask him if he had any old bicycles. He said no, but if I wanted that stripped-down frame . . . and boy, was it stripped! It didn't even have handlebars, pedals, or a seat; nothing. I asked him what he wanted for it and we struck a deal. I brought it home and set it down in the entryway. Every time I go in or out it's there. And I look at it and think, hey, it's a step in the right direction. A few days later I was working at the Born Market and ran into a really great guy from Andalusia named Senén. He delivers vegetables for a farmer out in Prat on his bicycle. We hadn't seen each other in a while. While we were catching up, I told him about what'd happened to me at the Encants flea market. That's when he offered me a couple of spare parts left over from some repair work he'd had to do on his bicycle; they were mine for the taking. He even said he'd help mount them. We left it at that, and that's how it went. Senén's a good guy. Now I'm a regular at the Encants. I keep buying parts, piece by piece. The frame is a big pile of scrap metal that, thanks to Senén, is beginning to take the shape of a bicycle. He keeps giving me a hand with the assembly and makes the necessary adjustments. I'm still missing the seat, a wheel, and the chain. Senén's promised that once we've got the whole thing put together, he'll fix it so I'll be able to pedal without any problems."

Sister Paula didn't reply. Maybe she was wondering if No-Sister-Salvador was a bit slow. She didn't know what I knew because he hadn't told her. That patchwork of metal wasn't just a bicycle to him, it was an airplane. And being able to pedal along the road on it was no different than flying at top speed through the sky of his wildest dreams. We stayed quiet like that for a bit longer. Sister Paula added, with the best intentions, "Apart from the bicycle, what else do you want?"

Half asleep, No-Sister-Salvador replied, "Nothing. Right now, if I don't have that bicycle on my brain, I'm happiest when I'm at home and thinking about absolutely nothing. Or when I hide behind a cart full of vegetables in the market and pretend to be just another head of lettuce. Or when I climb into this tower here and fall asleep . . . and don't even dream."

That's how the three of us fell asleep, snuggling together under the covers. I don't know if Salvador had any dreams that night. I hope he did. I hope he dreamed about his bicycle, all finished and put together. And that he'd seen himself joining some cyclists' club, pedaling alongside his Andalusian friend on a Sunday outing to Montserrat one sunny morning. I hope that's what he dreamed, because by the same time the next day, he was dead.

CHAPTER TWENTY

Tuesday, October 25, 1949

Eusebio drops me off not far from the pension. It's nine o'clock and I'm hoping Campillo will be able to revive me with a hearty bowl of stew. I've got a horrible migraine. My head is throbbing and I'm shivering cold. It must be nerves. Or maybe the wine. Someone calls out as I'm about to go inside.

"Hello there, Sergeant!"

It's a lady's voice, almost shrill. I recognize it instantly. Turning around, I see her at the wheel of a prewar Austin parked across the street, right next to the gardens. Señora Cedazo motions for me to come over. I remember her hands, those fingernails painted pale pink. She might as well have pulled me over to the car by the cock. I go.

"May I ask what brings you here, madame?"

"Don't be so formal, Legionnaire."

"All right. What's a girl like you doing in a place like this on a Tuesday at nine o'clock at night, with the headlights and motor off?"

"I went out for a spin in the car. Women are very independent these days, you know. You men are just as stubborn as ever, that'll never change, but now women can drive and get about on their own in the world. And if we want to go for a ride, we learn how to drive and do it. I spotted you going into the pension, so I stopped to say hello. Do you mind?"

"Not at all."

We exchange pleasantries back and forth, testing out the terrain for a while beneath the soft glow of one of Miranda's lovely wrought-iron streetlights. I'm on my feet with my arms leaning against the car roof. Señora Cedazo's looking up at me through the window. The lady has the same look on her face as when she was playing "The Bridegroom of Death" on the piano while I sang along and ogled her cleavage.

"Actually, I'm glad I ran into you. Now I can let you know first-hand what a bad-mannered young man you are."

"Why?"

"Well, I assumed you'd come to thank me in person for letting you borrow my camera. And not only did you neglect to do that, I'm beginning to suspect that I may never get it back," she said coyly.

"I'd planned on showing up on your doorstep tomorrow morning to do exactly that."

"As you see, I'm a few hours ahead of you. It's a family heirloom."

"In fact, I mentioned to your husband that I'd stop by. We had breakfast together."

"I know."

"He was very dressed up."

"Yes, he went to Madrid on business. He still hasn't returned. The truth is he won't get back until tomorrow."

"It's up in my room."

"What is?"

"The camera."

"Is that a proposition?"

"Come again?"

The major's wife lowers her eyes, abashed, saying, "You know what, why don't you get inside the car. It's chilly and we look like a pair of idiots talking out here like this."

I was thinking we could also attract a lot of attention. They say criminals grow more daring over time. It's not to show off how clever they are; it's more out of exhaustion. Unconsciously, they almost want to get caught. Then at least their worries will be over. That's why getting in that vehicle is such a bad idea. If the major appears around the corner, I'll have a pretty hard time explaining what I was doing in there. Now is the perfect opportunity to tell her that we've had a lovely chat, but it's time for dinner. Each in a respective place of residence, of course. But I don't say it. I shouldn't get into her car. I circle the vehicle, open the passenger door, and sit down.

She starts the car and we're off. We lurch forward and I am thrown against the back of the seat. Flirting with the wife of someone like Cedazo is arousing me beyond words. Even my headache has disappeared. Yesterday I rejected Carmela's air of cheap perfume and today I'm letting myself get carried away by the scent of the major's lady's throat. It's obvious that, at least when it comes to sex, I've got class prejudice. The madam who runs Melilla's choicest brothel is even more discriminating. All of her clients are faithful adherents of the Regime, but she makes a distinction between her religious clients and those who are merely right-wing. She prefers the latter, since they tend to be more straightforward and pay willingly for the services rendered. The former, on the other hand, have such a firmly rooted sense of sin that they take pleasure in committing acts of vice. They like to cross the line. That way, they get to confess about it later. According to her, they're demanding, cheap, complicated, and perverse. But as usual, the customer is always right. As long as there's cash being poured into her pocket, everybody is allowed in the door. So far, I still allow myself the luxury to pick and choose.

We leave the pension behind and cruise slowly around Miranda. She asks me about my life and is quite taken aback when I tell her about my son.

"Where's the mother?"

"Dead."

"You're a widower?"

"No. She was a Muslim girl from Melilla. We weren't married. In fact, the whole affair didn't last for very long. She died in childbirth."

"When did this happen?"

"Three years ago. I barely remember her face."

"So, do you find it pretty boring around here so far?"

"Not at all. Miranda can be quite a lively town, depending on the circumstances."

Unable to hold my gaze, she stares at the steering wheel as if looking at it for the first time, and speaking in practically a whisper, she says, "You say that because you don't live here. Aren't you nervous?"

"Why should I be? Didn't we agree that you're a modern woman with a driver's license, who, despite being married to an Army major, cruises around at night picking up men she's only met once before? All very normal and cosmopolitan, don't you think?"

We're on the bridge with the crowned lions. There's no one around. She glances over at me from time to time. Halfway across, she stops the car, shuts off the headlights, turns in my direction, and gives me a tantalizing kiss, right on the mouth. I seize hold of her as tightly as I can. Back in the Middle Ages, any merchant who wanted to transport goods between the Basque Country and Castile was forced, by law, to use this bridge. A tribute had to be paid in order to cross it. Now it's the major's wife who's making me pay the toll. She's a very clever woman. Despite the spectacular nature of the setting, kissing someone on this bridge has got to be one of the least risky depravities one could commit in Miranda de Ebro. There's only a dim glow from street lamps, and the houses lined up on either side aren't that close. Not only that, there'd be plenty of time for us to start up the car and continue on our way should another vehicle or pedestrian come along. The next day she could always say that the car had stalled. So we kiss on the bridge for a good while under the lions' indignant scowls, listening to the water of the Ebro flow beneath us. The major's wife really knows how to excite a man. I'm sure it won't be long before I find out why she doesn't use those same talents on her husband. She decides it's time to continue our little drive.

"Where are we going?" I ask.

"My house."

"What about the major?"

"I already told you, he won't be back until morning."

"Are you in the habit of doing things like this?"

"The macho Legionnaire doesn't like being driven around by a woman?"

"Something like that."

She grins. I shut my mouth. She knows she's got me trapped. The combination of lust and danger makes it hard to think straight.

"I don't want to go to your house. I wouldn't feel comfortable there."

"Especially if you happen to run into my husband, right?"

"I won't deny that's part of it. But it's not about being afraid. The first thing they teach you in the desert is how to forestall a surprise attack. But it'd be a bit unpleasant, don't you agree?"

She observes me, amused. Her brain seems to be racing a mile a minute. I can follow her train of thought as if it were my own. She decides that yes, although it would be very exciting to fuck me with the risk of her husband showing up, the disadvantages might outweigh the benefits. Señora Cedazo comes to an abrupt halt and I fly against the windshield. She makes a sharp U-turn and takes off, burn-

ing up the road. A window curtain is pulled hesitantly aside, and I see
the inquisitive face of an old man in a robe straining his eyes to see
through the gloom. If this is how Señora Cedazo tends to do things,
then the good people of Miranda must've memorized all her noctur-
nal comings and goings by heart. Undaunted, she doesn't seem to
care. She throws me a playful glance and says, "It's a good thing you
don't trust me. To be honest, José Carlos could very well turn up unexpectedly tonight, I'm not sure. It's a shame that all the discreet ho-
tels I know are so far away."

She holds the steering wheel gently, but drives with determined
confidence. We cross over the bridge once more as she slips down
Miranda's deserted streets. Before I know it, we're on a highway. I
don't know which one; I've lost my bearings. We leave the city behind.

The white light of the Austin's headlights cuts through the darkness. We don't say anything for a few minutes. She seems to know
where she's going. All of a sudden I feel the imprecise pressure of her
gloved hand on my thigh and get as hard as a carrot. The lady continues driving with her left hand while, without even looking at me,
she gropes at my crotch. She paws at my cock the same way she
handles the steering wheel, with a combination of tenderness and authority. She says unexpectedly, "I could start whining and tell you
some story about how my husband is impotent, wounded in the war,
and that it's been over ten years since we've had sexual relations. And
that's why we don't have children. And that I married very young and
can't quite resign myself to a chaste existence. Basically the sorry old
excuses of the kind of slut who tries to screw every new boy to set
foot in her husband's barracks. But that's not the way it is. José Carlos is a rigid man who's a bit fussy and has delicate feet. But he's
sexually active. Every Saturday he makes use of my body with the
precision of a Swiss clock. Before fornication, he performs the exact

same ritual as he does every night prior to going to bed. He carefully folds up his pants and shirt, piling them neatly on a chair; he removes his shoes and socks, heaves a sigh of relief, and places them in exact equidistance to the four legs of the night table."

"Why are you telling me all this?"

"Because I don't want you to think of me as some whiny little wife."

"Fair enough. But that's not what I think. What should I be thinking, by the way?"

"Don't be impertinent. I may not be a whiner, but I'm fairly unhappy. I never expected my marriage would be perfect, but I didn't imagine it'd be so dreadfully dull, either. We haven't had children, which is supposed to provide some distraction, so I've heard . . ."

"Get separated. The Church owes the Regime plenty of favors. The Vatican will annul the marriage, no problem."

"Listen, Legionnaire, what I need is a good screw, not someone to figure my life out for me. You got that?"

Her brutal words resonate throughout the car. The major's wife is a strong woman, as far as I can tell. She can take care of herself just fine. She apologizes.

"I'm sorry; it's just that I don't want any problems or complications. Every once in a very great while, I'll meet someone like you and am tempted to risk everything for passionate, physical contact. In my own way, I love my husband. Don't get the wrong idea; I have no intention of getting separated. The only thing for you and me to do right now, if you want, is give ourselves a good time for a short while. The way things are going, that's already asking a lot. If you lived near Madrid, then we could see each other again."

"Ah, you mean like when you go to visit your dressmaker, huh?"

She doesn't reply.

"We could've become friends," she states, "but you're Catalan and live in Melilla."

"How do you know I'm Catalan?"

Even in the Austin's dusky interior, I can sense her cheeks flush red.

"I don't know, by the last name, I suppose? And leave me alone. You've no idea what you're talking about. You think you're so smart, but you're actually just an idiot, like the rest of them."

That's the second time I've been called an idiot today. I'm getting annoyed.

"How can you be so sure about that?"

"Because you're here in this car with me."

"You're not going to believe it, but before getting in, I was thinking exactly the same thing."

"Only an imbecile would take such a risk. Not that I'm complaining. Anyway, why did you come to Miranda in the first place?"

This woman is leaving me completely floored. I'm too dumbfounded to reply. Luckily, she doesn't seem to expect an answer. She veers off to the right onto a dirt road for a few feet and stops when we're far enough away from the headlights on the highway. There's hardly any moonlight tonight; it's almost pitch-dark. Her tongue is quickly in my mouth again, practically massaging the back of my throat. After that, we both lose control. I push her toward the back of the car. She jumps over the front seat, laughing. One of the advantages of being petite, she says. I do the same, but with difficulty. Then it's me who's kissing her hard on the lips. I'm sitting down and she straddles me. This woman is a real live wire. She starts to peel off her blouse, while I fondle her small, full breasts. The sound of our still tentative moans is the only noise that breaks the silence. She starts to feverishly lick the scar on my head. All the ladies do. The old wound seems to attract them like a magnet. Who am I to stop them? I lower my head and let them lick it; lick it so hard it shines. Meanwhile, I take the opportunity to let my hands roam at will. The major's wife gets tired of my scar and rubs her hand against my fly, fumbles with the buttons, forcing me to pull my pants down. She slips a condom on before I even know it. I really want her to get on top and ride me hard. And when she does, the only thought in my head is that I wouldn't care if the ghosts of my father and Bartomeu Camús appeared before me right now. The major himself could show up brandishing a loaded gun. He'd have to pump my chest with a full clip of bullets before being able to tear this woman off me.

We hold each other. She's a good fuck. And, despite the strange situation, I experience, as on other occasions, a moment of truth.

I caress her breast as we cool down afterward. She amuses herself by curling locks of my beard around her fingers. I notice that she's had her gloves on the whole time.

Listlessly, I grab her wrist to check her watch. She doesn't get it for a second. Both our hands drop abruptly. I say it's too bad, but I'd better be getting back to the pension. It's absurd. It's not as if anybody's waiting for me, but I'm getting a little restless. Anyway, I feel pretty defenseless out here in the middle of this dark, empty field.

She replies, "Yes, it's such a shame you have to go."

We drive back to Miranda through the darkness without conversing. Señora Cedazo stops and I make as if to give her a kiss goodbye, but she holds up her hands. She doesn't want it.

"Get out," she says.

I follow orders and start to leave.

"Legionnaire . . ."

"What?"

She waves her hand aside in resignation, but then points at me seriously as if she wants to tell me something but can't quite work up the courage. Finally she lets it out.

"Be careful. Very, very careful."

I ask her why, but she's already on her way. As I watch the white smoke trail out of the Austin's tailpipe, it consoles me to think that cuckolding the major could be considered alternative tactics of warfare.

The car comes to a dead stop. She puts it into reverse and backs up in my direction at full speed. The major's wife lowers the window and sits there, staring at me, for a few seconds. She blurts out all at once, "I didn't meet you by accident."

"I figured that."

"Don't be rude, it's not what you think. You made a good impression on me the other day. Unlike some people, as I've said before, I do get bored in Miranda. I wanted you, but wouldn't have done anything about it, except that I felt I should give you a word of warning as well. People here are dying to know why a Legionnaire is going around asking questions about a certain what's-his-name."

"Eusebio Fernández."

"Doesn't matter. The problem is you've asked everyone but the authorities. And you didn't mention a word about it to my husband, either. It doesn't look good. And José Carlos is very suspicious. The man's as mistrustful as he is ambitious. He's had you followed. Since practically the day after you got here, he's been keeping tabs on every move you make."

"How do you know?"

"He told me, honey, he told me. It's not so strange; I am his wife, after all. He's gotten very worked up about the whole affair. Deep down, he's just as bored as I am. Even his feet don't seem to be bothering him so much. This afternoon he was yelling, 'That son of a bitch is hiding something.'"

"Why are you telling me this?"

"Because we've just had sex."

"Thank you."

"Don't take it the wrong way. The second you leave Miranda, I won't remember your name. It's pure survival instinct. I don't want to suffer. And now listen up good. Legionnaire or not, I have to say that when José Carlos wants information, he gets it."

"I'm not looking for trouble."

"I hope nothing happens to you. Or to your friend, of course."

"What friend?"

"The one you were trying so hard to locate. He seems to mean a lot to you."

"It's a personal matter, nothing out of the ordinary."

The major's wife is sharp, and doesn't buy it.

"Suit yourself. But I swear that if my husband catches you, after having confessed everything, you'll be begging for a bullet in the head to put you out of your misery."

She's disappointed. The lady was hoping I'd share my secret with her. She's got an odd expression on her face, which I can't decipher at first. Then I realize that she's no longer looking at me as a lover or a confidant, but as one of her husband's victims. Maybe she's right.

She starts the car up once more.

"What are you going to do?" she asks.

"Get the fuck out of here."

"Sensible decision. Good-bye."

She shifts into first gear and careens away. The wheels scorch the pavement yet again. Someone, somewhere, probably just said, "That's the major's wife on her way home." She has simply confirmed what I already knew, that Cedazo is suspicious. The good news is he'd never guess the real reason behind my trip to Miranda. And Bartomeu Camús's document doesn't affect him. I see the major's wife in my mind's eye and smile. The ambitious and dissatisfied woman, forced

to share her military husband's grim fate of wandering from one provincial city to the next, is a classic theme in pulp fiction.

She's dropped me off a fairly good distance from the pension. I start to walk. The grin on my face lasts less than ten seconds. It comes crushingly to mind that this is the same woman who applauded at executions. She, too, is the enemy. How can you make love to your own enemy? The migraine comes raging back and my mood sours considerably. I'm ashamed of myself. My father advised me to become an expert liar, the king of hypocrites. But you can't play a double game all the time. Eusebio and I were talking about that only a few hours ago. And I've just realized I wasn't being the least bit hypocritical back there with the major's wife. What good does all this rage do? What use are eight years of waiting for the right moment if the mere vision of a woman with tapering fingers and lacquered pale pink nails is enough to undo all my efforts? The major's wife is right; I'm not nearly as clever as I think. And if I was wrong about that, then it's possible I've been wrong about other things, too. I told her I wasn't looking for trouble, basically letting her know that I was up to no good. A complete and utter idiot. They say that love is blind. I don't know about love, but it seems that for some men, at least for me, lust certainly is. Is it possible for the torture victim to fall in love with the torturer; the prisoner with his jailer?

I've run into various ex-Nazis in Melilla over the years. They've taken on new identities and escaped to North Africa to become businessmen. The Generalíssimo's Regime protects them as much as it can. Most of them don't bother to keep a very low profile. One of these men, a former officer in the SS, told me casually about how, days before the Americans liberated the concentration camp he'd been assigned to, the guy disguised himself as a Bavarian chimney sweep, complete with brushes, rags, and a squashed top hat. He blackened

his face and hands with a bit of soot and ran away under the cover of night. His servant, a Jew who'd become his personal slave, was sobbing inconsolably over their separation when they said good-bye, despite all the suffering the SS officer had inflicted on him. Among other atrocities, the Nazi would force the man to lick his boots clean with his tongue or get him to copulate with his own sister like an animal for the fun of seeing what their offspring might look like. The officer admitted that once, while drunk, on a sudden impulse to punish his servant, he'd gone so far as to literally string the man up by his balls. It was a miracle they weren't ripped clean from his body. But despite all this, the Jew cried when his master abandoned him. "You see, those people are no better than animals," the SS officer said. If that son of a bitch had lived through half of the Jew's experiences, his more bestial side might have come out, too. For instance, if he'd seen his two-year-old child smashed to pieces against a wall and then fed to the dogs for breakfast; his parents killed right before his eyes with a bullet to the temple; or his wife and daughter being brought to the gas chambers as soon as they got off the cattle car. The Jew had some very profound reasons for losing his sense of self. My reasons are purely intellectual and sentimental. I've never experienced pure terror. Nevertheless, I've acted just as irrationally as that poor Jew. He deserves to be given every consideration, but I don't. I was almost about to jeopardize my entire scheme out of personal vanity. Señora Cedazo's seduction could have been a trap. And I would have fallen for it hook, line, and sinker. Yes, I most certainly am a poor idiot, a hopeless fool. With a little bit of luck, the whole operation will be over tomorrow. So much the better, because the longer it takes, the more chances I'll have to screw up.

Right now, deep down, I have no idea who I am. I don't minding admitting the swarm of ignorance and doubt teeming within me. For example, I'm not sure God really exists. And even if he does, the

way things are going, he doesn't seem to be wasting too much time
on us. And what about me; do I exist? How many times have I, protected by my secure life in the Legion, doubted whether or not I was
on the right path? In the Legion, you use force to earn people's respect. Some Legionnaires refuse to use an umbrella when it rains because they consider it too effeminate. They'd rather get wet like real
men. Actually, the Legion isn't even Francoist. It has its own distinct
and independent code of honor. Not long ago in Melilla, the major
of a regiment contracted a purveyor to supply the Legion with
footwear. The businessman had just gotten back from the Peninsula.
He'd spent a few years in prison for engaging in activities against the
Regime. The mayor of Melilla recommended a relative of his from
Alicante for the contract instead. The nephew was a member of the
Falange who was apparently going through a difficult time. The Legion responded that they preferred to give the work to the newly returned Red. They reasoned, "Your Falangist relative must be hopeless,
a complete idiot, if he hasn't been able to make some serious cash in
these last years after the war. He can't be trusted. The Communist, on
the other hand, will bust his ass to do a good job." We live in a kind
of permanent insanity. Civilization's values have been turned upside
down, and nobody is who they would have been under normal conditions.

I shouldn't have been a Legionnaire, but I am a Legionnaire.

It's not that late, but a deep quiet has fallen. Miranda is a welcoming place, full of history and rife with the dead. The members of
the democratic town council were the first ones to be killed in the
war. They were brought to Burgos. Every single one was executed.
On July 20, 1936, only forty-eight hours after the coup d'état, Miranda de Ebro already had a new, Francoist Town Hall. It's strange
how an entire city's way of life can change so much in such a short
time.

There's an abrupt flash of lightning. I quicken my pace. Thunder strikes. It begins to rain. All of a sudden it's pouring. It seems like some kind of joke. Cursing to myself, I take off my jacket and hat (I'm a fucking Legionnaire, aren't I?) and continue walking with my head held high, marching along ferociously, in case I run into somebody. Water runs down my back in buckets. But I keep going, withstanding the raindrops that rail against my face like needles. By the time I arrive at the pension, I'm soaked. Campillo's cream-colored Chrysler is parked outside the pension door, and I find it reassuring without quite knowing why. I go inside, stamp my feet on the floor, shake off some of the moisture, and stand there watching the old lady knit. Completely still and unaware of my presence, she keeps clicking away at her needles as always.

Campillo appears. His face changes expression when he sees me. He looks scared. After an effusive greeting, he says that he'd been waiting for me to arrive in order to lock up. He urges me to change my clothes immediately or I'll catch my death of cold. I push the man out of the way without even glancing in his direction. Glowering at the old woman, who hasn't missed a stitch, I say good night and climb the stairs. How does Campillo get her into bed in the evening?

The last thing I see before closing my eyes is my clothes, left to dry on the bathroom sink. They cover the floor in drops of water, forming a small puddle in the exact shape of Banyoles Lake.

CHAPTER TWENTY-ONE

By the time I woke up, No-Sister-Salvador had already gone off to work and Sister Paula was washing her face with a cloth and water from the jug. She stood with her back to me, so I could follow her movements without being seen. Sister Paula had taken off the white nurse's uniform and was wearing a bone-colored blouse with a gray-blue skirt. She unbuttoned the top and exposed her shoulder blades for a few moments, wiping them down with the wet fabric. I was an adolescent and, nun or not, those were the shoulders of a naked woman. I could barely take in what her hair looked like, only that the midlength locks just grazed her shoulders. I watched how efficiently she gathered the hair up into a bun, jabbed it with a clip, and deposited the nurse's hat atop her head.

She quickly buttoned herself up and I shut my eyes tight once again.

I could hear how she finished preparing herself for the day and then began to make breakfast. She woke me up gently.

"Listen, sir, you may be a fugitive, but that doesn't mean that you have to be a lazy good-for-nothing."

She'd prepared two glasses of lemon water along with some bread and cheese. "How long do you plan on staying here?" she asked as we ate breakfast.

"I don't know. As long as it takes the government of Barcelona to completely forget about my existence."

That's when she took up her change purse and handed me the entire contents of one of its compartments.

"Here, it's not much money, but at least this way I know you won't be wandering the world like some kind of tramp. You can take the train as decent folk do."

I didn't refuse her offering. In my own mind, I felt like she owed it to me.

"Thank you very much."

Sister Paula made me promise that if I did manage to escape, I'd keep in touch with her. I couldn't see any reason not to agree.

"You're a good boy. And I trust you. I did some thinking last night. I could never detain someone against his will. I only hope this obsession with fulfilling your father's last request doesn't lead you to ruin."

"I don't care where it leads me."

"I'm well aware of that, obstinate child! At least assure me that those bones you're looking for will be treated with respect, and if found, they'll be given a Christian burial."

It didn't cost me a thing to go along with everything she said. The requests were natural, coming from someone like her. In theory the losers were a faithless bunch, especially the son of a Republican soldier. The Regime was struggling to lead the country back to Christian values. But in reality they were the ones who threw bodies in the ground as if they were no more than sacks of meat, hair, and bones. They were the ones who made people disappear like slaughtered livestock; they were the ones who . . .

"I promise" was my reply.

"That makes me feel better."

At least you could talk to Sister Paula. And, more important, she'd listen. She never acted superior like the other nuns or administrators at the institution. And she didn't make you feel guilty. She wasn't intent on absolving all your sins before hearing what you had to say. And she didn't treat you like most of the decent and well-meaning people on the street did. They never knew how to react when faced with the boys and girls from the Charity Home. We felt their discomfort immediately whenever we'd go out. Or when somebody came to visit. We, with our shorn hair, obligatory smock, espadrilles, and ratlike stance, had to withstand their stares. And depending on the situation, you could tell that our mere presence was frightening to them. As one can imagine, it was very satisfying, almost pleasing, to have such an effect on others. After a funeral, members of the public would often come up to me on their way out. It wasn't hard to sense a guilty conscience lurking beneath the upstanding citizen's chitchat. They were convinced that a kid quaking in his uniform, a monumental scar gleaming on his shaved head, couldn't possibly have anything to hide. The catastrophe of his physical appearance was enough. With every scrap of misery on display, you didn't need to tell them anything. The general populace assumed that being cast off from society and most likely the orphans of Red soldiers made us inherently good somehow. They, on the other hand, encased in hats and polished shoes, felt an overpowering urge to confess, to reveal their most personal secrets without anybody asking them. They'd try to make you feel better by saying that, deep down, we were all the same. And that life out on the street was also very hard. It was unbearable. Well, maybe Sister Paula wasn't one of them. This meant that she was very, very smart.

Suddenly I said, "Sister Paula, I'm afraid of thinking too much."

"Why do you bring that up now?"

"No-Sister-Salvador is happiest not thinking at all. He said so last night. I think too much. And I'm afraid that means I don't have feelings."

"I don't agree. It's not true that the more you think the less you feel. It is one thing to reflect and another to judge. I do believe that being too judgmental makes it more difficult to love. Ginés . . ."

"Yes, what is it?"

"Tonight I'm going back to the Charity Home. I don't want to run away from anything. I'm not as brave as you are. And speaking of judgment, I don't want you to think badly of me, either. We are all the products of our experience. I am who I am and can't change overnight. I believe in my faith and my work. I'm satisfied if my presence can contribute to making the wards' lives at the Charity Home a bit easier and more humane. That doesn't mean that I'm incapable of seeing the contradictions that surround me, or my own hypocrisy. Don't judge me. You heard what I said before, the more you judge . . ."

"The less you love."

But it was impossible not to judge her. At any rate, religious types certainly weren't ones to talk about judgment. The Regime is a perfect example of how the secret to maintaining power lies in reconciling oneself to different truths. And that's exactly what Franco's followers do every day, relentlessly and without shame. The Regime is a sack so full of contradictions that it's a miracle it doesn't rip wide open. Sister Paula's well-intentioned inconsistencies weren't any worse than those of the Regime, with the difference that the dictatorship's contradictions were born out of bad faith and hers out of God.

We said the Rosary and then decided to read for a while. I attacked the new comic books that No-Sister-Salvador had brought. Sister Paula concentrated on the breviary she carried with her.

Salvador showed up around lunchtime bearing a potato omelet and a jug of milk. He also presented us with a bottle of Cerebrino Mandri that he'd managed to steal. He didn't let us dig into the meal until we'd had a generous spoonful each. The young man claimed the elixir was absolutely indispensable, given the circumstances.

"You, too, Sister. If you don't take care of your body, you'll end up neglecting your spirit. And that's a sin."

Normally, if you saw him in the market or on the street lugging around Señor Pau's bulky sample case, No-Sister-Salvador tended to look, if not menacing, at least tough. Being lame didn't help. Depending on the situation, I myself had seen him exaggerate his limp when it suited his best interests (to soften up a girl, for example). But when forcing a dose of Cerebrino Mandri on us up in the tower, it was his true self that shone through. Salvador was really a sweet and imaginative boy who'd followed the train tracks on foot from Lleida to Barcelona, in search of a sister whose whereabouts were unknown. He'd been taken in and adopted by the older man who lived in the apartment next door to us. And Salvador ended up being the pillar of our little community. He'd kept Señor Pau and my mother alive during the war and long after. He'd helped me out from the very beginning and he was still helping me out now. Even Sister Paula seemed to be at ease around him. They'd calmly and naturally grown accustomed to each other's presence in less than a few hours.

Salvador informed us, as we feasted on the omelet, that the coast was clear.

"There doesn't seem to be anyone keeping watch inside the building or out on the street."

"It doesn't matter. They're sure to come back," I replied.

"I guess. I'm the only link in the chain they've got. And they're not going to let that connection go."

"No."

"What do you mean, no?"

"You're not the only tie. There's my mother, too. They may be in Caldes de Malavella as we speak, interrogating her."

The possibility had only just occurred to me. The thought of her being mistreated by the authorities was unbearable. And yet it made sense. One of the first places where I'd thought to seek shelter was precisely that, my mother's house.

"You should've taken that into consideration before," Sister Paula interjected.

"Try not to worry too much, if you can help it," interrupted Salvador. "I know your mother. First of all she doesn't have any idea what's happened. And secondly she'll defend you to the death if there's the slightest hint that someone wants to harm you. That lady is smart, and if necessary, she'll spin their heads around like tops."

Once that was said, he got up and left, off to work. Sister Paula and I were alone yet again. I asked her when she planned on leaving the tower.

"I'm not exactly sure, but very late, when it's dark. I'd like to keep you company for as long as possible. We'll see."

Then evening came, with tragedy following close behind.

The sun had almost faded from view, bathing the tower room in the crimson light of dusk, when we suddenly heard sirens. Cars were screeching their brakes and parking down in the street. Then there was the crash of doors slamming and boots stomping about, confused with the shouts of men giving orders out on Plegamans Street. A vaguer, more confused noise came from the side of the building that faced Caputxes Street. It sounded like an army taking up positions for battle. The street seemed to be filled with people. I didn't have to look at Sister Paula to feel her quaking with fear. We sensed the military boots tramping up the stairs, but didn't actually hear them. This time a sharp kick sent the door flying off its hinges. The crash was followed by a barrage of enraged screams, punctuated by cries of panic. The building was surrounded. Policemen in uniform, guns cocked, crowded on the roof. More and more armed men gathered on the terrace. After jumping onto the neighboring roof, they headed straight for the tower. Seven or eight cops formed a human chain around the little turret, their bodies pressed tightly against each other, quietly waiting for further orders.

"Don't be frightened, I'll take care of everything," Sister Paula said, rapt with fear.

Just then, the Baron of Remei climbed onto our roof, a police officer at his side. No-Sister-Salvador was behind them, struggling against the grip of two guards. He was crying disconsolately, like a child who's lost sight of his parents on a busy street. He'd been given a thorough beating, the poor soul. His whole shirtfront was covered in blood. One of the men shouted at him to be quiet, but he cried even harder, the same as a little boy. The man punched him in the stomach, shutting Salvador up right away. My friend was bent over double in an almost implausible fashion, as if made out of rubber. Mouth hung slackly open, he gasped for breath. They let him go and he fell miserably to the ground, bleeding from the nose, his body a wreck. I turned away, trembling. I didn't want to look. It killed me to see him like that. Sister Paula was speechless at my side. It was all happening so fast. For a quick second I stole another glance. Salvador's distorted face was too horrible to contemplate. He'd been abandoned on the ground like a beast no one bothers to tie up because it's no longer considered dangerous. His expression was such a vivid picture of terror and pain that I might as well have been experiencing those feelings myself. Deep down, No-Sister-Salvador and I were one. That's when I began sobbing as well. I was only a sixteen-year-old boy, after all. Then the baron began to shout in the direction of the tower. Someone had passed him one of those ridiculous mega-phones, the kind that ringleaders brandish in circus posters. You could tell he relished being in charge. And he was an innate leader, skillfully ordering people about with the calm resolve that comes from years of experience. He addressed me in the same voice that he used when speaking to his peasants or servants.

"Listen, you son of a bitch. We know you're holding my daugh-ter in there against her will. Let her go immediately, do you hear? If you do, I'll give you my word as a gentleman to do everything in my power to ensure that the authorities treat you with as much leniency as possible. If not, I'll go up there right now and strangle you myself. What do you say?"

Then events began to unfold at breakneck speed. Everything oc-curred in a matter of seconds. Sister Paula's strong and assured voice rang clearly out of the tower window.

"Father!"

"Darling, are you all right?"

"Of course I am! Nobody is holding me against my will. I'm here because I want to be!" she cried.

The baron and the inspector looked up at us in stupefaction. Their faces were full of perplexity. It was as if they'd set the dial for one radio station and were hearing a completely different one instead. The baron was especially confused, opening and closing his mouth like a fish out of water. He couldn't speak and became extremely agitated.

"What have they done to you?" he cried, his face contorted with emotion.

The man was beside himself. Sister Paula continued to insist that she was fine, that no one had touched a hair on her head. In that in-stant No-Sister-Salvador staggered to his feet and tried to run for the stairwell door, dragging his gimp leg. He didn't pose any threat. The inspector proved as much by simply watching the young man with disdain. One of the policemen went over and blocked his path, just for fun. Disoriented, he backtracked, running pell-mell around the roof, like a chicken with its head cut off. The baron didn't know whether to focus on Salvador or on his daughter, up in the tower. On the verge of hysteria, he ordered the boy to halt immediately. But Salvador, more frightened then ever, didn't hear him. He scrambled about like a rag doll as the policemen laughed and pretended to try to catch him. The baron lost control.

"Enough!" he shouted.

Then he pulled a pistol out of his pocket, firing a shot above his head. The sound drove Salvador wild with fear. The baron commanded him to halt once again, getting within fifteen feet of him. He insulted Salvador, saying he'd kill him for what he'd done. The poor young man begged for mercy, insisting that he hadn't hurt anyone. Suddenly, the baron's gun was trained on Salvador. Up in the tower, Sister Paula and I both started shouting, telling the baron he'd gone mad and begging him stop. The inspector's laughter instantly dried up and he tried to intervene. But the baron, rabid as he was, paid no attention to the officer and fired his weapon. The bullet appeared to hit Salvador's shoulder. He dropped to the ground. A couple of policemen went over and helped him to his feet. Salvador began to wail like a baby and didn't let up. He touched the wound with his hand and, on seeing the blood, howled even harder. They propped him up against the balustrade of the building. Blood quickly began to pour out of his mouth. I was wrong, that great big son of a bitch hadn't gotten him in the shoulder; he'd ripped Salvador's chest open. The baron returned the gun to his pocket and swiveled around to face us, or rather me.

"You, poorhouse boy, listen up good. Let my daughter go; otherwise I'll finish off this piece-of-shit cripple you call a friend."

"Father, are you deaf? Let him go! I came here out of my own free will!"

"I've heard enough of that! My darling daughter must be drugged!"

Then the inspector went up to Salvador, who'd grown quiet all of a sudden. He was seized by a series of small convulsions. A pool of blood surrounded his quivering form. The officer inspected the wound and turned back to address the baron. He whispered a few words into the nobleman's ear. The baron looked at him and nodded in agreement. That was when Sister Paula and I both witnessed with horrific clarity how the very same inspector, with the help of a policeman, grabbed the half-conscious No-Sister-Salvador, picked him up and pushed him against the brick balustrade. At that point the poor kid realized what was happening and screamed in terror.

"Ginés, they're going to kill me!"

I somehow managed to find my voice and holler back.

"No!"

They flung him over the side, onto the street below.

There was a hideous scream, followed by the dull thud of a body hitting cobblestones. The baron leaned over the balustrade and spit down onto the street. All the air left seemed to have been forced out of my lungs. I vomited right there and then. Sister Paula shouted.

"Murderer! Murderer!"

The baron heard her and lifted his face toward the tower. Only then did he become fully aware of what he'd done. And that his only daughter was a witness. Not to mention that the other bastard—me—had seen it, too. There was no way to get out of it. He quickly calmed down. If the Barons of Remei had been around for over a thousand years, it was thanks to knowing how to react, and quickly, during crucial moments.

"Dearest, we're coming to get you right now!"

"Don't you dare!"

"Is he threatening you?"

"Of course he's not. And nobody else is, either!"

"I'm coming up there."

"No!"

"Enough nonsense. I'll be right there. You tell that poorhouse boy he'd best behave himself."

"Or else you'll kill him like you did his friend, is that it?"

"Darling, it's not what you think."

"I saw it with my own eyes. You're a murderer!"

"I'm coming up."

"If you do, I'll kill myself. I'll throw myself out the window."

I surveyed our surroundings. I didn't see how it was possible. The tower windows were too narrow for even a toddler to get through. Apparently the baron wasn't familiar with the building's construction, because he stopped short, shouting, "Don't say such things! Why are you doing this to me? What's wrong?"

"You're an assassin!"

"Enough. I'm coming up there."

"I'll kill myself!"

"Do you want me to send for your mother? Would you rather talk to her?"

"No. It's you I want to talk to."

"What do you want?" the Baron asked in a weary voice.

The man didn't understand a thing. He had no idea what had happened to his daughter and was positively certain that she'd been drugged.

"Sweetheart, those bastards must've forced you to take something."

"Nobody's forced me to take anything. And God forgive me, the only bastard around here right now is you."

"How dare you speak to me like that?"

"Because you're not my father anymore. You're a murderer. And a murderer doesn't deserve to be spoken to any other way."

"I've never seen you act like this."

"And I've never seen you kill a boy in cold blood. No—there's nothing wrong with my mind. I feel completely sober."

"But think about—"

"The only thing I should be thinking about is whether or not I'm going to accuse my father of murder."

"I cautioned him to halt and he disobeyed my orders. The lad was trying to escape."

"Don't treat me like a fool! Escape from what? More beatings? He was innocent! Do you hear me? Innocent!"

Sister Paula dissolved into tears. I was as quiet as a grave. Although unable to move, I trembled like a leaf. Let them come and do what they wanted with me. I couldn't tear the image of Salvador out of my mind. Just then we heard one of the policemen encircling the tower drag the clay pot away from our secret entrance and start to go inside. Sister Paula composed herself immediately. Wiping her nose on her sleeve, she shrieked in apparent frenzy.

"Tell them to get out! Make them leave or I'll throw myself out the window!"

It worked. The inspector ordered his men to retreat. They went back out onto the roof. Sister Paula addressed her father in an eerily distant voice.

"You tried to trick me. You are a killer and liar. Come closer; we have to talk."

"Talk? What about?"

"About what's going to happen to this boy I've got here by my side, for example."

At the mere mention of my presence, the baron grew furious again.

"What happens to him is none of your concern! Listen . . ."

"No! You listen to me, because I won't say it twice. I'm going to take off every stitch of clothing and climb onto the tower roof stark naked for the entire neighborhood of La Ribera to see. Do hear me? And once everyone's gotten a good look at every inch of me, I'll throw myself down onto the street."

"Have you gone insane?"

"No. You're the only lunatic around here. You don't think I'm capable?"

A dumbstruck silence reigned down on the roof. Meanwhile, back in the tower, Sister Paula shot me a wink and asked me to turn around. Even so, I snuck a peek as she peeled off a pair of thick stockings and threw them out the window at her father.

"No, dearest, don't!"

By way of reply, Sister Paula removed her coif and flung it out as well. The starched cotton twirled downward like a windmill and landed at the baron's feet. The blouse went flying through the air soon after. Sister Paula wrapped the white cape around herself. The entire situation would have been comical if I hadn't been so terrified. I peered outside to see what was going on. Small groups of people were gathering on all the neighboring roofs, watching the events unfold with undivided attention. The next item to take wing was a bra. She dangled it out the window, wiggling it back and forth. An isolated smattering of applause emanated from another building. The baron, although a cold-blooded murderer, proved unequal to the occasion. He begged, "Darling, please! That's enough! What do you want?"

"I want all these policemen out of my sight! Tell them to go away . . . Once they're gone, come up here and you and I will have a talk. Now!"

"All right, all right. Understood."

As the nun proceeded to put her bra back on, I watched in amazement as the policemen, armed to the teeth, filed off the roof and retreated down the stairs. She managed to keep them from invading the tower. Sister Paula had just saved my skin. Salvador's death made it very clear what would've happened to me. The Baron of Remei was the only person left on the empty roof. I watched him approach the tower, get down on all fours, and crawl inside. Not a minute later his head was poking out of the trapdoor in the floor. Sister Paula helped pull him up the rest of the way. He was carrying the articles of clothing she'd so recently discarded. The nobleman gave them to her and then took a look around, smoothing the front of his suit jacket down with his hands. He couldn't believe his eyes. When our gazes locked, I faced my own death. I should have lunged for his neck and strangled him right there and then, but I didn't. It wasn't my conscience that held me back, it was shame. I was covered in my own vomit.

"Isn't there anyone else here?" the baron asked.

"Where would they be hiding?" Sister Paula replied with disdain.

"I want to know if this gang has any more members."

"There is no gang. I wasn't kidnapped and you're an insane and dangerous murderer."

"You've no idea what you're talking about," he responded in a bitter voice.

Sister Paula asked me to leave them alone, so I went downstairs and waited outside. The moon struggled to cut a path for itself as the gusts of crisp autumn breeze sent banks of clouds racing through the sky. Clouds heavy and gray with rain consorted with tufts as plump and white as the sugarcoated fritters sold at the pastry shops during Lent. It was the same sky as always, but No-Sister-Salvador was no longer there to see it. That's the way of the world; an eternal firmament looming over the transient populace below. Policemen were stationed on all the surrounding roofs. They glowered at me ferociously.

They looked like hunting dogs, straining against their chains, dying to pounce on their prey. I couldn't escape. They'd finally gotten the nosy neighbors to disperse. I was on my own, with only the tower for company. I went up to the balustrade facing Plegamans Street and leaned against the brick. Down below, on the cobblestones, lay the crushed body of my friend No-Sister-Salvador. His death had not completely sunk in yet; I was still overwhelmed by Sister Paula's behavior. I heard father and daughter climb down the tower ladder not five minutes later. I peeked into the secret entrance and watched them leave. He went first and she followed. Then the baron drew up alongside the nun, putting his arm around her shoulders. Sister Paula was once again fully dressed, cowl and all. I wanted to approach her, but couldn't. A pair of policemen blocked my path. I saw them both head toward the door on the roof, which led down to my building's staircase.

"Sister Paula!" I cried out.

But she didn't even turn around. Maybe she didn't hear me. The wind picked up and I caught a bitter whiff of my own vomit.

CHAPTER TWENTY-TWO

Wednesday, October 26, 1949

I wake up in a foul mood and eager to get down to business. After checking to make sure that the gun is still hanging off the back of the nightstand, I head down for breakfast. It's a few minutes past eight o'clock. Campillo serves me yet another plate of fried sausage, battered and stuffed with rice.

"Did you sleep well?" he asks.

"Perfectly, why do you ask?"

"You were so soaked when you got back last night, I was afraid you might've caught a cold."

"Even in the wilds of Africa, Legionnaires are trained to withstand every kind of deluge; it doesn't matter if it's sand, water, or frogs."

Campillo's jaw drops. I can see exactly how many teeth he's missing.

"Frogs?" he gasps.

"Yes, sir. You've never heard of that before?"

"Never in my life! Are you sure you're not having me on?"

"Do I look like the kind of guy who goes around looking for cheap laughs?"

"No, no."

"I'll tell you all about those frogs one of these days."

I congratulate Campillo on the sausage and head for the Venta del Cruce without waiting to hear him say good-bye.

It's nine o'clock and Eusebio isn't there. A half hour later he still hasn't shown up. At ten o'clock I go back to the pension. Campillo is out. I ask the proprietress if she knows where her son is but don't expect a reply. Actually, she doesn't so much as tilt her head to listen. I push past her into the reception area and call Eusebio. Nobody answers. I don't know what to do. Luckily, Campillo, who must have heard me, opens the dining room door.

"Is there something I can help you with, Sergeant?"

"Let me borrow the Chrysler." My words shoot out like cannonballs.

"Come again?" he gasps in alarm.

"I need the pension's vehicle, the Chrysler."

"You mean my car?"

"Yes. It's an official mission. Don't worry; I'll make it worth your while."

"It's not a question of money."

"I'll only need it for a couple of hours."

"But why don't you hire a taxi? What about the boot camp? Why can't you take a military vehicle like you normally do?"

"Impossible. Discretion, Campillo. It's a matter of discretion. You understand."

"You're putting me in a very difficult position."

"Do you or do you not need the car this morning?" I ask, getting a little impatient.

"Well, I have to pick up some provisions around noon and—"

"I'll get it back to you way before then," I cut in.

"Where are you going?"

"Pancorbo."

"That's not very far," he admits, "but even so . . ."

"Are you trying to suggest that you don't trust me, Campillo?" My face takes on a fierce expression. I step toward the man, staring at him straight in the eye. "Am I to understand that you're afraid I may steal your car? Am I to understand that you doubt the word and actions of a gentleman Legionnaire?"

That last bit truly horrifies him.

"My God, no, nothing of the kind, it's just that this has never happened to me before."

Finally, in a tremulous voice and eyes full of supplication, he says, "Two hours. I can't let you have it for any longer than that."

He holds the keys out to me like a maiden who's defended her honor to the bitter end, a look of immense suffering on his face. I snatch them up with my fist and snap back, exasperated, "I've had enough. Don't worry so much, damn it. And no matter what, if anybody asks for me, tell them you don't know anything. Good-bye."

The car's interior is as neat and tidy as its owner. I ratchet the gearshift pitilessly into first. The car jolts to life. Campillo, pained, stands in the doorway beneath the carefully painted sign of his establishment. He observes my departure with a consternation exaggerated beyond measure. By now he's wracked with regret, but it's too late. Let him suffer.

I'm on the road to Pancorbo. It rained quite a bit last night. The sun's rays barely puncture the overcast sky on my way out of Miranda. I pull into a village whose main street is a dirt road full of mud. By mistake, I end up at a dead end. I feel leaden, overcome by a dreary, dense, and unsettled sensation. There's a goat tied to a straw-bottomed chair right in front of me. A baby lamb nuzzles one of her udders, while a woman seated in a chair nearby breast-feeds the child she's holding in her arms. I stop the car, get out, and walk up to her. The woman covers her breast and the baby's head with a handkerchief. I ask her if this is Pancorbo and she says no, this place is called Santa Gadea del Cid, but I won't be able to miss Pancorbo. She shows me the way without getting up, shifting her gaze between the handkerchief and the scar on my head. I get back in the car and turn around. Everything happens automatically, as if inevitable. I turn onto the main highway to Madrid. This time it's a straight shot to Pancorbo. I'm not feeling so hot. It's as though I'm lacking confidence, especially after that fling with the major's wife last night. That was a big mistake. It could have cost me my life. I'm seized by an urge to cause her physical harm. If it came down to it, I'd be perfectly capable of snapping her neck like a chicken's. My mood improves just thinking about it. The sky has cleared up. I spot what's either a falcon or an eagle gliding over the landscape of low, twisting oak trees. The bird must be hunting for prey. He doesn't know what today's catch will be; it could be either a hare or a field mouse. It's the same for me; I'm out hunting with no idea what spoils I may find. After crossing a deep gorge, I see Pancorbo appear. It's nestled at the foot of a castle in ruins. The houses are stacked along the narrow chasm. Driving into the village, I quickly find the main square, very spick-and-span. I park and walk beneath a passage of stone arches supporting the town hall. The train tracks are right in front of me. A river flows past down below on my right. A woman of uncertain age is scrubbing clothes at a public washing area. The fact that I'm about to see Eusebio brightens me up. The woman smiles when she notices me, baring a set of pink gums. I ask for Eusebio Fernández.

"Who?"

"Piojillo, from the bakery."

Her leer vanishes instantly. Bad sign, I think. But she still tells me where the man lives, while making it plain that the sooner I leave her in peace, the better. The family bakery is on the other side of the train tracks, next to a church dedicated to Saint Nicholas. The house is typical for the region, built out of a latticelike combination of wood and clay bricks. There's a sort of open courtyard alongside the entrance. I calm down on seeing Eusebio's truck parked there, next to a well. I knock on the front door. An old woman with a weathered and crooked face opens the door. She gives off the mingled odors of livestock, firewood, and soot. She looks me up and down when I ask for Eusebio.

"Who are you?"

"A friend. We were supposed to meet today at nine o'clock and he never showed up."

"Are you the Legionnaire?"

"Yes."

"Come in."

We climb a narrow staircase ending in a room that serves the dual purpose of entrance hall and dining room. There are two doors on the left and what looks like a kitchen off to the right. The space is large, simple, and austere. Fat clusters of garlic hang off the blackened and worm-eaten beams. There is a fire going in the hearth against the back wall. A vast wooden table covered in oilcloth presides over the middle of the room. It's flanked by two benches. The floor is littered with sacks of flour. The woman sits down on a low, straw-bottomed chair next to the fire. She picks up a woven grass fan and starts waving it in front of the flames. She doesn't speak. Why did she bring me up here? All at once the lady begins to murmur as if delirious, or slightly off her head.

"We're nobodies. There's not a soul we can turn to. The bakery is the only thing we've got in this godforsaken corner of the world. It's no wonder we love it so much, since we've got nothing else. We find shelter here, warming ourselves when night falls, while the bread bakes."

"Why are you telling me this, ma'am?"

"Because my family has suffered enough and I don't want to lose everything now that I'm an old woman. They've left me here by myself."

Before I could open my mouth, she went on.

"The children are at school, my daughter went shopping, and her husband is out delivering bread . . . I don't want anything to happen to them."

"Why should anything happen to them? Where is Eusebio?"

"He isn't here."

"Will he be long?"

"I don't think he'll be coming back."

"Where did he go?"

"I don't know. They took him away."

"Who?"

"Some military men. The officer in charge must've had sore feet, because he walked like a duck."

Suddenly the show's over. I have to get out of here fast. I turn tail and make for the door. The woman calls me back and motions for me to follow her. She opens one of the doors off to the left and we enter an immaculate bedroom punctuated by a tiny window. She turns on a lightbulb, but it does little to dispel the gloom. There's a trunk and two beds. A pitcher-and-bowl stand has a white towel with an embroidered fringe hanging off it. She tells me that this is where Eusebio and her grandson sleep. She pulls a cardboard box tied up with string out from under the big bed. She unties the knot and opens it. It's full of letters.

"Eusebio warned me that if you ever came by, I should give this to you. When the war ended, there were still lots of letters that never got sent. Often the prisoners themselves didn't know where their loved ones were. At least those poor souls died in peace, confident in the illusion that their last words had reached their destination. He tried to send them whenever he could, but it had to be done carefully to avoid detection. But he ended up getting caught anyway. Someone in Miranda reported him . . ."

"I'm in a real hurry, ma'am, and won't be able to take them with me."

"They're for you."

I don't have time to argue, so snatching up the box, I run down the stairs without bidding her farewell.

Well, this means it's all over. There seems to have been a shift in the already delicate balance. Cedazo has gone into action. I decide to put my faith in Eusebio's powers of resistance. He's got nothing to lose. As long as he doesn't spill everything, I've got just enough time to collect my things and wing it out of here. There's not much they can accuse me of even if he does talk. Tricking the Army into thinking I was writing that so-called report is the only solid accusation they have against me. As for the idea of digging up the bones, it never went beyond exactly that—an idea. I could always deny it anyway. On my way back to Miranda, I consider the chances of being able to carry out my father's last request. There aren't any. I haven't done a single thing right from the very beginning. I asked around for Eusebio Fernández for purely sentimental reasons. It was stupid and unnecessary. I could have found him later, after hauling Bartomeu Camús's bones away. Still, I don't consider my trip to Miranda a total failure. I discovered the exact location of the grave. Next time I'll get down to work immediately and succeed. At any rate, the only thing to do now is disappear as quickly as possible and stop pushing my luck.

The box of letters is next to me on the passenger's seat. I slam the brakes, jump out of the car, open the side door, grab the box, and throw it down into the ditch by the side of the road. The letters fly up into the air, scattering every which way. They're not my affair. I can't be held responsible for every piece of unfinished business in the world. I've got enough problems with my own.

Everything seems quiet when I get to the pension. Nothing's out of the ordinary. The pedestrians on the street are going about their normal daily routine. There doesn't appear to be anybody waiting for me. They've probably been keeping themselves busy with Eusebio. I have to move fast. I leave the motor running and go inside. The old woman behind the reception desk has finally changed position. She isn't knitting. A plaid blanket thrown over her shoulders, she stares steadily ahead. Barely glancing at the lady, I act as if I haven't seen her. I feel bad, but I've got plenty of other things to worry about. I grab the key. Speed is everything. The major will be here in no time.

I go up to my room. Before opening the door, I stand still and put my ear up to the wood for a few seconds. There's no one there. I go in to find the room turned completely upside down. It's been given a thorough search and no one's tried to hide it. Anxiety setting in, I take up the Marines duffel bag and stuff a few particulars inside; money and identification papers. I'm not planning on bringing anything else. Running over to the night table, I drag it away from the wall. My second firearm has disappeared. Now I really do have to make a run for it.

Slipping slowly down the stairs, I keep my ears open but don't hear a sound. I pull up short on reaching the reception desk. The old lady isn't there! Her customary place seems oddly vacant. It's uncanny. There is a hushed stillness. I backtrack up the stairs a few steps. It's just my nerves getting to me. So what if the old lady isn't there? She had to move someday. It was her constant immobility that wasn't normal. Maybe somebody took her to the bathroom, what do I care? I go back down those last few steps again and head toward the front door. Not a soul. That lovely Chrysler is still parked on the right, with the name "Pension Campillo" painted across the sides. Instinct tells me to get the fuck out of here right now. I'll grab the car and drive it as far as it'll take me. I'm leaving. I'll go collect my son and mother and then we'll all go down to deepest Africa to make my fortune. Afterward, when I'm good and ready, I'll put Bartomeu Camús's testimony to good use. About to step out the door, I hear a noise from behind that stops me in my tracks. A gravelly, but firm, cough. My heart pounds wildly in my chest. I turn around. It's the elderly Señora Campillo. She doesn't take up any more space standing than she does sitting down. Her cloudy blue eyes are boring into mine. She glides toward me like some kind of rheumatic ghost. I don't wait to find out what the woman wants; she's thoroughly unsettled me. I burst out the door and jump in the car. I turn the key in the ignition, turn it again, and again . . . It doesn't start. I seize the steering wheel with both hands. Looking up, I see the old woman standing in the pension door. She observes me fixedly, but with indifference. Leaning against the headrest, I close my eyes. I have to think. I remember that before rushing into the pension, I'd left the motor running.

When I open my eyes, the soldier Fontes is right outside, sweeping me up and down with his gaze.

A smile on his face, he's got a pistol in one hand, aimed at my head, and a spark plug in the other.

In no time at all, the car is surrounded by a swarm of policemen. Each one is armed and ready to fire. I spot a couple of Eusebio's letters, which managed to escape destruction, on the floor of the car. What should I tell them? I refuse to budge. As my father used to say, I'm going to the dogs.

Fontes opens the car door and makes me get out. He's still smiling. The guy doesn't say a word as he pats me down to see if I'm armed. Good. He still hasn't wiped that grin off his face, but at least he's keeping his mouth shut. The soul of a dog lurks within Fontes's body. If he were to die right now, he wouldn't go to heaven or hell. The guy would be sent directly to pet limbo. He takes my gun as he shoves the butt of his own against my kidney. I start to move. We head back to the pension. The old lady's place behind the reception desk is taken up by Eusebio's inert form. His cheeks and eyes are swollen and his face is covered in blood. He's completely immobile, and I can't tell if he's dead or alive. He's sitting up, leaning against the wall, hung low against his chest, arms hanging down. Someone's draped the old lady's plaid shawl across his shoulders, I guess as some kind of joke.

They tie my hands behind my back and push me to the ground. An all too familiar sigh emanates from the door leading to the dining room. I hear him, but I can't see anything.

"The Bible itself says it," the major begins. "'Vanity of vanities, all is vanity. What profit hath a man of all his labors which he taketh under the sun? One generation passes and another cometh, but the earth abideth forever. The sun also ariseth and the sun goeth down and hastens to the place where he arose . . .' And what happens? The next morning it rises in the east again. But that being said, we're only human. Everybody knows there's nothing new under the sun, but we persevere out of sheer vanity. Our vanity won't let us quit. If we didn't indulge ourselves with a little self-importance from time to time, our lives would be even more mediocre than they already are. Everyone has to satisfy their own egotism, their self-love, in accordance with their specific needs." The major plants himself right in front of me. He's still wearing civilian dress, complete with those patent-leather shoes. "Take a look at me. You could say I'm vain for refusing to let someone make a cuckold out of me and then live to tell the tale.

"I'm vain because I can't stand someone going around pretending to be a Fascist right under my nose and thinking that I don't know what's really going on.

"I'm vain for not being able to tolerate it when some little shit shows up at the camp and tries to make a fool out of me in front of my soldiers.

"I'm vain because I think I can aspire to more in life, and believe that real opportunities to get ahead only come your way once. And that's when you have to grab them."

"What've you done to Eusebio?"

"Nothing, we just asked him a few questions. The same thing we'll do to you. By the way, that was very clever, hiding the pistol behind the nightstand."

"You can't do anything to me. Let me go. Whatever it is you want, we can talk about it."

"Oh, we'll definitely talk, don't you worry about that."

The last thing I see is Fontes's highly polished boot, poised to kick me right in the face. Then the impact of a hideous blow to the head.

CHAPTER TWENTY-THREE

The two policemen on either side of me were bulky men, at least three times my size. Eyes to the ground, I saw four military boots, black, powerful, and steel-toed. They looked capable of doing quite a bit of damage. That's why I kept dead quiet. I figured my hide wasn't worth a cent at that point. I almost wanted them to hit me. Then they wouldn't be able to claim I'd tried to escape, which would give them the perfect excuse to heave me over the side the building, like poor No-Sister-Salvador.

I was quiet, real quiet.

I was a shit, scared shitless.

I didn't want to die. Suddenly I had two goals in life: honor my father's last request and avenge No-Sister-Salvador's death.

The two men clutched me stiffly by the arms. Seconds passed and they still hadn't done anything to me yet. My mind was a blank. Sister Paula had abandoned me and now I was all alone. Trying to stay as still as possible, I lost balance and faltered anyway. The policemen tightened their grip even more. Someone came out onto the roof and sidled up behind us. I could hear him breathing. I turned to see who it was. My face was whipped around by a hard slug. It was the chief of police, who, grinning broadly, said, "Don't look at me, kid. Don't look at me. Or else you're going to get it."

The two officers led me down the stairs. We exited the building by Caputxes Street and turned onto Plegamans, where the cars were waiting. Salvador's body was being taken away when I got there. A pair of orderlies lifted him up off the ground, grasping him by the knees and armpits. They didn't even put him on a stretcher. His body was simply tossed into the back of the paddy wagon. I caught a quick glance of his face. He looked sad. In the moment of impact, my best friend had known he was dying. I would never be able to forgive them.

They shoved me into a police car and took me away. I started to shake when it became clear that instead of heading for the station, we were actually leaving the city limits. The policemen traveling along in the back of the vehicle with me noticed and started to laugh. They told me not to be afraid; nothing was going to happen to me. Each time they said that, I grew more and more terrified.

I was taken to a mansion on the outskirts of Barcelona, where I was sent reeling onto the floor of some sort of garage. The door slammed shut, leaving me in the dark. The air was thick with damp and the fumes of engine grease, oil, and old tires, blended with months of accumulated dust. I didn't know what to think. It was obvious that I'd been forsaken by Sister Paula, and yet her father hadn't killed me. Why? An hour and a half later, the door opened and someone turned on a lightbulb. A maid in uniform entered, accompanied by two middle-aged men with indefinite, almost blurred, features. The older of the two cautioned me, without much enthusiasm, not to move and to be on my best behavior. He pointed the index finger of his right hand, as massive as a stone crusher's maul, in my direction. I imagined what that fist would feel like pounding into my face and obeyed. The maid, a pretty girl of about sixteen or seventeen, wouldn't even glance in my direction. She was carrying a sandwich wrapped in newsprint, a jug of water, and a chamber pot. She left everything on top of a straw-bottomed chair at the entrance and left, followed by the men, leaving the light on. I saw that the garage was empty, except for the chair and a low, small cot in one corner. There was a door, tightly shut, which probably led into the main house. I pulled a potato omelet out from between the sandwich slices and, famished, ate it all by itself, saving the bread for last. Between sips of water, I set to reading the torn sheet of newsprint that had been used to wrap my meal. It was the cover of the Barcelona daily, *La Vanguardia,* from a few days before. On the front page there was a picture of a soldier, his thin lips jutting out like two pot covers. He was a cavalry lieutenant of the Spanish Army. As a member of the Blue Division, he'd fought alongside the Nazis. He'd been awarded the Iron Cross of the Third Reich by the Führer himself. His name was José Acosta Láinez, and I couldn't help but wonder what his parents thought of the whole thing. But I couldn't carry such musings any further because, on the other side, between two oil stains, I read about how, in the region of Moscow, during the German troops' advance, they'd discovered a Soviet military facility in which hundreds of dogs had been trained to destroy enemy convoys. Each animal was assigned to a soldier. The beasts were weighted down with bags of sand, which were suspended off a small armature. The canines were trained to run between moving tanks. Then the soldiers would replace the bags of sand with explosives that were activated by remote control. I closed my eyes, and for one second I could see myself in a Russian uniform. I loved my dog very much but sent him off to be blown up along with the tanks anyway. I imagined putting my arm around his neck, petting the creature to calm him down, while slowly switching the sand for dynamite. Locked in that garage and having no idea what was to become of me, I was left with imagination as my only means of survival. And the only way to withstand the pain of having lost my friend.

I dreamed that night about the tower and the stories that No-Sister-Salvador used to tell me when I was little. We'd sit on the wooden floor, dusty rays of sun slicing like lances through the cracks and fissures in the partially bricked-up windows. He'd tell me stories that were "actual fact," as he liked to say. Some tales were adventure stories set in exotic countries involving explorers and their exploits with lions, hippopotamuses, and crocodiles. The explorers' fate—whether they were to get devoured or not—depended on the day. I never knew ahead of time, and Salvador always kept me on tenterhooks until the exciting conclusion. Years later I found out that most of those stories were lifted directly from comic books. I didn't care. I practically memorized each one and was later able to recite them perfectly from start to finish. The ones that left the biggest impression on me took place in an alley called Top of the World. The back wall of our building on Caputxes Street led to Plegamans Street. And Top of the World Alley was a little cul-de-sac that began and ended on that street. The tiny street was visible from up in the tower. Only an incorrigible storyteller like No-Sister-Salvador was capable of pointing out the mysterious contradiction between that small and insignificant passage, full of shadows and filth, and its name, replete with significance and mystery. It wasn't normal, he'd say. There had to be some sort of conspiracy behind it all, which, sooner or later, we'd eventually uncover. Maybe the top of the world really meant the end of the world. He'd delight me with sinister adventures involving spies, illegal business transactions, depraved souls, and assassins, or just depraved killers. And they all began and ended on that fantastical street, Top of the World. Often the crime stories involved one of the buildings that led to the alley. A kidnapper who had the daughter of an important tycoon locked up. Or a gangster who fabricated counterfeit money behind one of those closed doors. Sometimes it was a devious Chinaman, whose principal activity was to lead ferocious bands of armed warriors out of their warren in the Top of the World to murder peaceful citizens under the cover of darkness. Once in a while No-Sister-Salvador would make me slink over to the little street in order to check and see if anything out of the ordinary was going on. Or we'd survey the alley from high up in our tower perch, inventing all sorts of small incidents that, of course, seemed highly suspicious. Suddenly I remembered that Salvador was dead and began to tremble with a combination of sorrow and rage.

On the second day of captivity, the maid brought me two sandwiches and a pair of apples. She substituted the half-empty jug for a full one and the bursting chamber pot for an empty one. The man from the day before didn't bother to come in. Instead, he stood right outside the door and shot me a hard stare. I slid over to the food as soon as they'd gone. The two sandwiches weren't wrapped this time, but there was an envelope placed beside them. I opened it, and inside was a newspaper cutting showing photos of the tower on Caputxes Street. I read the article so carefully that I could practically reproduce it word for word. It described how a band of dangerous delinquents, along with a ward from the Charity Home, had kidnapped Sister Paula, the only daughter of a well-known member of Barcelona society, the Baron of Remei. Quick and efficient action by the police force had ensured her release without any harm befalling either captive or rescue team. One of the kidnappers, in a desperate attempt to avoid being apprehended, threw himself off the roof and died instantly. The Charity Home ward managed to escape, etc., etc.

Bullshit.

The baron had me brought to his study a few days later. He was sitting in his chair attending to an employee, probably his majordomo. The scent of waxed wood pervaded the room. Two framed

photographs were displayed on a round, low table. One showed the
baron and baroness with Sister Paula at their side. They were all much
younger. The other image was of Franco, shaking the baron's hand. . . .

"The maid has had an accident, sir. A tile fell off the roof right
outside here and landed on her head," the majordomo explained.

"Bad luck. Was she hurt?" the baron asked with disinterest.

"A gash on the head. She's lost a great deal of blood. They've taken
her to the hospital."

"Understood. Go down to Barcelona and send a little something
to her mother, so she doesn't come around here causing problems."

"Yes, sir. Shall we say ten pesetas?"

"Unthinkable. Maximum five."

The servant disappeared and seemed to slither, rather than walk,
across the carpet. The baron sat staring into the fire with his back to
me. Without deigning to turn around, he said abruptly, "I could
squash you like a fly right now. Nobody knows you're here, not even
my daughter. But I won't. She's far away, in America. She only agreed
to go on the condition that I would promise to respect your life. I
plan on keeping my word, as long as you agree to comply with the
arrangements I've made for you."

"What sort of arrangements?" I broke in.

The man became furious. I could tell he was longing to throttle
me right there. But he was able to contain himself and, of course,
didn't.

"I'm packing you off to Africa in the hopes that you'll keep your
mouth shut. It's not that I'm the least bit frightened of you. In a few
days' time the circumstances revolving around your friend's death will
be completely forgotten. I can wring your neck like a chicken's whenever I feel like it."

That's when he made that lovely and ever so poetic proposition.

"You may go to sea onboard a boat bound for Melilla or go to sea as a drowned corpse tied to a cement block beneath the docks. You decide."

The baron explained that although it hadn't been easy, he'd been able to shift the blame of the supposed kidnapping onto another Charity House ward; a kid who'd died of tuberculosis not long ago. They simply fudged the dates of the death certificate by pushing them back a bit. As for me, I was officially registered as an escapee.

"They'll file your case in no time, giving you up as a lost cause."

"What about Salvador?"

"Who?"

"Salvador, the boy you had killed . . ."

He slapped me across the face.

"I didn't have anybody killed!"

"Where is he?"

"What do you mean?"

"What did they do with him?"

"How do I know? What sort of question is that? He must have been brought to the morgue. I imagine he was given a municipal burial."

To that son of a bitch, No-Sister-Salvador was a crippled little louse who'd already slipped from his mind.

The baron fell heavily onto a sofa in front of the hearth. I could have slashed his head open with the letter opener. He said abruptly, "I'm getting old. I don't understand why my daughter is so concerned about you. I love my daughter very much. She's an intelligent girl. When I die, my brother will be the one to inherit the barony, and he's not half as clever as she is. Now he's decided to embrace the Falange as if it were some sort of religion. I spoke to him this morning. All he could talk about was how busy he was, preparing for the fifth anniversary of José Antonio's death, in three weeks' time. How vulgar! Years ago I was forced to accept the fact that my only daughter wanted to become a nun. And now, in my dotage, I must face that my noble title and family fortune will be passed on to my younger brother, a visionary who's capable of donating every last cent to the Falange."

I suppose that's why he suffered from nervous attacks, like the one on the roof, from time to time. One might even say that's why he killed poor, unfortunate Salvador and allowed his daughter to witness the crime. I didn't feel sorry for him at all.

He stood up and left the room, without glancing in my direction.

I was locked up in the garage once again, with the sandwiches, jug, and chamber pot. They brought me back to his study a few days later. This time it was different. The baron had a high-ranking military officer with him. I found out afterward that it was Captain Bajolmonte, the man who was to become my lord and master for the next two years. The captain inspected me like a calf at an agricultural fair.

"Stand up straight, you little shit!" the soldier barked.

I obeyed, even though I wasn't very afraid of him. I was growing weary of the whole thing and almost didn't care what they did with me.

"What do you think of the boy?" The baron addressed his friend.

"It won't work. He doesn't look a day over sixteen," the officer replied.

And it was back to the garage again. It didn't make sense. How could they expect me to look anything but sixteen, considering that was how old I was?

A few more days passed. I spent most of my time lying on the cot, barely touching my food. I didn't have any strength or will left. I assumed that the baron, for lack of a better plan, was planning on keeping me locked up like that forever. He'd promised his daughter that he wouldn't kill me. But letting me die slowly in his garage was another matter entirely.

One day two guards entered the garage carrying buckets of hot water and soap.

"We're going to clean you up a little. You stink something awful."

Did they expect me to smell as fresh as a rose? They stripped me down and gave me a thorough scrubbing, like you'd wash a dog. They dressed me in clean clothes, combed my hair, and brought me outside into the November sun. A car pulled right up and we got inside. I asked them where I was being taken, but they wouldn't respond. We rode in silence. Our destination turned out to be the port of Barcelona. They were sending me off to Melilla as if I were a barrel of dried codfish. Once onboard, I was placed in Captain Bajolmonte's care. There, with the blazing sun reflecting off the docks, I saw his famous tattoo of Christ in agony for the first time, inscribed with the legend "He forgives, I don't." The Legionnaire told me what to expect out of my immediate future.

"We couldn't sign you up for the Legion because it's too obvious that you're only sixteen years old. The baron will leave you in my care for two years, to work as my orderly. You'll live with me and do as I say, familiarizing yourself with the spirit of the Legion as you go along. At the age of eighteen, you'll enlist. If it's any consolation, you'll be able to go by your own name. The Legion will wipe your record clean. You'll begin a new career, which, by the look of you, I doubt will be very glorious."

"The Legion?"

"You should consider this opportunity as an honor. What more can a miserable wretch like you expect?"

I could have rattled off quite a list, but I didn't get the chance. A swift blow to the stomach threw me on the ground. The captain and one of the sailors grabbed me by the legs and hung me over the side, suspending me in midair above the ocean for a few seconds. I watched how, down below, the ship left a trail of foam in its wake. I tried to imagine what it would feel like to fall headfirst into the water and let myself get caught up in the swirl of the deep.

"What do you think?" I heard. "Should we let him drop or pull him back up again?"

I couldn't take it anymore.

I thought of my father and No-Sister-Salvador, dead, and my mother, half-crazy. I begged them to please lift me back onto the ship. I didn't cause any more trouble for the rest of the journey. I had ceased to be myself. For the first time I began to wear the mask. It was also the first time that I realized how easy it is to fool people.

I embarked for Melilla on November 21, 1941. A solemn atmosphere was still palpable in the air from the ceremonies of the day before. It had been the fifth anniversary of José Antonio's death. All of Spain, with Franco at the forefront and Melilla, the Pearl of Africa, behind, paid heartfelt homage to the memory of the glorious founder of the Falange. Every balcony in the city was still adorned with Spanish and Falangist flags, which were draped in black crepe. Government buildings flew the flag at half-mast. And I was no longer a poorhouse rat. Instead, I'd become a beaten dog, lacking in dignity and judgment, the servant and lackey of a Legionnaire, but at the same time, very, very angry. And very, very hypocritical.

CHAPTER TWENTY-FOUR

Wednesday, October 26, 1949

I arrived in Barcelona aboard the *Mar Cantábrico* on Tuesday, October 18, 1949. The steamship carried a cargo of over a thousand tons of cotton, destined for the Catalan textile industry, which was only just beginning to get back on its feet after the recession caused by the war. The craft was also loaded down with machinery and seventy tons of mineral oil in barrels. A lone passenger got onboard, too. It was yours truly, a full-fledged Legionnaire on his way to Barcelona. I spent the five days of that voyage dodging puddles of oil and the flecks of cotton that floated through the air. I'd lean against one of the ship's railings, gaze down at the ocean, and feel the rage build up inside me day by day. We disembarked first thing in the morning, and, as it so happens, it was raining. The jagged skyline down by the water was outlined against Barcelona's inhospitable, bitter sky. Although quiet as mummies, the buildings were early risers, catching the first rays of the sun. A mass of seagulls surrounded the ship. Some were poised above the water, while others perched on floating pieces of wood. The most audacious of them would land on deck, refusing to budge until a sailor came along to scare them away. That's when they'd calmly stretch their wings, stride forward a few paces, pick up speed, and take flight, screeching. The *Mar Cantábrico* eased itself toward the dock with an exasperating slowness, engulfed in dense, shiny water that was littered with filth.

I was dying to get on land. After stumbling down the gangplank, I was almost run over by a tramcar on Columbus Boulevard. I checked into the first pension I found, right there in Duc de Medinaceli Plaza. Having decked myself out as a Legionnaire, I hit the streets. Wearing that uniform made me feel invincible; doors seemed to open as I passed. Everyone looked at me. My plan was very simple, relying on the element of surprise for its success. I was hoping to catch the baron alone and liquidate him discreetly, making sure to give myself enough time to escape. Then, after getting a close shave and changing into civilian dress, I'd head straight for Miranda de Ebro. I took a taxi to the baron's office, located in a ritzy section of town, on Diagonal Avenue. I adjusted my hat to cover the scar on my head, undid another button on my shirt, twisted up the ends of my mustache with a touch of spit. After double-checking my weapon, I rang the door.

A fellow who was probably the baron's secretary informed me that the gentleman wasn't in. He spoke in the smug tone of a notary at the height of his powers. I put on my best ferocious Legionnaire expression to make it understood that I'd come all the way from Melilla on an urgent business matter between the Legion and the baron.

"Then why wasn't the baron informed of your arrival?"

The secretary's question was perfectly logical. It didn't faze me in the least.

"For reasons of security," I intoned mysteriously, "we've advanced the rendezvous a few days in order to avoid unpleasant surprises."

The secretary, a relatively young man, relented and begrudgingly admitted exactly what was keeping the baron out of his office.

"He's fulfilling a social obligation."

"Of what kind?"

"The baron is a patron of the monthly magazine *Our Friends*. Are you familiar with it?"

"No."

"It's dedicated to the world of canines. They organize a prestigious dog show every year; even international breeds attend. The last phase of the contest was on Sunday and many of the dogs on show belong to distinguished members of Spanish high society. Captain General Solchaga will be presenting the awards today during a private reception. The magazine is offering a small aperitif and the baron will give a short speech. Is the Legion also taking part in the contest perhaps?"

Gazing at him steadily, I ran my fingers over my beard and responded drily.

"There are no dogs in the Legion. We have goats."

"Of course, of course."

"Where is the event taking place?"

"At the Picadero Andaluz."

"Thank you."

I'd forgotten about how all sorts of recreational and sports clubs featuring an Andalusian theme had sprung up around Barcelona after the war.

An odd jumble of odors emanated from the Picadero Andaluz, located in a well-to-do neighborhood uptown. The stench of horse manure, a clue to the club's regular activities, mingled with the pungent aroma of the show dogs—drenched in cologne to hide their natural odor—and the heady fragrance of high-society perfume. I had the taxi wait for me outside. If everything went well, it would be a discreet and rapid means of escape. If anything went wrong, there'd be no need for a taxi. The Captain General José Solchaga's official vehicle was parked at the entrance to the grounds, adorned with the four-starred flag. The soldiers at the door let me through without asking questions. The men didn't even blink. They simply saluted and stepped aside as I walked in. I asked the first person I saw wearing a black-and-white uniform and a slavish expression on his face for the Baron of Remei. The place was filled with happy and contented members of Barcelona's ruling class. I recognized the captain general, despite his civilian dress. He seemed like an inoffensive old man. He was being congratulated for his upcoming retirement in a few days. The subject of so much considerate attention was the same son of a bitch who, after commanding the National Army's invasion of Barcelona alongside General Yagüe, had relentlessly pursued the poor souls who were trying to escape across the border by walking north on the highway to France. Although claiming to be pursuing the retreating Red soldiers, they actually began to gun down columns of fugitives, the immense majority of whom were civilians; families consisting of women, the elderly, and small children. As I approached the military figure, I heard people, in a Spanish heavily accented with Catalan, expressing their "undying affection," offering their "most sincere and admiring best wishes," and thanking him for his "gentlemanly, tactful, and prudent military prowess in the Catalan Zone." I was carrying a loaded gun. It was enough to make me want to murder the captain general instead of the baron.

I tried asking someone else, and was discreetly informed that the baron was in the bathroom, attending to his necessities, and would be back shortly. The opportunity was heaven-sent. I rushed to the lavatories and found him washing his hands, back toward the door. The man wore the uniform of the Falange. There was no one else around. He appeared taller somehow. I pulled out a knife and went up to him, twisting one of his arms behind his back while holding the blade point up to his throat. His other arm hung stiff and cramped at his side. That always happens. When the brain goes into panic, it sends a message saying, "Don't try to do anything with that free arm, you won't have time, and he'll cut your throat."

"I've come on behalf of No-Sister-Salvador. He sends his regards from the great beyond. Don't you remember me? I'm the one you sent to Melilla."

I instructed him in a very low, threatening voice to lift his head and look at my face in the mirror. I wanted the baron to see my reflection so he would know who was killing him, just in case his memory failed.

"Look at me, asshole. My face is going to be the last thing you'll see in this world. Then I'm going to rip your artery open with this knife. Don't think I can't. I learned how to do many things in the Legion, thanks to you. For example, I was trained to kill silently and in cold blood."

The man, about to shit with fear, lifted his head ever so slowly. When I saw his features head on, I was shocked.

"Who the hell are you?"

"The Baron of Remei."

"Liar. Where is the baron, you son of a bitch?"

"I'm the baron, I swear. What do you want?" he asked, terrified.

"Don't fuck around. One corpse more or less doesn't matter to me."

"I'm telling you, I'm the baron. On my word. I'm afraid you're looking for the wrong person."

The jerk didn't care who got snuffed, just so long as it wasn't him. His eyes bulged after hearing my brief description of the baron.

"You're referring to my brother!"

"What?"

"The Baron of Remei that you're looking for was my brother, may he rest in peace. He passed away four years ago, of natural causes. If he had some sort of a debt to repay you, don't worry, I'm sure we can come to an agreement. There's no need for violence. I'm a great admirer of the Legion."

I was disoriented and didn't know what to do. That was the last thing I'd expected. I pressed the blade a bit harder against his throat. The tip sunk a quarter of an inch into the flesh and blood began to flow. The sissy dissolved into sobs. I said to him, "You're right. I've come to settle an old debt. And you're the one who's going to pay."

He saw death approaching and lost control of his sphincter. Those sobs turned into moans. I was covered from head to toe by the fetid reek of the new baron's excrement.

I was incapable of killing him.

"You may have gotten lucky today, but don't tempt fate. I was never here. You've suffered from a minor intestinal disturbance. Understood?"

"Understood."

"That's good, because if not, I'll be back to liquidate you. And I'll take my time about it. I'll cut your belly wide open and watch your intestines tumble out. Then I'll tie them in a bow around your neck and strangle you."

The baron started vomiting before I could finish. He was so frightened that I managed to put away the knife and pull out my gun, stunning him with a blow to the head. I left him lying there in his own vomit and excrement.

On our way back to town, the taxi driver mentioned, very discreetly, that I must have stepped on something at the show, judging by an unpleasant odor emanating from my person.

"With so many dogs running around loose, it's inevitable."

"You're absolutely right," I responded. "The place was full of dogs. Very elegant ones, I'll grant you, but dogs nonetheless. And one of the biggest ones shat all over me."

"That's bad luck."

"Yes."

"Where are we going?"

"To the Plaza Duc de Medinaceli, so I can put on my civilian clothes and pick up a suitcase. Then you'll drop me off at the train station."

"Are you going on a trip?"

"Yes. Are you familiar with Miranda de Ebro?"

"No. Where is it?"

"It's in the province of Burgos. I'm going to do a favor for my father."

"The best kinds of favors are the ones you do for your father."

"You can say that again."

I didn't bother to shave. It wasn't necessary. The Baron of Remei would keep quiet. The rest you know well enough. I didn't manage to kill the Baron of Remei last week and, by the looks of it, I won't be able to satisfy my father's last request, either.

Shaken awake by the jolting of the truck, I'm lying in the back of the vehicle, my hands and feet bound to a metal ring affixed to the chassis. Eusebio's inert body is splayed out next to me. He's obviously dead, from the way he lists from side to side with the vehicle's fits and starts. They didn't even bother to tie him up. I can't move. My entire body aches. Aside from that kick in the face, I must have gotten a good beating before they threw me in the truck. I have no idea where they're taking me.

After driving on the highway for some miles and then turning onto a patch of dirt road, the vehicle comes to a stop. A man I don't know lifts up the tarp covering the back and climbs up onto the truck bed. He releases me from the ring, unties the rope knotted around my feet, and drags me outside. Another man, also dressed as a civilian, is waiting for him. It's strange. I don't see any military around. It's as if the major was acting completely on his own. I have no idea what's going to happen. He's a much more dangerous character than I thought. They could do whatever they wanted with poor Eusebio. With me it's different; I'm a sergeant in the Legion. It's taken me eight years to form this thick hide of mine. It's not going to be that easy to tear off.

The two men carry guns and force me to walk in front of them. The first thing I see is the tree in the shape of the letter Y. So Eusebio blabbed about that, too. They push and shove me toward the landmark. Cedazo is there, his jacket wrinkled and his patent-leather shoes soiled. He walks up to me with his characteristic gait, as if treading on cotton balls. When we reach the pine tree, I notice the rosemary bush that had been growing up around it is no longer there. In its place is a long, shallow hole. Fontes, the only soldier in sight, is keeping vigil over two men who are crouched down in the ditch. His rifle is trained steadily on them. They're sweaty and covered in filth; hands and faces caked in earth. The cavity deepens beneath their two shovels. I know them. They're the ones I hired last week in Barcelona. It appears as though they've ended up carrying out what they were hired to do, excavate. But for somebody else. They must have been waiting around in Logroño and instead of getting picked up by me, found themselves thrown into the back of an Army patrol vehicle. Eusebio didn't leave out a single detail in his confession. I don't hold it against him. Unfortunately, talking didn't stop the guy from getting beaten to death.

A shove sends my body reeling to the ground, facing the pit. I look up. My two would-be assistants are staring at me with profound loathing. They'd crush my skull with those shovels if they got the chance. I didn't mean to deceive them, but thanks to my own stupidity, they've fallen into an unexpected trap.

The major says, "See that hole your friends are digging? It's a technique I learned from the Nazis. Executing people can be quite a chore, depending on how you go about it. Packing the bodies into the trucks, unloading them, then digging the graves. All that's unnecessary. It's much more practical to bring the offenders to the location where they're about to be buried. After walking to the site on their own two feet, they dig their own graves. When they're done, you simply get them to kneel in front of the cavity. Once you shoot them in the back of the neck, the offenders fall into the graves all by themselves. Then it's simply a question of covering them up, which is relatively easy. It'd be impossible to find a more hygienic, practical, and efficient technique."

They force me to my feet and pull me aside, while the other two continue digging. The major sits down on a stone. I'm standing in front of him, bound and retained by two men. Cedazo painfully struggles to take his shoes off, but he can't. The patent leather seems to have fused to his skin. He orders one of his men to help while pulling a paper out of his blazer pocket. Barefoot and relieved, he begins to read. At the same time, one of his cronies sets to polishing up those patent-leather shoes. He recites:

"'These are the words of Bartomeu Camús, which I leave as a testimony of everything that I witnessed as an unclassified prisoner, from the end of 1938 to the beginning of 1940. In the capacity of master carpenter, I was hired to work in the house of Dr. Antonio Vallejo-Nágera, major of the Military Psychiatric Service of Franco's Army.' Tell me, Sergeant, are those words familiar? You wrote them yourself. Yes, you'll have to forgive me. I'm afraid I intercepted that letter you sent to Melilla. It was very unfair to keep such an interesting document to yourself and not share it with friends. This Bartomeu or Bartolomé guy reveals some devastating information. He mentions the names of some very important people in Spanish society who are, no doubt, anxious to protect their good names. People who would pay good money to keep such a well-documented statement from coming to light. Bad luck, Sergeant. Now Camús's declaration and all the information concerning the case are mine. And I don't plan on sharing. Right now you're nothing more than a little worm squirming in the mud. I'm the one who's going to end up with the cash. Actually, the purpose of my trip to Madrid yesterday was to lay the groundwork for future negotiations. The results were very promising. The concern expressed by those implicated was enough to convince me of the information's veracity. I might as well have come across a treasure chest. Well, admittedly, you're the one who discovered the treasure, but—"

"My father did," I break in.

"Oh really? Well, it's mine now. I got back from Madrid this morning. I wanted to go straight to Campillo's place and slice your balls off right then and there. But I was so worked up that I decided to visit one Eusebio Fernández in person first. A matter of routine, pure and simple. I wanted to find out why a sergeant in the Legion who had come to Miranda to look for Camús's treasure would be so interested in a guy who delivers bread. It was five o'clock in the morning, but you won't catch a baker asleep at that hour. On the contrary, they're wide awake, working. You can't imagine how surprised he was. I hadn't even said hello, and the man started shitting in his pants, spilling the beans all over the place. Of course, out of everything he told me, there was one item in particular that caught my attention. He confessed that aside from making away with the treasure, you planned on disinterring a Red who'd been buried anonymously, back when Miranda was still a concentration camp. A Red? What Red? And here's a coincidence; the Red in question was named Camús! The same name that appears in the document! And I, who as a rule don't believe in chance, asked him, 'And why would he want to do a thing like that?' He told me, 'To fulfill a promise that he made to his father on his deathbed.' It was all I could do to not burst out laugh-

ing. What a joke! I assumed the wretch was having me on. That's
when we laid into him. The harder we hit the fellow, the more he
swore he was telling the truth, that those had been your very words.
The man was already broken down when we got our hands on him.
You might say that after a couple of well-placed blows, he was already
halfway to the next world. But something still remains unclear. That's
why I need your help. I refuse to believe that you've done all this just
to carry off the bones of a dead man, to keep a promise. In other
words, start talking. And don't think that being a Legionnaire will do
you any good. You're not going to get any mercy from me. And you're
not going to get any money for what you know. The most you can
hope for is to save your life."

It's a lie. I don't believe him. Not even God himself will save me
if they dig up Camús and don't find anything. I'd be too dangerous
a witness for Cedazo's business plans. I've got to escape. And I'm
going to take my mask off; it will be useless to me now.

"Eusebio told the truth."

"So it was all for a promise, huh?" Cedazo says, visibly restrain-
ing the urge to slug me again.

Behind my back, I hear the rhythmic sound of the two men fill-
ing shovels with dirt, lifting them up and emptying them over the
side of the pit.

"Yes. My father couldn't stand to think that the very person who'd
saved his life should be wiped off the face of the earth as though he'd
never existed. When we forget those who have been taken from us,
we condemn them to death twice over."

The major gets extremely agitated. Turning bright red, he strides
barefoot in my direction, taking care not to tread on any pebbles.
Looking down at me, he says, "Don't give me any speeches, you son
of a bitch! I'll tell you a story. Something I personally experienced. It
took place a few days after the end of the war. I was temporarily

assigned to a unit in Extremadura. There's a village there called Ta-larrubias, in the province of Badajoz. We arrived at the place in a couple of trucks and took away forty-two men. Among them, there was a fellow who claimed to be one hundred and fourteen years old. During May of '39, we spent the nights of the seventeenth, the twenty-third, and the twenty-eighth executing every single last one of those men. There were no witnesses and we kept to the task at hand. The Regime authorities were saying that a third of the Spanish male population should be exterminated. It was a bit like ripping out weeds—a dirty job, but necessary. We buried them on the side of the mountain, in three different mass graves. Those forty-two people haven't been heard from since. The grave diggers might as well have been blind, deaf, and dumb. The relatives didn't dare leave their homes when we passed through town. The mountains of Spain are filled with burial sites like that. Over ten years have passed and the villagers still act as if nothing happened. Nobody wants to cause trouble, not even the victims' families. Nobody gives a shit about that ridiculous statement of yours. It's all the same to them whether the forgotten dead are killed twice or two hundred times over. Once again His Excellency's leadership has proven infallible. We did what was best for Spain. And we did it quickly, with no regrets."

"Those families remain silent not from forgetfulness, but from fear. It's normal."

"It's good they're frightened. As long as they're scared shitless, the authorities can calmly go about the business of building the country back up. Once the new State is up and running and those fucking Democrats realize that we were the first ones to really screw the Communists, then nobody will ever mention the war again."

"That's not true. In order for there to be reconciliation, there must be forgiveness . . ."

"Who said anything about reconciliation?" he cuts in. "We won the war, imbecile."

He didn't let me finish my sentence. I merely wanted to add that in order to be able to forgive, it's important not to forget. After a few moments' consideration, I decide to keep silent. He motions to one of his men, who hastens over and puts the major's shoes, now restored to their former brilliance, back on. The major ties his laces and stands up, advancing slowly toward me. Fontes smirks at me, and I notice a trail of drool slipping out of the corner of his mouth. He doesn't lose sight of the two men digging the hole. The major, with one of those icy grins, says very slowly, "I'll tell you what I think. Before dying, your father confided in you about the existence of Bartomeu Camús's document and why its recovery was so important. He let it be understood that there was another part to the treasure buried along with the body of his friend, perhaps even more important than the document, who knows? It could be further top-secret information about high-ranking members of the Regime. That's why you've come here to dig up those bones. That's the real reason; it's not for the sake of some promise. Am I wrong?"

"Completely."

"You're so stubborn. What I if proposed that we split the treasure fifty-fifty? Well, we'll split whatever it is that's left to discover, of course."

"You won't find a thing when you dig up Camús. Be satisfied with what you've got. I don't want anything from you. You can keep it all for yourself and leave me in peace."

"How generous!"

Cedazo plants himself directly in front of me, whacking my face so hard that my head whips backward. Fontes giggles and the major silences him with a glare. He says, "I see you don't want to cooperate. That's too bad."

I'm dragged over to the truck again. Then they toss my body, bound by hand and foot, alongside Eusebio's corpse. I take in his inert features. Eusebio looks happy. But that won't do anybody any good. None of his relatives will be able to find consolation in his peaceful countenance. I don't care what sort of face he was left with, but I do wish that we'd gotten a chance to talk more. You never forgive yourself for those missed conversations. I try to loosen the knots, to no avail. It's impossible to escape. They leave me there for an hour, keeping an eye on me all the while. I'm just as curious as the major is to find out if there are any more surprises hidden among Bartomeu's remains.

Some men pull me roughly out of the truck, untie my feet, and lead me back to the pit. The major and Fontes are there. They chat among themselves without even glancing my way. On closer inspection, I realize that the cavity is enormous. At least seven feet deep. The bodies of the men who dug it are lying at the bottom, shot in the back of the head. Cedazo is insane. As I'm about to turn around, one of his thugs gives me a hard shove. I fall down into the pit, on top of one of the bodies. I try to get up but my hands are bound. It's impossible. I hear the major issue an order. I look up and am met with Fontes's inexpressive and smiling face, holding a burlap sack. It looks pretty full. He begins to empty out its contents on top of me. At first I can't tell what it is. The pieces are hard and white, but don't feel like stones. They fall in a sharp tumult all over my flesh. I close my eyes. When I open them again, I see bones; a tibia, a foot, a piece of rib. . . . Farther off, a skull has rolled into a corner. Then comes Cedazo's preternaturally calm voice.

"Allow me to introduce you to Camús, Sergeant. He may be a little fragmented right now, so to speak, but it is indeed him, I assure you. At least, that is what we dug up."

In the end those grave diggers in Melilla were right. Nine years underground is sufficient for a dead man's bones to fit into a potato sack. The major goes on, as if it were the most natural thing in the world.

"What do you think? Aren't you going to say hello? Take a good look at him, because one could say that he's got your fate in his hands. We didn't find a thing."

"I already told you there was nothing to find."

"Well, I still don't believe it. You can't fool me."

"I'm a Legionnaire!"

"A Legionnaire! You're pathetic, that's what you are!"

"Untie me and get me out of here!"

"Since when does a twenty-four-year-old sergeant start giving orders to a major, and a war veteran to boot? Is that what they teach you in the Legion? What happens if I don't untie you? Or worse, what if I stopped you cold with a bullet in the ass? What do I have to be afraid of, the scandal? Or perhaps you're considering breaking into a rendition of 'The Legion Is for Me'!"

He begins to chuckle and everyone else joins in. In the midst of a fit of hiccups, he adds, "So you think your buddies are going to come running up from Melilla to save you, huh? 'The Legion Is for Me.' Oh, I'm so terrified . . . I can't believe it, when are you going to come to your senses? You're a dead man. I can do whatever I want: a shot to the head, a rope around the neck. Or simply inflict some minor wound and then bury you alive. Nothing would happen. And do you know why? Look." He pulls out a doubled newspaper from the interior pocket of his blazer and unfolds it, waving a page in my face. "This is today's schedule for the Generalíssimo's trip to Portugal. He's going to Fátima. His Excellency will worship the Mother of God in the very place where she appeared to those dear children Francisco, Lúcia, and Jacinta. That Franco, a religious man and the conqueror of atheist Communism, should get down on his knees to worship this miraculous Madonna is exactly what Spain expects. The

Generalíssimo will visit the sanctuary of Fátima today and observe the most severe religious unction. When he and his wife receive the Holy Communion, the intense emotion of that instant will be communicated to all the faithful present. Spain itself will be inundated with torrents of heartfelt sentiment and pride. That's the way Spain is now. The country is concerned with things like that and nothing else. The population certainly isn't interested in the ravings of a half-crazy Legionnaire like you. When compared to the immense ocean of His Excellency's fame and glorious journeys, your case is a minuscule splash in a puddle. Everyone in Spain is focused on Franco these days. No one's going to pay attention to the son of a Red who shows up here to dig up some other Red. If that isn't enough, that second Red left behind a testament, which, if it came to light, would have serious repercussions in times like these, when we've got glory coming out of our ears. Right now you're a shadow. You're nothing and you'll leave nothing behind. You can't do anything for me. Camús has given me the chance to attain a much more comfortable position in life. You, on the other hand, are merely in the way."

I realize to my horror that Cedazo is stupid enough to actually kill me.

"You can't go around assassinating people," I say.

"Another thing I learned from the Nazis is that it's easy to eliminate people like you. The trick is to stop thinking of people as humans and instead consider them as nothing more than pieces of shit. It's getting late. What do you have to offer me?"

"What do you want?"

"Whatever you've got, fool! Something that might save your skin."

Señor Pau always told me that life is a one-way street. No matter how far you wander, it's impossible to turn back. Life becomes much simpler for whoever learns to accept this simple truth. "That's when you realize, Niso, how important it is to make the most out of what we've got, of who we are and what we've become." Well, I don't seem to have learned that lesson very well. Cedazo asks me to tell him something that'll save my skin and I have nothing to offer.

They lug Eusebio's body over to the cavity, flinging him down roughly on top of me. I turn to see if his features are still frozen in an expression of happiness. It's hard to tell. His face is smashed into the dirt. All I can make out is the back of his neck. What's clear is that it's impossible to breathe when lying facedown at the bottom of a grave. That means he's good and dead. The position itself goes against nature. All of a sudden I can see myself lying facedown in the dirt, practically tasting the ocher in my mouth. As a small boy, I'd sometimes get the urge to eat the soil from the flowerpots out on the balcony. Shit! I long to struggle free of the rope, but it's no use. I try to crawl out of the hole with my hands tied. Leaning my chin against the edge of the cavity, I strain to somehow jerk myself upward. I hear Fontes giggle again. He sidles near and, with a swift kick to the head, sends me flying back down again.

Cedazo had said, "Right now you're a shadow. You're nothing and you'll leave nothing behind. You can't do anything for me." Then I start laughing, too, at the top of my lungs. It's a fantastic feeling. I laugh and laugh. Hard. Cedazo pulls a gun out of his pocket. He doesn't like the way I'm acting, doesn't understand it. The guy must assume that being such an idiotic Legionnaire, I'd rather die than share the rest of the treasure with him. He aims the gun while hollering at me to shut up, but I only cackle louder. My hilarity comes in part from being scared to death. But also because Cedazo is wrong when he claims that I'm not leaving anything behind. The envelope that I left with Carmela at the Venta del Cruce will probably reach its destination within a few hours. It contained Bartomeu Camús's original declaration. I gave her quite a bit of money to waste some time, catch the bus to Vitoria, and mail the envelope addressed to my mother from there. That's why I'm cracking up so hard. Thanks to that letter, I'm going to leave a lot of things behind. My mother knows why I'm here and the reason for my visit. She'll also know what happened if I don't come back. Eventually, once she's somewhere safe, my mother will make Bartomeu Camús's accusation public, no matter what the consequences. The major won't get a single peseta out of it. I'm also leaving behind my son. Someday he will come to get me. In the letter I make him promise to do so. The same way I promised my father that I would find Bartomeu Camús. The poor kid is going to have more work cut out for him than I did. Or maybe, on the contrary, times will have changed and he'll be able to do it openly, without having to hide. And if my son can't comply with my last wishes, then his son will. That's the way it is and the way it always will be. There's always a son, a brother, a mother, a grandfather—always somebody. That's why I can't stop snickering. My peals of laughter project upward toward the major's gun, which is aimed directly at my head.

How can he have the guts to kill a full-fledged Legionnaire like me?

I was searching for one thing and found another. Could it be that the way to find what you want is to go looking for something completely different? In order to discover a pile of bones—do we have to search for oblivion?

I lift my head. Cedazo isn't there anymore. Fontes is training a rifle directly at me. I can hear Cedazo's resigned voice saying to him a few steps away, "Come on; let's annihilate this son of a bitch. I'll give you twenty *duros* if you hit the scar on his head. Come on, be quick about it, it's getting late, and we still have to fill in this fucking hole."

The major doesn't want to get his hands dirty. Or maybe, to him, I'm not worth the trouble of staining his suit. That's why he's left the job for his dog, Fontes, to take care of. The soldier stares at me greed-ily, spurred on by the possibility of extra cash. He focuses intently on my scar and I get the feeling that instead of simply lodging a bullet into it, he'd lick the distorted flesh if he could. Releasing the catch of his weapon, he begins to move silently around the edge of the cavity, keeping the gun trained on me at all times. He's taking aim. I follow him with my eyes until I can't twist myself around any farther. Now he's the one laughing, not me. I can hear his giggles spilling out from behind. I kneel down and lean my head to the ground. I'm tired and can't take it anymore.

If you ever go to the cathedral Santa Maria del Mar and stand be-neath the main façade, you'll see right in front of you, across the plaza, a queerly shaped building built on top of an arch on that very same street. This L-shaped structure is Number Six, Caputxes Street. The old run-down edifice doesn't have the precarious novelty of the build-ing across from it, whose inverted pyramid shape is due to the builders' decision to make each floor a bit larger than the next. Neither does it evoke a splendid past, as some of those stately portals throughout the neighborhood do, even on tiny alleyways of no importance. If you go inside and climb up to the roof, you'll find a little tower, built at the back of the building in such a way that it looks like a mere continua-tion of the façade leading over to Plegamans Street. Since the streets are so narrow, it can barely be seen from down on the ground. It's not a coop for pigeons or chickens; it isn't even a laundry room. The little space is an authentic tower some fifteen feet high and approximately twenty-five to thirty feet square. It's crowned by a steeply peaked roof, open to the four winds, which is covered in old, yellowed clay tiles, en-crusted with moss. I went up there often with my friend and com-panion No-Sister-Salvador, who treated me like an equal, even though I was only a child and he was already a young man.

I gather together my last ounce of strength and wrench myself upward. Screaming, I leap beyond the bounds of the grave's rectangular outline toward the patch of blue sky above.

A shot goes off behind me.

It's over. I'm fucked.

Catalan, a romance language like French, Spanish, or Italian, possesses a complex history that stretches back more than a thousand years, and has survived despite the rigors of time and circumstance. Catalan enjoyed its heyday during the Middle Ages, when it was the official language of the kingdom of Aragon. There it was spoken by everyone—including popes, kings, philosophers, poets, doctors, scientists, and writers. In 1713, at the end of the War of the Spanish Succession, Aragon was unified with Castile and both Catalonia and Aragon became part of the Spanish Empire (though in Catalonia the fighting continued through 1714). Thus began the Decadência—a period of decline in Catalan culture, when written Catalan fell into disuse. The upper classes began to speak the language of the court in power: Spanish. The nineteenth century saw the onset of the Renaixença, a period of intense interest in and promotion of Catalan literature and culture. This upsurge continued into the twentieth century, during Spain's very brief Second Spanish Republic (1931–1939), when, once again, Catalan became the official language of Catalonia. The twentieth century brought two dictatorships to Spain—those of Miguel Primo de Rivera (1923–1930) and Francisco Franco (in Catalonia his government was in control from 1938 to

1975). Catalonians were persecuted during both regimes and speaking or writing in Catalan was strictly regulated.

While Franco was in power, Catalan was forbidden almost everywhere outside the home. Catalan speakers were alienated from their native tongue in an effort to exert total control over their lives. As an example of this in the novel, Genís's father is forced to communicate in Spanish with his family while being held prisoner. Citizens were not allowed to use the Catalan spelling of their names under any official circumstances: not for birth certificates, school records, marriage licenses, or even death certificates. It is for this reason that, throughout *For a Sack of Bones,* our hero's name changes from "Genís" (the Catalan spelling) to "Ginés" (the Spanish spelling) depending on the moment and the context. This was a conscious part of my overall effort to show readers the extent to which a person's identity was shaped by oppression during this period in Catalan history.

After Franco won the Civil War, his repression of the Catalan language reached radical—and nearly genocidal—extremes. This was especially true during the first years of the Regime, which coincided with the Nazis' early victories during World War II. Slowly, over the years, the brutality of certain aspects of this persecution diminished. But up until the very last minute of the dictator's life, there were no significant legal changes made in favor of Catalan.

Until democracy was established in Spain in 1977, Catalan was forced to survive through clandestine means—a language without a country. Even today, Andorra is the only independent nation to designate Catalan as its sole official language. In Catalonia and other regions of Spain, Catalan must share the privilege of its official status with Spanish. It is also spoken in the small French province known as Pyrénées-Orientales and the Sardinian city, Alghero. One revealing consequence of these years of oppression is deftly illustrated by a quick look at statistics regarding the contemporary use of Catalan.

Because Catalan was for so many years an untaught language, these statistics must be broken into two categories—one for those who understand Catalan and one for those who both understand and speak the language. Today there are about 10.4 million people who understand and roughly 7.6 million who speak Catalan.

To this day, and despite its suitability to every aspect of daily life—be it government, education, or literature—Catalan continues to struggle for full acceptance in Spain and to suffer from the complexity of its role as determined by the Spanish constitution. In *For a Sack of Bones,* I have used the persecution of Catalan as a plot element in an effort to show one key method of control employed by the dictatorship in power. I hope that I have, in writing this novel, brought out the importance of a people's language and culture and shown how the loss of these can impart damage not incomparable to violence done to the body.

ACKNOWLEDGMENTS

My gratitude to Doctor Castellarnau, a good writer, whose
aid with medical questions was invaluable.